BLOOD AND FIRE
New Stories of the Vampire Wars

Edited and Co-Authored by
JONATHAN MABERRY

V WARS

BLOOD AND FIRE
New Stories of the Vampire Wars

Edited and Co-Authored by
JONATHAN MABERRY

With

JAMES A. MOORE

JOE MCKINNEY

KEVIN J. ANDERSON

LARRY CORREIA

SCOTT SIGLER

WESTON OCHSE

YVONNE NAVARRO

Ted Adams, CEO & Publisher
Greg Goldstein, President & COO
Robbie Robbins, EVP/Sr. Graphic Artist
Chris Ryall, Chief Creative Officer/Editor-in-Chief
Matthew Ruzicka, CPA, Chief Financial Officer
Alan Payne, VP of Sales
Dirk Wood, VP of Marketing
Lorelei Bunjes, VP of Digital Services
Jeff Webber, VP of Digital Publishing & Business Development

Jonathan Maberry, Editor

Jeff Conner & Tom Waltz, Associate Editors

Richard Sheinaus, Designer

Robbie Robbins, Associate Designer

Trevor Hutchison, Cover Design

ISBN: 978-1-63140-027-8

17 16 15 14   1 2 3 4

IDW

www.IDWPUBLISHING.com
IDW founded by Ted Adams, Alex Garner, Kris Oprisko, and Robbie Robbins

Facebook: **facebook.com/idwpublishing**
Twitter: **@idwpublishing**
YouTube: **youtube.com/idwpublishing**
Instagram: **instagram.com/idwpublishing**
deviantART: **idwpublishing.deviantart.com**
Pinterest: **pinterest.com/idwpublishing/idw-staff-faves**

CONTENTS

"APOCALYPSE TANGO" PT.1

Jonathan Maberry

—1—

The Barkey Family Farm
Town of Ulysses
Potter County, Pennsylvania
The Eve of the War

There was so much blood.

So much.

So much.

Too much.

Luther Swann felt like he was swimming in it.

Sinking.

Drowning.

The floor seemed to tilt under him and he took a few, slow, wandering sideways steps, one hand fumbling for a wall, a rail, a table, anything. He found the edge of a couch, steadied himself, then froze, suddenly afraid to look at the fabric he was clutching.

It was wet.

And warm.

And so wrong.

Turning his head was so hard, so difficult; it felt like someone was squeezing his neck, grinding his bones. He was gritting his teeth as he looked at the couch.

It wasn't a couch, of course.

His questing hand had overshot the edge of the couch and grabbed something else.

A shoulder.

What was left of a shoulder.

Torn cloth. Torn everything. The sharp ends of bone pressed against his palm.

He snatched his hand back but then held it as far from the rest of him as he could manage. Fearing it. Loathing it. Wanting to cut it off. Wanting to shove it into boiling water or scrub it with lye soap.

The scream, which he'd been holding in for so long burned in his throat, bubbled, burst out. It was too shrill, too loud, too long. It tore the tissues of his larynx and it kept going. It wouldn't stop.

It couldn't stop.

He saw movement through the fireworks in his eyes. A shape. Big and blocky. A blur of an arm, the whip of a hand.

Then the crack of a flat palm that hit his cheek with such shocking force that Swann's mind and heart and voice went numb in an instant. He slammed into the wall, rebounded, and then hands were on him, grabbing his shirt, spinning him, ramming him back against the wall. A face was there, close. So close he could smell coffee and cigarettes on hot breath.

A voice, speaking from an inch away.

"Shut. The fuck. Up."

The words spaced, staccato, like bullets hitting a wall.

The hands shook him. Pulled him forward and then slammed him back again.

"You fucking hear me, Doc?"

"Y-yes," stammered Swann.

The man who'd struck him stepped back. Swann blinked his eyes clear and looked up at the hard, angular face of Special Agent-in-Charge Jimmy Saint. The other FBI agents all stood staring at Swann. There was very little compassion on their faces.

There were so many different emotions in their eyes.

Shock.

Jaded indifference.

Contempt.

Fear.

A lot of fear.

AIC Saint stepped back to allow Swann to fall or stand. He stood. Barely. Requiring the wall to manage it.

Jimmy Saint was a fourth generation Spanish-American. Spanish, not Mexican, as he often pointed out. His family name had once been Santa Domingo. Changed at Ellis Island to Saint. He had fair skin and intensely black hair. His jaws were always blue with five o'clock shadow, even after a fresh shave.

"Are we good, Doc?" asked Saint.

Swann nodded.

"Doc…?" prodded Saint, who was never content with anything but a verbal response.

"I'm good," said Swann, and saying it actually helped. It steadied the floor beneath his feet.

Saint smiled. He had a big, white smile that Swann thought was totally false and yet completely infectious. Saint knew it was, too. He used it to control moments like this, and it shifted the power in any room to him.

Swann pushed off the wall and stood on his feet. The room took a last spin and then settled back into place. Into structure and form, into something quantifiable.

And that was the problem.

The clearer his mind, the more precisely his senses were focused, the greater the horror. He stared at the gore on his hand. This was someone's blood. This was tissue that made up skin and muscle and brain and bone.

This was part of a person.

He looked around.

This place—this home—was a charnel house. The thing on the couch, the thing he'd accidentally touched, only vaguely human anymore. It was meat. The humanity had been stripped away and what was left did not total up to a complete person. There were pieces missing.

There were shapes on the floor. In other chairs. On the steps.

They were vaguely human, too.

But not actually human. Not anymore.

He struggled to find a lexicon with words to describe this.

"I—" he began and stopped. Swallowed. Licked his lips. Tried it again. "I thought this was over."

Saint gave him a pitying look.

"Really? Over? It was almost a goddamn war, Doc," said the agent.

"Terrorists. Bombings. We had cities in flames last year. Have you been to L.A.? Have you been to Trenton?"

"I've been everywhere," said Swann. "I was in this from the start."

"I know, Luther, it was a rhetorical question. You should know that this was never going to be over. That ceasefire? That non-aggression agreement? Did you really think anyone really gives a cold, wet shit about that?"

Swann turned away. "Yes."

There was no comment from Saint.

"I really believed we'd reached some kind of understanding," said Swann. "I thought there'd been enough killing to…I don't know. To wake everyone up. And we went months without any significant violence. Months."

When he turned back to the agent, he caught a fleeting glimpse of another expression. Not pity this time. Not contempt.

The agent half turned to hide it.

Was it a smile?

"Yeah…I saw that quote on your website, Doc. What was it? 'Mankind must put an end to war before war puts an end to mankind.' John F. Kennedy, am I right? You thought that the players all listened to their better angels, came to their senses and decided to—what?— live in peace, happiness and puppies?"

Swann stiffened. "Is idealism or optimism a crime now? Do you want to add them to the list of human frailties? Right along with compassion and common sense?"

Agent Saint was amused. "Much as I'd probably enjoy debating political philosophy with you over a couple of beers, for now let's focus on this, shall we? I'm not picking a fight here. I'm trying to give us all a perspective check. This is the third incident of this kind in the last eleven days. One in Bradenton, Florida, one in Solana Beach, California, and this one. Three states. If we presume it's the same killer or killers, then crossing state lines makes it a federal crime. Either it's the work of a serial killer or incidents of renewed aggression by vampire cells operating on U.S. soil. And I'm inclined to think these were done by Bloods."

Swann wanted to sneer at the street term. Ever since the first outbreaks of what the press had come to label the "V-War," street lingo had nicknamed all vampires—regardless of species—as "Bloods," and all non-vampires as "Beats." Swann resisted using the slang. He found it vulgar and somehow disturbing.

"We haven't gotten back the lab work on the other attacks," he said, keeping his eyes locked on Saint so he didn't have to look at what lay around them. "We don't know that these attacks are in any way related. There hasn't been an outbreak-related incident in four months."

5

"You ever heard the expression 'calm before the storm'?" asked Saint. The agent took him by the arm and led him to the other side of the room, away from any listening ears. He dropped his tone and leaned close. "Doc…Luther…I know how much you want this to be over. So do I, believe me. I know someone who turned. And I knew three of the agents who were killed in Philadelphia. I have a personal stake in this and I'm not taking sides. I'm really not. However, if this is a new outbreak, then we have to confirm that and notify the proper departments so that we can respond appropriately."

"'Respond appropriately', Jimmy? You do know what that will mean, don't you? There are people in Washington and in the military— people we both know—who would love a chance to explore solutions that could be worse than the problem. And internment camps would be just the start."

"I know, I know," said Saint patiently. "I read your articles, I saw the interview you did with Yuki Nitobe. You think this will escalate into ethnic genocide."

"Don't you?"

Saint spread his hands. "I don't know, and it's above my pay grade to speculate."

"That's a bullshit answer, Jimmy. It's cowardly."

If the agent took offense, it didn't show on his face.

"Let's just work the scene, okay? Once we have the facts then we can talk about what they might mean. First things first."

He patted Swann on the shoulder, gave him another of those smiles, and went over to talk to the Bureau's forensics techs.

Swann said nothing.

Instead he forced his revulsion down into a box along with the emotions that kept trying to break him. He needed to see this scene. To become part of the investigation.

He looked at the scene.

The scene.

There were two lights in the room, both with off-white shades. Both shades were spattered with blood that turned the available light into a red-gold gloom. The farmhouse was modest-sized with an open plan so that a conversational grouping of sofa, loveseat and chair occupied one-third and the dining room and kitchen filled the rest. The red-gold light glimmered on the stainless steel handles of a vast old farm stove, gleamed on the half-dozen water glasses on the half-set table, sparkled on the silverware laid out for either lunch or supper—and shimmered on each and every one of the thousands of drops of bright red blood that spattered the floor and ran up in wild patterns on the walls. The light danced along the blood patterned on the outstretched leg of a woman who lay partly hidden by an overturned chair.

Swann closed his eyes for a moment. "God damn it," he breathed.

The kitchen was painted with blood, with great arterial sprays that slashed up and down the walls; blood pooled like great red lakes on the linoleum floor, gathered around the bodies. Swann looked at the woman's leg and saw that she was not sprawled behind an overturned chair. The leg was all there was of her there. The rest was in a corner where it had been thrown.

Gretchen Barkey, according to police reports.

What had *been* Gretchen Barkey.

Her husband, Roger, was bent backward over a shattered side table, his arms and legs splayed, his mouth thrown wide as if to scream in protest for the things which had been done to him. Swann looked at him, looking into him. His heart and lungs were gone, torn away, nowhere to be seen; his intestines lay like purple ropes across his thighs. Roger's throat was as savage a ruin as his chest. Swann could only stare.

He turned away, but there was no turning away because everywhere he looked, in every corner, there was horror. Another man, perhaps a farmhand or a family friend, was huddled against the radiator, his hands still clamped around it, but his back had been torn out, the flesh ripped into long tatters that showed the red of blood and the red-gray of meat and the white of gouged vertebrae.

Fireflies seemed to be crowding at the corner of Swann's eyes.

Here in the living room area was the body he'd touched. A young man, but his face was completely gone, and Swann picked the name out of the initial police report. Hal, Barkey's son.

Seventeen years old.

Seventeen going on eighteen.

Seventeen going on nothing at all.

Hal—if that ruin really was Hal—had the handle of a broken knife in his hand. The blade had been snapped off and placed with great delicacy in the precise middle of the coffee table.

7

A long smear of blood and the scuffle of bloody footprints showed how hard Hal had fought to get away. To fight back. Maybe to protect his parents and the others.

The dining room looked like a storm had raged through there. All the chairs were overturned and smashed, and the big oak dining table was on its side. Swann stared at it and saw that the three-quarter thick oak had been splintered by some powerful force. It would have taken a sledgehammer at least to do that kind of damage.

The other part of the scene was sprawled in the open area that joined living and dining rooms. There were two children lying in a tangle on the floor.

Children.

A boy of about ten and a girl of sixteen. Youngest son and middle daughter.

What had been done to them was…was….

He backed away, unable to see it, to contain that kind of horror, to compute that degree of utter and inhuman savagery. It was like nothing he had ever seen. Ever. Not during the first V-War, and not since. Not even the photos of what the outbreak's Patient Zero, Michael Fayne, had done to the women he murdered.

This was something new, something horrible, vicious and fierce. Something insanely cruel.

"God in heaven…" he murmured, speaking not to the others but to his own worst fears. "It's starting again."

"THE COURT OF THE CRIMSON QUEEN"

Jonathan Maberry

The Court of the Crimson Queen
Undisclosed Location
The Eve of the War

The throne on which she sat once belonged to Marie Laveau, reputed to be the Voodoo Queen of New Orleans. It was made of exotic woods and carved with the faces of *loas* and saints.

The stone top of the table beside the throne came from Bran, in the immediate vicinity of Brasov in Romania. The castle is one of three presumed places where Vlad III, the voivode of Wallachia who had defeated the Turks and who impaled twenty thousand of them outside of his capital, Târgoviste. There were other relics in the room from Poenari and Corvin Castles, other sites tied to Vlad the Impaler.

The room—her throne room—was large and damp and buried deep beneath a building whose innocence and mundane function was so at odds with what went on in the sub-basement as to deflect even casual speculation. The walls were soundproofed against screams. The flooring was made with impermeable materials that would not accept a stain and could be thoroughly cleaned after even the most extreme use. The walls were hung with decorative rugs depicting scenes from the *Old* and *New Testaments*, and many from the *Apocrypha*.

The Crimson Queen sat on her throne. Robed in red and black, velvet and lace. Her face hidden behind a mask of carved ivory that once served as the funeral mask of an Ethiopian princess. On either side of the throne were pale-skinned vampires of a certain species. *Draugr* of

Scandinavian extraction. Two of them had been farm boys from Minnesota. The third still played offensive fullback for the Vikings. The fourth was an actor who had played a superhero in two low-budget films. After they had turned, they were screened and then recruited into the Court of the Crimson Queen. Into the Red Guard, the military elite. Through the fury of the first War of Human Aggression they kept the Queen safe. All of them had spilled lakes of blood in her defense.

In front and to one side of the throne was a slender knife-blade of a man with laughing eyes and a cruel mouth. He was dressed all in black except for a small red handprint embroidered over his heart. His real name had been checked at the door along with the identity he wore in day-to-day life. Like everyone in the court he had adopted a *shadow* name. A war name. Like the combat call-signs of the enemy soldiers. Incognito was only one of the many pathways to safety.

The name he chose when he was appointed Chief Executioner for the Court was one deliberately selected to strike fear into everyone— vampire and human. It was grandly theatrical, which was a choice because if one played a grand role then others would, because of social conditioning, come to treat you with elevated deference. For that purpose, he affected an attitude of haughty malevolence. His actions, in defense of Queen and Court, had become legend, and like all legends, those actions were deliberately and carefully exaggerated. The legend grew according to a specific plan, and was reinforced by the old world formality used by all of the members of the Court.

He was Mephistopheles.

Apart from serving the Queen's pleasure and exacting her justice, he was also her chief advisor and chancellor. A role he played with absolute devotion, tireless dedication and total loyalty. Mephistopheles knew that he was living an affectation, but he did it because he believed with heart and soul in the Queen and her vision for her people.

For the vampires.

All vampires.

The Court of the Crimson Queen had no boundaries, no borders. It obeyed no laws other than its own, and dealt justice and punishment according to those laws.

For the last twenty minutes the chancellor and his queen listened to a young woman, who wore a black tank top and jeans and whose shoulders were covered with tattoos of bats flitting among stars and comets. Her nails were painted black and she had red streaks in her hair.

"It's getting worse every day," she said. "Last month, a cop pulled my friend Celia over, too, just because she has a fang plate."

Fang plates were popular decorative frames for license plates that were shaped like a gaping mouth filled with vampire teeth.

"She's not a Blood. She never turned. She's just a friend to the Bloods, like a lot of people are."

"What did the officer do?" asked Mephistopheles.

"Well…not much, but he hassled her and searched her car. Frisked her, too, and I don't know if that's legal. I think he was copping a feel. Celia's pretty cute. Big boobs, you know? The cop did a pretty thorough pat-down."

"What did he find?"

The Goth girl paused. "Um…well, there were a few magazines. You know, *Dark Times* and the *Time Magazine* with Luther Swann on the cover. And…maybe she had a poster from the *One Blood-One Beat*."

"*One Blood-One Beat*?"

"You know, the fundraiser concert in Austin for homeless Bloods they had in March? Celia was there and she got a poster for me. Got it signed by Arcade Fire and Katy Perry and Lady Gaga."

"They're not Bloods," said Mephistopheles.

"Most of the performers weren't. It was a fundraiser. Mostly for those families who got firebombed before the war ended."

Mephistopheles nodded. "Did this police officer harm your friend? Did he molest her further?"

"No, it wasn't like that. But the cop was rough on her. Told her she was a traitor to her species. That kind of stuff, you know."

"Words," said Mephistopheles, and shrugged.

"Yeah, but ever since then she's been getting crank phone calls. All from blocked numbers, but it's nasty stuff. Obscene stuff. And people telling her she's a sinner. One caller said he was going to fuck some sense into her. Sorry for the language, but that's what he said. Celia's car's been booted three times for no reason. They keep telling her it was a computer error that tagged her as having outstanding tickets, which she doesn't have. And her dad is being audited by the IRS. He's just a dry-cleaner. He's not political at all, and suddenly the IRS decides to audit him?"

Mephistopheles held up his hand to stop her rant.

"What do you want from her majesty?"

The girl colored and looked suddenly sheepish. "I…"

"Go on, girl," said the Queen. Her accent was soft and Southern. A rich contralto. "Speak your heart."

"I guess I don't know what you could do. Maybe nobody can do anything." She wiped at a tear. "It's just that it's getting bad again. There's that skinhead gang that's been messing up gay Bloods in New Orleans. Some restaurants are posting signs saying that they won't serve Bloods because of some new health regulation. Everywhere you look there are right-wing religious nuts handing out those pamphlets. You know the ones: *Suffer Not a Witch* and *Abomination or Salvation? It's Your Choice.* Crap like that. I mean…people are getting stomped. Female Bloods are getting gang-raped. It's bad and it's scary and I don't know what to do."

Tears fell down her cheeks and hung from her chin. She covered her face with her hands as soft sobs trembled through her slim body.

Mephistopheles turned slowly to face the queen.

The Crimson Queen's eyes glittered like jewels behind the ivory mask.

"Girl," said the queen quietly, "listen to me."

The Goth girl raised her eyes. Her mascara had smeared and run in black lines down her face. Her nose was running and she looked very young and very frightened.

"We have friends in the IRS," said the queen. "That can be taken care of. We have friends everywhere. Give Mephistopheles your friend's address and phone number. We'll help her find a new apartment and get her an unlisted number. I'll have one of the Red Guard watch over her. If anyone moves against her they will bleed for it, do you understand?"

The girl nodded. "Thank you…"

The queen raised a hand to silence her. "But you need to tell her to be more careful. We have many friends among the Beats. Many. But there are many more of them who hate us and would like to see us all dead. There are people who want to build camps and gas chambers for us. There are people who would like us rendered down to soap." She traced the cold lips of her mask with a forefinger. "War is coming, girl. Do you know that?"

"People…people talk about the V-Wars starting again."

"It won't be the same war," said the queen. "This will be different. The Beats have learned a lot about us since the first war. Just as we have learned about them. And from them. The war that's coming will be very different. And when it passes, the world will be a different world."

"Does it have to happen?" asked the girl. "Do things have to get that bad?"

The queen sighed. It was a sound filled with such deep sadness that the girl's tears started anew.

"It is already that bad. All that's required now is a single spark to light the fires."

"What kind of spark?"

The queen, however, did not answer.

"THE ENEMY WITHIN" PT. 1

Yvonne Navarro

— 1 —

There is nothing in the world like a southwestern Arizona sunrise. She hasn't been a lot of places in her life—besides New York City, only Tucson and Phoenix a couple of times—but Mooney Lopez knows all the way to her core, to her very *self*, that this is the truth. More dawns than not, the clouds and the rays of the sun are just right as they spill over the mountain peaks. It's like watching lava spread across everything above your head, not just the sky but eternity itself. Forever is made of wild shades of azure and crimson crashing against a lower layer of melted gold and blinding angelic-white, almost like heaven and hell have flipped and each is trying to regain its original position.

Perhaps that's exactly what's happened, Mooney thinks as she squints into the beams circling upward. God reduced to DNA and science, and vampires rising and trying to claim the planet. It isn't such a stretch in belief, even without listening to the doomsayers on the third- and fourth-rate cable channels in the middle of the night.

But out here, in the chilled air that hangs between dark and light, the end of the world seems so far away. How, she thinks, can there be war anywhere when she is surrounded by such beauty and peace, such clean and endless quiet?

A coyote's call, almost like high-pitched laughter, rakes across the stillness and makes her jump, a reminder that in the desert nothing is ever truly what it seems. Was this a lone coyote a mile or more away, or a human smuggler masquerading as one? It's too far out for her to be sure, and sound does strange things, unearthly things, when it sails on the cold, inverted air, spins around the prehistoric rock formations and slips through the spines of a hundred thousand cacti. What sounds like a thirty-five pound member of the canine family can, if she isn't careful, turn out to be a carniovore of a much more familiar and dangerous type.

The wind ripples through the rattlesnake pattern of her hair, grown long and fast since the awakening of her vampire DNA. Mooney breathes deeply, turning in a slow circle to taste the breeze from all directions. Nothing—no coyote, no human, not even a jackrabbit. That in itself is odd since this is prime foraging time, when the temperature is too cold for snakes and although the light is slowly overtaking the night there is still plenty of shadows to hide in. Has something scared them into stillness, or kept them inside their hidden burrows? Not even a single whistle floats on the air, and at this time birdsong should be rapidly increasing.

As if in answer to her question, something suddenly glides over-head, a shadow darker than the sky but not quite silent to her over-sensitive hearing. Mooney glances up and sees the silhouette of a great horned owl, one of the more feared of the desert's predators. This one has a wingspan of over four feet as it sweeps past, the ominous outline of certain death to anything it can carry away. For a moment Mooney is stunned as she imagines the end of a small mammal's life within that taloned grip as it rips its prey apart and feasts.

She shudders, then gives herself a sharp pinch on one thigh to snap herself out of it. It must be the cool night air, the stillness, the sweet caress of the fading desert stars that's mesmerizing her. She makes an effort to focus as she studies her surroundings, the rocks, the scrub, the up and down landscape until she's finally convinced. No, not a thing out here tonight.

Mooney takes her time walking back to her 4Runner, enjoying the rays of the sun as it crests the mountains and spills over the land, warming the air and waking the desert's creatures. By the time she opens the driver's door the air is filled with sounds of birds whistling and singing to each other, sometimes escalating into a screech as a pair fights over prime perch space. Rabbits move here and there, freezing if they think she's seen them, as if doing such a thing could protect them. Sometimes she feels just like that, like her idyllic life could just suddenly shatter if she takes just one wrong step. Somehow she's gotten herself into a position where she wants for nothing—she has fresh food, money, a job that ensures a future for herself and her children. What could exist beyond that? The escalating vampire-human war might be all over the news—the face of that Asian reporter, Yuki Nitobe, is practically burned into everyone's retinas—but it's only a bunch of faraway stories on LED screens. Here in the southwest, in tiny Sells, Arizona, the townspeople, she, and the law seamlessly coexist.

For now.

– 2 –

The guy is there, standing halfway between the door and her 4Runner, when Mooney comes out of Robles Market. She always stops here to get a cold bottle of water after checking in with Chief Delgado before the start of her shift; he'd fill her in on anything special that might be going down, give her a few printouts of the baddest bad guys hiding out in the desert on this particular night, and send her on her way with his half-sincere, half-sarcastic caution of, *"Be careful not to do anything anyone will have to look at too closely."*

"Hey," he says in an easy voice. "How're you doing?"

She stops and eyes him, taking in more information in a two-second scan than an ordinary human can get in a ten-minute interrogation. At six-foot three-inches, he's taller than the average Native American around here, although he does have straight black hair. His skin is the color of saddle leather, the good quality kind, but he's young enough so that it hasn't taken on the texture of boots left too long in the sun. He's wearing the standard Sells outfit of jeans and a long-sleeved cotton shirt with cowboy stitching, although he's gone for Asics athletic shoes instead of cowboy boots. His eyes are hazel, which rules out Native American…Mediterranean, perhaps? His smile is slight but genuine, showing a glimpse of good white teeth in a face handsome enough to make most girls do a double take.

Oh, and he's a vampire.

"My name's Josh," he continues. "Word around here is that you're Red Moon."

"Mooney," she corrects automatically. "I go by Mooney."

He nods. "That's better anyway. Not so old-fashioned."

Smooth words, she thinks. But if this stranger thinks he knows her, even a little, he's way off. "Do I know you? There must be a reason you're asking about me."

"Other than we're two of a kind?" His smile widens and there they are, incisors that taper to an unmistakable point. Although his expression doesn't waver, his fangs change everything about the way he looks—the Cowboy Joe countenance vanishes in favor of a more vulpine appearance that looks somehow disturbing and…*hungry*. Suddenly Mooney has a flash of what she must look like to normals— specifically the way she'd shown her own fangs to Chief Delgado the first day she'd bitten someone—and she doesn't much like the image that sticks in her head.

"Not by a long shot."

He shrugs. "By one factor, anyway. You've got your hair all stuffed into that cap, but I've seen it loose. That rattlesnake pattern is awesome. And everyone in town seems to be talking about the shit you can do." Josh waves a hand at himself. "Me? I've got nothing like that to brag about. The best I can say is that I'm from Florida."

Mooney's eyes narrow. Maybe, but she seriously doubts he's the only vampire in the world whose junk DNA had given him nothing but a pair of stereotypically pointed teeth. Whatever his latent ability is, he just isn't revealing it. And what's that crap about him knowing what she looks like with her hair down and what her abilities are? He's starting to sound like some kind of stalker.

One thing becoming a vampire did was get rid of her fear about speaking up. Well, among other things.

"So what's your deal?" she asks. Her tone is sharp, but she doesn't try to soften it. Mooney's in uniform and she puts her hands on her hips, noting the way his gaze follows her movement and pauses on the weapon at her hip. A nice way to emphasize that if he's bullshitting her, he risks both the wrath of a vampire and the scrutiny of the Border Patrol. "You been following me?"

Josh starts to shake his head, then pauses. "Not exactly," he amends. "But I admit to asking around. I'm new in a really small town and kind of an outsider—I'm sure you understand why. Just trying to figure out if I was the only one."

"You're not," Mooney says. "You and me, plus one other guy I've

16

never met. He stays to himself and he keeps out of trouble, so I don't even know his name. That's just the way I like it."

"Sure, I get that. I'm not trying to invade your space or anything."

She studies him without saying anything, and he lets the silence go on while she does it, not shuffling his feet or looking away. A patient guy with nothing to hide…or is he? "There's a little place in the strip mall on Main Street," she finally says. "The Desert Rain Cafe. I'm working right now but I'll be done with everything by about 8 a.m. We could meet for coffee."

Josh's expression brightens. "Hey, that would be great. I'll see you then. And thanks."

He touches his eyebrow with a forefinger salute that seems half-gallant, half-cowboy, then heads over to a dusty Ford pickup. The movement and the truck fit her overall impression of him. Mooney shakes her head and watches him drive off. Florida, huh? Maybe he'd come out here to get a taste of ranch life. If that was it…dumb move. There are a lot greener places than the ass end of a desert Indian reservation.

– 3 –

Mooney doesn't make it to the cafe until after eight-thirty, but she catches a glimpse of him at a table with a mug in front of him. He was probably nursing a cup of black coffee just like Mooney herself does almost every morning, taking tiny sips that would let her savor the taste but not put too much of a load on her stomach. There are still plenty of smells and tastes she likes, even if her gut can't process them anymore. She suspects—or hopes—coffee with plenty of cream will always be one of them.

When she pushes into the restaurant she sees that Josh has someone else with him at the table. He stands as she approaches, then leans over and pulls out one of the empty chairs for her. "Really glad to see you could make it, Mooney." He indicates the wan-looking young woman seated to his left. "This is my friend, Rose. She got into town this morning."

Mooney nods at the woman, who's a vampire but looks all of sixteen and is probably jailbait. Her best guess about Josh is early twenties, and she can't help wonder exactly where Rose is staying. The thought makes the back of her scalp tingle unexpectedly, as if she's suddenly been stuck with pins.

"I'm nineteen, if that's what you're thinking about," Rose says suddenly. "I've always looked younger than my age, and even more since I got hit with the vampire virus."

"Right," Mooney says agreeably, although she doesn't believe it for a second. She rubs the back of her head and leans back, outwardly relaxed, inwardly taking it all in. A nod to the girl behind the counter gets her a cup of coffee with lots of creamers, and Mooney opens each one and pours it in while waiting for the conversation to start. When neither Josh nor Rose says anything, she realizes she is going to have to open things up. It doesn't take a rocket scientist to figure out Rose is an unexpected addition and Josh is derailed by her presence. "So are you from Florida, too?" she asks when she'd stirs in the last creamer.

"Minnesota."

"You two know each other already? Before Rose got here, I mean." Josh chuckled. "Of course. We—"

"—met last year when I was visiting family in Naples," Rose interrupts. When Mooney raises an eyebrow, Rose gives her an almost acidic look. "Florida, not Italy."

"I know where it is," Mooney says.

"She borrowed her cousin's car and went for a drive," Josh puts in. "Got lost and ended up running out of gas in Clewiston, where I lived. I gassed up the car and turned her back in the right direction. We've been exchanging emails ever since."

"Right," Mooney says. She looks back at Rose. "And now you're visiting here. Pretty long way from Minnesota."

Rose's expression is set. "I go where I want."

"No doubt." To Josh, Mooney says, "So what brings you way down here to begin with? As you can see, there's a whole lot of nothing going on in Sells, Arizona." She grins. "Probably a big disappointment to your girlfriend here."

"She's not my girlfriend," Josh says a little too quickly. Rose's eyes darken but she stays quiet. "Just a friend, like I said."

That strange tingling feeling comes again, a little stronger this time and accompanied by a faint feeling of being *pushed* somehow. Mooney fights the urge to rub her scalp again. "That's great, but you didn't answer my question. What brings you here? And you, too, Rose. You just visiting Josh, or are you planning on staying?"

"When I turned, my parents didn't take it too well," Josh says. "Neither did their friends. Don't get me wrong—they're good, God-fearing folks, all of them. I guess they just couldn't understand that I was still the same as them…mostly."

Mooney frowns. "I'm not following."

Josh leans forward, as if that will somehow make her understand. "My folks are very religious. All their friends are from the same church, and mine were, too. In their eyes, me turning into a vampire made me some kind of demon. Suddenly I was evil, a killer who was going to eat their children and spread death and pestilence among them. When word got around—and my parents didn't even *try* to keep it a secret—I became an instant outcast." A note of bitterness creeps into his tone, although Mooney can tell he's trying to keep his voice even. "My parents put my stuff on the front lawn so that everyone could see them purging their home of the ungodly beast that used to be their son, my friends wouldn't look me in the eye much less talk to me, and my boss fired me under the guise of downsizing."

He'd had her at the word *outcast* although she doesn't show it. Finally, a use for all the training the Border Patrol has put her through, classes on neutrality, diplomacy, functioning in stressful situations, ad infinitum. "So this is your fresh start," she says. When he nods, she asks, "But why Sells? There're plenty of places with a lot more going for them than a one restaurant town in southwestern part of Nowhere, USA." In her peripheral vision Mooney sees Rose's expression flash into one of utter agreement. She files that away for future reference.

"But that's exactly why I *want* to be here," Josh said. "Down here no one cares about what you are as long as you mind your own business, right? I ended up in a cheap hotel room off Interstate 75, spent days researching. I learned about you from a tweet that I caught completely by accident on some thread about illegal aliens." He glances sideways at Rose. "It doesn't take a genetic scientist to figure out what you're doing on the night shift out in the desert, and when you spend a little extra time working over it, it's not a hard leap to figure out that the Border Patrol arm of Uncle Sam is looking the other way. Hell, they may even be *asking* you to do what you do best."

Mooney feels dangerous heat start to build beneath her jaw. "And what's that?"

Josh holds her hard gaze for a moment, then says carefully, "Surviving." He pauses for a beat. "Isn't that just what we all want? To survive?"

The anger dissipates and Mooney feels her muscles relax a bit. "I suppose that's what everyone wants."

"Exactly." Josh seems almost excited. "See, that's why I picked Sells, right? I've been asking around, sending out some feelers, and telling people like us to meet up with me down here. Think about it. There's plenty of free food and no one cares where it comes from as long as the regular townsfolk remain untouched. The local law, the Border Patrol—they all look the other way, right?"

Mooney's jaw tightens at the picture he's painting of her hometown but she says nothing. Funny how she wants to rise and defend Sells without even thinking about it. But the way he's wording it, the townspeople, and her with them, are starting to sound like a bunch of cold-hearted sociopaths. Are they really that bad? Sometimes the truth is a bitch.

"And if there aren't any humans handy," Josh continues, "there are always desert animals, right? Coyotes, rabbits, javelinas—a year round buffet that will never run out. It's paradise but without God breathing down your neck." He nods to reinforce his words. "In fact, I'd say the idea was actually a Godsend, exactly what I'd been searching for."

Rose finally speaks. "We already have a few people like us who have joined up, and more are on the way." Her eyes glitter. "This place is pretty tiny, you know. It won't be long until the vampires actually outnumber the substandards—"

"The what?" Mooney asks. This time it's like someone giving her a mental *shove*. Rose? Mooney doesn't like the idea of this brittle teenager trying to invade her mind, or worse, influence her; without changing her expression, she pushes back, hard. Across the table, Rose winces suddenly, as if she's been stung by an insect, then scowls. Now that Mooney knows Rose is the source, maybe her resistance will put an end to this weirdness.

"Substandards," Josh tells her. "Non-vampires."

"I'm not sure I like where this is going," Mooney says slowly.

"Come on, don't be so dense." Josh taps a finger on the tabletop for emphasis. "There's a war going on out there between the humans and the vampires. In lots of places it's out in the open and downright brutal. People and vampires are dying, but mostly people. Seriously, the *vampires* are the stronger species, Mooney. Dominant, top of the food chain. Another couple of weeks and we'll have enough people who've come here to form a small army. *We'll* be the ones in control, calling the shots and making the decisions." He leans across the table until he's close enough for Mooney to smell his breath. Was that bloodscent? "Choosing our *food*."

She opens her mouth to say something, but nothing comes out. Was it wrong to want to eat, to take steps to feed your family and your spouse? Is she any different from them? She clears her throat. "How many vampires are we talking about here?"

Josh shrugs. "I don't know how many will answer the posts we've been making around the Internet. A dozen? Fifty? Who can tell? If we're lucky it'll be enough to take over. Think about it. We're genetically superior; we're stronger, faster, better at all these great things depending on our DNA heritage. Why should the substandards tell us what to do and when we can do it? They may have been top dog in the past, but there's a superior predator around now." He sends Rose a smug look. "And no one's going to ostracize us anymore, or try to put us in some bullshit relocation camps like we're something out of fucking World War II history."

Mooney nods but inside her thoughts are bouncing back and forth like a metal bead in one of those old handheld pinball games. Some of what Josh says makes sense, even sounds attractive. Other stuff...not so much. Sure, she hates being an outcast, she always has—and no one knows better than her what that feels like. But she isn't so sure that amassing an army of physically superior beings in Sells is the answer to anything. There aren't any soldiers here, no one's trying to make her or the other vampire in town do anything.

"And while we're growing," Josh continues eagerly, "you can be a huge help. You can help supply the best source of food out there: those illegal aliens or drugs smugglers—that you catch in the desert almost every single night." His expression is a hundred percent triumph.

"They're people, not game," she manages.

Josh waves his hand. "*Pah.* Tell me that when the subs roll in some kind of tank to fire into a crowd of protesting vampires like they've already done in a couple of the bigger cities. 'Crowd control,'" he announces in a high-pitched voice. "My eye. The puny humans were getting nervous and Big Daddy Government wanted to flex its muscles, keep the nasty little vampires in their places. Or maybe just try to get rid of a nice big bunch of them right on the spot, give the ones who didn't die a big hint to go somewhere else."

Chief Delgado might be one of her bosses now, but Mooney doesn't have to struggle to remember when he had come to her trailer and told her she needed to leave Sells after she'd defended herself by biting a boy who'd grabbed her. Outcast then, yes, but now? Not so much. Yeah, some people still look suspiciously at her, but a lot more seem to have grown quite comfortable, not only with her presence but with the idea that she's defending them.

But will they stay that way?

Mooney pushes back her chair and stands. "I'm not interested in being part of any army. I've got a good life here, a *quiet* life. I fit in just fine, I've got a job and make a good living."

Josh smirks. "Yeah, for *now*. How long do you think that's going to stay once the war reaches Sells? You're not that far from Tucson, or Phoenix. The humans and the vampires are already clashing in both cities. There are probably less than three thousand people in Sells." He looks smug. "When this puny little town gets overrun, whose side are you going to be on?"

"The right one," she retorts as she yanks her cap over her hair and drops three bucks on the table to cover her check. She strides out of the cafe and over to her truck before the other vampire or his lank-looking sidekick can get in a final comment. There she stands for a moment and gazes at the street beyond the small mall that houses the cafe and a few other businesses. Sells wasn't much, mostly Indian reservation folks with families and an over-abundance of single mothers struggling along below the poverty line. What chance would these people have against vampires, of any kind, if they decided to move on the town? Illegal aliens and drug runners were bad but at least they were human. Vampires would be a lot harder to kill.

Mooney shakes her head and climbs into her truck. She needs to get home to her babies and try to clear her head. Kill vampires? Does she really think that? They're her kind, aren't they? And yet she had been human not so long ago, and on some level, isn't she still? She works to protect humans every day. Who would prevail in the end? Isn't that the side she wants to be on? What will happen to her children if she's killed in some gunfight, either with illegals or, God forbid, in this war that Josh—and let's face it, everything she hears on the news—insists is coming? Doesn't she need to make her alliances now so that her children will grow up in a world that's better than the one she experienced? Jesus, she's so confused.

Which side *is* the right one?

"APOCALYPSE TANGO" PT. 2

Jonathan Maberry

– 2 –

The Barkey Family Farm
Town of Ulysses
Potter County, Pennsylvania
The Eve of the War

"Okay, we're going to do this the right way," said Jimmy Saint to the gathered agents and technicians, "and that means no mistakes. No one screws up and no one screws around. Everyone here is a professional and we will all conduct ourselves as such. We don't want another Des Moines."

Swann watched as Saint looked from face to face, appraising each of them, taking the measure of each of them. The reference to Des Moines hit the right note on everyone. It had been a critical case during the early days of the V-War where an accidentally contaminated crime scene resulted in a vampire terrorist slipping through a net. The vampire, a Russian *upor*, went on to kill four children in random attacks and then set a bomb in a school that resulted in eighteen deaths and forty-seven wounded, some of them critically. It was one of the worst-case mishandlings by the Bureau since Ruby Ridge. The press had been brutal and relentless. The agents who mishandled that case were dismissed with prejudice, and the SAC was transferred to North Dakota.

The team that had come from the Philadelphia office were seasoned and experienced, but the other two agents here were from a tiny regional subagency. From what Swann knew of the FBI, to get a posting like this you had to either be a screw-up or bottom of your class at Quantico.

Some of the forensics people looked green, too. Or, maybe they were just young. Swann had encountered an alarming number of people in the military and in law enforcement who still looked like teenagers. Some of the techs here were younger than his own graduate assistants.

Saint had brought two senior agents with him, Whitcomb and Roth, both of whom had worked cases during the first outbreak.

Saint's briefcase lay open atop an equipment box that stood in one of the few spots of the farmhouse that was not stained with blood. The AIC removed a pair of clipboards and handed the first to Whitcomb. "You're the evidence man. Everything that gets collected gets logged on that. The techs will bring everything to you and you will damn well make sure everything is logged and secured. *Capiche?*"

"Yes sir."

"But I don't want you touching anything that hasn't already been bagged and tagged. Nothing. Tell me you understand."

"I understand, sir."

"Good." Saint turned to the rest of them. "Now everyone else tell me you understand. Chain of evidence is holy writ. Nobody—and I mean no-fucking-body—makes a mistake. When in doubt, you ask me. I will be happy to observe and advise. Do you understand?"

He got a brisk chorus of "Yes, sirs."

Saint nodded and handed the second clipboard to Roth, the other local agent. "Sally, you sketch out the crime scene. We have preliminary sketches from local law, but I want trained eyes on this." It was a dig at the township and State police, but Swann knew that it was also said to buck up the confidence of the local agents. Sally Roth straightened and said she understood.

Saint then gave orders to the lab techs. Everything was to be photographed, measured, tagged and bagged.

The team got to work.

Swann drifted over to Saint. "What about me? Frankly I don't know why they send me out on these things. I don't know anything about forensic evidence collection."

"You're here to advise."

"On what?"

"On what species of Blood did this."

"But I—"

"Correction, on what species of Blood *could* have done this. No one knows them better than you."

"I have no idea."

"None? Come on, Luther—look at the bodies. At the bite marks."

"You have me confused with a forensic odontologist, Jimmy," said Swann. "I can't tell one bite mark from another."

Which was a lie. He'd now studied photos of hundreds of victims, and while he wasn't a bite-mark expert in the traditional legal sense, he had helped to build the VBMI—the Vampire Bite-Mark Index—by helping to match attack patterns with folkloric descriptions of vampires. He actually could tell, to a high degree of probability, one bite pattern from another, but he didn't want to. Looking at a washed, bloodless corpse in a city morgue was bad enough. Seeing victims at an actual crime scene was something else entirely.

In its way, this was almost as hard to do as when he used to roll out with Special Ops teams on missions against terrorist V-cells. He'd done that several times, mostly with V-8, General May's pack of pet attack dogs. The last time he went into the field with them, just before the peace, Swann had been badly wounded. His body was criss-crossed with scars. His soul, far more so.

"Luther," said Saint, "do your best, okay? We need to work this as a team."

Swann was about to reply when he was interrupted by the *whoop* of a siren. A single note. He followed Saint to the door and saw an unmarked SUV with a magnetic dome light pulling to a stop in the turnaround out front. They watched as a very tall, very thin man unfolded himself from the backseat.

"Ah," said Saint. "The Angel of Death arriveth."

"Who?"

"Dr. Spiro Nyklos."

"Oh…shit."

He'd heard of Nyklos. He was a clinical psychologist on the government payroll who had spent the last twenty-five years as a consulting profiler for the FBI and other investigative agencies. In the early days of the outbreak, Nyklos had been one of the most frequently seen talking heads on news programs. Swann had also read some of the man's reports. They were cold, precise, but alarmist. He believed that the vampires constituted a grave threat, not only to national security, but to the human race as well. He was the first person to suggest the internment option. There was a rumor that he had made a case to the White House to declare all V-positive persons to be enemy combatants, which would effectively cancel out their Constitutional rights.

Swann believed those rumors. And it had earned Nyklos the nickname of the Grim Reaper.

"What's he doing here?" demanded Swann. "Did you call him?"

"No," said Saint quietly. "I fucking well did not."

However, the AIC went out onto the porch to meet Nyklos. They spoke quietly for a moment and the doctor handed Saint a letter. Saint read it, nodded, handed it back. They shook hands.

"We're, um, happy to have you join us, Dr. Nyklos."

Dr. Spiro Nyklos was a six-and-a-half foot tall Greek-American with a thick head of coal-black hair and eyes set so deeply into dark pits that at any distance his head looked like a skull. He always looked emaciated and unhealthy on TV, but in the glow of the swirling red and blue lights, he looked cadaverous. As he stepped into the house his eyes darted here and there and Swann could almost hear relays clicking inside the man's head. He wondered if he actually thought in sound bites. Then Nyklos saw him and those dark eyes stopped. His stare was invasive and prolonged.

"Dr. Swann," he said with a half-smile on his lips.

"Dr. Nyklos," Swann said, nodding. Neither offered to shake hands.

Saint eased himself between them with the deftness of a boxing referee. "Luther, Dr. Nyklos is here to observe and advise."

"Advise on what exactly?"

Nyklos showed him yellow teeth. "Classified."

"Bullshit. Unclassify it."

"Sorry. I'm not at liberty to do that."

"You are aware, I'm sure, that I'm the presidential advisor on this crisis," snapped Swann, aware of how waspish he sounded. He rarely pulled rank—or even respected the rank they'd given him—but his dislike of Nyklos bordered on contempt.

"Then I recommend you discuss this matter with the president," said Nyklos. "In the meantime, I am here at the behest of General May and the Congressional Committee on Nonhuman Affairs."

"His, um, papers are in order, Luther," said Saint, who's face was wooden.

Nyklos turned away from Swann and snapped his fingers for one of the agents to provide him with protective shoe covers and latex gloves. He put them on while studying the crime scene.

Swann and Saint exchanged a long look.

Swann mouthed the word "Asshole." Saint turned away to hide a smile.

The Grim Reaper moved from body to body, pausing to bend low and look into dead eyes. Green flies, late for the season but empowered by the cooling meat, buzzed around him and the bodies, sometimes landing to lay their thousands of eggs in the ragged edges of wounds. Swann trailed a few feet behind Nyklos, careful not to step in any of the puddles of blood, trying to see the scene as Nyklos saw it, hoping that it would give him some idea of what the man was thinking.

Nyklos looked at the two dead children and began to move off, then he stopped and came back to stand over them. Swann and Saint joined him and for a long moment the three of them stood in a loose half-circle around the corpses. Their bodies had been forcibly dismembered and the parts thrown into a heap. Hands and feet, elbows and knees pointing in all directions.

The girl must have been pretty, good bone structure still padded by the roundness of baby fat but showing the elegance of the womanly face that would have blossomed if not for this. Her flesh had a waxy, nearly translucent veneer, unpinked by the loss of all the blood that pooled around her. Both of her eyes were open, but they looked flat and distorted by the loss of fluids. Her lips—bled pale and pulled tight over her small teeth—were rigid with the beginnings of rigor mortis.

Dr. Nyklos grunted.

"What?" asked Saint.

"Have these bodies been moved?"

"A little," said the AIC. "When the responding officers came in the lights were off. One of them accidentally kicked the boy's body."

"His arm," said Nyklos.

"Sir?"

"He kicked the boy's arm." The profiler pointed to a smear that fanned back from the dead boy's forearm. "His arm was moved. See?"

"I see it," agreed Saint.

"Has this already been photographed?"

Saint confirmed that it had been.

"May I move it back into place?" asked Nyklos.

"Why?"

"May I?"

"Okay, but I'm going to need to know why you're doing it. And I'll have to note that it was done."

"Fair enough."

Nyklos squatted down and gingerly lifted the limp wrist. Rigor hadn't yet set in and the severed arm moved easily. Nyklos settled it into place at the beginning of the smear, where clotted blood indicated it had originally laid. The profiler grunted and stood up.

"Can we have the girl's body lifted off?"

Saint ordered two forensics techs to do it, and the body was placed on a plastic tarp and set down out of the way.

Nyklos sighed and shook his head.

"Why did you do that, Spiro?" asked Swann.

"Stand on this side and look for yourself."

Swann frowned and came cautiously around to the other side and stood next to Nyklos. For a moment Swann saw nothing but the same tragedy from a different angle. Then, just as Nyklos was about to reach a bony finger out to show he what he meant, Swann saw it, too.

"Oh, my God," he breathed.

"What?" demanded the AIC, and he crowded in beside Swann. The three of them stared down at the boy as he was now revealed.

Saint said, "Oh…shit."

The boy was on his back, with his left arm stretched high above the shoulder, the elbow joint wrenched so that the forearm cut left at a sharp angle; his left arm was hanging straight out from the shoulder, and leaning down toward the floor, but the forearm was raised as if in surrender. The boy's left leg was raised so that the thigh went out in a horizontal line from the hip joint, the knee bent at a right angle; and the right leg was straight down except where the knee was twisted to cant the lower leg sharply to the right.

"Jesus Christ," said Swann. "Could that be…could that have been an accident? Some kind of spasm?"

"No. I know cadaveric spasms, and this is not that kind of thing," Nyklos said. "This is deliberate. Look how precisely the limbs are arranged."

Swann didn't want to look.

But he couldn't look away. The horror of the murders was bad enough. The thought that this might be the fuse that could make the V-War erupt all over again, that was bad enough. The *slaughter* of these innocent people was bad enough. He didn't need this to be worse. To be more complicated.

But it was.

One by one the forensics techs and FBI agents came over and stood around the corpse. With the girl's body gone it was easy to see. The message was there to be read as it had been intended.

A message.

A statement.

The boy's four twisted limbs formed the crooked arms of a swastika.

"THE ENEMY WITHIN" PT. 2

Yvonne Navarro

— 4 —

Mooney runs into Josh a few times over the next couple of weeks. In Sells, it's hard not to cross paths: one grocery store, a couple of convenience stores with gas pumps, a few other stores. And, of course, one restaurant. He wasn't making a point of seeing her, but he wasn't avoiding it, either. Just a new guy making his way around town and familiarizing himself with everything. He'd see her and give a wave, then go on about his business. No big deal.

His creepy ex-girlfriend is something altogether different.

At first Mooney isn't sure when Rose went from odd and slightly annoying to creepy-stalker-woman, then she realizes that although Josh might consider Rose just a friend now, at sometime in the past they had been a lot more than that. Mooney doesn't care one way or another; he's interesting in the way a man or a woman always examines someone new, but the things he'd said had obliterated any chance of that going further. And those very things make Josh warrant more than an assignment to the just-another-guy category. It's more than the training she's been given by the Border Patrol, the classes and videos and PowerPoint presentations. He has, perhaps, one toe over the line of fitting the profile of a terrorist, except that all he is right now is a lot of big talk. No threats, exactly, just grand and great plans. That those plans involved war could be an issue, but Mooney has significant logic problems believing he can pull off any of what he said. And if she can't take it seriously, would Chief Delgado, or his boss higher up the pay grade? She doesn't want to look like an overreacting teenager and end up with them no longer taking *her* seriously.

And pallid, thin-faced Rose just accentuates that possibility.

Yeah, she's stalking Mooney, at least as much as she can given she doesn't seem to have her own vehicle. Mooney doesn't feel like the vampire is dangerous, but she's bothered by it, unnerved in the way a person feels when she keeps finding the same door in a dark, old house open after she *knows* it was shut. Rose never says anything to her, which is too bad—that would give Mooney the push she needs to just confront her and have it out. But Rose is always just a bit too far away, there are always a few other people between them to act as roadblocks, or she always disappears behind a building or into a door-way before Mooney can get to her. It's like Rose wants to lure Mooney somewhere private, but Mooney isn't having it; she isn't afraid of the other woman, vampire or not, but she doesn't *trust* her…or Josh, for that matter. Both of them have hidden agendas and Mooney can't decide if she wants to be a part of that or not. In all honesty, she wishes they would just go away so that things can be like they were: her, the illegals, the Border Patrol, a perfect triangle in the way it protects the people of Sells and Mooney's children alike. It wouldn't be the first time she's wished time would turn back on itself and undo a few things. As much as she wants to deny it, there's always the chance of another war between the new vampires and the humans—anyone can see that. Hell, in most of the large cities around the world, it's happened twice.

And Mooney has a nasty feeling that Josh and Rose are trying their damnedest to bring it right here to Sells.

– 5 –

She sees the first trio of new vampires drive into town two days later.

Mooney's sitting on a lawn chair in front of her trailer, soaking up the strong summer heat and enjoying the quiet of the afternoon. Her babies are napping inside after their noon meal, a couple of small jackrabbits whose drained carcasses she'll toss into the desert during her shift tonight. One of the passengers glances her way as the car drives slowly past, but his gaze doesn't linger; the way he scans the street makes it seem like he's looking for an address. Josh's, no doubt, if what he'd said was true and he'd been posting around the Internet for others to join him. He's probably posted in some chatrooms, on a bunch of blogs…he might even have his own Facebook page. Nowadays a little time online, a few connections, and some well-placed comments could take you around the world in less than twenty-four hours. There were probably entire online vampire communities, all of which were being religiously monitored by Uncle Sam's minions. Mooney herself is probably regularly watched, but that's okay. She is what she is and doesn't have anything to hide from her employer or anyone else.

She watches the car as it rolls down the street, committing the license plate number to memory so she can run it through the system later on. With her rattlesnake-pattern hair stuffed under a plain black baseball cap, there's nothing to separate her from any other Native American woman sitting outside her place; the ground is dust and scrub, the paint on the trailer faded from the harsh sun, her vehicle pulled at an angle in front and covered in the same Arizona dust. Most of the townies know where she lives even though there are no toys strewn in the front yard dirt; Mooney keeps the twins' outside playtime to the backyard and rarely takes them out in public. They're growing and learning faster than human children, but they need to be old enough to understand actual language and the difference between right and wrong before mixing with human children. Having your kid bite someone else's is bad enough, but when yours is a vampire and the other a human…yeah, bad business, indeed.

On her way to meet the Chief later on, Mooney sees a couple more vampires; these two are in the same late-teenager group but trudge past the Desert Rain Cafe beneath the weight of hikers' backpacks, the kind pros use when they know what they're facing in the desert and what they need to carry. Even a vampire can get dehydrated under the fireball hanging over Mother Nature's earth. Their faces are flushed with heat but they seem happy enough, chatting as they walk and shift the weight on their backs, occasionally consulting a well-crumpled piece of paper—a map? Not exactly the type Mooney had imagined rushing into Sells to populate Josh's so-called army. As she thinks back on it, neither had the three she'd seen earlier. Not much of a look at them, but even so: the car had been some kind of newer hybrid thing with a couple of college stickers on the back bumper. But it could all be a masquerade, the curtain behind which his newfound soldiers had been instructed to hide. That made five so far—*if* she knew about them all, and Mooney suspects otherwise. Yet no one had said anything about any newcomers, and she hasn't noticed any strangers shopping or in the cafe.

34

What Mooney really wants to do is stay the hell away from them and let her own life go blissfully onward, but maybe it's time to do a little research on Josh and his weird little shadow whether she likes it or not.

—6—

"Hi, Mooney. How've you been?"

She turns at the sound of Josh's voice behind her in the aisle of the grocery store. Not surprisingly, there's Rose, following at his elbow like a tail attached to a cat. "Fine, thanks. You two?"

He lifts one side of his mouth. "Can't complain." He starts to move past but Mooney steps into his path and plants her feet. "Where are you staying?" she asks. "Haven't seen many of your newcomers show up. Given what you said, I kind of expected a bunch by now."

"There's more than you realize," Rose blurts. "Staying with us." Josh shoots her a shut-up look, but it's too late.

"Where's that?" Mooney asks. "Maybe I'll stop by later. Introduce myself."

Josh stares at her and she can almost see him weighing options. When he opens his mouth, Rose grabs at his arm as if to tell *him* to keep quiet, but he shakes her off impatiently. It was an odd turnabout. "We're off of Artesan Road," he says after a beat, "about a half mile after it starts to curve southeast."

One of Mooney's eyebrows arches. "Only thing I know way out there is the Marcos place. Hasn't been lived in for years."

Josh nods. "Yeah. It's not much but it's site built. Pretty sturdy and cooler than a manufactured place. I used my savings and bought it as-is from the bank for fifteen thousand bucks, cleaned it up a bit. It's livable."

"Sounds good," Mooney says. There's a sudden, faint prickling in her scalp; before it deepens, she shoots Rose a warning glare. The feeling stops as abruptly as it started, confirming her belief that Rose has some sort of telepathic ability. Mind control? Maybe, but to what extent Mooney has no way of knowing. And she doesn't want to find out.

Mooney does, however, want to have an accurate count on how many vampires were now in Sells. "Why don't I come by this afternoon?"

Rose looks decidedly unhappy but Josh's smile is wide. "Looking forward to it."

— 7 —

If the goal was isolation, Josh and Rose have picked the perfect location. The house is almost out of the town's boundary and there's nothing else out here, certainly no neighbors. Josh had claimed it was livable, but Mooney remembered the Marcos place (she couldn't stop thinking of it that way, and she'd never known Josh's last name) as being a pit and it wasn't much better now. New it had been the standard low-income government housing that had been built for all the Indians around Sells, both in and out of town. But that had been years ago, and the cheap construction hadn't held up well under its former owner's no-maintenance lifestyle. Juan Marcos had carried a formidable temper exacerbated by a drinking problem he hadn't cared to fight, which was exactly what he did—with his wife, his two teenaged sons, and anyone in town he decided shouldn't be breathing his oxygen. About ten years ago he'd gone drinking one weekend and launched himself at the wrong *ranchero* in a bar in Mexican Sonoita, just over the border, and gotten dead for his trouble. His sons had split for bigger cities and his wife had packed up her clothes and walked away from the four-room house with holes in almost every wall from Juan's fists. Bank of America had reclaimed the house but no one wanted to live at the edge of nowhere when Sells itself was already in the middle of it.

Mooney pulls up in front of the place and puts the 4Runner into park. *Wow,* she thinks as she eyes the sagging porch roof and the outside walls showing cracked and missing chunks of stucco. *I wonder what he considers unlivable.* Like most of the other houses in Sells, there's no indication of air-conditioning or a swamp cooler; most folks make it through the days with fans and open the windows to let in night air that's chilly year-round. The windows are closed against the daytime heat and Mooney can see that new light-colored curtains have been drawn to thwart the sun on the south-facing side.

She climbs out and stands for a few moments, examining the hard-packed dirt that stretched around the house. Off to one side are the remains of some kind of wire fence, a chicken coop or maybe something to keep rabbits away from a home garden. Not much else, although she can just see the rear bumper of a car around the back corner. Mooney walks over to that side to see if it's the car that drove by her place; she'd run the plate and found it legal, but now she's just curious. Twenty steps forward brought it in full view and what she sees makes her eyes widen.

Her oversensitive hearing picks up the sound of a door opening and she's back at the front corner of the house before Rose can actually step outside. Rose looks at her but doesn't bother to ask what Mooney has been doing. "You coming in or what?"

Not the most enticing of invitations, but before Mooney can comment, Josh pushes past the teenager and gestures at Mooney. "Never mind Rose," he says. "I think the Arizona heat makes her cranky. Please, come on in."

Mooney bites back a sarcastic remark and nods. "Thanks." When she steps past Rose on the cracked landing, the girl starts to reach for her. An instinctive feeling of loathing blasts through Mooney's senses; she yanks her arm out of the girl's reach and, without realizing it, opens her mouth and hisses at her. Rose freezes. "Don't touch me," Mooney says in a low voice. "Not ever."

"Now, ladies," Josh says as he slips between them. "Let's not quarrel."

Rose looks away like a sullen teenager, but Mooney glares at him. "That was condescending," she snaps.

He flushes. "I apologize. I didn't mean it the way it sounded. Seriously."

Her mouth set, Mooney steps past him and into the living room of the ramshackle house, surprised to find it almost empty. There's a small couch on one side over which has been tossed one of those five-dollar throws, and a table that looks like it might collapse at any moment under the skimpy weight of a couple of books and an old lamp. Besides that, not much except…

Six people—vampires—sound asleep on blankets in sleeping bags on the filthy floor.

"What is this?" She keeps her voice lowered without intending to.

"Don't worry," Josh says. "You won't wake them." Beside him, Rose chuckles under her breath, an ugly sound that works on Mooney's nerves.

"So," Mooney says, "I counted twelve cars in back. How many vampires are here and where are the rest?"

Josh gestures first at a couple of open doors on the back wall of the living room, then toward the kitchen of to the left.

"There's maybe another twenty or twenty-five in the other rooms. Most of them came in two or three to a car, but a few had 'em packed into vehicles like sardines. The more the merrier and all that."

Mooney frowns, then on impulse reaches out with one boot and prods at the leg of the nearest slumbering vampire. It's a guy, face pale and still beneath a head of badly-cut straggly brown hair; he doesn't stir, even when Mooney pushes hard enough on his knee to move it a good three inches. "What's wrong with them?" she demands. "Are they sick? Why won't he wake up?"

"They're just groggy," Josh answers, a little too quickly.

"Groggy?"

"We partied a pretty hard last night," Rose puts in. "Plus food's a little scarcer than we thought it would be, so they're not as chipper as they might be otherwise." There's no mistaking the sarcastic emphasis on the word *chipper*.

Mooney looks at her. "By food, you mean blood."

Rose shrugs. "I say it like it is."

"The desert is full of animals," Mooney says flatly.

"We all know animal blood isn't what vampires really need," Josh says. "How about you help us out with that, Mooney?"

Her eyes widen. "What?"

Rose steps closer to her. "With the FOOD part. Real food—you know, *blood*. As in human blood, like from a few of those illegal aliens you're probably running across every night at work." Rose's lips stretch into an almost sinister smile, wide enough to show the tips of her fangs. Bloodsmell washes over Mooney as the other woman exhales and Mooney automatically steps back. Her gaze cuts to the figures at her feet and she realizes that she can see marks here and there on exposed skin. Not big, but still…bites? Bruises?

"Seriously, you think I'm going to bring you humans to dine on?" She looks at Josh and Rose, not bothering to hide her expression of disgust. "You want me to make up a dinner menu for you, too?"

"Not the worst idea I've heard," Rose fires back. "I—"

"Shut it," Josh interrupts. "Come on, everyone knows why the

Border Patrol hired you. What's the big deal about sharing?"

"What I do on the job stays on the job," Mooney retorts. "And in case you don't get it, there a big difference between me doing what I do for work and kidnapping people to bring them to you." He opens his mouth to argue, but Mooney holds up her hand. "This isn't open to negotiation."

Josh's look of disappointment is overshot by Rose's cold words. "Too bad. But hey, we appreciate *you* stopping by."

She leaps.

Mooney knows next to nothing about the young woman beyond she's a vampire, a likely runaway, and has an unreturned crush on Josh. It's said that every vampire had some kind of history in the DNA that had been reactivated, some relation to a forgotten myth or long-lost fantastical tale. Rose's connection might be anything from an Irish fairy to Godzilla, but all that matters right now is that she isn't nearly strong or fast enough to take on Mooney. As quick as the rattlesnake heritage in her bloodline, Mooney steps to the side and whips out her hand. It fastens tightly around Rose's throat before she can so much as squeak, then Mooney's fangs, each tipped with just a drop of her paralyzing venom, are hovering just above the skin beneath Rose's jaw.

"Don't. Move." With Mooney's warm breath tickling her ear, Rose shudders in response but that's all.

"Oh, hey now," Josh says in a mild voice. "This is not where I thought this conversation would go." Wisely, he stays where he is. "I'm thinking Rose misconstrued things."

Without letting go, Mooney walks the girl backward until her back is against the wall. "You think?"

"Please, Mooney." Josh nods toward the people on the floor. "Rose is just overreacting. All these extra mouths to feed have spread us a little thin, and some people "—he looks sideways at Rose—"don't think straight when their stomachs aren't full."

Mooney's gaze centers on Rose. "Is that what this is, Rose? A misunderstanding?"

Mooney's grip has loosened just enough for the other woman to nod slightly. "Yes," Rose manages to get out. "M-Mistake."

Mooney releases Rose with a sideways shove that sends her reeling into the wall all the way to the left. "I hope so," Mooney says. This time her gaze focuses on Josh. "Because I'd hate to see what might happen if things *really* got off track."

Josh steps toward her. "Mooney—"

"Don't," she snaps. "Both of you need to just stay away from me. Find your own food, and *don't* try to do it in town, either." She looks from one to the other. "Clear?"

"Very," Rose says from where she's slid down the wall and into a sitting position.

Mooney doesn't wait around to hear what Josh has to say.

"APOCALYPSE TANGO" PT. 3

Jonathan Maberry

– 3 –

The Perkins Homes Housing Development
Southeast Baltimore, Maryland
The Eve of the War

"Yo! Bitch!"

Those two words rang out, hard as gunshots. It froze the woman in place. She huddled where she stood, afraid to turn and look. Afraid that if she looked, she would see monsters.

The monsters, however, did not require her attention.

They required *her*.

They came running. A pack of them. Sneakers slapping the ground. Grunting like hogs. Laughter threading through the noise of their approach.

There were six of them.

A feral pack that had staked out this corner of Perkins Homes. It was a dangerous neighborhood before the V-War. It was worse now. A series of firefights between the *Red Africa* V-cell and their rivals, the *Africa Screams,* had escalated into wholesale slaughter. Two SWAT teams were sent in, and were promptly torn to pieces. The National Guard came in next and tanks rolled down Eden Street, blasting at the barricades and firing into houses. For six hours on one bad Thursday the skies above Perkins Homes were filled with Black Hawk helicopters. The papers called it an American Somalia. They tried to make it about race, about black and white.

But that wasn't it. It had *always* been that, so this was something new.

At first it was Blood versus Blood, to establish hunting grounds.

Then it was Bloods versus Beats.

It stood as one of the worst confrontations of the V-War. Up there with the Battle of Butcher Holler in Kentucky and the South Miami Slaughter.

Now it was a ghost town. A no-man's land populated by drifters, the homeless, addicts, and a few of the elderly who survived the war but had no money to relocate. People who were deliberately ignored by a system that regarded them as inconvenient logistical problems.

The woman on Eden Street was one of those.

Sixty-eight, but older than her years. Bent from forty years working a press in an industrial cleaners. Scarred by the machines, scarred by beatings. Always hungry. Always alone.

She stood there, hunched over, wondering what kind of horror was coming up behind her.

Robbery? She had fifteen dollars left out of her pay. If they took that, she wouldn't eat for the last two days before next payday. Not the worst thing that could happen. She'd gone hungry so many times before.

Rape?

She'd survived that twice. Both times in her forties, when she still had some of her looks. Enough that a rapist thought her worth attacking. It was the coldest of compliments paid by a vicious world.

What else did she have that they could want?

If she had been two blocks closer to home, and maybe fifteen years younger, she would have tried to run for it. Tried.

And they'd have run her down.

The running feet were right behind her.

The laughter was in her ears.

They slapped the ground with their feet as they fought their own youthful momentum. Then they were there. A ring of them. Five.

Five monsters.

"Hey, bitch. Where the fuck you going?" asked one of them. It didn't matter which one. They were all alike. All monsters.

They circled her like savages. Poking. Pushing. Slapping her hands away as she tried to cover her face. One of them tore her purse off her shoulder. That was gone. No money, no food. No house keys. No Social Security card.

Gone.

All gone.

"Let me see your face, bitch," said one as he plucked at the scarf she wore around her face. And from the way he said it, she knew what they were going to do.

Knew.

Her knees wanted to buckle. Her bladder wanted to let loose. She clenched everything and tried to stand. Tried to keep herself together. For a moment longer. For however long she could.

"Let me see," said another of them.

Then they were all saying it.

"Show us!" they cried. Over and over, like kids playing a game. Like Romans at the Circus. "Show us!"

They began running in circles around her. Plucking at her. Darting in to try and catch the scarf between thumb and forefinger. Making a game of it. Making it last. She slapped at their hands, and it made them laugh even more. She pressed the scarf to her face, and that made them laugh, too.

"Please," she said, and the single syllable broke into pieces as she said it.

"Show us!"

Then one of them caught the tail of the scarf and yanked it. Ripped it off. Tore it from her with such force that it spun her whole body. She staggered three steps and then dropped to her knees. Her kneecaps struck hard and pain exploded through her body.

Two of the monsters pulled out cell phones and began taking photos.

"Instagram, bitch!" one of them laughed. It made the others laugh, too.

The cameras flashed and flashed, catching her in the light. Catching her ragged clothing. Catching the lines of pain on her face. Catching the glistening tears as they rolled over the thousand wrinkles on her face. Catching the curve of her fangs.

Her fangs.

Her fangs.

So long. So sharp.

So useless to her.

She was one of the first to turn, she knew that. It had terrified her. At first she thought her gums were receding because of some disease.

The people at the clinic had done tests. They found nothing. They told her to see an orthodontist. As if she could ever afford such a thing.

Then the stories began to break.

Michael Fayne in New York.

The Bradley twins in Omaha.

All the others.

She knew what she was, and she didn't.

She was a vampire. She knew it. Everybody knew it.

But she didn't know what kind.

Some ugly kind. Her fangs kept growing until they pushed through her lips and hung like walrus tusks down her chin. They were heavy. It jammed her other teeth together. The TMJ gave her migraines. The pain never really let up.

She took to wearing a scarf. Easier to get away with in winter. Harder in summer. Most people, if she was lucky, thought she had skin cancer and wanted to hide. The others knew.

Of course they knew.

Like these boys knew.

They pushed her. They jumped in and out to poke her. They taunted her and dared her. One of them pulled open his shirt collar to expose his throat.

"Come on, you toothy old whore. You know you want it. Take a bite."

"Please…" she begged. "God, please."

The boys closed in around her.

If God heard her screams, He did not care to answer.

"THE ENEMY WITHIN" PT.3

Yvonne Navarro

— 8 —

She goes back three days later.

Not because they had ignored her warning—that would have been easier to take—but because the desert is going to hell and the only thing Mooney can think of to do is ask for Josh's help.

"What the hell do you want?" Rose spits at her after she opens the door.

Before Mooney can answer Josh pulls Rose aside. "Being rude doesn't help anything," he says mildly. He gestures past Rose. "Come on in."

Mooney eyes the shadowy room behind the two vampires. Like before, nothing moves in there. So much for Josh's army. "No, thanks," she says. She doesn't think she can stand to see those silent figures lying on the floor. She clears her throat. "I-I came to ask for your help," she says awkwardly.

Josh's eyebrows lift in surprise at the same time Rose chortles from behind him. "That's rich," she says. "Like we would—"

"Would you *stop* already?" Josh snaps. "You're not in charge here, remember?" Rose's mouth abruptly closes into a sullen line and she glares at Mooney. "You were saying?" Josh prods.

Mooney hesitates, not sure how to word what she needs without it sounding like she's giving permission. "I know I said you needed to stay away from the townsfolk if you…hunted," she finally says, "but maybe you'd like to ride along with me on my shift tonight, give me some…assistance if I need it in any encounters with illegals." She doesn't bother to add that the encounters are escalating not in frequency but in violence and ratio, to the point where she's almost outnumbered despite her superior abilities; the word is something big is going down tonight, movement of a substantial amount of product that'll require the appropriate escalation in guards.

Josh looks at her thoughtfully. "I think we could do that."

"Just you," Mooney says. Seeing Rose's hate-filled look, she adds, "My truck only seats two."

Rose hisses something under her breath but Josh ignores her. "I'll follow you in my truck, but Rose has to stay here anyway." Mooney wonders why but Josh doesn't bother to elaborate. "Is this common?" he asks instead. "Like in those so-called live cop shows?"

"No," Mooney answers. "And it's off the record—so far off the record that it never happened."

Josh nods. "I understand. Do you want me to meet you somewhere? What time?"

Mooney looks him in the eye. "If you're up for it, now."

— 9 —

A cool, moonless night, the sky filled with millions of stars and the clear air heavy with the scents of desert plants and animals. It would be perfect except for Josh's truck following her and the certainty that without him she'd be heading into a situation she can't handle.

The drug cartels haven't taken well to having their livelihoods diluted by the sudden success of the Border Patrol's countermeasures. Rumor has it they believe there are rogue agents killing their people and keeping the spoils. It's easy to see where this comes from— Mooney leaves no bodies and the drugs and vehicles leftover from her encounters are quietly taken care of, the drugs destroyed and the vehicles confiscated to be sold at auction. Rather than limit their attempts to smuggle goods across the border, the response of the cartels has been to double, even triple, the guards on each drug run. Mooney's good, but even she has a hard time when the number of opponents climbs into double digits.

Any wish that Josh not be there dissipates as they follow a scrub-choked tire trail around to the backside of a small hill and right into a trap.

Rough shouts of *"¡Alto! ¡Alto!"* bounce through the air and the sudden headlights of a quarter dozen vehicles sting Mooney's vision as she slides to a stop. Behind her Josh does the same, the front of his worn pick-up truck *thunking* lightly into her bumper. Someone yanks open her driver's door and screams "Get out!" in heavily-accented English. She lets the man pull her out then moves on ahead as he pokes her in the back with his weapon. Besides the obvious scents associated with the vehicles, she can smell sweat, meth, and gun oil.

And fear. Yeah, plenty of that.

"I count fourteen men," Josh whispers from her left side. "Might be more still in the—"

"No talk!" bellows the man striding behind Josh. He jabs at Josh's head with the barrel of his rifle. Josh makes a growling sound deep in his throat that only Mooney hears, but he stays in place, waiting to see what's ahead. Ultimately that isn't much beyond a lot of shouting and questions that Mooney can't—won't—answer. It takes less than three minutes before their lack of cooperation gets them the ultimate verdict.

"Shoot them," commands a man who has consistently given orders to the others but not gotten his own hands dirty. Mooney knows he says the words in English on purpose.

The man in front of her squeezes the trigger, but he's a half second behind Mooney's sideways leap. Somewhere to her right another man screams, then everything turns into blurs and flashes of gunfire, like stop-motion scenes from a black and white horror movie. Mooney strikes and bites, over and over, leaving paralyzed and dying men all around her as she moves in a pattern too rapid and erratic for any of them to follow. Those who fall because of her are clean and silent kills, and it takes a few moments for her to register that Josh's method is the polar opposite. He's biting and slashing and beating his targets; the aftermath of his attacks are on the ground in twisted, bloody piles, some still alive but too mutilated to move.

The end of it is not silent.

They win, yes, but at what cost? Mooney feels no guilt about the dead she drags into piles for the clean-up crew that will come within an hour after her call into headquarters, but she can't say the same for the five torn and bleeding men she watches Josh toss into the bed of his truck. And yet, has she not done the same in the past, brought home food for children? Yes, but at least her "spoils" had been paralyzed, their deaths and draining painless. These men are still alive and still in pain, their moans floating on the spare desert breeze like the songs of lost ghosts.

"To feed the troops," Josh tells her with a bloody grin. She had asked for his help so she can't deny him payment, but it still horrifies her. He's covered in blood—his face and hands, his clothes, even his hair are matted with gore and dirt, as if he'd wallowed in the blood of the dead. Had he? Mooney has a sudden, horrifying image in her mind of herself becoming irreparably involved with Josh and his small but growing army. If things change in their world, if the war between the vampires and humans does actually make its way to Sells, will she end up doing the same thing? Will her children? The idea of a future like this makes her want to retch.

"Make sure you dispose of the bodies properly," she tells him. "They can't turn up later, in or out of town." She hears her voice, emotionless, even businesslike, but she suddenly doesn't like herself. She doesn't want to be this kind of individual, human or vampire.

But is it inevitable?

– 10 –

Mooney sees the backpacker as he strolls into town around midmorning on a Friday, after she's finished her check-in and paperwork at the end of her shift and is about to head for home. She's avoided anything to do with Josh for almost a week, but he and his budding army are always in her thoughts. It isn't hard to peg the traveler as a vampire, and she imagines him finding his way to Josh's place after a couple of hours of asking around. Great, she thinks. Another one for the ranks. Then, as she drives past and glances at him, his gaze locks with hers.

She has no idea why, but she slams the brakes hard enough to dump her workbag and phone onto the passenger floorboard.

"Hey," she calls. She gestures for him to come over. "New in town?"

The guy looks at her, then gives her dusty truck a critical scan before crossing the highway to talk to her. When he sees her Border Patrol uniform, his shoulders relax and the slight front line between his eyebrows smooths out. Inside Mooney chuckles; it's usually the other way around.

"Yeah." He isn't sweating but he looks hot and thirsty, not exactly tired but tired of walking. "I caught a ride down from south Tucson but the guy let me out at Three Points." He glances back across the road at the small green sign that announces SELLS. "It's been a long hike from there to here."

"Thirty-five miles? Yeah, I'd say a trek," Mooney agrees. She sticks her hand through the window. "Agent Lopez," she says. "Or just Mooney."

He takes her hand and gave it a good, firm shake. "Mooney," he repeats. "That's a great name. I'm Tyler McKinzie."

"What brings you to Sells, Mr. McKinzie?"

"Tyler, please. I'm looking for a guy named Josh Mulleneaux." He gazes at her for a beat. "I'm a vampire."

"Yeah," Mooney says. "I guessed that." He's tall and has the lean build of an athlete. Beneath hair that falls to his shoulders in dark curls, Tyler's eyes are a bright crystalline blue shot through with odd flecks of fiery gold. She's never seen anything like them and has to force herself to look away. She exhales, disappointed; it had probably been too much to hope that someone like Tyler would just stumble into Sells for no particular reason. He actually reminds her of a young Greek god right out of one of her old history books. Below the sleeves of his t-shirt, his pale, muscled flesh bears matching tattoos of green vines interspersed with flames that wind around his wrists and fore-arms to disappear beneath the fabric.

"Is there a problem?" Tyler asks. She glances at him, but there's nothing confrontational in his tone.

She shrugs. "No, I suppose not. So you came down here to join up with his army, huh?"

Tyler looks confused. "What army?"

"That whole idea he's got about getting vampires together to take over the town before the war makes its way to us," she answers. She doesn't bother to hide her impatience. "Because, you know, this place is such a strategic location. Or something."

"Hold on," Tyler says. "That's not why I came here. The forum I was in when I picked up on the invite talked about this being somewhere we could go to get away from the war, just stay out of it. Like consci-entious objectors."

Mooney stares at him. "Excuse me?"

"I'm not here to fight anyone, Agent Lopez." Tyler gazes around him, squinting at the desert. "If that's the deal, I might as well just turn around and head back to Oregon." He sighs. "Probably easier to survive in the wilderness there than here anyway."

Mooney leans over and unlocks the passenger door, then pushes it open. "Get in," she says. "We have some talking to do."

– 11 –

"I am—was—majoring in environmental project management," Tyler tells her as he sit on the other end of her couch. "That all went haywire with the vampire emergence."

"Why?" Mooney asks, even though she already has a good idea.

Tyler shrugs and looks at his hands; the fingers are entwined so that it almost looks like he's praying. "Prejudice, fear, distrust, anger—you name it. Who can pinpoint one thing in a situation like this, where social norms and culture are destroyed so quickly? There's no 'normal' anymore, no pattern to follow that might lead anyone, human or vampire, to a stable future. There IS no stable future." He glances up at her. "You can't even blame one side or the other. I envy the way you've been able to stay in this town, the way the humans have accepted you and you feel safe living among them. You do, right? Feel safe among them, I mean."

Mooney thinks about it before she answers. "Well," she answers finally, "it hasn't been all roses, but yes. I feel safe." She pauses again. "For now."

Tyler is too intelligent to ask why she would put a caveat in her answer. Before he can say anything else, the twins charge into the trailer from the backyard, flinging themselves at Mooney amid laughter and childish screams. They seem more like three-year-olds, their growth apparently as accelerated post-birth as it had been inside Mooney's womb. When they realize someone else is in the trailer besides their mother, both suddenly stop in place and stare at Tyler, as still as rabbits frozen under the shadow of a hunting hawk. The only problem is that the current that shoots around the room is decidedly not prey looking at predator, but the other way around. Mooney sees Tyler's shoulders tense, ready in case the kids leap for him.

She clamps a hand around each child's wrist. "This is my friend," she tells them firmly. "His name is Tyler." Without releasing them, she continues. "My girl is Sitol, and my boy is Judum."

Tyler peers at them, relaxing bit by bit as they do the same. "Excellent." He grins. "If I give you my hand to shake, you have to promise not to bite me."

The twins look to Mooney, and she nods. "No bites," she instructs. "I'm not kidding." They almost look disappointed, but each one shakes Tyler's hand, then stands obediently in front of Mooney. After a few seconds, she laughs and pushes them toward the door. "You can stop protecting me now. Seriously—back outside. You know the rules, straight to the back yard and stay there."

She and Tyler watch them go; the energy leaves with them like tiny tornadoes. "How old are they?" he asks.

"Couple of months."

"Wow," he says. "That was fast. I take it their father is a vampire?"

"Don't assume," Mooney snaps before she can stop herself.

Tyler blinks. "Sorry."

She holds up her hand. "No—*I'm* sorry." She hesitates, then decides to just spit it out and be done with the whole, ugly thing. "Their father was an illegal who raped me. He and his *compadres* left me for dead in the desert." Her mouth lifts at one corner. "Obviously I survived, and not long after that I caught the virus. I was pregnant but didn't know it. The virus affected the babies, although no one, including me, knew I was carrying twins." Her smile this time is almost proud. "They grew almost as fast before they were born as they are now."

"Wow," Tyler says again. It isn't an empty sentiment—he is clearly impressed. "That's an amazing story, in all aspects." He shakes his head. "To endure what you did—"

"I'm no good at turning the other cheek," Mooney interrupts. "And I didn't. I found all three of them and killed them." She looks away for a moment. "Not very New Age, but it let me move on."

He eyes her. "It's not for me to judge," he finally says. "Yeah, I advocate forgiveness, moving forward rather than backward, coexisting rather than fighting. Even so, given the same set of circumstances, I can't say I would have done differently. You never know until you go through the exact same thing, and really, who can say that?"

"So you don't think I'm a monster?"

"I don't think anyone is a monster," he replies. "Not deep inside."

"You're wrong about that," Mooney replies. "You haven't seen the things I've seen. You haven't seen *Josh* the way I've seen him."

When Tyler has nothing to say in return, Mooney pushes to her feet.

Tyler does the same. "I'll head out," he says. "Catch up with you in the morning?"

Mooney opens her mouth to agree but the words won't come out. She can't, she realizes suddenly, stand to think of him out in the desert, unprotected and vulnerable—a vampire hippie child in a part of the country that given the chance will, literally, eat him alive. "Stay here," she says before she can change her mind. She points at the couch. "The kids and I will be in the bedroom. I'll get you a pillow and an afghan."

He looks at her dubiously. "Are you sure? I don't want to be a pain—"

"I insist," Mooney says in a voice that doesn't leave room for negotiation. "Get out from under all that weight you're carrying and relax for the first time in…what? Weeks?" He doesn't elaborate but she guesses she's close to the mark. The time has passed quickly and it's getting on toward evening; time to call the kids inside and settle everything down.

She decides that in the morning, she and Tyler will pay a little visit to Josh and Rose, and she *will* get to the bottom of their charade.

– 12 –

Mooney and Tyler pull up in front of Josh's dilapidated place close to ten o'clock. Neither has slept much; Mooney heard Tyler moving around now and then in the front room, checking the refrigerator for cold water, tossing on the squeaky and fairly uncomfortable couch. She imagined him standing at the window and looking out at the desert, the cold night sky shining with stars and not much of a moon, perhaps wondering what the hell he'd gotten himself into and if there was an "undo" button somewhere he could push. She's wondered the same thing now and then.

The house has an odd feeling about it, like it's deserted but…not, or maybe that there's something weird but unseen going on. Mooney can't quite put a name to it, but in a few minutes all the secrets Josh and Rose have been keeping are going to get a big dose of daylight. Tyler follows her up to the door but when Mooney raises her hand to knock he touches her on the shoulder and points to where it's already open a couple of inches. Mooney hesitates only a second, then gives it a nudge. It swings open to the living room and the air that spills from the opening is still night-cool and smells of stale bodies and…blood. Her eyes narrow but she pushes inside anyway, with Tyler right behind her. Her eyesight adjusts to the dim interior instantly and she jerks to a stop; not expecting it, Tyler stumbles into her back, then rights himself. A half second later he, too, focuses on the scene in front of Mooney.

Mooney hears Tyler's intake of breath just before her voice rises, as loud as she can and not actually scream, and splits the dusty silence in front of them. "What the *fuck* is going on here?"

Josh's head snaps up from his position on the floor across the room, about ten feet away. His back has been to the door and he'd been so focused on what he was doing that he never heard them come in, hadn't even known they were there until Mooney spoke. The inside of his mouth is dark with blood and a scarlet, viscous line of it dribbles down his chin, making him an almost stereotypical carica-ture of the vampires seen so often in old horror flicks. The difference, of course, is that this was real, and he has the potential to be very, very dangerous.

"Mooney!" Josh had been wrapped around the side of a young woman half-covered with an old army blanket, but he comes to his feet and quickly yanks the covering up to her chin. Not fast enough, though, to keep Mooney from seeing where he's been feeding on her shoulder. "Good to see you," Josh manages. He tries to look composed. "Who's your friend?"

Mooney doesn't answer, glancing pointedly at the girl on the floor. She even recognizes her as one of the backpackers who'd come into town last week.

"I was just checking to make sure she was all right," Josh says. He speaks sluggishly, like someone's who's just finished with an overly large meal and grown sleepy.

"You've got blood on your chin," Mooney says. Her tone makes the words sound jagged, sharp at the end of every syllable.

"What? Oh…" He swipes the back of his hand across the lower part of his face then looks at the stained skin like he doesn't understand it. Finally his thoughts seem to click back into place. He laughs. Actually *laughs*.

"Well, I guess you've found me out." Josh wipes his bloody hand down the side of his jeans.

"I'm guessing this isn't exactly the kind of kinship he was promising in chat room postings," Mooney says to Tyler. She glares back at Josh.

"And it's damned sure not the collection of soldiers you tried to sell to me."

Josh's gaze flips on Tyler. "Hey, you're one of mine!"

Tyler's mouth twists in disgust. "Not in this lifetime *or* the next. You're a liar." He pauses. "And some kind of freaking…cannibal."

Josh laughs again, deep in his belly. "Cannibal? Oh, that's *rich.* Cannibal!"

A noise catches Mooney's attention and she sees Rose sidle into the room from one of the bedrooms. She has that same intensely satisfied air about her, the L-tryptophan slowdown after a huge Thanksgiving dinner. "What's going on?" She sees Mooney and scowls sleepily. "What are you laughing about?"

Josh points at Tyler. "The new guy—he called us cannibals!" He chuckles again while Rose just stares at him, then makes an effort to rein it in. "Think of us as more like a…winery, but for blood. We collect, sample, and age the product."

"You're drugging them," Tyler says. "You have to be. I can't believe they'd be your buffet this willingly."

Rose shrugs languidly from her spot at the kitchen door. "We might be giving them a little something to make them more agreeable."

"Looks like you're partaking, too," Mooney says. "It's not enough you're feeding on your own kind, the two of you are druggies besides."

"No," Josh says. "It's secondhand, like cigarette or pot smoke. We didn't consider that." He inclines his head, looking thoughtful. "But we learn from experience. For instance," Josh waves his hand at the sleeping forms, "we've learned that the younger they are, the better their blood tastes. And the younger the blood, the stronger it makes us. It's the best of the best, a bottle of exquisite champagne compared to cheap beer."

A chill runs down Mooney's spine. "We're leaving," she says flatly.

"Why the hurry?" Rose asks unexpectedly. Before Mooney can blink, the girl is standing in front of her and Tyler; faster, Mooney could have sworn, than she had been previously. She locks gazes with Mooney, then points at the array of sleeping vampires. "Why don't you take a taste or two? This one here is from somewhere in Louisiana." She pushes at one of the forms and Mooney thinks she hears a faint groan. "Spicy." Rose's last word sounds more like a hiss than anything else and Mooney feels inexplicably frozen in place. Suddenly Rose raises her head and sniffs, then leaned toward Mooney. "You smell interesting, like—"

"Let's go," Tyler interrupts. He yanks Mooney backward and pulls her outside, his swiftness pretty impressive in its own right. He keeps going, propelling Mooney toward her truck until she moves on her own again and climbs into the driver's seat. Instead of walking around the truck, Tyler leaps over the back bed and lands in a crouch by the passenger door.

Mooney frowns and rubs at her slightly numb face, then turns her head back toward the house. Rose and Josh stand at the doorway, watching them and smiling faintly as though they share the best secret in the world. Rose leans over and whispers something in Josh's ear and his eyes narrow as he stares at Mooney. He straightens and starts toward her truck.

"Stop right there," Mooney says, and comes up with her Berretta balanced on the window frame and aimed at his head. Josh halts midstep, his gaze unaccountably hot as he meets her eyes. "Stay away from me," Mooney orders. "Both of you. Stay away from me, Tyler, and anyone, human *or* vampire, in Sells." When neither Josh nor Rose respond, she adds, "In fact, it's time for you to move on."

"That's impossible," Josh says flatly. "All the people inside—"

"—will stay right here," Mooney finishes for him. "I'm sure when they wake up from whatever you've been pumping into them, they'll find your invitation stinks, just like Tyler did. You *will* leave them here, and then they can decide what's next."

"That's not your decision," Rose says hotly, but Mooney won't look at her; she knows better this time. The girl has strengthened her nasty little ability to control others, and who knew what would've happened if Tyler hadn't been there to pull Mooney away.

"This isn't negotiable," Mooney says. "You have until noon tomorrow to get the hell out of my town."

"Or what?" Rose asks with a sneer. "You'll run us out?"

"Exactly."

Josh gives an ugly laugh. "You and what other army?"

Mooney's expression is icy as she put the truck into gear.

"The United States Border Patrol."

– 13 –

"Did you mean what you said to them about the Border Patrol?" Tyler asks later. They'd gone back to Mooney's to hang out before her shift started, when Mooney plans on introducing Tyler to Chief Delgado as well as to her supervisor. If the meeting goes well, she's considering asking if she can take him on a ride-along later in the week, an official one with all the requisite paperwork and such, the polar opposite of her under-the-table and ultimately bloody liaison with Josh. If Tyler can deal with it, good and bad, who knew? Maybe he'd consider a new career.

"Probably not," Mooney says now. "If he ignores me, I really don't know what I'll do." They're sitting on the couch while some inane sitcom plays on the television with the volume turned low. The twins are giggling in the bedroom, which doubles as their playroom when Mooney wants them inside. "It would be one thing if Josh and his evil twit were attacking humans, but vampires feeding on vampires? I can honestly say they probably won't care." She looks at her hands. "All over the world the vampires and humans are fighting. The BP might not like that so many vampires are coming into town, but ultimately the order would likely be sit back and hope Josh simply feeds on his food supply until they all die."

Tyler pushes his hair out of his eyes. "Can't blame them for that I guess. We're stronger, faster, and a lot of humans are dying at vampire hands. And so we're going to what, ask the humans to protect us against ourselves?"

"Right," Mooney agrees. "Humans kill each other, vampires kill each other. Not much difference, you know?" She pauses. "Except at times it still seems so damned *strange* to think of myself as not human. I mean—"

The center of the trailer's front door suddenly caves inward with a terrific crash.

Mooney yells in surprise as metal edging, splinters, and pieces of faux paneling whip in all directions. Mooney instinctively ducks, registering that Tyler does the same. She crouches on the floor, wedged next to Tyler in the tiny space between the coffee table and the old couch. As her vision clears more pieces of the door are bashed into the trailer's interior; she glimpses a hand ramming again and again at the sides of a widening hole in the locked door. By the time she and Tyler scramble back to their feet, the last piece of the door shatters and Josh knocks it aside and steps through. Not surprisingly, Rose is right behind him.

Dangerous heat slides up Mooney's spine and spreads across her face and down to her hands. "Get out of my house." Her voice is smooth, like velvet. Deceptively slick. "Right now."

"Nope," Josh says. He sounds happy and for a moment, standing in the wreckage of the trailer's entrance, he almost looks like the soldier he'd claimed to be. "I'm looking for something," he announces. "You see, Rose told me something about you after you left our place this morning. You never mentioned it, so we decided to come and find out for ourselves."

Rose sidles around him and raises her head, breathing in deeply. "Oh, *yes*," she purrs. "I was right. She has *children* in here."

Mooney grinds her teeth. Not a sound has come from the back bedroom—she taught the kids early on that if danger threatened they should stay quiet and hidden unless they absolutely had no choice but to defend themselves.

"My kids are not your lunch special of the day," Mooney snaps. "And me telling you to get the hell out of Sells didn't mean you should break into my house."

"Pretty obvious you're not welcome here," Tyler says from beside Mooney. His words are low and grating, almost like a growl.

Josh chuckles. "So what? You think this is like some old movie where vampires have to be invited in? Welcome to the twenty-first century, lover boy."

Without warning Rose lunges past Mooney and streaks down the short hallway toward the bedroom. There's no time to consider how much faster the girl is now compared to when they'd first met; with a shriek Mooney is after her, leaping on top of Rose's back as the door to the bedroom slams open and Rose spies the twins.

She goes down under Mooney's weight, screaming the whole time for Josh. "I was right, I was right! She has two kids—get them! *Get them!*"

Mooney snarls and shoves her forearm under Rose's chin, cutting off the words and yanking the woman off her feet. Rose fights like a cornered javalina, kicking as she claws at any part of Mooney she can find. To protect herself, Mooney keeps her face turned to the side and pushes hard against Rose's shoulder as she drags her backward, but that means she can't get in a position to bite. Both of them are slamming against the walls of the narrow hall as Rose thrashes crazily, but at least Mooney is putting distance between Rose and the kids. Mooney knows there's movement and noise behind her, but she can't worry about that now.

Until Josh attacks her from behind.

Mooney gasps as she goes down. Rose is underneath her, screaming anew and digging deep, fiery furrows into the exposed skin of Mooney's arms. She feels Josh snapping at her head and neck like a dog but her hair is in the way; he keeps jerking his head to the side in a futile effort to get the strands out of his mouth. Then the vampire's weight on top of her doubles as Tyler launches himself at Josh and tries to drag him off of Mooney, succeeding only in adding himself to the mix of bodies crammed into the tiny space.

Sandwiched between Rose and the two men, Mooney is damned near suffocating—Rose seems to have form-fit herself to Mooney while the weight above keeps Mooney's lungs from expanding. Black spots dance in Mooney's peripheral vision, a warning of what's to come if she doesn't find a way to get out of this pile-up. But no matter how hard she tries, she can't move, can't even adjust; the vampires on either side of her have been feeding on the blood of their own kind and have grown stronger as a result; she doesn't know what Tyler could do, but right now it doesn't seem like much.

Someone slips, a body part moves sideways…then there's unobstructed flesh in front of her. Mooney's fangs shoot out instinctively and she bites down; venom pulses into the bite. But almost nothing happens, a twitch, that's all; are vampires immune? It's something she's never even considered, and if true, a crippling handicap.

Mooney's strength is giving out. It's an unequal battle: her and Tyler, normal—whatever *that* means—vampires against those of their own kind who have amplified their abilities via cannibalism, who are stronger, faster, *better*. They will lose this battle, and then what?

Her children will become food.

"*Nooooo!*"

Mooney hardly recognizes her own scream. She gives a last ditch effort at galvanizing her own strength, and perhaps that of Tyler's, but it doesn't help. They are both fading under the energy and sheer power of Josh and Rose, losing the battle. Except…

Suddenly her twins are there, adding their childlike cries to the chorus of screams.

Sitol leaps for Joshua and Judum goes for Rose. Her precious children are like Mooney, snake-swift, even if they are young and have nothing in comparison to the power of the attackers. Also like Mooney, their bites are toxic, but they lack the control, instinctive or automatic, that maturity gives them over the amount of toxin they expel.

Judum sinks his fangs as deeply as he can into the first thing within reach, Rose's bare calf. Her shriek is still trying to escalate when Sitol wraps her arms around Josh's head and her open jaw fastens tightly on his cheek. Like Rose's, his bellow is over before it can find full volume, abruptly cut off as the massive dose of rattler venom causes his lungs to convulse, then cease to function entirely. He becomes dead weight on top of Mooney at the same time that Rose goes limp beneath her. Mooney wheezes then gratefully sucks in air as Tyler drags the paralyzed Josh backward and rolls him off to the side; in another moment, he helps Mooney to her feet and the twins run to her and hug her knees. In any other world, they might have been normal toddlers.

"That was not fun," Tyler manages. He is covered in bruises and a dozen bleeding gashes; one cheekbone is swollen enough to make the eye above it barely more than a slit.

"Ouch," Mooney says and touches it lightly with her forefinger. "That has to hurt."

He laughs, but the sound is short and painful. "Thanks for the sympathy but you'd better save it for yourself. You look like you got run over by a concrete trunk."

"I feel like it," Mooney admits. She looks down and strokes the twins' heads. "You guys were supposed to hide."

Sitol looks up at Mooney with a solemn expression. "Help Mommy." Judum, already a man of few words, nods.

"Can't argue with that," Tyler says. He looks past Mooney. "I think they're dead."

Mooney grunted. "Couldn't happen to nicer people." She nudges the kids toward the door. "Go out back until I call you." She waits until they're gone then grabs the closest dead-weight appendage. "These two are headed for a deep desert grave," she says. "One no one will ever find."

"Good thinking," Tyler agrees. "What about the ones back at their house?"

"I think we'll wait for them to come around and explain what happened. Take it from there." She shrugs. "They might want to stay, depending on what they left behind. If they don't, I'm sure they won't get any objection from the townspeople." She made a face.

"And can they stay if they want to?"

Mooney tilted her head, considering. With the war on all fronts, there would be enemies and allies on both sides. Vampires against humans. Humans against humans. Vampires against vampires. A sort of worldwide civil war where the strong will subjugate the weak. But what then? If the vampires prevail, will they be any different from the way the humans have always been? Not a chance.

"Absolutely," Mooney finally answers. "If the war really does make it all the way down here…

"We might need to even the odds."

"APOCALYPSE TANGO" PT. 4

Jonathan Maberry

— 4 —

The Barkey Family Farm
Town of Ulysses
Potter County, Pennsylvania
The Eve of the War

The front door whipped open and one of the agents burst into the room. "Agent Saint, I think you better see this."

Jimmy Saint, Luther Swann and Spiro Nyklos hurried outside after the agent.

"What have you got?" asked the AIC.

"We were checking the barn and outbuildings when we saw it," the agent replied. "We must have missed it before, in the dark, but now that the sun's up…well, you'll see."

They made their way up the gravel path to the huge red barn. The paint was old and dark and to Swann it looked like dried blood. The tarpaper shingles on the pitched roof were worn and paled to ash by too many unrelenting summer suns. As they drew nearer Swann began to feel an atavistic dread of what they would find. The swastika, the dismemberment and savagery inside were already bordering on too much for him to handle. Since the V-War ended, Swann had been dealing with paranoia about who was who and who was what. He'd been in therapy for it. His nightmares were filled with horrific images of the whole country burning, of unrelenting bloodbaths, of a world plunged into a species war that would not and could not end. In those dreams, death came hunting for his two children, Jenny and Brian, and his ex-wife, Trish. It came hunting, and it found them.

Sometimes, in his dreams, it was his children who became the hunters, their mouths filled with wicked teeth, their eyes filled with madness.

Swann was sleeping too little and drinking too much. This war was wrecking him and he was only a civilian advisor. He could only imagine what thoughts and fears simmered inside the heads of soldiers who had been in battle and who were waiting for it all to erupt again.

The peace that had lasted now for months was always thin, always stretched to the breaking point. Swann was realistic enough to know that. He'd warned about it. He'd cautioned them to deal fairly and negotiate honestly with the various militant vampire groups. He pleaded with them—and at different meetings with vampires—to strive toward a lasting peace because there was no way to win any war that might start up again. No way. It was, in genetic terms, the equivalent of mutually assured destruction. Neither side could truly defeat the other without burning down most of the world to do it.

He saw Saint and the agent round the corner of the barn and for a moment that left him and Nyklos, both lagging behind the others, alone together.

He cut a look at the psychologist.

The man was smiling.

"What—?" asked Swann.

"Mm?"

"You're smiling. What's funny? Am I missing something?"

"You are a very intelligent man, Luther. PhD, tenured professor of folklore, published author. You were the voice of reason throughout the epidemic. You were the first person to advocate for a truce. You have, I hear, stood up to General May, to the Joint Chiefs, and to congress on numerous occasions on behalf of a balanced response to the vampire threat. A lot of people respect you."

"Yes, I'm wonderful. Is there a point to this or have you started a resumé service?"

Nyklos chuckled. "I note it for context. During your TV interview with that Asian reporter—"

"Yuki Nitobe."

"—you brought up the question of ethnic genocide. Before that interview it was not part of the national conversation. After that interview, it was the conversation."

"The topic had to be raised. So what?"

"Luther…have you ever stepped far enough back to try and see what effect that had on the type and frequency of violence in the war? No? I don't believe that. I think you know full well that by raising the issue of genocide groups within the vampire community became radicalized. That's when the first V-cells were formed. That's when disparate vampire groups began joining together to form the Blood underground."

"That's hardly my fault, Spiro."

"You say that," said Nyklos with a shake of his head, "but you can't even meet my eyes when you do. One doesn't need to be a psychologist to interpret that."

Swann said nothing. They were almost at the corner of the barn.

"Luther," continued Nyklos. "You're probably one of those people who call me the Grim Reaper. You probably think I'm a villain because I've advocated for extreme responses to the vampire threat. But let's be clear on one thing—had you not lit the fire of hysteria, I would not have needed to suggest a way to keep the world from burning."

With that Nyklos pushed past Swann and rounded the corner of the barn.

Luther Swann stood for a moment, fists balled, teeth bared in anger and tried—tried—to tell himself that the psychologist was totally wrong, totally unfair, totally blinded by his own agenda. He tried.

But he couldn't sell himself on that as anything but a lie.

His hands slopped open and empty at the end of limp arms. He closed his eyes and for a few moments could do nothing except breathe.

Then he opened his eyes, took a breath, and followed the others to the far side of the barn.

He saw the three of them standing there, staring open-mouthed at the side of the barn.

Swann saw a kitchen mixing bowl sitting on the ground. It was filled with dark red paint.

Except that it wasn't paint.

It was blood.

A basting brush lay on the ground, the bristles stiff with drying blood.

And on the wall…

Someone had used the brush to draw a smiley face. Round, with dots for eyes and a wide, grinning mouth. With fangs.

Then a long vertical slash had been struck through the face.

Swann had seen that image on t-shirts and buttons, on bumper stickers and as Facebook icons. He'd heard of soldiers being reprimanded for putting stickers with it on their helmets or rifle stocks.

Above that was a symbol. A cross, and overlaid upon it at the crosspiece, was another swastika. All of it painted in clotted blood.

Beside these images were words:

GOD HATES YOU

GOD WILL NOT ABIDE YOU

WE ARE THE SOLDIERS OF GOD

– 5 –

In Maryland Airspace
The Eve of the War

The helicopter had a pressurized cabin that was sealed for conference-quality quiet.

The silence was crushing Luther Swann.

He sat in the last rows of seats, by the window, face turned to peer out at the landscape rolling beneath the Sikorsky S-92. The only other passengers were AIC Jimmy Saint and Dr. Spiro Nyklos. Each of them sat in an envelope of silence. Saint had made a dozen calls since the disturbing find at the murder scene. Nyklos had spent the entire flight on his laptop. Swann could only imagine what fires he was lighting with the news.

The facts had been coming in all day, and with each report, the situation got worse.

The bodies had been transported to the State Police medical examiner's office and a team of doctors was performing emergency autopsies. Everything was fast-tracked.

The preliminary reports from the coroner verified that each of the victims had been bitten multiple times. Casts taken of three sets of bites demonstrated that the attacker—human or animal—had performed those bites using abnormally large teeth. Long and pointed.

Scans of the bites and the casts were being uploaded to several critical databases, including the VBMI.

The possibility that these attacks had been done by ordinary humans was fading, but the questions were mounting.

The graffiti on the barn was the kind frequently seen in areas where rogue groups of humans had committed attacks on vampires. Why would it be at the scene of an attack on humans by vampires?

And...why the swastika?

That made no sense to Swann.

In the first round of tensions between the newly infected vampires and the uninfected humans, politics had played a big part, but never once had Nazism surfaced as an element. The V-cell terrorist groups had operated more like the IRA or Al-Qaeda, with some similarities to the old Weather Underground, Symbionese Revolutionary Army and 1960s-era Black Panthers. There were apolitical kill groups who modeled themselves after the Manson Family, but even they didn't use the swastika either.

Not even the five V-cell attacks in Germany took that stance, and there were neo-Nazi groups active in that country even today despite the German Criminal Code forbidding it.

So what did this all mean?

The helicopter flew on and Swann sank deeper into depression. He prayed that this wasn't what it seemed.

If it was a vampire, then he prayed that it was a single killer. Maybe a serial killer who had become infected. There had always been a fear of that.

Let it be that, thought Swann. Let it be only that.

Horrible as that was, it was an aberration. It wasn't a call to arms.

He was jolted out of his reverie by the snapping of fingers. Not Nyklos this time. It was Jimmy Saint. The agent rose from his chair, a cell phone tucked between shoulder and ear, a new coat of stress painted on his features.

"Thank you, doctor," he said. "Please keep me posted. And, I don't need to tell you how important it is that this stays within the circle of this investigation. That means you don't talk to anyone and all reports come directly to me. Are we quite clear on that?"

He listened.

"Good. Thank you."

Saint ended the call and stood in the aisle between Swann and

Nyklos. He weighed his cell phone in his hand thoughtfully, his eyes half-focused as he looked inward at his thoughts.

"That was Dr. Singh at the San Diego County medical examiner's office."

"Wait," said Swann, "how's he involved with the Barkey autopsies?"

"He's not. He just got the full lab work on the Solana Beach kills… and, I'm afraid they match what we found in Bradenton."

"Which is what, exactly?" asked Nyklos. He sat with his legs crossed and fingers steepled. Swann wondered if he was actually trying to look like an evil mastermind. Who sits like that? Ever?

Saint chewed his lip for a moment. "We've…been keeping a few things under wraps. No, wait, before you gentlemen jump down my throat, remember that this case is still classified as a domestic federal murder investigation. Until now there hasn't been anything that conclusively ties the two pervious series of murders to the outbreak."

"'Until now'?" prompted Swann.

The AIC looked uncomfortable. "Actually, we had some information about Bradenton that we've been sitting on. We hoped that it was isolated and that it could be handled carefully and quietly." He nodded to Swann. "We really don't want this to blow up, Luther. Trust me. No one does."

Nyklos said nothing. He studied his steepled fingers and Swann saw his lips twitch.

"Come on, Jimmy, what's happening? What have you found? Did the M.E. find anything in the saliva or bite patterns?"

"Yes," said Saint, "but it isn't what we expected to find."

"Then what is it?"

"Three things," said the AIC. "The Meyer family in Bradenton and the Rodriguez family in Solana Beach were both killed by the same person or persons. We have conclusive matches from castings of the bites. And we have shoe prints that are a match, but which don't match any of the victims. That's the first point."

"So, a traveling vampire killer," suggested Nyklos. "Acting alone or with a team?"

"That's still to be determined, though we believe that there was a second and possibly a third person at each of the first two scenes. Too early yet to tell about the Barkey scene."

"What's the second thing?" asked Swann.

Saint looked really uncomfortable. He took a breath before he answered. "The District Twelve medical examiner's office in Florida and the San Diego Country M.E. have determined with one hundred percent certainty that both families—the Meyers and the Rodriguezes—were vampires."

The silence was crushing.

"Wait…" said Swann. "What?"

"They were vampires."

"All of them?" asked Nyklos, leaning forward now.

"In Florida the victims were a husband, wife and baby. The wife and baby were both vampires. The husband was human and apparently helped to conceal their conditions. In Solana Beach both parents had turned, as had two of the three daughters."

"This is something new," said Swann. "Whole families?"

"I know—it's a statistical anomaly and not a very pleasant one. It skews the math in terms of outbreak projections. But, that's really not the point, is it?"

"No," said Swann. "The victims were vampires?"

"Yes."

"What are we seeing here?" asked Nyklos. "Are the vampires turning on each other?"

"No," said Saint. "That's the third part. And…maybe it's the worst part."

"How so?" asked Swann. "How can this really get worse?"

"Doctor Singh in San Diego was able to get DNA from saliva in the bites. He got the results today, and they match what we got from Bradenton last night. It's what I'm afraid we're going to find from the samples we took this morning in Lancaster."

Swann and Nyklos waited. Nobody seemed to be breathing.

"The DNA is something we've only seen twice in confirmed cases since the outbreak. Once in Brooklyn and once in Bucharest. And now we have it at both of the first two crime scenes. And, quite frankly gentlemen this is scaring the living shit out of me."

"Jimmy," said Swann slowly, "what did they find?"

"The DNA was mixed as if the saliva came from two sources, and at first that's what we thought. That an animal had gotten in and fed on the bodies after the killer had left. But the DNA analysis is conclusive. The samples from Florida and California match exactly. We have human DNA and we have animal DNA. Bonded together. One creature."

"What kind of animal?" asked Nyklos.

Saint looked at him and then at Swann. *"Canis dirus."*

"Canis...? You mean this is a wolf?"

"No, doctor," said Swann in a hollow voice. "He means that this is a werewolf."

— 6 —

New Hope, Pennsylvania
The Eve of the War

The eye of the moon looked down at the car moving along the winding black tongue of a road. On one side of the car were endless fields of early season corn, the green stalks not yet heavy with the ears that would burden them by late August. The stiff blades of each plant dueled and parried with the other stalks crowded against them. On the other side of the road was a patch of dense forest that dropped down into hollows and climbed up the slopes of short mountains.

The whole region was quiet in the deathly way of farm country in the late evening. The hands and the farmers were all asleep with their alarms set for five o'clock. Aside from the white van, the road was empty.

The man behind the wheel looked human.

He had human skin and a human face. Human hands rested at ten and two on the knobbed steering wheel. The smile on his face was not human.

It was not a wolf's smile either.

There is no precise name for the kind of animal he was.

The kind of creature.

He smiled at the winding road as if he saw much more than was there. His eyes jumped and twitched and were as bright as polished glass. His tongue—which was very long and very dark—flicked out now and then to lick his lips as if searching for missed traces of the blood. Of the meat.

His belly was full, but that didn't matter. He was always hungry.

Always.

Always.

Always.

The Sirius radio was tuned to the Disney Kids station. Happy songs.

For and by children. Delicious little voices singing for the joy of it.

He licked his lips again and felt his groin throb.

He sang along to the songs.

And drove.

His mind was a furnace.

"TENOCHTITLAN WILL RISE" PT.1

Joe McKinney

—1—

Ernesto Ramirez's grandfather was dying. For several days he'd been unwilling to stare that truth in the face, but it was impossible to look away from it now. The man who'd raised him, who'd taught him to read and filled his nights with stories of life as a boxer and a soldier and a journalist, who'd kept him off the streets when the cartels came looking for new recruits, was dying. The coughing and the fever had left him weak and wasted. He looked small, breakable, sad. The man had been a pro fighter once, but now his hands felt as delicate as a baby bird in Ernesto's grip.

Earlier that day Ernesto had gone downstairs to fetch the old retired doctor who lived on the first floor of their apartment building. The man had taken one look at Papa's swollen neck, listened to his labored breathing, opened his mouth and looked at the back of his throat. The doctor rose from the bed, shaking his head. "He has diphtheria," he said.

"What does that mean?" Ernesto said. He was thirteen years old and he'd never heard the word before. "What does he need to get better?"

The doctor let out a long, tired sigh. "He needs a hospital, my boy. I can't even be sure it is diphtheria. He needs tests and some powerful medicines."

"Then I'll take him. I can find a car. I know how to drive." Ernesto spoke defiantly, almost daring the doctor to contradict him.

"It would be too much of a—"

The doctor broke off midsentence. A white spotlight pierced the window, momentarily filling the room. With it came the thropping of helicopter blades. The next instant the aircraft veered off, turning its spotlight on the apartments across the street from their building.

The doctor turned toward the window, all expression slipping from his face. Beyond their little apartment building Mexico City was burning, the flames painting the pre-dawn sky with an angry orange glow. For ten days now the cartels had been at war with the government, and the fighting was growing worse with each passing hour.

"He'd never make it," the doctor said. "He's too weak to travel. And with that fighting out there…" The doctor shrugged.

"Then I will go. I can buy the medicine. I have some money."

"My boy, it's not that. I'd give you the medicine, if I could. It's the government. They've seized nearly everything."

"But there might be some somewhere. At the hospital, maybe."

The doctor shrugged again.

Ernesto took a seat on the edge of the bed and wiped the sweat from his grandfather's brow with a damp towel. The old man's breath was coming in ragged, painful pulls. His eyes were open, but he wasn't conscious. All at once Ernesto felt short of breath. He loved that man so much. He was his world, his rock.

Ernesto stood up and faced the doctor.

"Please write down the medicines he needs. I will get them."

The doctor didn't even try to object. He simply nodded, then went to the kitchen table to write a note.

– 2 –

But daylight came and went without the medicine. Ernesto had wanted to leave hours earlier, but couldn't. A crowd had gathered in front of his apartment building. From his fourth story window Ernesto had listened to their chants with mounting worry. It had started with a group of women trying to break into the apartment building across the street. From the bits of yelling he could make out, it sounded like they meant to lynch a woman who had turned into one of the *Cihuateteo*, one of the Blood Mothers. They held up posters on sticks bearing pictures of their missing children and screamed to have the *Cihuateteo* on a bonfire. Then the cartel soldiers had showed up with their guns, their faces hidden behind bandanas. Angry chants for justice turned into screams of pain. Government soldiers had moved in about an hour later and tried to restore order. The firefight had raged all that afternoon and most of the evening. A missile fired from a helicopter ended the skirmish just a few minutes ago, and even with the windows closed the air still smelled of burning wood and plaster and gasoline.

He'd have to go now, while there was a lull in the fighting.

If he delayed any longer, he might as well not go at all.

"Papa, can you hear me?"

His grandfather's eyelids fluttered open, revealing yellowed, blood-shot eyes, crusted over with gunk.

"I have to go. The doctor says you need the medicine as soon as possible."

The old man tried to speak, but could manage only a phlegmy rattle at the back of his throat.

"I'll be back by morning. You'll be strong for me, won't you? You'll hold on?"

His grandfather squeezed his hand. It was the only answer he could muster.

"I'll be back. I promise."

And with that, Ernesto Ramirez gave his Papa's brow a kiss, and rose to cross the battlefield that was Mexico City.

— 3 —

The smell of burning flesh hit him square in the face the moment he stepped into the street. The missile he'd heard a few minutes earlier had done terrible work. The apartments across the street were unrecognizable. Where before there had been a nine-story building of gray concrete and glass, there was now only a charred metal skeleton. A vast hill of rubble blocked the street to the north. Dust hung in the air and coated the cars and the bodies abandoned in the street so that they looked like the ruins of some ancient city covered by volcanic ash. Columns of smoke rose into a gray-black night sky all around him.

He put his arm over his face to keep from breathing in too much of the ash and smoke and started over the mound of rubble. Ernesto was picking through the jumble of bricks and tangled rebar when he heard gunfire close by.

He stopped and listened.

It was close. He thought it might have come from the alleyway off to his left.

He heard men yelling, and then the sound of people running in the dark just out of sight.

He pressed himself flat to the rubble and tried to be invisible.

"They're coming back!" a man yelled from the alleyway. "Take cover!"

"Gunships!" another man yelled.

Ernesto glanced over his shoulder and saw three dark silhouettes skimming over the roofs of Mexico City's endless sprawl. The helicopters were streaking in his direction, angry as hornets.

He hadn't left his apartment building since the fighting started ten days earlier, but from his window, and from the roof where he gathered rain water in buckets after the water and electricity stopped working, he had seen enough helicopters to know nothing good came from them.

He clambered down the far side of the mound of rubble as fast as he could go and veered toward the burned out skeleton of the Apartamento de Guanajuato. The Army had hit it once, he figured, so they were less likely to hit it a second time.

He hoped that was the case anyway.

He cleared the rubble just as a rocket hit a building farther up the street.

Ernesto dropped to the ground and clapped his hands over his ears, but the concussion from the blast was still loud enough to deafen him.

Two more rockets shrieked overhead and exploded somewhere off to his left.

The pain was intense. He climbed to his feet but could barely stand. The city swirled around him, and he felt like he was moving in slow motion. He swayed like a drunk. There was a fierce ringing in his ears that pulsed in time with his heartbeat. Ernesto dropped to one knee. Red-hot embers filled the air and caught in his hair. He swatted at the back of his head like a man being attacked by bees. Somehow he managed to stumble back to his feet and ran into the darkness of the burned out building to his right.

He didn't make it far, though.

It was dark, and he hit something hard. The impact knocked the wind from his lungs, and he pitched over backward into the black ash that carpeted the ground.

– 4 –

Ernesto's ears were still ringing when he came to, but his headache had settled down to a dull roar. He pushed himself up to his hands and knees, spitting out the ash that clung to his lips.

He stood and looked around.

He'd managed to go farther into the bowels of the building than he'd first thought. All around him glowing red embers floated on the breeze like fireflies. But they were the only remnants of the battle he'd witnessed. There was no more gunfire, at least none that sounded close, and no thropping helicopters circled overhead. The only sound was the murmur of the wind as it passed through the burned timbers of the Apartamento de Guanajuato building.

The silence was broken by the sound of a woman gasping for air.

Instinctively, Ernesto ducked into a crouch.

Where the cartels were concerned there was no such thing as honor. Certainly not for the brand of honor his grandfather had taught him. If there were cartel soldiers here, it wouldn't be beneath them to strangle a woman as bait.

Especially if they thought he was part of an Army platoon sent in to finish the helicopter's job.

He strained to listen against the dark, but heard only the woman's dying gasps.

The sound was coming from the next room, and Ernesto slowly made his way to the shell of the doorway for a look, carefully putting one foot down in front of the other to avoid snapping the burnt wood and brittle plaster piled on the floor.

He made it as far as the door before he stopped and let out a gasp.

It was a Blood Mother, one of the *Cihuateteo*, flat on her back, her distended belly framed between her upraised knees. Ernesto wanted to back away, but couldn't. He was riveted to the spot like his feet had grown roots.

She must have been crushed by falling debris, he thought. He could see one side of her rib cage was smashed and partially flattened. She could barely breathe. The diseased rattle in her throat fascinated him.

It was the same sound his grandfather had made when he'd promised to return home by morning.

The woman, vampire or not, was dying.

He watched her for a long moment.

She knew he was there, of that Ernesto had no doubt. She labored to sit up, but couldn't move her burned body beyond a few spastic twitches. She tried to reach for him, and as she did a noise somewhere between a gasp and a snakelike hiss escaped her lips.

But the effort was too much for her, and after a few ineffective grasps at the air between them her gnarled hands fell down to the ground in a puff of ash. Her dead, open eyes stared up through the burnt skeleton of the building, where the sky had finally cleared enough for the starlight to shine through.

Though he was terrified, Ernesto stepped closer.

He stood over the corpse, filled with both wonder and disgust. There was something sexual about her that held his gaze, even in death. It was her scent, musty and raw, but it made him funny inside. He felt his cock start to stiffen, and he didn't know whether to be disgusted with himself or give in to the strange urges he was feeling to touch her.

The woman wore only a loose-fitting, knee length skirt. It was covered in dark stains that Ernesto thought might be blood. It was hard to tell. Whatever it was had turned dark and crusty. Her bare and swollen breasts were tattooed with the skeletal faces of Aztec gods he didn't recognize. Her hips were wide, and as he traced the curve of them he caught sight of her hands. They'd looked gnarled before, but now that he was standing over her, studying every inch of her, he could see that the skin of the first and second fingers had fused together, as had the skin of the third and fourth. Where before there had been a pair fingernails, the fused fingers now ended in one long wickedly sharp claw, so that her hand resembled the talons of an eagle.

He couldn't stop sniffing the air. He wondered how something so ugly, and so pitifully dead, could turn him on the way she was doing. Her face was twisted and unnatural, the mouth grossly out of proportion to the rest of her. Her jaws hung open, her mouth red as blood. The skin around her lips shiny with scales. She had no nose. Just a red, inflamed hole where the cartilage that had formed the bridge of her nose had once been.

It was ghastly.

But her face wasn't the worst of it.

The really awful part, the part of her that touched a primitive fear inside him, was her horribly distended belly. She was grotesquely fat, but only there, in her belly. It rolled over the waistline of her skirt and sagged between her thighs, forcing them open. It wasn't like a pregnant woman though. He'd seen lots of pregnant woman. This was different, somehow hideous, as though she'd eaten far more than any human body was meant to hold. She looked ready to pop, in fact, her abdomen marked here and there with lumps.

He stared at her belly, tracing the stretch marks along her skin, until he realized that one of the lumps was in the shape of a child's hand.

Ernesto jumped to his feet, fear coursing through him like a live current.

He couldn't bring himself to look down, to see again that child's hand pressed against the flesh. It was true what they said; the *Cihuateteo* ate children. Ernesto stood there amid the skeleton of the burned out building, trying to process that, but it was a truth too horrible to wrap his mind around.

Those little fingers.

Shaking his head, he tried to convince himself that it wasn't real. It was just a trick of the shadows. It was his mind running away from him. After hearing for the past six months the horror stories of the *Cihuateteo* who roamed the streets at night, his mind was turning shadows into nightmares. It was his imagination and nothing more.

But when he dared looked again, the fingers were still there.

He backed away in horror, certain he was about to vomit. Then his back hit one of the blackened ribs of the building and he stopped moving and stared at the scream frozen on the dead vampire's face. High above him the clouds shifted again and a silvery wash of moonlight threw the woman into stark relief.

So that was a *Cihuateteo*, he thought. One of the Blood Mothers.

Not for the first time he wondered how anybody could worship something so hideous, so cruel and monstrous.

But worship the *Cihuateteo* they did.

And the *Cihuateteo* fed off of that worship. They seemed to thrive as much on that adulation and supplication as they did on the blood and meat of children.

Ernesto had paid close attention to the TV over the last eighteen months. That was when the first case of vampirism started, some American actor in California. After that, vampires had appeared everywhere, all over the globe. But not the same as the vampires he'd seen in the movies. These didn't wear capes and tuxedos. They were strange, each of them different from all the others.

He'd seen an American doctor on the TV named Swann who said the vampires were the result of reactivated junk DNA, lingering fragments of the biological songbook that made up the human chorus. That was what he had said, a human chorus.

What that meant in Mexico was the *Cihuateteo*, the Blood Mothers. There had been others, especially in Mexico City, but the *Cihuateteo* had wiped them all out.

Blood mothers did not abide competition.

From the TV he'd learned that the Aztecs considered childbirth a form of battle. They conferred full warrior status on women when the birthing time came. But those who fell in the battle, who lost their lives while giving birth, were doomed to return as the *Cihuateteo* and haunt the crossroads and eat the children they found as a way of reclaiming the babe they'd lost.

So went the folklore, at any rate.

The truth was more complex.

Mexico, since the earliest days of Spanish conquest, was made up of two separate races: the Hispanics—tall and slender and pale skinned, who could trace their lineage back to the Spanish; and the Indio—shorter, darker, who were of Native American stock. It was a racial divide that had found a middle ground in mixed bloodlines like Ernesto's family, but nonetheless still defined Mexico's culture. The wealthy, the ruling elite, and the beautiful actors and actresses you saw on the TV, tended to be Hispanic, while the poor tended to be the dark skinned Indio. On the TV they played the stupid, overweight housekeeper or the drunken gardener. They were the comic relief.

But they made up a huge percentage of Mexico's people, and it was from their villages and towns that the cartels grew. The cartels had long worshipped the god of money and violence, but also the old ways of the Aztecs too. They dreamed of a world where Tenochtitlan, the ancient Aztec capital buried beneath the streets of modern day Mexico City, would rise again.

When the *Cihuateteo* appeared, the cartels took them as a sign that their dreams were becoming a reality. They located the *Cihuateteo*, sheltered them, fed them, worshipped them, and carried them into battle against the government. Their battles had raged all over Mexico for six months, but ten days ago, the fighting finally entered Mexico City.

The Blood Mothers were here.

"APOCALYPSE TANGO" PT.5

Jonathan Maberry

– 7 –

The Office of the White House Chief of Staff
Washington D.C.
The Eve of the War

"Werewolves, Luther?"

Bill Gabriel, the president's chief of staff, sat behind his half-acre of polished mahogany, fingers laced on the printout of the report from the San Diego County medical examiner's office.

"I'm afraid so, sir."

"I thought that was a rarity in terms of this outbreak."

"Very rare, sir."

"How many cases? Worldwide, I mean. Documented cases."

"Four."

"Four?"

"The most prominent, of course, being the Bronx District Attorney Hugues Charles."

"Big Charlie is hardly a homicidal maniac."

"No."

"Then what are we looking at here?"

"I'm not sure. At least not yet." Swann shifted nervously in the leather guest chair. He was acutely aware of the hard stares from the other two men in the room. Spiro Nyklos and General May sat in the other two chairs. Neither had said much since this meeting began. Their silence felt somehow threatening to Swann.

Gabriel opened a drawer and removed a thick file folder, placed it on the desk and began rifling the papers until he found the one he wanted. He peered through his reading glasses.

"Big Charlie outted himself and has willingly submitted to a battery of medical tests. Granted, some of them were conditional for his run for office, but his compliance is a matter of record." Gabriel touched a word on the document. "'*Loup garou.*' That's his species, am I correct in that?"

"Yes. *Loup garous* are a specific type of werewolf from rural regions of France. Big Charlie is of French extraction, so our initial supposition is that lycanthropy follows the same rules as vampirism. And the *loup garou* apparently possess the ability for deliberate theriomorphy."

"Which is what, exactly?"

"They can change at will into a wolf. Genetically-speaking the *loup garou* shares DNA with *canis lupus lupus*, the European forest wolf, a subspecies of the common gray wolf."

"But that's not what these reports say about the attacks here in the States," said Gabriel. He consulted the ME's report and read the Latin. "*Canis dirus*? What exactly is that, Luther? Is that an American species?"

"That's just it, sir—the *canis dirus*, or 'dire wolf' was a species here in the western hemisphere. It's about the same size as the gray wolf, but with a heavier build. It was probably stronger and faster. But…it's extinct."

"Extinct? Is this a recent extinction? Something that was the result of deforestation or—?"

"No sir," said Swann. "The dire wolf was hunted to extinction more than ten thousand years ago. It was a brute, with longer teeth and a much stronger bite than modern wolves."

"So this is an American wolf," insisted Gabriel. "In terms of genetic origin?"

"Possibly. There's some discussion as to whether the species migrated northward from South America."

Gabriel nodded and sipped coffee from a mug that bore the presidential seal. Swann waited. Nyklos sat like a statue, his dark eyes unreadable. Jimmy Saint looked enormously uncomfortable, which Swann could understand. Saint had inherited a case that seemed to be accelerating downhill. Solving it could be a career bump; failing to do so could break him.

Gabriel peered at Swann through the thin vapors rising from his cup. "Should we be looking for a second causation here? Is this something other that I1V1?"

"I don't think so, sir," said Swann. "I think this is the Ice Virus and I think we'll find out that it triggers the same gene."

"How is that possible? Vampires and werewolves?"

"Well, sir, this is something I mentioned the first time we met, and the first time I spoke to the congressional committee. Our problem may be in our definition of what constitutes a 'vampire.' We've already seen ninety-two species, which includes eighteen sub-types that don't have a corollary in the literature. That still leaves nearly two hundred known species from world folklore as possible new actual species. Not to mention the hybrids. We're seeing more and more of those, and some of the American melting pot gene pool may be resulting in the new species. We still don't have a grip on the science yet. However, the tricky part is coming up with a definition of what a vampire is. In the broadest terms, a vampire appears to be a person who has an abnormal need to feed on one of several vital substances. Mostly blood, but we've encountered flesh-eaters as well as some who appear to feed on hormones, moisture, trace elements like iron and copper, salt, saliva, tears, and—if the study at Johns Hopkins bears it out—life energy."

Gabriel glanced at Nyklos, who merely shrugged.

"My point," continued Swann, "is that we may now have to consider lycanthropes to be a sub-species of vampire. The werewolf and the vampire are closely linked in many cultures. In Belarus, for example, when a werewolf is killed, it comes back as a species of vampire called a *Mjertovjec*. The *Loogaroo* of Haiti were believed to be witches who shed their skins at night to become vampire/werewolf hybrids. The Romanian *Pryccolitch* is a vampire/werewolf hybrid, as is the Portuguese *Lobishomen*. In Greece, when a wronged person is killed—a common source for vampire legend—it is reborn not as a vampire but as a werewolf called a *Farkaskoldus*. And there are plenty of others. Remember, Mr. Gabriel, the public perception of what constitutes a werewolf and a vampire are purely Hollywood and fictional constructs."

"So…does that mean the moon, silver bullets…all that doesn't apply?"

"We don't know enough about them," said Swann. "How could we possibly make that call? Going purely on folklore, the phases of the moon were never really a factor. Werewolves could shapeshift either at will or when driven by passions, or in some cases by using some kind of magical charm—a ring, a belt, a pendant. As for silver—I would think that any living thing could be killed by a silver bullet just as easily as by lead bullets. The exceptions being those vampire species we've encountered who have a hypernormal wound repair system. They can be killed, but not as easily."

"If this killer—or killers, as the case may be," said Gabriel, "is a werewolf, and if werewolves are now to be classified as a vampire subspecies, then how do you account for the fact that the victims were vampires?"

"How do I account for it?" said Swann with a grunt. "I don't. It doesn't make sense to me."

Jimmy Saint spoke up for the first time since the meeting began. "I thought vampires and werewolves were enemies."

"According to what source?" asked Swann.

Saint colored. "Um…movies, I guess. *Underworld*?"

"That's Hollywood," said Swann. "There are almost no known cases of vampires and werewolves encountering each other in folklore or myth." He turned back to the chief of staff. "I'm afraid this is something new."

— 8 —

New Hope, Pennsylvania
The Eve of the War

The smiling man pulled the van off the main road and onto a narrow farm lane that was heavily overgrown with weeds. They whisked along the sides of the vehicle as it bumped and thumped along. The headlights picked up a young deer standing wide-eyed and uncertain and the driver accelerated to try and hit it, but at the last moment the animal jumped off the cracked blacktop and vanished into the overgrown brush.

Disappointed, the smiling man's mouth lost its grin for almost three full seconds. But then memories of the things he'd done made his smile blossom again. He was too happy to let a small, missed opportunity spoil his mood.

He considered switching the radio to the news channel, but he already knew what they would be talking about. Philadelphia.

Thirteen bombs.

Thirteen wake up calls.

Boom, boom, boom.

Thirteen ANFO bombs. Each one was ninety-four percent porous prilled ammonium nitrate, that would act as an oxidizing agent and absorbent for the fuel, which was six percent number two fuel-oil. The smiling man had first learned how to make it from a Wisconsin Conservation Department booklet entitled "Pothole Blasting for Wildlife." Very useful. Very instructive.

He'd made the first of those bombs for the people he was now going to meet, and taught several of their people how to make more. The thirteen in Philadelphia and the ninety-seven en route to other destinations.

So much fun.

He smiled at the memory. At the remembered smells. At the test firings he'd set off to demonstrate the blast PSI and radius. At the cool feel of the ball bearings as he ran his hands through the barrels of them. Pea sized. Beautiful.

So beautiful.

He sang along with an old Hannah Montana tune.

Pumpin' Up the Party.

How appropriate, he thought.

The van's headlights splashed against the front wall of a farmhouse, and he slowed down, lowered the volume, and coasted to a stop a few inches from the bottom porch step. As he turned off the engine, the front door opened and three people stepped out.

Two of them he discounted immediately. Muscle. Protection. Nothing.

The third person made his smile grow.

She was very tall and pale, with masses of curly black hair and lips as red as all the sin in the world. She wore a plain cotton dress that whipped around her thighs in the night wind. Her arms and feet were bare. The dress has a keyhole neckline that showed the shadows that sculpted the inner curves of her breasts.

Annabelle.

He smiled at her. Devoured her with his eyes. Stripped her naked and bloody with his mind.

Annabelle.

He got out of the van but left the keys in the ignition.

One of her guards came down to meet him, blocking his view of the woman.

"Were you followed?" he growled.

The smiling man ignored him and began walking around him. The thug placed a hand flat on his chest. He was a big man and his hand looked like it could easily palm a basketball. The smiling man looked down at it and then at him.

"Don't," he said.

"Answer the question. Were you followed?"

"You're being rude."

"Answer the fucking question before I—"

The smiling man killed him.

Just like that.

One moment the thug was alive, and the next he was not. His throat seemed to explode and he pitched sideways trailing blood as he crashed onto the steps. The smiling man did not appear to have moved, though his left hand was now raised, his fingernails slick with blood that glistened like oil in the moonlight.

The second thug spent one second gaping in dumb confusion before he moved—but after that he moved very fast. He whipped open his jacket and tore the Glock from its clamshell holster. He was so fast, he got it out and pointed it at the smiling man.

Except that the smiling man was no longer there.

In the space of heartbeat the hulking form seemed to blur, to melt, to lose all normal shape and structure. There was a sound of tearing cloth. Buttons flew through the air.

In the next heartbeat a gray shape slammed into the second guard and bore him back and down with such force that blood flew from chest and throat and face and mouth. The thug landed harder, splayed like a starfish, screaming and thrashing as the gray shape crouched atop him, muzzle buried deep in the ruin of his chest.

The dying guard's scream rose and rose and then ended on a wet, soft, gurgling note of finality.

The creature raised its dripping face from the steaming body and glared with fire-yellow eyes at the woman. At Annabelle. She leaned against the porch rail. She was smiling.

The wolf changed again.

A heartbeat later it was the smiling man, kneeling naked over the dead guard. His face was a mask of crimson except for the bright whites around his irises. Strings of meat hung from the corners of his mouth.

"Was that necessary?" asked Annabelle. "They were stupid but they were pretty."

The man looked down at the corpse. He bent and licked at the blood, "Prettier now."

"They'll be missed."

He shrugged. "Not by me."

Annabelle sighed, pushed off the rail, came close and then lowered herself slowly to her knees. She leaned across the dead man and ran her tongue up the side of the smiling man's face. As she tasted the blood, her eyelids fluttered and she shuddered.

"So much prettier," she murmured.

Together they bent their heads to a shared feast.

"TENOCHTITLAN WILL RISE" PT. 2

Joe McKinney

– 5 –

Ernesto heard boots crunching on debris behind him. He ducked down, glanced around, and saw shapes moving in the darkness out by the street. They were coming toward him, several men armed with machine guns.

They might be cartel soldiers, or perhaps government troops, he couldn't be sure. Still, it didn't matter. The cartel soldiers would just as soon kill him as speak to him. And the government troops, if they even remotely suspected him of being a cartel soldier (and what else would he be, a young man, out past curfew, but a cartel soldier?) would put him in one of the Indio relocation camps he'd heard so much about on the news. Either way, his grandfather would die. He couldn't allow himself to be caught.

Ernesto ran into the darkened recesses of the shattered building and hid.

From the darkness he watched the approaching group. It looked like about a dozen men. They were dangerous, of course, but a known element. He had seen many men with guns.

It was the woman with the distended belly walking among them that caused his blood to run cold.

A Blood Mother!

Seeing a dead one had been frightening enough, but here was one walking around, and supported by her cartel troops. What would she do to a boy found amid the rubble? The other one had eaten a child. Would this one do the same to him?

He was too scared to even think of an answer.

Ernesto stood up, determined to run, but managed only to hit a burnt strut above him and knock it to the ground.

The noise caused the scouting party to stop their scan and train their weapons in his direction.

He barely noticed the rifles, though.

The Blood Mother was staring at him, sniffing the air, trying to catch his scent.

Ernesto stared into her black, empty eyes, and he ran for his life.

— 6 —

He was still running when the helicopter suddenly appeared overhead.

He'd seen hundreds of helicopters in the last few days, but none like this one. The others had all been noisy airborne junk that leaked smoke all over the sky. They were big and green and looked like they might fall to the ground at any moment.

But not this one.

It was big, like the Mexican Army helicopters he was used to seeing, but it was black as the night sky. It moved like a ghost over the rooftops, without lights, lethal and predatory.

And it didn't make a sound.

It seemed to be tracing the streets and back alleys, looking for something. The grace and terrible beauty of the thing captivated him. It was like some enormous bird of prey, turning and turning in the sky, ready to dive for the kill at any moment.

But when it suddenly veered away from its course, its engine screaming with the strain for the first time, it took Ernesto's breath away.

He wasn't prepared for the rocket that shrieked up from the next street over.

It lanced up from between two low, concrete buildings and caught the helicopter just forward of the aft rotor.

For a moment, the black bird seemed to have been swallowed by a fireball. Bits of glass and metal flew through the air. The shrieking of the engines suddenly became a low, agonizing groan as the aircraft struggled to hold its course.

But it was doomed.

Ernesto didn't know anything about aircraft, but even he could see the thing was going down. The helicopter shuddered, seemed to shake in the air, and then went into a tailspin that sent it careening into a nearby office building. Ernesto watched the chopper bounce off the face of a building, its rotors getting caught up in power lines that snapped like whips in the air before it crashed into the street less than a hundred feet ahead of him.

For the second time that night, Ernesto felt like his feet had grown roots.

He couldn't move.

The helicopter was burning. Power cables sparked and sizzled in the rainwater puddles that gathered near the curbs.

And for the briefest of moments, a terrible stillness spread over the city.

The silence was cut a moment later by men yelling in victory. Guns went off in celebration. He could hear the voices of cartel soldiers yelling cries of *¡Viva Tenochtitlan! ¡Viva Tenochtitlan!*

The soldiers were coming closer.

He could hear the echo of their boots as they ran through the demolished streets.

Ernesto turned back to the burning helicopter. That had to be Army, and that almost certainly meant armed soldiers. He had no intention of joining in the fighting, but he'd seen enough already to know that the fight just might come to him, like it or not. If those were soldiers on that helicopter, and they almost certainly were, they'd have weapons. It couldn't hurt, he figured, to have a weapon if he needed it.

He glanced to his right. The cartel soldiers were coming, but they were still far enough away that he could make it.

If he hurried.

He ran toward the helicopter, but stopped about twenty feet from it. The aircraft was spewing black, oily smoke, and even at this distance it felt like somebody was trying to push a wire brush down his throat. Ernesto pulled his t-shirt up over his face and entered the crash site.

The helicopter was twisted, its spine broken. On the way down it had torn through power lines, and now those cables wrapped around its rotors and its fuselage, making it look like some giant insect in chains. The front of the aircraft was smashed beyond recognition. The fire seemed fiercest there, for a constant jet of smoke roiled through the broken windshield. He could see two blackened bodies inside the smoke, but they weren't moving.

The passengers inside the cargo area hadn't fared much better.

The ceiling had buckled with the impact, and six of the men in the forward part of the hold had been crushed instantly. One had been sliced in half. All of them had limbs bent at sickeningly wrong angles.

Oil leaked from the ceiling. Ernesto could hear it pulsing out of the aircraft's cables like blood from an open wound. The smell, even through his shirt, was enough to make him gag.

Then he spotted the weapon. It was a fancy black machine gun, like the kind he'd seen in the American movies.

None of the cartel soldiers had weapons like that.

And come to think of it, none of the Mexican Army soldiers had weapons like that either.

He tried to pull it out from under the seat where it lay, but when he did, an arm came with it. Ernesto let go of the weapon. Metal groaned. Smoke and sparks came up from under the seat, and the next instant it fell over, kicking up more smoke.

Behind the smoke was a corpse.

A badly burned corpse.

Ernesto turned his head from the sudden waft of burnt flesh that hit his nostrils, but the glimpse he'd seen of the man forced him to turn back.

The man was Anglo. Ernesto could tell that even though the man's face was charred and blistered from burns. The goggles he wore had melted into his eyes. The helmet, and the camera mounted above it, was also fried. His uniform looked like American military issue, but there was no insignia, no names, nothing. The soldier had been equipped with a lot of gear, a *lot* of it, and as Ernesto looked over it he realized this wasn't anything he'd ever seen. This had to be an American crew of commandos.

He rocked back onto his heels and thought about that for a moment. What would American commandos be doing here? And why weren't they wearing any insignia? Were they U.S. military? Were they mercenaries?

Someone made a noise behind him.

Ernesto leapt to his feet, and nearly hit his head on the helicopter's collapsed ceiling.

Toward the back of the helicopter, a man was groaning and swatting ineffectively at the pile of debris on top of him. Like the others he wore military clothing devoid of insignia, and like them, his face was burned. But he was alive.

"Who are you?" Ernesto said in Spanish.

The man could only groan in pain.

Ernesto knelt down in front of the man. In addition to his burns, he was bleeding from his nose, his mouth, and a bad cut just below his left ear. The man's short hair was soaked with blood and hydraulic fluid. But he was definitely alive.

"Are you American or Mexican?" Ernesto asked.

The man stopped struggling against the debris. He looked exhausted. *"Ayúdeme,"* he said in a voice that was little more than a gasp.

Voices behind him.

Ernesto glanced over his shoulders. From somewhere in the darkness he could hear men laughing and shouting. Cartel soldiers. He couldn't let them find him here. If they did, they'd scavenge the weapons off these soldiers and probably feed him to one of the Blood Mothers.

He turned his attention back to the commando.

"Who are you?"

The American didn't answer.

"Tell me who you are," Ernesto insisted. "You're American, I know that."

"No," the man said.

There were more noises out in the street. The cartel men were getting closer. The soldier claimed he wasn't American, but the cartel men wouldn't believe that for a second. Not with all the amazing guns and equipment on the helicopter. No telling what they'd do to this man. Captured army soldiers were usually beheaded with chainsaws and their corpses put on display in public places. The cartels liked to make an impact with the violence they practiced.

What horrors would they do to an American soldier?

He shuddered as several ideas came to mind.

"If you want me to help you, tell me who you are," Ernesto said. "You're are an American Special Forces team, aren't you? What are you, a SEAL?"

The man closed his eyes against the pain of his injuries, but they flew open the next instant as a burst of gunfire sounded from somewhere close by.

The American looked from Ernesto to the darkened street outside. The voices were coming closer. He looked back at Ernesto and seemed to make a decision. "I'm Command Sergeant Major Juan Perez," the soldier said. His voice was rough from the pain. "United States Army Special Forces, Delta Force Team Four."

So the man was U.S. Army Special Forces, Ernesto thought. No wonder there were no markings on his uniform, no indications of rank or even of what country he fought for. He'd heard of these men. Delta Force, he knew, was something similar to the famous SEALS that had killed Osama Bin Laden all those years ago, but a little different. He didn't exactly understand the difference, but he knew this man was a whole lot more than a normal soldier.

And in that moment, Ernesto also made a decision.

"Come on," he said. "We need to get you out of here."

There was a lot of debris on top of the soldier, but his seat had shielded him from most of it. To Ernesto it looked like the crash must have ripped the man's seat from its mounts and flipped it upside down. The man was under it and his face was smashed into the floor, his neck bent at a painful angle, but at least the seat had blocked the jagged pieces of the fuselage from slicing him to ribbons.

From behind him, the voices of the cartel soldiers were getting louder. "*¡Viva Tenochtitlan!*" they called. They sounded like drunks singing corridos in the streets. "*¡Viva Tenochtitlan!*"

Ernesto turned back to the American soldier. He didn't have much time. The cartel soldiers would be on them in moments.

The commando was held in place by a web of seatbelts. Ernesto pulled at the buckles, but they wouldn't budge.

He was about to ask the American how to work the harness when he saw the scabbarded knife clipped to the man's chest. He thumbed open the clasp and slid out a glinting work of art. There was nothing fancy about it. The hilt was a solid black piece of molded plastic, the blade a highly polished five-inch piece of double-edged steel. But it was perfectly balanced. Ernesto held it in his hand and knew that if he were to throw it he could bury it to the hilt in anything from wood to brick.

"*¡Ahí está!*"

Ernesto looked behind him. The cartel soldiers were rounding the corner down at the end of the street, and they'd broken into a sprint. They'd be on him in no time.

But before he could turn his attention back to the knife, and the harness that held the American Delta Force man in place, he saw another figure turn the corner behind the wild cartel men. She moved with lanky, lurching steps. Her arms seemed too long, too tapered at the hands. Her head lolled from side to side with each step, for her legs were bowed and oddly bent. But it wasn't her legs that caused her to move so erratically. He realized that with dawning horror. It was the distended belly sagging between her thighs that impeded her gait. They had a Blood Mother with them.

"We have to go," he said to Delta Force man. "Let me help you."

Ernesto felt around for a part of the harness that wasn't straining against the soldier's uniform and pressed the blade into the fabric. It cut through the nylon webbing like it was wet paper and the soldier collapsed in a heap on the ground.

The American groaned in pain.

The cartel soldiers were getting close. Their chanting had turned into excited yells, like boys heading out to the *futbol* field.

The helicopter crash had knocked a hole in the side of an office building, and through the wreckage of the aircraft and the crumbling façade of the building, Ernesto spotted a small tunnel that was just big enough for him to pass through.

The American, though, would never fit.

Even without the pack on his back he might be too big.

Again Ernesto tried to figure out the complex network of buckles and straps that held the pack in place. He looked for a buckle, some sort of release, but he couldn't make sense of it.

"I have to cut it off," he said.

The American groaned again. Ernesto couldn't be sure if he was hearing anything he said, or if he even understood Spanish, but there wasn't any more time to explain it. He put the knife to the straps and was shocked all over again at how easily the knife slid through the tough fabric. Like it wasn't even there. He'd never seen anything cut so effortlessly.

With the pack free Ernesto rolled the man over onto his back and grabbed a strap that hadn't come loose with the rest of his gear. He pulled with everything he had and the American came loose from the rubble and slid with him through the hole in the twisted wreckage.

The cartel soldiers entered the wreckage just as Ernesto cleared the helicopter's cargo area and pulled the American behind a mound of shattered concrete. The cartel men started fighting over the weapons and the gear almost immediately, yelling and shoving each other like children fighting over toys. A moment later someone fired off a machine gun. There was silence for a moment, and then laughter and cheers.

Their noise covered his movements. It would have been quicker if he'd have been strong enough to throw the soldier over his shoulder in a fireman's carry, but he couldn't even lift him to his feet. His only chance, he knew, was to drag the man into the darkness of the building beyond the rubble.

The office building had suffered a lot of damage. The helicopter crash had done some of it, but not all. It had been badly damaged in the early days of the fighting. The first floor was wrecked. None of the windows had glass in them. The walls had been chewed to shreds by gunfire. Soaked and rotten knots of insulation hung from the ceiling. What furniture was left was upended and broken. Everything else had been reduced to piles of splinters on the floor.

There was a stairwell close by, and Ernesto pulled the American toward it.

Moving the man across the floor was hard work, and Ernesto was panting by the time he reached the lower steps. He mounted the first few steps, walking backwards, but when he tried to pull the American up he slipped and landed hard on his elbows and lower back.

He nearly cried out, but managed to choke it back in time.

Wincing, he sagged against the stairs and listened to the men rummaging around inside the helicopter. They were cheering like they'd just burst open a *piñata*. And then one of them must have found the pack Ernesto had cut loose from the American's back.

"Hey," he said. "Hey, look at this."

Ernesto sat up, his bruises momentarily forgotten.

"It's been cut," another man said.

"There's one alive," the first man said. "Find him!"

Oh no, Ernesto thought.

He stood up, grabbed the American's shoulders. "Come on, come on. We need to go."

"He couldn't have gone far," another man said. "Who has the flashlight?"

"Shit," Ernesto muttered. They'd see the tracks the American's heels had left in the muddy concrete ash. Surely they'd be able to follow him through the hole.

"We have to go!" he said to the American. "Get up, please."

The man's arm moved. He slapped clumsily at Ernesto's shoulder. Ernesto grabbed his arm and steadied it.

"I've got you," he said.

"Help me up," the soldier said in Spanish.

Ernesto guided him to his feet, then threw the man's arm over his shoulder.

"Where are you taking me?"

"Somewhere safe," Ernesto said. "I need you to climb the stairs though. I can't carry you."

The man tried to speak, but couldn't. He stifled a cough and seemed to lose consciousness for a moment.

"No, no," Ernesto said. "Don't do that. You need to stay with me."

The man caught himself, and stood with great effort. He turned a pair of bloodshot eyes on Ernesto and blinked, like he couldn't quite recognize him.

"I'm...okay," he said. "Who are you?"

"A friend."

Ernesto led him up the stairs.

The second floor had fared a little better than the first during the fighting. There was no electrical power and everything was dark. The building's sprinkler system had discharged, leaving a mildew smell clinging to the furniture and puddles of water standing in the carpet. Their shoes squished as they crossed the floor.

"Where are we going?"

"We have to get out of sight."

They went over to a window and Ernesto helped the man get down on his back between the couch and the wall. Ernesto crept over to the window and slowly peered down at the street. The cartel soldiers were still wandering around, still yelling, still firing off the fancy weapons they'd just found, but they seemed to have lost interest in looking for the man Ernesto had led away from the crash.

That was good, he thought. Now all he had to do was stay put and keep quiet. They'd be gone in another few minutes.

"What about my team?" the American said. His voice sounded like it had been passed through a woodchopper.

"You have to be quiet. The cartel men are still out there."

The American lowered his voice. "My team…what happened to them?"

"I'm sorry," Ernesto said. "Your friends are all dead. They died in the crash."

The American lay back on the floor and closed his eyes. His chest was bleeding, Ernesto noticed. His uniform on his left side was soaked through. As gently as he could he opened the soldier's body armor panels and lifted the shreds of the man's torn uniform, exposing a nasty-looking cut about twenty centimeters long. It started near the front of the man's shoulder and curved down, under his arm, toward his back.

It wasn't as bad as he thought, though. There was a lot of blood, but it wasn't deep. Ernesto searched the man's remaining gear until he found a small first aid kit. Inside were bandages and alcohol swabs, some iodine, water purification tablets, a few other things he didn't recognize. He unwrapped an alcohol swab and dabbed it over the cut.

The American barely flinched.

When it was as clean as he could make it, Ernesto pressed a gauze bandage to the deepest part of the cut and held it there a moment.

"I need your help with this," he said to the American, and put the man's hand over the gauze.

But when he let go of the man's wrist, his hand and the gauze fell away. At first Ernesto thought he had finally passed out from the pain, but when he looked again he realized the man was fighting down anger, and probably grief too. The dead men back at the helicopter must have been his friends, Ernesto figured. Probably closer even than that. He'd read stories about the American Special Forces teams in the newspapers, and he'd even watched a few of the documentaries on the TV with his grandfather. Their fighting ability was legendary. Men like that must look on each other as brothers.

The breath hitched in the man's throat. He brought the gauze up to his wound and pressed it there with a grimace.

Ernesto looked back toward the street.

He was watching the cartel soldiers as they searched the doorways of a building across the street when the American spoke again.

"You never told me your name."

Ernesto didn't look away from the window. The men were fighting amongst themselves now, arguing again over who got to use the weapons they'd seized. Two men squared off against each other. One of the men had a black pistol in his hand. The other had a small black machine gun. The one with the pistol called upon the others to shoot the other man for taking the machine gun from him, but before any one could come to his aid, the man with the machine gun fired. The man with the pistol, a skinny boy barely out of his teens wearing a dingy white t-shirt and jeans way too big for his narrow hips, crumpled to the ground in a heap.

He'd always felt a deep disgust for these men. Men just like them had killed his father and mother when he was just a little kid. His father had been a journalist. Ernesto's grandfather had told him his father was a brave man, a man of principal and integrity. Others were too scared to write about the cartels, but not his father. He'd written about the cartels with relentless honesty. Ernesto had even read some of his articles. They made him proud. Ernesto's father had been one of the few who dared to name names of cartel leaders and call corrupt government officials out, despite their threats and the warnings of his peers.

The cowards put a bomb in his father's car.

Now, looking down on the men in the street, Ernesto's expression turned mean. For a long time, and like pretty much everyone else in Mexico, he'd been deathly afraid of those men, but now he saw them for the street thugs they really were. They were criminals, not soldiers, not religious zealots, or even gangsters. They were street thugs hiding behind bravado and bullets, nothing more. They had made the *Cihuateteo* their goddess, and he couldn't help but smile. As far as Ernesto was concerned, they'd gotten the deity they deserved.

He held his chin high. "I am Ernesto Ramirez," he said to the Delta Force man.

"How old are you, Ernesto?"

"Thirteen."

The American tried to raise himself up on his elbows, but the pain was too much for him. His head fell back to the carpet and he let out a low, aching groan.

"So what's your story, kid? What's a thirteen-year-old doing out in this? Didn't anybody tell you there's a war going on?"

"This is my home," Ernesto said, his voice suddenly heated. "I know there's a war going on."

The man studied him for a long moment. "Yeah, I guess you would. But you didn't answer my question. What are doing out in this?"

Ernesto bowed his head. "My grandfather is very sick."

Saying the words out loud made him feel very tired. He'd been such a fool to think he could do this. What was he against the cartels and the mobs and the Army and the *Cihuateteo*? Just a boy. What had the American called him, a kid? It was all too much for him.

But then he jerked his head around and stared at the American. "They'll come looking for you, won't they?"

"Who?"

"The other Americans."

"What Americans?"

"Like you, other Delta Force soldiers. Your helicopter has some kind of beacon on it, right? They know where you are. They won't leave you here like this."

"Who said anything about Delta?"

Ernesto was growing impatient. "Your name is Juan Perez. You are an American soldier with Delta Force. Some kind of sergeant."

Perez's eyes narrowed with suspicion, but he didn't answer. He studied Ernesto's face for a long moment, and then his hand came up to the spot on his chest where his knife had been. Ernesto watched him, uncertain what he'd do if the American demanded the blade back.

"Yes, they'll come looking for me," Perez said at last.

"I knew it! You have doctors, right? Someone to work on your injured soldiers? You could help my grandfather."

Perez said nothing.

Ernesto reached into his pocket and took out the paper Dr. Rivera had given him before he left the apartment and held it out for Perez to see. "I have a list of the medicines he needs. You can help him, can't you?"

Perez looked from the note to Ernesto. "Son, you saved my life, but I don't know if I can…"

"Don't you see? He'll die without help."

"Ernesto, I can't…I can't make a promise like that." He nodded toward the window. "Not with all that going on out there."

Ernesto was ready to beg him, to plead with him, to scream at him if he had to, but before he could utter a word, the fighting and the gunfire down in the street abruptly ceased.

Ernesto and Perez traded a worried look.

"Go take a look," Perez said.

Ernesto nodded and went back to the window.

The cartel thugs had gathered in a huddle, their weapons slung over their shoulders. Ernesto followed their stares to a nearby corner and gasped.

"What is it?"

"A Blood Mother," Ernesto said in a whisper.

He watched the *Cihuateteo* as she waddled down the street. Her belly was huge. It sagged down between her thighs like an enormous melon. There was blood on her face and more obscuring the tattoos on her breasts, as though she had just fed, and as she got closer Ernesto realized that she was the same vampire that had spotted him when he found the dead *Cihuateteo* near his apartment. Had she tracked him here, latched onto his scent somehow?

She made her way past the cartel men to the helicopter. She stuck her head inside the wreckage, and to Ernesto it looked like she was sniffing the carnage she found there.

"What's going on?" Perez said. "What are they doing?"

"Shhh," Ernesto hissed. But when he turned back to the street he saw it was too late. The Blood Mother had backed out of the helicopter, and she was staring right at him.

The cartel men followed her gaze, then scrambled toward the building, jumping through the broken windows on the first floor.

"Oh no," Ernesto said. "No, no, no."

"What is it?"

"They know we're here. They're coming for us." He grabbed Perez's shoulder and tried to coax him to his feet. "Come on, we have to go right now."

Perez seized up in pain. Through gritted teeth he said, "No. No, wait."

"We have to go!"

"I can't," Perez said. He shook his head. "I can't."

"We can't stay here."

"Here, help me up."

"What do you want me to do?"

"Grab the straps on my shoulders. Yeah, that's right. Now help me up."

Ernesto did as Perez asked. He grabbed the straps and pulled up as Perez struggled to get to his feet. The process took a long time. Too long, Ernesto thought. He could hear the cartel men forcing their way through the debris that blocked much of the first floor. Shoving harder, he got Perez on his feet. The American couldn't stand up straight, and he kept one arm wrapped around his ribs like a boxer who's been hit too many times, but he was on his feet. He turned to Ernesto with watery, bloodshot eyes and asked him to hand him his pistol.

"You can't fight like that," Ernesto said.

"I can shoot a pistol with a few broken ribs," Perez said. "Now go on, get out of here."

There wasn't time to argue. The cartel men were charging up the stairs like a pack of wild dogs.

"Go," Perez said. "I got this."

Ernesto could hardly believe the calm in the man's voice, like it wasn't an act. He was clearly in pain. The man could barely stand. But he was calm and focused, and Ernesto felt a mix of admiration and jealousy, wishing he could have even a small measure of whatever drove the American.

Perez brought the pistol up to a ready position and blinked the sweat out of his eyes. The smile he'd favored Ernesto with a moment earlier changed into a hard, cruel line as he focused his attention on the top of the stairs. "You better go now," he said.

Ernesto didn't know what to say, so he merely nodded.

He turned to leave, unable to shake the feeling that he was some-how betraying this man, that he was acting like a coward.

"Hey, kid."

Ernesto stopped and looked back over his shoulder.

"I hope you get the help your grandfather needs."

At that moment, Ernesto would have begged him to come with him all over again, would have started the argument again, but before he could speak the cartel men burst from the stairwell, firing wildly as they charged. Ernesto dove behind a bench and crawled on his belly away from the shooting. He chanced a quick look back and saw the American firing one-handed at his attackers. Several cartel men dropped, only to be replaced by more. There was a steady stream of them rushing out up the stairs.

And then he got hit.

Ernesto saw Perez's body shudder and twist violently. The arm he'd used to cradle his ribs fell to his side and he sank to his knees, but he returned fire the whole time.

Seeing the American fall was all the motivation Ernesto needed.

He jumped to his feet and ran as fast as his legs could carry him. He expected the air to swarm with bullets, but all the fire seemed directed behind him.

He was running at a full sprint when he reached the stairwell at the opposite side of the building. Ernesto charged through the door and made it down four steps before stopping short, a scream caught in his throat.

There, standing at the foot of the stairs, her belly sagging with her latest meal, was the Blood Mother.

"APOCALYPSE TANGO" PT. 6

Jonathan Maberry

— 9 —

Loews Madison Hotel
Washington, D.C.
The Eve of the War

L uther Swann and Jimmy Saint sat on stools on two sides of the
corner of the long hardwood bar counter. Swann stared moodily
into the depths of his third martini. His head was swimming and
he found it difficult to keep his eyes focused.

Saint was taking it slower, still working on his second schooner of
Stella Artois. He'd eaten three bowls of mixed nuts, though, and his
face had a hypertensive salt flush.

They'd spent two hours with the chief of staff, another hour with
General May—a meeting dominated by Spiro Nyklos, who seemed to
have the general's ear—and then retired to the hotel where Swann
was staying. The hotel was much more expensive than Swann would
have chosen, and more expensive than was necessary for a consultant
paid by taxpayer's dollars. Even so, they made a great martini. Karlsson's Gold Vodka from Sweden, a faint nod in the direction of dry
vermouth, straight up with three olives.

Saint had expressed some disgust when he ordered it. "Martinis are
made with gin. Anything else is a crime against good taste."

"Never developed a taste for gin," said Swann. "Besides gin is made
from juniper berries. Karlsson's is potato vodka, so this is me getting
my vegetables."

They drank for a while in moody silence.

It was Saint who broke it. "I didn't call Nyklos in," he said.

"I didn't ask."

"I know, but I wanted you to understand that. Him showing up was as much a surprise to me as it was to you."

Swann sipped his martini, said nothing.

"And, look," said Saint slowly, "about earlier. When I, you know…"

He did a little hand flip in imitation of a slap. "I…shit, Luther…I'm sorry."

"Don't be, Jimmy. To quote the vernacular, I was losing my shit. Probably would have totally lost it."

"Even so. Hitting you was out of line. If you wanted to file a report—"

"Oh, for Christ's sake, Jimmy, buy the next round and we're square."

Saint did. They clinked glasses and lapsed once more into brooding silence, though it was more companionable than earlier.

"He's dangerous," said Swann.

"Hm? Who? Nyklos? Yes, I'm aware of it. He and General May are tight, going back to the Bush administration. Nyklos did some consulting at Gitmo. There's a rumor he came up with the phrase 'enhanced interrogation' as a way of soft-soaping the torture scandal."

"Jesus."

"Worked, too. He's as much a political spin-doctor as he is a psychologist. The annoying thing is that he's almost as good as he thinks he is. His profiles have helped us catch several of our Most Wanted. When the outbreak happened, General May began courting him to come up with profiles of vampire predators."

"I read those reports. Most of them are bullshit."

"Are they?"

Swann ate an olive and didn't answer.

The bar was empty and the bartender—a pretty Irish woman with intensely red hair and very interesting cleavage—was drying wines glasses and hanging them on an overhead rack. Every once in a while she cut a look at Swann and gave him a small but very pretty smile.

Saint caught Swann smiling back and grinned. "You have a friend," he said. "Play your cards right and you won't have to sleep alone tonight."

"Not shopping to buy right now," Swann said, lowering his eyes. "Been trying to work things out with Trish."

"Trish? As in your ex-wife Trish?"

"Yup."

"I thought she hated you and wanted to—and I'm quoting here—see you burn in hellfire for a million years."

"Yeah, well. There's the kids and all."

"Boy and girl, right?"

"Brian and Jenny. Six and seven. Trish has custody, but I get to visit. Lately she's been asking me over for dinners, so maybe there's something there. A chance."

Saint studied him for a moment, then nodded. "If you get that chance, man, take it. I didn't try hard enough with Amelia and now I never see her. It's like she's totally gone from my life. Lives in Houston. Married to some guy who owns part of the Astros. They have a kid on the way."

"Damn, Jimmy, I didn't know."

Saint waved it off. "Not trying to be maudlin here, Luther. My point is I had a window and I waited too long. If Trish is inviting you over, then she's reaching out. Reach back."

"That's the plan."

"And tell me to go fuck myself if this is none of my business, but…"

"Go ahead. Ask it."

"Do you still love her?"

Swann sipped some of the martini, thought about it, took another sip. "I think I could fall back in love with her," he said.

It was a sad thing to say and they both understood it. The kids.

Saint patted him on the forearm. "I hope it works out for you. Family is everything. It's why most of us do what we do."

"Even you?"

"I don't have kids," said Saint. "But I have two sisters and a slew of nephews and nieces. My mom's still alive, down in Miami. And I have cousins. So…sure, I'm doing this for my family. And my friends. And my country."

Swann nodded and they toasted on that.

The vodka was kicking Swann's ass and he was about to tell Saint that it was time to cash it in, when both of their cell phones began ringing.

They exchanged a glance, knowing immediately and with perfect certainty that this was not a coincidence. And any call at this hour could not be good news.

Could not.

Reaching for his phone took real effort. He didn't want to know anything whoever was calling wanted to tell him.

Saint was just as slow reaching for his.

Swann thumbed the button and said, "This is Swann."

"Dr. Swann," said General Aldous May, "there's been an another incident."

"Good God, another attack on a family? Where?"

"No," said the general, "I'm afraid it's a good deal worse than that. I've sent a car for you. They should be there any minute."

"General, I'm exhausted and I've had a couple of drinks. I'm in no shape to—"

"That doesn't matter, Dr. Swann. We need you right now."

Swann saw two tall, burly soldiers enter the hotel bar. They spotted him and angled sharply toward him.

"What's happened, General?"

"You haven't seen the news?"

"No, I—"

"It's Philadelphia."

"What about it?"

"It's burning, doctor."

– 10 –

Starbucks Coffee
Doylestown, Pennsylvania
The Eve of the War

They sat on the porch and watched the traffic.

It was a rustic porch in front of a building that had been, among other things, a traveler's inn and a wagon stop before it became part of the Starbucks chain of coffee shops. The table was wrought iron, and the chairs were aluminum. The coffee was in paper cups and a bag was torn open to reveal a half-eaten chocolate caramel muffin.

The men were as unalike as possible.

The man on the left was short, fat, bald, ugly, and badly dressed in an old off-the-rack suit that had probably first seen wear during the Clinton administration. It had seen hard years since.

The man on the right was tall, very thin, ten years younger, and dressed in hipster clothes. Sneakers, skinny jeans, an earth-color sweater over an untucked dress shirt. A bow tie identical to the one Doctor Who wore a few seasons back. Thick-framed glasses with only a touch of correction. A two hundred dollar haircut designed to look like it was bed hair on a windy morning.

They drank their coffee and watched the cars, watched the people, watching rich ladies walk absurd little dogs, watched teenagers move like tides back and forth through a town that possessed no nightlife.

The fat little man played with a ring. It was small, silver, with a flush-set garnet.

The hipster had an identical ring. He wore his on his thumb.

A girl walked past. Late teens. Very nicely built, with a bobbing blonde ponytail and buds screwed into her ears. She passed close enough for them to smell her.

When she was out of earshot, the fat man said, "*Givenchy Dahlia Noir L'Eau.*"

"Nice," said the hipster. "Good catch. Soap?"

"Nivea."

"Oil of Olay," corrected the younger man.

The fat man sniffed, pursed his lips, nodded. "Oil of Olay."

"The skin cream is Nivea," said the hipster.

"You are correct. It's over sweat, though. Gym. Washed but didn't shower."

The hipster nodded. "Had tuna with onions for lunch. Strong, but not recent."

"What kind of onion? I'm thinking Vidalia."

"Vidalia. Albacore tuna, though."

"Hunh…didn't catch that. Younger nose."

"You should stop smoking," said the Hipster. "Helps with the sense of smell."

"Fuck that," said the fat man. "I smoke to deaden it. I don't smoke, I can smell everybody's shit, no matter how good they wipe. Don't get me started on public bathrooms."

"I hear ya."

"And taste? I was always really sensitive," he said. "Before, I mean."

"Yeah."

"Now? Fuck."

"I know."

"I can't go near a McDonalds. I can tell when some asshole's put their finger on a beef patty."

"Really?"

"Shit yeah. That's why I smoke. I don't want that kind of detail when

I'm trying to eat."

The hipster leaned slightly closer and dropped his voice. "What about the taste of…you know? Doesn't it kill the taste of that?"

The fat guy shrugged. "The fuck do I care? I'm doing cow's blood."

"Seriously? Since when?"

"Since the end of the war. I don't tap anybody for so much as a thimbleful. No way, Jose. I don't need that kind of hassle."

"Shit."

"What? You're still feeding on…" He nodded to the people on the street.

"Not that way, no. I belong to a club."

"Club? Like what? One of those wannabe things?"

"Sure. The Funeral Parlor up in New Hope. Always Goth chicks willing to give up half a pint just to get boned by one of the Undead."

"Undead? Seriously? They still think we're dead? After everything in the papers? After that *60 Minutes* special?"

The hipster shrugged and took a sip of his coffee. "People believe what they want to believe. When did facts ever matter more than a wet fart?"

"True, true," agreed the fat man. "Still…they give up the O-pos *and* they let you bone them?"

"Hand to God," said the hipster, holding up a hand.

"Shit."

"Shit."

The fat guy thought about it for a while. They watched the crowd.

The hipster was just about to say something else when they heard the screams. From inside the Starbucks. They turned to see people running toward the doors. And running out. People had stopped in the street and were staring at their smart phones. A black man two tables down gaped at his laptop screen.

The black man said, "Jesus Christ!"

He said it very loud and with absolute horror in his voice.

The fat guy and the hipster stared at him, then at each other, then around at the crowds. Those who didn't seem to know what was going on huddled with people who did. The murder of concerned voices rose steadily in volume.

Without saying a word to each other, the fat man and the hipster got up and hurried over to where the black man sat. He saw them coming and said, "Do you *believe* this shit?"

"Believe what shit?" asked the fat guy.

"What's going on?" asked the hipster.

The man spun his laptop around to show a live news stream from ABC News in Philadelphia. A reporter stood on the street yelling so she could give her report above the din all around her.

"…three explosions reported in Philadelphia, bringing the nation-wide total to eleven. Wait, we're getting word now…wait, is this confirmed? Okay, folks, we're getting word now that four more bombs have exploded. Two more in New York and two in Chicago."

The fat guy and the hipster leaned over the black man's shoulder and watched in horror at scenes of carnage. The network kept switching to various live and taped feeds of burning buildings, burning hospitals, flames erupting from the mouths of commuter tunnels, burning bridges.

Burning cars.

Burning people.

The banner under the reporter read: America Under Attack.

"Holy shit," breathed the fat guy.

"What *is* this?" said the hipster. "What the hell is happening?"

The black man shot him a hard look. "What's happening? Open your damn eyes, son. *They're* happening. They're back and they're trying to burn it all down this time."

"They?" asked the hipster weakly. "Wh—who?"

"Why…the fucking vampires," growled the black man. "Who else would do something like this?"

"No…"

"Don't fucking tell me no. My cousin Trey died in the first V-War. He was with the Philadelphia SWAT team and he got himself killed. And it wasn't some crackhead, neither. He was killed by a vampire. And now look at this shit. We gave them a chance. We said we'd be able to make peace and live together and all that shit."

"All that shit…"

"And look what happens. The vampires are back, god damn it. Blowing shit up all over the country. They're back and they want us all to fucking roll over and die. God damn bloodsucking parasites." The man was seething. "I hope we nuke them all the way the fuck back to Transylvania or wherever the fuck they come from."

The hipster and the fat guy said nothing. They dared not.

They began retreating from the black man and from the horrors on the screen.

The man's words followed them, though.

"This time, I hope they kill 'em all. I really hope they kill every last one of those bloodsucking, unholy sonsabitches."

They retreated all the way to the end of the porch. People were shouting in the streets. Hugging each other. Crying.

Yelling.

Cursing.

Everyone.

The hipster looked around and saw two other people that he knew, for sure, were vampires. One of them was a member of a V-cell, but even he looked totally confused. Totally lost by this.

That made no sense to the hipster. If someone from a V-cell didn't know, then what really *was* happening?

There were no answers. Not now.

Not while the dying was still going on. Not while Death Himself had come visiting.

Death, certainly.

The Angel of Death to be sure.

Come to America.

But whose hand held the torch?

If not vampire…then humans? Both choices were filled with complications and neither offered an answer that might work.

Who then was doing this?

Who?

Why?

And where would it all end?

The hipster didn't know. Neither did the fat guy.

So, like vampires all across the country—like *people* all across the country—they ran home to be with their families.

Boom.

Boom.

Boom.

"TENOCHTITLAN WILL RISE" PT. 3

Joe McKinney

— 7 —

Ernesto barely had time to raise his hands to guard his face. Despite her ponderous belly, the *Cihuateteo* moved with alarming speed. She seemed to rush up the stairs in a blur of color, her tattoos flashing angrily. She was on him the next instant, her hands on his wrists, pushing him to the ground.

He let out a weak cry, but it did no good. The next instant he was on his back and she was on top of him. Her breath reeked of blood. She made a noise like a strangled growl. Her teeth looked like two rows of glass shards in her gaping maw. Ernesto fought with everything he had, twisting and bucking beneath her. He tried to turn to one side and then the other. He kicked and writhed, but she was incredibly strong. He had no idea a woman could be so strong. Nothing worked. He was pinned to the stairs. Her hands were tight as vice grips on his wrists. Her belly pressed against his, pushing his shirt up to his armpits as he struggled to get out from under her.

He raised a knee and tried to push her away but couldn't get under her belly. In desperation he kicked out, and connected with her shin. She howled in pain. Her grip loosened and he pulled his hands away. Before she could get her hands on his wrists again Ernesto balled his fists and slammed them into her face. He kicked again, catching her just below the knee. It was enough to throw her off balance, and she fell face first to the stairs below him.

But she didn't stay down long. She lifted her head, fangs bared, and her black eyes were filled with hate.

Ernesto turned and ran up the stairs, taking them two at a time.

She was right behind him as he rounded the second story landing, and again he was shocked at how quick she was. He could feel her hands clutching at his back as he climbed higher, terror propelling him upward and upward.

She couldn't match his pace. She was quick, but he was faster, and by the time he reached the sixth floor landing he was a full flight of stairs ahead of her. He reached the seventh floor landing and hit the door, throwing it open.

He didn't go through it though. With the door slowly closing again, he crept as quietly as he could up to the eighth floor and listened. She was making a lot of noise down there, but she was still coming. Praying the door wouldn't give him away, he pushed it open just enough to slide through, and then carefully guided it back into the jamb.

He backed away from the door, praying the diversion would work the way it did on the TV.

"Please, please," he said.

He imagined her climbing the stairs to the seventh floor, tired but angry, and seeing the door as it clicked back into place. She'd push the door open and sniff the air the way she'd done down in the helicopter, and maybe she'd go wandering through the halls, pushing open doors as she looked for her next meal. But then he had to stop thinking about it. He was starting to scare himself all over again, thinking of those glass-like teeth of hers and the stink of blood on her breath. He shivered and backed away from the door a little more.

He glanced behind him. He was standing in a dark lobby, the carpet wet from the sprinklers and smelling of rot. Beyond the lobby were a few offices. He thought maybe he could hide back there somewhere, stay out of sight until daylight. The fighting was always lightest in the mornings and he figured even vampires like the *Cihuateteo* needed to sleep eventually. It was his only hope.

But he'd only made it halfway across the lobby when the door behind him exploded open. He spun around and saw the *Cihuateteo* standing there, chest heaving, her distended belly rising and falling with every breath. She opened her mouth wide, fangs bristling, and that was all it took. Ernesto turned and ran.

He jumped over the receptionist desk and ran into the hallway behind it. The carpet was slimy with standing water and his feet slid out from under him. He hit the wall hard, and if the plaster hadn't been so damp he would have seriously hurt himself. He got back to his feet, looked over his shoulder and saw her coming around the receptionist desk. He sprinted for a doorway halfway down the hall.

The door was unlocked, and he pushed through it.

He closed it, locked it, and backed across the empty room to the window. A soft, struggling sound caught in his throat when he saw the room was completely bare. There was absolutely nothing he could use for concealment. The ceiling was made of movable panels, and in desperation he thought maybe he could get up there and hide among the pipes. He jumped for the ceiling, but missed it by a good two feet. He'd never be able to reach it. Not without something to stand on.

He stared around in full panic.

There was nowhere to go.

Nowhere, he realized with dawning horror, but the window.

– 8 –

Ernesto grabbed the bottom of the window and gave it a good heave.

Nothing happened. It didn't budge.

Behind him, the Blood Mother pounded on the door. It shook in its frame and he knew it wouldn't hold her long.

"Come on," he pleaded with the window. "Come on, why won't you open?"

She hit the door again. She was screaming behind the door, a hideous noise like pigs must make when they die, and it sent a chill over his skin. He turned to the window, his feelings of helplessness overwhelming him, until his gaze caught on the window latch.

Locked, he thought. The damn thing is locked.

He flipped the latches and pulled the window open. A cold wind whipped at his face. The sounds of a city caught up in battle filled the room. Mexico City was dying, and this was its death knell.

This was *his* death knell.

He put his head out the window, and as he did he thought of the images he'd seen on YouTube from 9/11. Papa had shown him video of men and women holding hands as they jumped from the burning buildings, falling a hundred stories to their deaths. At the time he'd stared at the computer screen in disbelief. He'd felt angry and sad and frightened, but mostly, just confused. It had seemed a mystery to him then that people could jump to their deaths rather than rush down the stairs, even if those stairs were on fire. Wasn't a fighting chance, no matter how thin, no matter how cruel and painful, better than certain death?

He thought as much as he stuck his head out the window.

And saw the narrow, decorative ledge that belted the building.

It was within arm's reach of the window, an easy leg swing down.

It was a way out!

He stepped through the window just as the door to the office exploded open behind him. He glanced up to see the Blood Mother standing in the doorway, her sagging, tattooed breasts heaving with exertion.

She took a few steps into the office.

Ernesto looked down. The ledge was only two feet below the window, and it looked wider than his foot was long.

But it wasn't the ledge he saw.

The building dropped away like the edge of the world. His stomach leapt up into his throat and his vision swam with vertigo. He'd been filling himself with false courage when he thought about jumping. Now that he was staring down at the street so far below, the cars there small enough to hide behind his thumb, he knew he never would have gathered up the courage to jump. Even with the threat of being eaten, of ending up as a hand pressed against the underside of the *Cihuateteo*'s belly, he never would have found the courage.

But she *was* coming, and the ledge was right there.

Ever so carefully he stepped through the window and lowered his right foot down onto the ledge. Like so much of the construction in the area the building was made of gray concrete and uneven workmanship, but it never occurred to him that the ledge would crumble. He couldn't think that. He couldn't.

The *Cihuateteo* was getting closer. He could hear her bare feet squishing on the wet carpet. Moving as quickly as he dared he brought his left foot out and lowered it down. He still held onto the edge of the window, though. The wind was picking up, filling his shirt like a sail. He pressed his face against the concrete wall of the building, unable to control his breathing. The blood was pounding in his ears and when he finally managed to open his eyes he was looking at his right hand splayed against the wall and it was shaking uncontrollably. He couldn't move. He was truly crippled with fear.

And then he felt the Blood Mother's hand on his left wrist and he jerked it away with a startled cry.

The motion put him off balance and for a terrifying moment he thought for sure he was going to fall. He pressed forward, smashing his cheek against the side of the building. It was cold but it was solid, and in that moment it was his whole world.

The Blood Mother howled behind him. Ernesto's left cheek was up against the wall. To look at her he would have to turn his head, and he wasn't sure he could do that. The idea of moving away from the wall, even an inch, even a fraction of a centimeter, was too much for him. Instead he began the slow process of moving away from the window, baby steps, right foot left foot, right foot left foot, a centimeter at a time.

The Blood Mother roared, and Ernesto turned his head toward her. It was a mistake.

She was leaning out the window. Her gaping mouth had changed shape just a little, almost like she was smiling. That smile unnerved him almost as much as the drop below his feet, and it took him too long to realize that she had something in her hand. What was that, a rock?

The question was still forming in his mind when she chucked it at his face. He flinched and it caught him on the shoulder instead. It careened off into the night. He looked down to watch it fall and his stomach did another back flip. He struggled to regain his balance, and for the second time pushed his face against the concrete, wishing for all the world that he could just melt through it and be on solid ground again.

The Blood Mother snarled. Ernesto met her gaze and for a moment he felt a rush of triumph. She'd tried to shake him loose, but he'd held on.

His elation didn't last though.

The Blood Mother stepped out of the window and balanced herself on the ledge. She too stood with her face pressed against the wall, the claws at the end of her right hand close enough to his hand he could have reached out and touched her. If the threat of falling scared her, she gave no sign of it.

And then she started after him.

He slid his feet along, staring back at her, unable to look away, until he came to the next window. With fingers made numb by the fear and the cold wind, he tried to lift it. It was locked, of course. Of course it was, he thought. But the edges of the recessed window frame gave him something to hold on to, and with a surer grip he was able to speed his pace. He crossed to the other side of the window, and still holding onto the window's edge, pounded a fist against the glass.

He couldn't hit it very hard though. He didn't dare. Even the slight force he was using made him feel like he was going over backwards.

He gave it up.

The Blood Mother was gaining on him, getting closer with every passing second. She was almost at the window. Her back was arched to make way for her enormous belly, but not even that slowed her down. She seemed surefooted as a goat.

Ernesto kept moving. He was concentrating on the next window, refusing to look down, when he heard something crunch behind him. He turned and saw the Blood Mother had made the window. She was holding a piece of crumbling concrete that she'd torn from the window edge with her claws.

Her gaze met his.

She held the concrete up so he could see, gestured at him with it like it was a piece of fruit she wanted him to taste, and then tossed it into the air.

He couldn't help himself.

He watched it fall.

His head swam with a sickening wave of vertigo. The rock fell and fell and fell for a very long time. When the crack finally came, all Ernesto could think of was his corpse down there in the street, smashed and shattered, every bone broken.

He nearly vomited.

The Blood Mother let out a low, menacing growl, and came after him again. Ernesto went as fast as he dared. He passed another window, and then another, and suddenly found himself at the corner of the building. He glanced back at the *Cihuateteo*, less than two meters behind him now, and slid his arm around the corner.

Though the wind was fiercely cold, his palms were wet with sweat. His grip felt uncertain on the concrete, but he had to go on. He couldn't wait any longer. He slid his leg around so that he was hugging the corner. Then he began the slow process of transferring his weight from his left leg to his right, shifting his torso bit by bit until he had rounded the corner. A crosswind bit into him and whipped his hair around his eyes. The back of his shirt billowed with air. And still he maintained his focus, until he was staring at a burning orange sunrise coming up over the urban sprawl of Mexico City.

It was beautiful and terrifying at the same time. Very few buildings in the city were taller than four stories, and the rooftops below him looked like a dappled sea of molten copper.

But there were helicopters too.

They skimmed over the buildings and hovered over alleyways, hunting their targets. Looking down he could see dead bodies in the streets. So many buildings had burned, and many more were burning still, their fires leaking columns of greasy smoke into the morning glow. In the far distance he saw the Templo Mayor Museum, the site of the old Aztec main complex. It alone seemed to have escaped the privations of war. Perhaps, he thought, the whole world would burn, except for that building. And maybe the cartels were right. Maybe the glory of the old Aztec capital, Tenochtitlan, would rise again from the ashes.

But the thought was gone the next instant. His attention turned from the crucible of battle to the ledge ahead of him. Some twenty feet away, the ledge hit a dead end at the building's elevator shaft.

"No," he said. "No, no, no!"

Behind him, the Blood Mother's clawed hand appeared at the corner. For a moment, Ernest thought of charging her. If he was fast enough he could get there ahead of her and shove her back before she even saw him coming. He knew from his own experience he wouldn't have to shove hard. It was all too easy to lose one's balance up here.

But she was faster than he was, and she peered around the corner before he could move that way.

Once again he turned back to the ledge ahead of him.

There was a window midway down the length of the ledge.

It was his only hope.

Ernesto slid along the ledge until he reached the window. He grabbed the edges and pulled himself across to the far side and tried to lift it.

It was locked.

He beat on the glass. He started to scream, but then he remembered the knife.

He still had it.

He reached into his back pocket and let out a cry when his hand found the hilt. He passed the knife to his left hand, turned it upside down, and started pounding on the glass with the butt of the hilt.

The window shook but didn't break.

He hit it again, harder this time, desperation making him reckless, and nearly fell over backwards. He grabbed the edge of the window and steadied himself.

The Blood Mother had rounded the corner with no trouble. She was closing in, her jaws working up and down like she could already taste him. He held the knife up so she could see, but she showed no alarm. Her black eyes, depthless and utterly cold, showed no emotion but hatred. She meant to kill him, and nothing he could do was going to stop that.

But he was sure going to try.

He backed away from the window, the knife held high, and readied himself for her. As soon as she put a hand on the window edge closest to him, he would lash out, maybe slice those claws off, or maybe put a painful gash in her arm. Either way, he was going to give her hell.

And then she was at the window. She grabbed the far edge and pulled herself forward, her body tensed and ready to strike. Ernesto adjusted his grip in his sweaty hand. The Blood Mother inched closer, then reached for the edge of the window closest to Ernesto.

He was about to slash the knife down on her wrist when the window exploded outward. Something big and bulky crashed through the window, colliding with the Blood Mother and sending her over the edge with a scream of rage and surprise.

In shock, Ernesto watched her fall.

She hit the ground a long moment later with a grotesque, wet-sounding splat. Even from ninety feet in the air, and the Blood Mother small as a doll down there, he could see the contents of her stomach had ruptured on the pavement. He saw a tiny arm, and a part of a foot, and in horror he looked away.

And saw a broken office chair on the pavement next to her.

A chair?

"Hey kid, are you gonna stay out there all day, or what?"

Ernesto turned his attention back to the window, back to the American soldier standing there. Perez was one solid wound from his hair down to his boots, but when he smiled his white teeth shone through the grime and the blood.

He held out a hand to Ernesto. "Come on, let me help you inside."

Ernesto reached him, but Perez suddenly pulled his hand away. "Hey, put that knife in your other hand first, okay?" he said. "That thing is sharp."

"Oh. Yeah, sorry."

He helped Ernesto inside and then fell against the wall, hugging his ribs again.

"Thank you," Ernesto said.

Perez nodded.

"I thought you were dead."

"Yeah, things got kind of tight there for a bit, but body armor will do wonders sometimes." He put an arm out so Ernesto could slide his shoulder under. "Here, help me to the roof."

"The roof?"

"You want to get out of here, don't you? I just got word. They're sending in a ride to get me. I'll take you, too."

"But…I can't. My grandfather…"

"If we get to the roof, do you think you could guide a pilot to your apartment building."

"Uh, sure," Ernesto said. "Yeah, I could do that."

"Good, then get me to the roof. Let's go get your grandfather."

"APOCALYPSE TANGO" PT. 7

Jonathan Maberry

– 11 –

The Situation Room
The White House
Washington, D.C.
The Eve of the War

Luther Swann stood up with the others as the President of the United States entered the secure room. Luther had met the POTUS twice before, during the most heated days of the V-War, but they'd never had anything beyond a formal conversation. However, when the president saw him he nodded and offered his hand.

"Dr. Swann, thanks for joining us," he said. "Sorry it's under such dreadful circumstances."

"I hope I can be of some assistance, Mr. President."

The president clapped him on the shoulder, gave him a grim nod, and took his place at the head of the table. The others crowded into the room were a who's who of the real power players in Washington. Two of the Joint Chiefs—Army and Marines—the National Security Director, the directors of the FBI, ATF, CIA, NSA, and Homeland, the Secretary of State, Bill Gabriel and General May.

And Spiro Nyklos.

It was a crowded room. Everyone had laptops or tablets open. The far wall was set with many large screens, and most of the screens had smaller windows open. The pictures shown on those screens were horrific. Like something out of a disaster movie, except this was real.

Each image was a live feed from either a news station, a ground team, or a satellite.

"Bring me up to speed," ordered the president.

The director of Homeland ran it down.

"Mr. President, the first bombs were detonated in Philadelphia. Thirteen confirmed explosions. Then six in New York, five in Chicago, nine in Los Angeles."

The chief of staff took the ball. "All state and local agencies have been mobilized. FEMA is on standby. All off-duty police and military personnel have been called in. Same for firefighters and EMTs. We are coordinating with hospitals in each city."

"What are the targets?"

"They're strategic hits," said General May. "In Philadelphia we lost police headquarters, the National Guard depot, the control tower at International Airport, and two major emergency hospitals. Jefferson and Pennsylvania Hospitals in Center City. Bombs went off in the tunnels for the Market-Frankford and Broad Street subways. Two bombs were detonated on I-95, effectively blocking traffic approaching Center City. And three bombs have caused significant damage to the Ben Franklin, Tacony-Palmyra and Walt Whitman bridges. A bomb that we believe was intended for the Betsy Ross Bridge detonated on a ramp from I-95, so that bridge isn't damaged. We've shut it down, though."

"What about New York?"

"Holland and Lincoln Tunnels were both damaged. And we have a major blast in Times Square. The other three bombs damaged the Brooklyn and George Washington bridges and the tower at LaGuardia. Significant damage in most cases. Traffic is gridlocked. It's a shitstorm."

The general ran through the strikes in the other cities. The pattern was the same. Bridges, hospitals, airports, tunnels.

Everyone at the table looked stricken and frightened.

"Casualties?" asked the president.

"Too soon for any accurate estimates," said the director of Homeland. "But we have to assumed thousands. The tunnels and bridges alone…"

An aide, who had been speaking quietly into a phone, interrupted. "Mr. President, three more just went off in Seattle."

"God Almighty," whispered the president. "What is this? Who the fuck is doing this? And how the fuck can something like this happen?"

No one wanted to answer.

No one met his eyes.

"Is this al-Qaeda?" demanded the POTUS.

The CIA director cleared his throat. "There is no indication of that at this time."

"Then who?" He looked pointedly at Swann. "You tell me, doctor. Is this the V-War again?"

Swann didn't dare answer.

So, Spiro Nyklos answered for him. "I believe that is *exactly* what we're seeing," he said.

The president turned cold eyes on him. "And why is that, Dr. Nyklos? What makes you so certain?"

"Because," said the psychologist, "this is exactly what I predicted would happen. This was inevitable."

The room was dead silent.

"The Vampire War never ended, gentlemen," said Nyklos quietly. "The lull we had was just them preparing, getting smarter, getting organized, getting ready...for this."

The president turned slowly to Luther Swann.

"What do you say to that?"

Swann felt tears burn in his eyes. He wanted to reach across the table and punch Nyklos' teeth down his throat.

What he said was, "I...think he may be right."

"WAR TORN" PT.1

James A. Moore

−1−

It was like a Hollywood scene, really. Old Hollywood, back when the movies were black and white. San Francisco was buried under a nice, thick layer of white fog. Not just the stuff that creeps on the ground, but the heavy moisture that covers the entire city and makes seeing anything more than two feet in front of your face almost impossible.

Seeing as I'm a monster, it worked to my benefit.

I had about fifteen guys with flashlights—torches would have been better for the old movies, but, hey, you do what you can—firearms and knives out to cut me to ribbons. The bad news for them? I was feeling exactly the same way.

I heard people say that this is now a war. And I guess that's true enough.

The thing about wars is you don't get asked to participate. You just kind of get sucked into them. Sometimes, even when you're the one everyone is calling the root of all evil, it's not because you were planning it.

Back when I was in elementary school, me and Rio used to play at war all the time. It's what you do, right? Pick up a stick and just like that it's a rifle. Or a sword, or a light saber, depending on the war in question. Okay, in Rio's case he had an awesome plastic light saber that glowed and made noises, but he was cool enough that now and then he even let me use it. Rio. That dude's been my best friend as long as I can remember.

But I was talking about wars, wasn't I? Yeah. In this case the racial war to end all racial wars. The "Vampire Wars." I hear there's about a dozen different movies planned. Me? I'm not so much interested in seeing them if I'm being honest here. The idea leaves a bad taste in my mouth.

If you look back far enough, I guess I got my invitation into this war. I was asked to play along by my sister when she was setting me up as the bad guy and pointing a bloody claw right at me for all the things she'd done.

What am I talking about? Back before the Vampire War started I was just a low level enforcer for the Triad running things in San Francisco. Money was decent, pressure was low and I got along just fine. Rio set it up, because, again, he's my buddy.

Then the fever hit, and I changed. Listen, we've been over this. I got sick, I got better. Then I kept getting better. I became a vampire. There's different types. Which is kind of cool I guess, but also causes all kinds of troubles.

Legends from the past, from different cultures all over the damn world, really, say this has maybe happened before and we forgot about it. Those who don't learn from the past are doomed to repeat it, that's how that old saying goes, I think. Anyways, there have maybe been vampires before. The kind I became is called a Hopping Ghost. Mostly because the muscles in the legs and the joints around those muscles lock up like rigor mortis. Back before she screwed me over and framed me for the shit she was doing, my sister Anna helped me get over the worst of the leg pains by showing me a lot of yoga stretches. I do the stretches, I get to walk. Kind of unfair when you think about it. I mean, rigor mortis wears off in corpses. Me? I guess it's the price I have to pay for all the benefits that come with my new condition.

That seems like forever ago.

Anyway. Back to the story. I had a good time working as an enforcer and then the virus got me and I made the news a couple of times and got interviewed. And I got a finger pointed at me when some bad murders took place. And then somebody stole my sister and told me to stay out of it. I'd have left it alone but they stole my sister, so of course I followed.

Yeah. Not my best move. I got set up to look like the heavy in the murder of a bishop who was screaming about the evils of vampires. Then for the murder of a country singer with more fans than brains who said the vampires were God's judgment. I got set up for the death of a senator's son and then for the deaths of the senator and his wife.

The senator, like the bishop and the country crooner, was very much against vampires. You can see how that would look, right?

So after I got back from making a damn fool of myself, I decided the best thing I could do was hide. I figured given a little time the worst of the shit would blow over and I could get back to my life.

And maybe that would have worked, but then the actual Vampire War started.

I know I should have paid better attention, okay? I'm sure you're there shaking your heads and thinking what a loser I am for not giving you all the details about how the war started, but I'll give you a counter-argument: Google that shit. This isn't about the war. It's about me and, okay, how the war made my life turn into a steaming pile of nastiness.

Johnny Lei, by the way. You've been reading this far you maybe should know what my name is. It's Johnny Lei. I'm the bad guy in this. At least that's what they keep saying. Someone figured out about the old legends of my kinds and I've been called The Hopping Ghost, all capitalized like that, and now and then they put my name at the end of it, just in case you don't make the connection automatically. Kind of like some people still felt that they had to put Presley at the end of Elvis, I guess. Most people got the notion—hell, I got the notion and the man was dead before I was born—but some people gotta put a whole name there, just to clarify.

I'm the bad guy. How the hell did that happen?

Well, I guess that's what we're here to talk about, right? So let's get to it.

— 2 —

I was laying low, I already told you that. I don't know what set them in my direction. Maybe it was Anna trying to recruit me to her side. I don't think so, though. Much as she maybe wouldn't have minded me suffering, I can't believe she'd have risked our parents getting hurt. When she made her move and broke away from home, she was sure they were out of harm's way. So I can't see it.

On the other hand, people change.

In any case, the police came knocking when I was minding my own business.

Listen, I said I was laying low. What I was doing was hiding my sorry ass in my bedroom and hoping it would all go away. The police and the

FBI were after a monster. They were looking for a white-furred thing with a cat face and a mane of white hair. That thing looked nothing like me. Okay, it *was* me, yes, but they didn't know that. My monster-face was sort of like my secret identity. Until I showed it I could hide myself pretty well. When I caught the virus and changed, my hair went white. A little hair dye and I was almost as good as new.

123

There were a few blurry photos of the hopping ghost. There were a *lot* of witnesses. The witnesses were cops, because I broke right through their ranks when I was investigating the murders and the disappearance of my sister. I also tried very hard to leave all of them alive. I might be a trashy enforcer for the Triad, but I never wanted to be a killer.

We don't always get what we want, right?

Remember that part about being an enforcer? Well, I worked for a man named Robert Kang. To me he was just Kang, or Sir. No Robert, or Bobby or any of that stuff. Back when I was hunting for Anna he was cool about everything. He told me he had my back and he meant it. After I came back and things only calmed down a little bit, he gave me some work and slid me money under the table. He's that sort of guy. Once you're on his team he's there for you.

He was the one that picked up the phone and called me when the cops were on their way to my house. Kang himself.

I won't forget that.

I was watching *Judge Judy*, and eating take out from the place downstairs in my building when he called and said the cops were on their way. By the time that registered, I heard the sounds of them coming for me.

I really didn't have time to thank Kang. I just killed the call and grabbed my cash.

I'm maybe not the brightest guy out there. I get that. But I'm all about survival and after what happened with Anna I made it a point to have a stash of essentials. Those included a backpack with two pistols, four clips of ammo, a big wad of cash and three pairs of underwear, because you never know how long you're gonna be on the run.

I had the backpack over my shoulders and I was halfway out the fire escape on the fourth floor before Kang knew the call was over. Seriously.

Soon as I grabbed my things I made the change happen and went monstrous. I change like that, I don't look the same. I probably already said that. I've seen pictures and looked in the mirror a million times. My hair goes long and I develop a serious case of fur, all white. My teeth grow longer and rounder, my ears get pointy. I look kind of like a cat when it's done, but a damn big cat. Say goodbye to Johnny Lei, short but handsome Asian stud, and say hello to the Albino Were-Cat of Chinatown.

Certain things change along with my appearance. I get stronger and faster and my senses get clearer. I never really thought about that stuff when I watched werewolf movies but it makes sense I guess. I get the benefits of the different body type. My hearing grew sharp enough to let me hear the men coming up the stairs inside the building and outside on the fire escape.

The building I lived in is old, and there's only so much you can do to make it look pretty, but it's solid. So my plan was to sneak down the metal stairs of the fire escape and get to the ground while they cops were coming in through the hallway. It's worked in the past, believe me. Louis Lew—LuLu to his friends—guy that lived one flight up from me used to make runs for it all the time and the cops never seemed to catch on.

Here's the thing. Guy that used to live one flight up? He never murdered a US Senator. Turns out the cops think that's more serious than boosting the occasional car for a joy ride like LuLu did.

I slipped out the window with my backpack snugged on nice and tight and two big bruisers in full riot gear were right below me. I could see how surprised they were right through the visors on their helmets. They could probably see how surprised I was by the girly scream I let out when I spotted them. I'd been hearing the cops inside and out, but it didn't really register until I saw them.

It takes about four seconds for your entire world to go straight to shit. Just for the record. First second, I'm caught red-handed slipping from my family's apartment.

Second second, one of the heavily armored and armed SFPD SWAT guys is bellowing for me to stop right where I am and put my fucking hands on my fucking head.

Third second, I'm going over the side of the railing and hoping I can land on my feet this time, because a few times in the past I've managed to break the fall with my face and my ass. Same second, the other cop is drawing his weapon and firing. I have to give mad props here and say he was faster than I would have thought possible. One fluid move and he had me dead to rights but it was too late, I was already going over the side. He fired and I felt the bullet like someone had bumped me in the chest on a crowded street.

Fourth second, I'm twisting around, trying to catch the railing because the impact has sent me off course and I just know I'm gonna kiss the concrete with my face again. I swear that was all I was trying for. But Quick Draw has fired a second and third time and I'm reaching and instead of getting a railing I'm grabbing hold of the one that was screaming. The railing is anchored to the wall of the building with heavy steel bolts and lots of them. The cop is standing free and easy and maybe off balance. I felt a little resistance, just a little, and then we were both falling.

Four stories down. Did I mention that? Four stories down and I managed to land on my feet that time. The impact was hard, I admit it. The muscles in my legs flexed and my knees bent just right and I still felt the jolt all the way to the top of my head. Around the same time my body told me I'd taken three bullets to the chest. Say this for the sonovabitch with the gun: he was a damned good shot.

Lucky me, I'm tougher than I look and with my monster-face going I'm already a scary looking bastard. I stood up and staggered and caught myself before I could fall flat.

The cop I pulled down with me wasn't as lucky. He did a face plant on the ground. I saw it. Four stories is a long drop and while you can take that sort of fall and live through it, a lot of damage can happen.

I heard his neck break even through the sound of his faceplate shattering. He crumpled over himself, a horribly awkward somersault gone wrong, and his body rolled backward with way too much fluid motion. I heard the vertebrae in his back breaking along with his ribs.

God damn it. The worst part? He lived through it. Officer Martin Collins, fourteen-year veteran of the SFPD got his back broken beyond any possible human repair and he lived through it.

I saw his partner stomping down the stairs, heard him screaming, saw the gun in his hand aiming my way again and I ran. There were no clear thoughts in my mind right then, just white noise and fear and that one question going through my head again and again: who the hell told the cops where I was?

"SUICIDE GAMES" PT.1

Jonathan Maberry

−1−

New Hope, Pennsylvania
The First Day of the Second V-War

They lay naked and bleeding on the living room floor.

Sweaty.

Gorged with meat and with passion.

Annabelle's breasts, heavy and full, heaved and trembled as he crouched over her, thrusting into her. First as a man, then as the wolf. Back and forth, the perversion of bestiality adding fuel to their fire. She clawed at him with jagged nails, bit him with wickedly long teeth. Together they screamed their way into their third orgasm.

He threw back his head and howled, his body caught halfway between wolf and man, his hips pumping and pumping with insane frenzy as he came and came.

On the kitchen table were two heads. They stared, glassy eyed, mouths open as if preparing to speak. Necks ragged and torn. Looking down with sightless eyes at the rutting pair.

At the two things that growled and rutted and came over and over again.

With each grunt of his body against hers, Annabelle spoke a single word.

"Rancid."

It was not a statement, not a self-aware description of their coupling.

It was a name.

His name.

Rancid.

Across the flat plates of his pectorals and running in a line from his heart down to his cock were tattoos. Crosses. Swastikas.

Sometimes separate. Sometimes overlapping.

Dozens of them.

Six times six of them.

And across his back in burning red ink were the numbers 666.

On each buttock was tattooed one half of the front cover of the *King James Bible*. Put there permanently so that every time he squatted to shit it was through the Word of God.

Rancid.

"Rancid," she gasped.

"Rancid," she cried.

As he came, the seed he ejaculated inside her was hot.

So hot.

Hellfire hot.

Annabelle believed with every fiber of her being that he was exactly what he claimed to be.

The Beast of the Apocalypse.

Come at last to fulfill prophecy.

Come to bring about the End of Days.

Come to Bethlehem to be born.

Coming inside her.

Fulfilling prophecy as he filled her with his seed.

Annabelle screamed and screamed and screamed… and smiled all the while.

"WAR TORN" PT. 2

James A. Moore

— 3 —

So here's the thing. There comes a point where, no matter what you do, you're going to come out of things on the wrong side. What do I mean? I mean it was one thing for me to be a suspect in the murder of a senator and a bishop. It was a whole different story for me to have eyewitnesses saying that I threw a cop down from a four-story landing and then fled the scene.

I told you my side of the story. According to Joe McPherson, the three-year cop who shot me three times, things went down a bit differently. He said I opened the window, caught the two cops by surprise and threw his partner from the landing. One time he said I laughed as I ran past him, the other times he just sort of glossed over that part when they asked him. Either way, he made me out to be the heavy and they listened. To be fair, I'm sure plenty of people would have loved to interview me and hear my side, but I was too busy trying to stay out of jail.

In the absence of my side of the story, the media found plenty of people to talk for me. Neighbors, kids I went to school with, and complete strangers who swore they knew me back when, were all over the place. Just like that, I became the flavor of the week.

What's the flavor of the week? If you run a diner, that's whatever your special is that the chef made four hundred servings of. If you're Baskin Robbins, it's the ice cream you're pushing. If you're the news, it's whatever story is getting the best ratings. It might be another Kardashian getting knocked up or slapped around by her ex-husband. It might be a politician sending dirty selfies of himself to his assistant.

It might be the evil vampire overlord who broke a cop's back and laughed while he was escaping. Believe me, it was a good week to be a bad vampire, at least if you wanted the press all over you.

I just wanted it all to go away. Instead the rumors started. There were plenty of those. Like I said, people I knew and people I didn't know were suddenly privy to my secret plans for world domination. It was crazy in the worst possible way. I've heard the term "media frenzy," but I had no idea. Seriously. Chum in shark-infested waters doesn't make that sort of splash. No one got into my family's apartment, not that I heard of, but there were all sorts of stories that sprouted. I mean, okay, the cops got in there. Of course they did. They'd been on their way to question me, after all. Hell, my folks probably opened the door and never suspected a thing. But by the time they got the door open I was already down on the street and running.

I made it to Rio's place. One look at the news and as tight as we are, he had to send me on my way, but he had some rainy day money set aside and he knew it was about to rain all over my ass, so he handed it over without question. He took exactly long enough to make sure I wasn't bleeding to death and slap a few pieces of cotton gauze over my wounds. I was going to live long enough to walk out the door at least. Rio's one of the good guys. Tommy was next on my list. He let me stay at his place for the night and we listened to the news about Martin Collins and watched the interviews start.

The police chief was pissed. I don't blame him. He was trying to be calm and professional, but it didn't take any special senses to see that he was angry and stressing. Somebody had just ruined one of his people. Really ruined, I mean.

Tommy very carefully pulled off the bandages Rio had put in place and then got his tweezers and some rubbing alcohol. Thing about bullet wounds is they have to be reported to the police. Thing about police was that just then they were looking to own my ass, so going to a real clinic wasn't going to happen. Tommy watched a lot of reality TV. He would have to do.

"What are you gonna do, Johnny?" Tommy's voice was as stressed as mine. We both knew this was the sort of thing you don't hide from. His hands were steady while he worked the first bullet from the wound.

I guess it was my healing factor at work. The wound had almost closeded itself, so getting the lead out took a bit of extra work. I tried not to cry when I answered.

I shook my head. " I don't know. I need to find out what happened."

"What do you mean?" Tommy looked at the first bullet and dropped into a tea cup. It didn't look all that big. I was trying not to scream my head off from the pain but it was just a little thing, really.

"I mean someone had to point the cops at me. Somebody's got an agenda. I need to know who I pissed off." I let out a little yelp as he started on the second wound. I resisted the serious temptation of slap the shit of out him. Those tweezers were not gentle.

"Anna?" He let out a satisfied grunt as the second bullet popped from the wound. I let out a sound too, but it was not at all satisfied. Some might even call it a little girly.

"No way. She wants me, she won't involve Mom and Dad."

"This one's gonna hurt." Tommy looked at me and pulled out a small blade. Normally he used that one for whittling on little wooden toys he made when he was really bored or really stoned. He sold the things for a few bucks at one of the shops down the street.

The knife was very sharp and cut into my flesh nice and easy. The wound was small and hurt a lot. I can pretty much guarantee I cried a bit. When the bullet came out, Tommy wrapped my chest up a second time, apologizing for the pain.

Tommy and me watched the news on his couch, and while we watched I grew more and more certain that my life was over. When the phone rang Tommy answered it. Tommy looked my way and handed the phone over.

"Hello?" Butterflies doesn't cover it. I knew who was calling, but still, I was a nervous mess.

Kang spoke as soft as ever. "What happened?"

"It was an accident. I got shot and the cop went over with me. I landed better."

"You know I like you, Johnny. You're one of us. But this? Its too much. You're in shit I can't help with and shit I can't be a part of. You need to leave town for a while and we can see if things calm down, but I need you gone."

Kang let me go just that fast. Loyalty be damned. I can't blame him. When I gave the phone back to Tommy, Kang had a chat with him that I wasn't supposed to hear but did anyway. It came down to the same thing. Kang told Tommy to cut me loose before I became a liability.

Tommy and Rio have been my buddies for as long as I can remember. We went to elementary school together. Hell, Tommy taught me most of what I know about fighting, and believe me, he taught me a lot.

When he got off the phone he shook his head. "You can stay the night, bro, but I gotta let you go after that."

He said it like he expected me to be pissed, but I knew the score. Part of the deal with being in the Triad is loyalty. That goes both ways. Kang had been good to me, but the heat was too much and that meant if I was associating with them they were going to get burned badly. It isn't just about me. It can't be, not when you're dealing with the sort of business the Triads handle. If I had stayed a possible suspect they'd have kept me for as long as needed. Instead I became the guy that almost killed a cop. No denying how bad the manhunt was going to get.

And then there was the media.

Listen, the Vampire War had started at that point. Not just a skirmish like what happened when me and Anna were causing problems, but the bigger deal—the one that started with a hundred or so bombs getting set off all over the place. There were a dozen different groups already claiming they were on the side of the good guys in this thing and then doing everything they could to prove otherwise. I'm not saying there were stories every day. There were rehashes of stories, but that's different. But there were enough. In London, a man went on a killing spree when he was caught feeding on a little girl. The people who tried to stop him…well, it was a bloodbath. Eventually the cops managed to take him down in White Chapel. Can you guess what they were calling the guy who ripped out the throats of a dozen men and women while he was running through the area? If you guessed Jack the Ripper, you ain't wrong. He was news for a week and then he was a reminder of everything that is wrong with vampires.

A woman in Des Moines thought her baby was a vampire so she set the infant on fire. Infant. Too young to do anything but cry and poop, but that didn't stop her. There was a case in Queens where one poor bastard got beheaded because his neighbors claimed he was a vampire. According to the press he probably was, but who the hell can say with any certainty? He looked human enough. Not all of them are like me. Not all of them can hide what they are. I don't even know what will happen when I die. Will I revert to my old self, like happens in the old movies? Or will I go full monster-face? I guess if I'm dead it won't matter much.

But enough of the morbid stuff. I'll save that for the next time I'm having a pity party. Let's get to the parts you want to hear. Like when they blew up my home.

Fox News, CNN, ABC, GSN…They all have their own agendas, which ultimately come down to ratings. My family pretty much always watched GSN and I was okay with that, especially because Yuki Nitobe always came across as a straight shooter with me. No one was more surprised than me when they jumped on the anti-vampire band-wagon. Maybe they were just following the leads, same as everyone else, but it sure felt like a knife in my back while I was recovering from three slugs in the chest.

They hurt and a lot, but because I'm not quite like everyone else these days I could help my body get over that stuff. All it took was a little life force. I'm a vampire. I already told you that. But I don't drink blood. Philosophically you could say I drain the soul, or the *chi*, or the life essence. I suppose scientifically you could say that I'm pulling the energy from someone else's bio-electrical field and making it mine. Point is, I can take from others to feed myself. I try very hard not to take too much. I'm also a practicing vegetarian. That last part is sort of a personal in-joke. I can take what I need from any life form. It doesn't have to be human. I prefer to take it from trees and lawns. Sometimes it kills the lawns, sometimes it doesn't. Either way, I feel better about doing that than I do about feeding on animals and people. I've fed on both when I had to and much as I hate to admit it, I loved it. I loved it too much, like a junkie loves heroin. The difference is, I can't just say no. I need to feed or I die. So I try to stay away from the pure stuff.

At any rate, before I made it to Rio's place after the cops tried to get me I fed on a tree and when that wasn't quite doing the job, I managed to catch a cat unawares. The cat let out a yowl like you wouldn't believe and I might have let out a noise or two myself when that rush of life force hit me.

I healed a bit. The cat died. There I said it. I killed someone's cat. I didn't like it. I had to do it.

When I got to Rio's place I was mended enough that I could have gone on indefinitely. I would have ignored the slugs still in me, but Tommy insisted on getting them out. He didn't have to cut too deep. I think they were trying to push themselves out of my body. I'm not really a hundred percent sure on how all of the healing factor stuff works. I just know I was mending and fast.

Anyhow, I was at Tommy's place when the news came on and my dream babe was talking about how I'd allegedly tried to kill the cop and the other cop had shot me and they were looking for me in the hospitals in the area.

That led to "experts" telling everyone how there are different types of vampires and how bullets may or may not even hurt me. Listen I'm still trying to figure out how there can be experts in this sort of thing. I figure in this case expert means someone who studied the virus. I doubt there's gonna be an illustrated book out any time soon going over the types of vampires that are out there and what does and does not work against them. Then again, you never know what the hell's gonna show up on the internet and Amazon.com, right? I mean Rio told me there's books about girls having sex with dinosaurs and if anyone would know, it's Rio. If there's porn of it, he's probably seen it.

I'm trying to make light of this, you know? I'm really trying. It's not always so easy. I can pick on Rio all I want, but there's every reason to believe I'll never see him again. I can't. I can't go back home.

I don't have a home to go back to. It's gone.

I stayed at Tommy's place for one night and in the morning he was cool about it and ran down the street and loaded us up with coffee and Egg McMuffins. I ate. I drank. I watched the news.

And on the news there were armies of people in front of my old apartment building. *Armies.* I'm not kidding about that. I could barely see the street because of all the people who were standing out in front of the place and waving signs.

Want to know the part that pisses me off? All those signs were in English and most of them were held by middle-aged soccer moms and a few guys in business suits. Mostly they were white. There weren't many of my neighbors out there holding signs and protesting. They were busy being elsewhere. I couldn't blame them.

Now listen I got nothing against soccer moms. I think they serve a purpose. I'm not really sure what it is, but I'm sure it exists. Me? I wanted to play soccer, I went down the street and I played. But these people? They were holding up signs talking about how I was the Anti-Christ and demanding justice for Officer Martin Collins. I could even understand that. I would maybe have liked a little justice for Johnny Lei, too, but I could see it.

Still, I watched the news and there was my girl, Yuki, standing in front of my apartment building and talking about the horrible things I had done.

My chest felt like someone had parked a car on it. I mean that. I could barely breathe. And Tommy is right there next to me on the couch shaking his head. He went back into his bedroom and did exactly what Rio had done. He came out of his bedroom with a wad of cash and he put it in my hand.

"Get out of here, Johnny." His words were not unkind. "Go on and get the hell out of Chinatown for a while. They're gonna come looking for you and everyone knows we're tight. So you need to run while you can." His voice was all business, but I knew he hated doing it. I nodded my head and got up. No hard feelings.

I was almost out the door when the front of my apartment building exploded.

"SUICIDE GAMES" PT. 2

Jonathan Maberry

– 2 –

The Situation Room
The White House
Washington, D.C.
The First Day of the Second V-War

"My question," said Luther Swann, "is what kind of event we're seeing?"

The president leaned his elbows on the table. "Explain."

"Well, sir, we have two events here…possibly three. On one hand we have these terrible attacks across the country. As much as I hate to say it, I think we'll discover—either through evidence or a formal statement by the perpetrators—that members of one or more vampire cells are responsible for these attacks."

There was a rumble of angry comments, but the president raised his hand and the voices fell silent. "That's one event. What are the other two?" he asked.

"The murders in Bradenton, Solana Beach and Ulysses," Swann continued. "These are families of mixed nature—human and vampire. The graffiti we found today suggests a radical religious group. They used blood from the murder victims to write a message: 'God hates you. God will not abide you. We are the soldiers of God.' We've seen that kind of extremism before, however there was the added symbology of the swastika. Jimmy Saint, the lead FBI investigator, says that there was similar graffiti at the previous murder sites, though *not* the swastika. That's new."

The president looked over at the FBI director, who nodded. "The presence of the graffiti was being kept out of the press for now. We were concerned about pushback because of the content of those messages."

"Pushback like this?" suggested the president, gesturing to the scene of fiery destruction on the many screens.

"Yes, Mr. President. We felt it was best to keep it quiet for now."

"It's no longer quiet," said the director of Homeland Security. "This is already on the Internet."

"What?" snapped Swann, the president, and three or four others at the same time.

"One of my people just sent this to me." The Homeland director hit some keys and threw an image onto one of the big screens. It was a photo from inside a small house. The same three sentences that had been on the barn wall. Also written in blood.

He hit another key and the image changed. Same statements on a different wall. The FBI director was hunched over making a quiet but impassioned phone call.

"How long has this been up?" asked Swann. "Who posted it?"

"We're running that down now," said Homeland. "It's popping up all over."

The FBI director looked up from his phone. "My office was just about to call me about this. They flagged it, too. The posts are going up from cyber cafes in different places. Hundreds of posts. My tech team thinks the messages were pre-set with timers because of how many and how fast they're going up."

"Can you take them down?"

"We're trying, but—"

Before the FBI chief could finish one of the screens showing news coverage switched its graphic from a flaming hospital to the wall of the small house in Bradenton. Those words seemed to burn on the screen. Yuki Nitobe, the reporter for Global Satellite News, was already making the connection between the murders and the bombings. Swann knew her well, having met her during the beginning of the outbreak at the hospital where Michael Fayne was brought after his arrest. Where Fayne committed his last series of brutal murders before SWAT cut him down. Where Nitobe had come close to being his last victim. Now she led the press in their crusade to demonize the vampires while conversely exposing the government for their brutality. All in the name of news ratings.

As they watched, she asked the question that was both inevitable and inflammatory.

"Are the attacks on cities across the country being done in retaliation for unprovoked attacks on vampire families?"

"Oh...Christ..." murmured the Homeland director.

"That's what everyone is going to think," said Swann.

"Of course they are," said Nyklos. "It's the natural question to ask."

"But it's the wrong question," insisted Swann.

"What do you mean?" demanded the president.

Swann turned to him. "Sir—the DNA from the bites at the first two crime scenes prove that the killer was not human. He was a werewolf. That was the other thing I wanted to say."

"I'm aware of that. What's your point?"

"We may be seeing the beginning of a three-way fight."

General May said, "Not possible. There have only been a few cases of werewolves."

"That we know of," countered Swann. "Look, I've been saying all along that we've never had an accurate count on how many people have been infected. The I1V1 virus spread everywhere. There is no statistical model that supports the low number of people who had presented as vampires. There should be more. Many more. Not just hundreds more, but possibly tens of thousands more. Some models suggest that as much as five percent of the population should have become vampires, and there are other algorithms that give higher numbers. None of the math works for the low frequency we've seen. I told congress that all our military aggression and harsh legislation has accomplished is to drive the vampires underground. To make them more cautious. To make them hostile, suspicious and paranoid—and with good cause. We misplayed this from the start, Mr. President. After the first wave of the infection, what did we do? We went to war with them. Immediately... and without hesitation. We immediately began labeling the infected as terrorists."

"They *are* terrorists," said Nyklos.

"No. The first attacks were random and arguably the result of psychic trauma brought on by the radical physical and chemical changes triggered by the vampire gene. It was only after we gave them the label of terrorist did they start acting like terrorists." He wheeled on Nyklos. "Spiro, earlier today you tried to tell me that this is my fault, that it was my bringing up the subject of ethnic genocide that the vampires began forming V-cells. I'll take whatever share of the blame is mine, but the overall handling of this by the government sparked my comments, which means all of us here are responsible for lighting this fuse. All of us."

"That'll be enough, Luther," said Bill Gabriel quietly.

"Fuck you, Bill," growled Swann. He stabbed a finger toward the screens. "We started this. *This*. If we handle it wrong from here out, then the war we have is the one we made."

The room was dead silent.

The president sat back in his chair and studied Swann with unblinking brown eyes. The commander-in-chief's face was grim and set, with deep lines etched around his mouth and between his brows.

"You may well be correct, Dr. Swann," he said slowly. "When future historians write about this war, we may be painted as villains, or as co-conspirators in something that could have been handled differently. Perhaps even handled better. That's for the future to decide. My concern—*our* concern—is the present. Right now. No matter who is to blame for initiating the conflict, there is no excuse for this level of atrocity. American cities are burning, doctor. American citizens are dying. The security of our nation and, yes I will say it now and for the record, the future of our *species* is at stake. The vampires have clearly become organized. They have launched a coordinated series of strikes against America and I have to make a decision as to how this nation will respond." He looked at the other men at the table, his eyes moving from one to the other. "They have asked for war. It is regrettable. It is tragic. But we have no choice but to take whatever action is necessary to respond to this threat and to eliminate this as an ongoing danger to our country."

His words hung in the air, burning like cinders that refused to fall.

"Mr. President," begged Swann, "please…"

"That will be enough, Dr. Swann."

The room erupted into noise as each of the gathered men began making calls to their agencies or departments.

Swann began to say something else, but Bill Gabriel laid his hand on his forearm and leaned close. "Listen to me, Luther. You need to learn when to shut up."

"I can't just—"

"You can get yourself thrown out of here and what will that accomplish? You want to do some good? You want to have the chance to influence policy? You want to regain the president's trust so that you'll have the opportunity to be heard when crucial decisions are being made? Then shut up and wait. Now isn't the moment. The president *has* to do exactly what he's doing. The entire country and the rest of the world will be expecting him to punch back. If he doesn't, we may never regain the trust of the people or—and listen to me here—the trust of the enemy. Yes, I said trust. They need to know that we are serious or they will never agree to peace talks down the line. That's how this works. Once the fight is started there has to be hard punches thrown back and forth before there's even the chance of a meaningful peace. I know it sounds crazy, but welcome to global politics. Saber rattling doesn't end wars. Bloodying your saber does."

Swann stared at him in open horror.

His mouth worked but no sound came out.

Bill Gabriel gave him a sad, tired smile. "War has never been about right and wrong, Luther. Never once in the history of the world."

"WAR TORN" PT. 3

James A. Moore

— 4 —

Where were you when the Challenger Shuttle exploded? Where were you when the World Trade Towers went down? There's maybe fifty questions like that around the world that everyone can relate to in one way or another, I guess.

Where were you when your world ended?

I was in Tommy's living room and heading for the front door. Yuki Nitobe was talking and the next second there were screams and Yuki was ducking down as the building behind her, my building, where I'd grown up my entire life, blew apart. Five stories of brick and glass and wooden doors and all of it went to pieces in an instant.

I've seen the film a million times. I've seen it a million more times when I close my eyes and try to remember my mom and my dad.

Listen, San Francisco is used to a few bad disasters. Most of the buildings are designed to withstand good-sized earthquakes and those that aren't have been tested again and again by minor tremors and by earth shakers alike. My dad pointed out to me and Anna the parts of the Bay Bridge that got rebuilt after a quake back in the '80s made a section collapse. He showed us buildings where they'd had to rip away the debris and start from scratch. There were even a couple of spots in my old apartment where you could see how he'd patched the plaster after a quake shook it free. You had to look carefully though, because my old man was always good at fixing things.

I close my eyes, I can see the front of that building rolling out in a wall of fire and smoke. According to the news reports and the forensic specialists, someone used a homemade bomb. Most likely it was just gasoline and a cloth wick. Whatever the case, it did what a hundred years of earthquakes had never managed to do and it blew the shit out of my home. Whoever did it was smart, see, they put their little explosive on top of the gas line for the building, or at least close enough that they caught it.

I see the explosion. I also see the pictures from later that night, when the firemen were still working at putting it out completely, because whatever sort of shut-off valve is supposed to let them shut off a gas line like that was damaged—or maybe deliberately broken, no one is really sure—and they had to call in extra engines from other departments to get it under control.

Here's the thing about those pictures: All the soccer moms were gone. They left when the fire started. I guess they had to go home and pick up their kids. But maybe it was the news people and maybe it was just my neighbors, I can't say. Someone had put up three big stuffed dummies. They were wearing old, ratty clothes and two of them had pictures of my face on them. I think someone must have pulled them from my Facebook page because they were me smiling and I knew the shot well enough. I was at Fisherman's Wharf with Tommy and Rio and a bunch of other people and we were having fun. The only place I ever saw that picture before was on Facebook. It's one of those pictures that, you know, was never really a picture at all, just a digital shot from someone's cell phone. Anyway, two of them had that face. The third one was supposed to be my monster-face I guess. It had white hair and big teeth and red eyes. There were three dummies of me in front of my apartment. Someone built them and put them up in the area even when my place was burning.

They put those up there and either set them on fire or maybe the flames from the apartment did that. I don't know. Either way, they took their time. While the building burned behind them.

I remember looking at that picture the first time and my ears were ringing and I still could barely breathe, and you know what I heard past the ringing in my ears? I heard that seven people were unaccounted for, not including me. I was supposed to be on the run and hiding. But my folks? No one knew if they were at home. The fire was too intense for anyone to investigate, and my folks and five of my neighbors were all missing.

I tried calling my dad's cell phone. No answer. Same with my mom. I even tried calling Anna, but she didn't answer, either.

And they call me the bad guy.

I'm not ashamed to tell you I kind of lost it.

— 5 —

Funny thing about terrorists, arsonists and glory hounds. They like to take credit for things, sometimes even if they didn't do them.

Turns out that can be a mistake. Know how I know? Because I went after three separate groups that claimed they were responsible for the fire bombing of my apartment building. There might have been more, but I stopped at three. I'll get to the reasons.

Like I said, maybe I wasn't really completely myself. I was scared, yeah, but not so much for me. I was scared for my folks and I was seriously pissed off. I was supposed to leave Tommy's apartment immediately, but as soon as the report came on I sat down on his couch and he looked at me for a long time and chewed on his bottom lip and probably thought about whether or not he should speak to me and what he should say.

He was worried and he had reason to be, because about two seconds after I heard about the fire I started stressing. And sometimes, when I get stressed, the monster-face shows up all by itself. I didn't think about it. I didn't think about much of anything except my mom and dad, but I was in full freak mode for a while and pacing around his place and sneering and scowling and making all kinds of noises. And I was thinking about doing someone some damage.

Tommy got smart. Whether or not he was supposed to help me, or anyone else in the Triad was supposed to have my back, he started calling around and trying to get information. He got it.

The first ones to take credit were a gang of douchebags that called themselves the Servants of God. I'd heard of them and we were never going to be friends. See, they were a little gathering but they were growing. They started out as a group that said vampires were brought about by the "sins of man," and maybe they would have been ignored, but then some loser went and killed a bishop. That helped their cause a lot.

Yeah, *that* bishop. That was what started getting them some serious attention and their leaders were the sort that made sure they got exposure at every major incident of vampire-on-human violence. And somewhere along the way I guess they decided it was time to start showing that sometimes people have fangs, too. No one had actually seen them commit any crimes, but there was a lot of buzz that they were behind some of the more public demonstrations against vampires. And burning effigies in front of buildings was exactly their speed.

And some idiot took credit for burning down the building where my family lived. The mistake they made was being just a little too public about it. I didn't have a lot of trouble locating their local San Francisco meeting hall. They were on Facebook and Twitter and had their own website where they were good enough to put down an address.

Thing about San Francisco is I know my way around. It didn't take me long to get there.

They were meeting in the basement of the Eighth Street Congregational Church. All of them sitting on little plastic chairs that I guessed were probably normally reserved for Sunday schoolers and maybe the local meetings of Alcoholics Anonymous. I let myself in.

I was angry and they were celebrating. There were sixteen people in that room and they were cheering themselves on, pleased as all getout by what they'd done. Most of them were teenagers, and they were all dressed in their Sunday best and they were drinking fruit punch and eating sugar cookies and there was one blonde girl with too much make-up and a jelly belly doing all the talking. She was going on about how since they'd announced their part in the situation they'd had over a dozen people calling in about joining the group. She couldn't have been happier about those numbers.

You ever notice how there's always someone that has to rain on everyone's picnic? Well, that was what she accused a guy named Dennis of doing. Dennis was going on about the possibility of retaliation, and warning against letting in any new members without checking into their backgrounds and Jelly Belly was starting to say that he was raining on that old picnic right around the time I came into the room.

Looking back on it, I could almost call it funny. Every last one of them grabbed at the crosses around their necks and a couple of them actually held up their jewelry as if they expected me to back away hissing and spitting like I was Dracula.

Imagine their surprise.

"Which one of you burned down my home?" I tried to be calm, I really did. I didn't kick down the door and I didn't throw a tantrum. I just came into the room with my monster-face in place and asked my question.

The last time I saw a group scatter that fast was when I saw the cops set off their flashers at an underage keg party. That had been in a park. This was in a room with exactly one door and I was standing in it. They were like bumper cars, slamming into each other and knocking the chairs across the dirty tile floor.

Not a one of them tried to answer me. They were all too busy screaming for Jesus or the cops to come save them. I screamed too, and that got their attention. Listen, in addition to the monster-face, I also have a different voice when I'm vamped out. Anna used to say I sounded like a train whistle when I let out a proper screech. I guess there must be some truth to it, because it's definitely loud and every one of those fools acted like a bat hearing a dog whistle and freaked the hell out. The last time I'd done that had been with a bunch of police officers. Their response was to shoot at my ass. These bastards didn't have guns.

I focused on Jelly Belly first, screaming and demanding answers. She wasn't much good to me. Instead of answering she pissed herself and started crying. Next on my list was Dennis, who was a little bit more together and answered my questions with a minimal amount of blubbering.

While I was dealing with him, most of the rest of them escaped into the night. I bet the 911 response boards lit up about three seconds later.

Dennis told me the truth. I'd bet money on it. What he confessed to was putting up the effigies along with several other members of the good, Christian Servants of God. I came very close to clawing his face open, but in the end I stopped myself. Not a one of them got hurt by me.

I managed to get the hell out of there before the police showed up. After that I was on the way to the next group I wanted to chat up.

The second target of my anger turned out to be a single guy. He was fifteen and making all kinds of claims on his computer. I wouldn't have located him, not on a bet, but Tommy helped. His cousin is good with computers and found out where to look.

I left him crying, too. I didn't touch him. I didn't even think about it. But I trashed his computer and I trashed his porn collection. I figured that was enough.

After that I managed to find myself a hotel room. It was cheap, and the sort of place where they don't ask too many questions. On the way

I grabbed a burner phone, because I had to say a couple of goodbyes and I didn't need the cops kicking down the door to my new place when I was doing it.

Okay, maybe goodbyes is the wrong term. Mostly I needed to talk to Rio. He was my best bud, right? I had to clear the air with him and I needed to see if he could do me a few favors.

I called and left a message because he didn't answer.

I took a quick shower and found an unpleasant surprise waiting when I got out. No, not the cops or something worse, just a change in myself I never saw coming. The white fur that I had always hidden before was starting to sprout on my chest and arms and legs and other places, too. I tried forcing it back where it belonged and it didn't go away. I'd always managed to dye my hair and call it done, you know? Hide my monster-face and the fur went way. But for the first time the damned stuff was just there, all over me in uneven patches.

I looked closely in the mirror and really, really studied my face. It was different. My jaw line was broader and my nose looked wrong. Too short and a bit flat. My eyes were too big, like "my, Grandma, what big eyes you have" too big. Doesn't take a rocket scientist, you know? My face was wrong because I wasn't going back to Johnny Lei anymore. At first I thought about freaking out over it, but after a couple of minutes of hyperventilating I decided it was stress. Anna once told me that bushy eyebrows are a sign of stress. I figure if that's true then maybe monster-face is a sign, too. Not enough research done on the subject, so I chose to believe it.

I shaved my face extra close and then I waited for Rio to call.

While I waited I watched the news and learned more about my enemies.

Third time lucky, right? My last target was the one where everything changed, partially because I found the people I was looking for and a little because I bit off more than I could chew. Like a minnow trying to steal a shark's dinner.

So I told you about the holy rollers and I told you about the geek. I didn't say much because they aren't really all that significant to the story, but they had their parts to play, right?

Here's the thing. They were small. Okay, the bible-thumpers were stupid, the sort of stupid that could have gotten them killed, but they were more talk than action.

And then there's the Divine Right. Sounds like they should be a bunch of holier-than-thous, too, and I guess they were, but not in the traditional sense. White Supremacists. They thought they had the right to rule over all other races because they were white and so was Jesus (Yeah, I know, Jewish. I'm not a member, that's just apparently part of their beliefs.). Some people with that sort of attitude keep it to themselves and the world is a better place. Others, like the Divine Right, believe they have to prove what they claim. If they'd been like the nutcases in the church basement things would have gone differently. These guys? They were more like the Klan, but on crack cocaine with a side of steroids. Most of the members had criminal records longer than my arm. Know how I worked for the Triad? Yeah, I didn't have a record. I'm not that stupid. These guys? It was like a badge of honor to get busted for kicking the crap out of some Mexican near the bus stop or for raping a girl who dated outside her race. Those kind of guys.

I didn't know much about them when I went for their headquarters. I just knew they were another batch of assholes claiming to have burned down my apartment building. I wasn't all there, okay? I was worried about my folks and stressed about what I was going to do with myself and I wanted to vent a little steam and so I picked the wrong fight.

Hindsight is always clearer. Isn't that what they say?

When I started this I was telling you about the guys who were looking to kill me. I guess it's time I finished that tale.

The Divine Right made claims on video. That's what makes them different. It wasn't just a bunch of losers posting on the Internet with nothing to back their claims. These assholes actually showed a piece of footage from inside the apartment building. I don't know for sure that it was taken right before the fire. I just know they'd been there. And they had footage taken on someone's phone of the fire when it was just starting.

There's this shot of Yuki Nitobe in front of the building but it's from the other side of where she was when she was making her news report. Instead of her calm face, I saw the same explosion while looking at the back of her outfit. I could hear the same startled scream come from her when the whole thing went boom. One camera in a crowd of people protesting my existence. Maybe the cops will figure it out someday and maybe they won't. Not that it would matter at this point.

Funny the things you remember. I can barely recall the sound of the explosion on the TV, but I can still hear Yuki screaming.

It was enough for me. I watched that footage from a motel room and I felt my blood pressure jump. Rio called me back around the same time.

"Johnny? Hey, bro. I'm not supposed to talk to you, you know that, right?"

"It's why I got the burner, man. Don't worry. I won't call from this phone again."

"Dude, no one can find your folks..."

"Yeah, I get it. I know." What else could I say? My tongue felt too thick in my mouth and my jaw hurt. I looked at the mirror on the wall and saw that my face was too long. My monster wanted out.

"Rio. I need you to look something up for me, okay? On your computer. Or maybe you could ask around if you can't find it?"

"Anything, man. What's up?"

I told him about the Divine Right. He said a few words that his mom would have washed his mouth out for. Even now. He's old enough for college and she'd have been brushing his teeth with Tide. Seriously.

He told me he'd call me back. While I waited I checked my clothes and my weapons. I didn't have that much to check, really. Everything I had got burned right? But I checked it anyway.

Rio called back and he gave me an address, but he didn't sound happy about it and he tried to warn me away. I thanked him and hung up. I pulled the battery from the burner and trashed it, just in case. If the Feds were watching Rio they might start tracing calls. He didn't need any part of how badly I was planning to wreck the bastards that burned my apartment down.

Like I said, hindsight is clearer.

— 6 —

That fog was a thing of beauty. It let me get close to my prey without being seen by anyone at all.

I let my monster-face shine through and hid my white furred self in the white swirling mists.

And then I circled the garage where those bastards worked a few times. Don't get any ideas about the garage being a real one, by the way. There was a sign that said Lowell's Auto Parts and Garage, but the building obviously hadn't been used to repair cars or sell parts in a long time. The brick face of the thing was covered in slogans ranging from crosses and swastikas to American flags and racial slurs. The sort of place I personally have always found way creepier than abandoned houses. Old empty houses are old and empty. Places like that garage are filled with hatred. Empty doesn't get you killed.

I smelled them and I smelled their beers and their pot. And every step I took around that building just increased my anger.

By the time I attacked, I was ready to break some bones.

What I was not ready for were the cameras and the guns.

And I wasn't ready for how the lights inside went dark just before I reached the door.

I maybe should have paid better attention to the local news. If I had, I would have seen Jelly Belly and her friends going on about how I'd almost killed them. If I had I would have seen the reports from the computer geek where he claimed that I broke into his place and threatened to kill him if he told anyone. Being a brave geek he risked my wrath. Okay, maybe I would have gone after his narrow butt, too, but I was a bit busy.

Those reports that I ignored were treated a bit differently by the press. They had a party showing the few pictures they could of me and claiming that I was on a rampage. They interviewed Yuki Nitobe on her own channel because she had been at my place when it went up. She didn't call me any names but she didn't do me any favors, either. Instead she pointed to several cases of vampire on human hate crimes and predicted I would maybe be on the look out for the people who burned down my home.

So it seemed the guys who were really responsible were waiting for me when I came in to get them. I'm guessing they saw me coming or had motion sensors set up. Whatever the case they went dark as I approached.

And then the lights came on. Not a lot of them, just a few flashlights burning outside the building. Enough to let me know where a couple of the bad guys were.

There were four of them outside. The fog was a lovely thing. I took them down one after the other, and no one knew where I was or what to do about it. The first one never even heard me coming before I hit him the back of his head and dropped him like a sack of rocks. I think that fourth one was just catching on when I knocked him cold.

Then I went for the door and I knocked just as hard as I could, hard enough to send the metal door sailing into the garage and the darkness that swallowed the place.

You know what the big problem with fog is? It hides things other than just sights. It muffles sounds and it maybe even masks a few scents. I thought there might be six or seven guys there. And while I'm not too cocky, I was angry enough I figured I could take them.

It was eighteen and they were armed and waiting. Thanks to Yuki, they were waiting for a monster to attack.

They got one, too.

And when they saw me and what I'd done to their door, they opened fire.

Let me tell you something and believe me, I can't make this clear enough. I am not bulletproof. That was the bad news. The good news? Neither were they.

I came into the room in full monster-face and I roared when I came in. "Who burned down my house?"

I kind of expected a few screams and maybe a little pants-wetting. To be fair that was what I'd gotten earlier.

I got screams. I also got more of the language that would have Rio's mom scrubbing tongues. And then I got the bullets.

First dude that unloaded on me was carrying a shotgun. He aimed and fired and I felt the buck shot pepper my stomach and thighs. And I let out a scream that had half of them staggering and the others aiming and firing.

The scream was not intentional. Mostly it was fear and pain. I did not dive bravely into combat right then and there. I tried to run. The bullets stopped me. Something hit me in the left thigh and I swear I was looking down and I saw the meat and the bone that blew out of my leg and all over the floor.

I hit the ground a second later, and the pain was too big for me to explain it to you. I mean that. Still, I have to try. I told you about the reason I'm called a Hopping Ghost. The rigor mortis-like tendon problems. I've dealt with those and they hurt more than anything I experienced before them. But I could overcome that. With stretches and patience I could get around and I could walk.

Yeah. That shit doesn't work when you have bone sticking out of your leg. I hit the ground and I whimpered and I forgot all about the pistols I was carrying. I forgot all about who might have burned down my house and whether or not my folks were alive. All I could focus on was the pain.

And you know what? The Divine Right has earned the term *hate group*. I was down and out and they kept firing. Bullet after bullet and shell after shell hit me until I was pretty sure I was already dead.

If I'd still been human in the strictest sense I would have been. Doesn't matter that they didn't shoot me in the head, because basically most of my organs were confetti.

When they stopped the air stank of burnt cordite and blood. My blood.

Vampire, remember? Vampire, but not a bloodsucker. One other time I got torn up so badly I couldn't hope to recover. You know what happened then? Instinct took over. Not human instinct, but vampire. And it happened again, only this time I let it.

I've tried to fight against that part of me. I've fed myself on trees and plants and occasionally on animals and I've done everything I can to avoid ever hurting people. Okay, I mean really hurting them, not just a little slapping around when they forget to pay the bosses.

And this time I let it happen. I fed on them, every last man in that room because I was hurt and I was angry and they were killing me. It's just that simple. It was them or it was me and I wanted to live.

The rush was incredible. I took from them, I drank them in and much as I wish I could say it horrified me right then I didn't care if they were dying. I ripped what I needed from their bodies and pulled it into myself. And watched them fall. They staggered and moaned and dropped their weapons, a few of them actually vomited even as they let out their wails of pain or sorrow. I heard them scream. There were howls of agony and gasps, and those gut-wrenching wails I mentioned. I never knew anyone could sound that miserable. I watched them *burst*. They vomited blood from their mouths and their eyes, they secreted the stuff from their skin, even as their flesh withered and shrank on their bones. Their hair wilted and turned as white as mine. I was aware of all of that, but none of it mattered. Instead all I really noticed was that I was healing.

The bone in my thigh put itself right. I felt the muscles twist and pull themselves back together same as the bones did. Flesh mended.

Nerve endings screamed and danced and I did the same. I don't think it could have been pretty.

But, my God, it felt so good to be alive.

I got to my feet despite the shaking muscles and electrified nerves and I screamed again, that same loud shriek I can make when I'm all out vampire and Johnny Lei is hiding inside.

And even over the screams I heard the sirens outside.

I don't know all the details. I may never know them, but I can make a few assumptions. First, I would bet whatever money I make in my life that the Divine Right did not want to die that night. There are fanatics out there who will sacrifice themselves, but none of those freaks were the type. They were the kind who use religion as an excuse to do what they want, when they want. Truly devout nutcases might have been armed, but the drugs, booze and porn in that room wouldn't have fit with the proper fanatics' life style.

Second, I don't care if they were on the line with the cops, there was no way the police showed up that fast. Because from the time I got there to the time I killed the Divine Right couldn't have been more than a minute, maybe a minute and a half.

San Francisco PD just ain't that fast. I was set up. They were set up. I don't know by whom, I don't know how, but I know it. The police were outside and they weren't alone. I guess maybe they did what Rio did and found the information and got ready for my attack. That's possible…I like that idea better than the thought that maybe Rio called the cops to help them arrest me. Anything is possible, right? I mean, come on, vampires are real.

I didn't open the door to surrender. I planned on busting through the police line and getting out of there. Going to jail wasn't on my schedule—and in hindsight I don't think it would have been jail I got hauled off to, but maybe one of the places I hear they've set up for "studying" the vampires they capture—and trying to explain the dead guys was not happening, either. The last time I fed on a person I was overwhelmed by how good it felt. I said then that I could understand how people could get hooked on drugs and I guess that's still true. But right then, after I fed on those guys? I was too high to care. I was buzzing and I felt invincible.

Still, I'm not bulletproof. Even when I think I should be.

I came out the door in a rush, and I took in the shapes in the fog. There were a lot of them, but I could only just make them out through the strobing police lights and the headlights from the squad cars.

The car that was closest to me was dead ahead and I could see two shapes partially shielded by the open front doors. You know, I always thought that was a Hollywood thing and that cops would never shield themselves that way, but there they were and there I was.

And I looked at the flashing lights on top of that car and used them as my target. I ran as hard as I could, as fast as I could and that's very, very fast.

And the cops opened fire. The first step I cleared was a big one and I think I made it halfway to that car before the bullets started. Those skinheads were rough. These were worse. The top of my left foot exploded. Seriously. I barely even felt it, but I saw it. And I went blind in one eye for a few seconds. I think I got a bullet through that eye, but I can't guarantee it. The pain was very big and very brief. All of the damage was brief, too. Because I was feeding.

I didn't even think that time. I didn't try to stop it. Maybe I was still too high on the good feelings and maybe I just didn't care right then. The bullets hit me and they tore me apart. And I fed as I ran, drawing life force from the very people who were shooting at me.

I cleared the first car in four strides and I jumped as hard as I could. I think I covered close to thirty feet with that jump. I guess there's more than one reason they call me a hopping ghost.

There's not much I can tell you that hasn't already been on the news. Three cops and one federal agent died. Seven more were hospitalized for whatever I did to them and eventually they recovered, but according to the reports they never quite made full recoveries. All but two of them were forced to retire because of the trauma to their nervous systems.

Do I hate that it happened? Yeah. Matter of fact, I do. But it was them or me and like I said, I wanted to live.

The attack on the cops? No one can really prove much about that. The fog was too thick. They fired at me and I ran and if anyone took footage I guess it was too distorted. The only clean shot I've seen from outside that building showed up as little more than a blurry image—I recognized the tennis shoes I was wearing, but beyond that there's nothing.

But inside the garage where the Divine Right met their ends? That's a different story. They had cameras running. I guess they wanted to get footage of me attacking them. Maybe they even wanted to get footage of them killing me. They were the sort that would have found a way to post it.

There's footage of my monster-faced self getting shot again and again. I don't think it was supposed to be seen by anyone, but the vampire groups managed to leak it. I think they wanted to show vampires as victims because the first leak was only me getting shot. Later the rest of the footage aired, too. The part when the Divine Right got wrecked by me. Murdered by me.

I've watched the footage so many times that it's almost painted on my eyelids.

Mostly I've watched it from a dozen different hotel rooms. And now and then I check out my Facebook page. I do it under a different name, of course. Lots of messages on there, groups condemning me for being a vile cop-killer and others praising me as a liberating force. They're both insane, both sides. I'm just trying to survive.

And I've gotten a few emails I can't respond to. I've looked at them, but I can't answer them. I'm afraid if I do the feds will know. There are people trying to get me to join them, to help them fight this war. Madness.

I travel mostly at night and sleep mostly in the daytime. I have to, because something has gone wrong with me. My monster-face is changing, becoming more cat-like. I used to think I looked a little like a house cat. These days it's more like a lion. If I shave my face as close as I can, I can still pass for human for a little while, but it doesn't last long. The fur grows back pretty fast.

It was foggy that night. But not inside the garage where I killed over a dozen men. Everyone got a good look at my face on those cameras.

I guess it's a good thing my face is changing. Maybe it means if they catch me they can't prove anything.

Just like I can't prove anything. I can't prove that someone told the police where they could find me. I can't guarantee that my folks are dead. I can't say without a doubt that the Divine Right hideout was a set up, or that the cops and feds were warned in advance that I was going to be there.

There is no proof. There's just my guts telling me that I got set up and that it isn't over yet. I think there's someone out there trying to make me suffer, or maybe just trying to make me out to be the bad guy in all of this.

I'm out of San Francisco and I don't think I'll be going back. I headed north first and now I'm heading east. I'm not really sure where I'm going just yet. I just know I can't go home. Even if they hadn't burned my home down, there'd be no way I could go back. Like Kang said, I'm too hot.

Like I said, I'm the monster of this story.

"SUICIDE GAMES" PT. 3

Jonathan Maberry

— 3 —

New Hope, Pennsylvania
The First Day of the Second V-War

They were wrapped up in a thick blanket in front of the fireplace when the phone rang. Annabelle raised her head and glared at the screen display.

"It's him."

Rancid didn't open his eyes. "Fuck him."

The call went to voicemail. Then a second later it started ringing again.

"Persistent fuck," he said.

"He'll just keep calling," she warned.

"So? Turn off the ringer."

"I can't. *We* can't." She hit the button. "Yes?"

She listened for a few seconds then lowered the phone and ended the call.

Rancid opened one eye. "What?"

"It was him. He said to turn on the TV."

He crawled a hand out and found the remote, aimed it at the TV, turned it on.

"What channel?"

But the question was moot. It was on every channel.

The official count was up to sixty-three bombs in fourteen cities. Coast to coast.

The reporters were at that edge of hysteria where they shouted nearly meaningless comments at the camera as hell opened up behind them.

They watched, rapt, for half an hour, switching channels, seeing from a dozen different angles what they had wrought.

When the phone rang again, this time it was Rancid who snatched it up.

Without preamble the caller said, "I didn't ask for this. I asked for something that would wake them up. Something that would get attention."

"Well," said Rancid, "don't you think we *have* their attention?"

There was a long silence on the other end of the line.

Rancid and Annabelle bent to listen. They could hear him breathing. Then…

"What the hell was all that with the swastikas, goddamn it? Who told you to do that?"

"Just something I thought up on the spur of the moment, like."

"Why, for Christ's sake?"

"Pissing in the punchbowl."

"What?"

"Clouding the issue. You said—"

"I know what I said, and I didn't say anything about swastikas."

"Consider it bonus material. The FBI will love it. The press will love it. And they'll never fucking figure it out. And even if they do, it won't be what they think."

"Christ."

"Don't be such a pussy," said Rancid. "This is good stuff. If your people can't use this to get you reelected then you need better people."

"This is not about me getting reelected."

"Oh, come on, senator. We both know exactly what this is about. I just gave you one hundred reasons why you'll always keep your seat."

"Wait—how many?"

"One hundred."

"Jesus H. *Christ.*"

They waited through another long pause, enjoying the sound of agitated breathing. They could almost hear the caller's heartbeat.

Annabelle covered the phone and whispered in Rancid's ear. "I think he's hyperventilating."

"He's probably jerking off."

They sniggered quietly while they waited for him to speak.

"Listen to me," said the senator. "This is over. The money's all been transferred. We're done. I don't think we need to talk again. Ever. You understand me?"

The line went dead before Rancid could answer.

Annabelle snorted. "Another satisfied customer," she said.

They laughed and laughed. And as each new report came in of another explosion, they laughed until they cried. And then they made love again and again as America burned.

"SOLITUDE"

Kevin J. Anderson

−1−

The monsters hit the RV in the middle of the desert—three hairy beasts, howling, drooling, snarling. Their bodies were bloated with an overabundance of muscles and fangs; their skin bristled with shocks of black fur that would have made a porcupine seem cuddly. As they tore at the metal side of the vehicle, their claws made an awful fingers-on-chalkboard screech. The walls of the big RV didn't offer much more protection to the people inside than the perceived weak spot of the spiderweb-cracked windshield.

The overlapping chorus of screams was such a loud racket that I couldn't tell how many victims were inside, but if I had to guess—judging from the make and model of recreational vehicle—it was probably Mom, Dad, a boy, a girl, and maybe even an obnoxious yap-yap dog. I doubt this was the family vacation they had expected to have.

Yeah, another example of the American Dream falling short. Been there.

The recreational vehicle was one of those big palatial monstrosities—the kind retired people call a "camper," but is basically a spa on wheels. It was decked out for state parks and fishing trips, not boulders, washouts, and other typical desert undercarriage-killers. This one looked new, with a good paint job, although smeared with the reddish dust from the canyon lands.

I don't know how the hell they had gotten the RV all the way out here in the deep desert. In this part of southern Utah, a person should know where he's going. The scenery is bleak but spectacular; the sky is wide and clear and blue, as if washed clean, except for crisscrossing vapor trails of jets going to and from the Air Force bases. The "roads" are faint dotted lines on the map, and in actuality they're little more than ruts and suggestions across the landscape. It's not a place for blundering amateurs.

As I rolled up on my ATV, on which I don't feel any obligation to follow roads—dotted lines or otherwise—I could see the lopsided way the vehicle sat on the rutted desert road. A flat tire, probably a broken axle or universal joint, too.

This was by no means an off-road vehicle; it didn't have the suspension or clearance to go on roads like this. What was the idiot thinking, driving all the way out here? The only unpaved road that sort of vehicle was rated for is the gravel parking lot of a Good Sam Campground.

Sometimes you have to wonder what people are thinking. Definitely contenders for the Darwin Awards, if anybody still keeps track of those.

In a national park like Arches or Zion, you expect lowest-common-denominator tourist yahoos who don't know what they're doing, but here in isolated Bureau of Land Management territory, you almost never see anyone else—and that's the way I like it.

I love the desert, and I feel I belong out here. The tough and unforgiving environment makes a person strong and self-sufficient, gives you the time and silence to figure out things—or just to have a little bit of peace. The desert rewards those who understand it and punishes those who don't.

The three monsters—werewolf types, if I had to put a label on them—rocked the RV back and forth, which only increased the terrified screams from inside. I heard a gunshot, and a bullet hole punched through the side door of the vehicle. Then another shot blew out the passenger-side window.

At least somebody inside had the good sense to carry a firearm; unfortunately, the shooter didn't have any skill. Both bullets missed. Bad luck.

With the passenger window shattered, I could hear the screams even louder. The three monsters let out a victorious howl. With the passenger-door window shot out, which was clearly a stupid tactical move from the people inside, the werewolves could get a good grip. They tore the door right off its hinges. The racket was deafening.

If I wanted this much noise in my daily life, I would have stayed in Afghanistan.

After coming back from over there, I couldn't leave my nightmares behind, but I could leave everything else. I threw in the towel, turned my back on civilization, and came out into the isolated Utah desert, where I hoped to find a little solitude. There's a lot of emptiness in these hundreds of square miles of BLM lands. Once every few months, I'll make the long trip into Mexican Hat to load up with supplies, and then I head back out. That's all the contact with people I need or want. I have no TV, no radio—no interest and no cares.

Now it looked like I was going to have to head even deeper into the desert. Why is it so difficult just to be left alone?

My ATV engine is loud enough, especially in the desert silence, but the three werewolves were so intent on their victims they wouldn't have heard a full brass band. I roared up to the stranded vehicle, grabbed my weapons from the back…and combat training kicked in.

The monsters were like a comedy routine as they all tried to pile in through the open door at the same time. The victims were trapped inside like fish in a barrel. I heard the tearing of skin and muscles, the sucking and cracking of limbs being torn from torsos, screams of terror taking on a different note of despair and agony.

The third monster lagged behind his buddies and I killed him as he was trying to climb inside the vehicle to share in the Winnebago banquet. I kicked the carcass aside.

Sensing something wrong, the second werewolf smashed out the whole spiderwebbed mess of the windshield, popping it onto the RV's hood. He sprang out onto the hood after it and glared at me with blazing yellow eyes, curling his black lips back to show off his fangs—which might have impressed a dentist or a taxidermist, but I didn't care. His muzzle was splattered with blood; torn ribbons of flesh and muscle dangled from his mouth. He flexed long, curved claws and coiled his muscles as if he was auditioning for a "don't let this happen to you" steroid-abuse commercial. He let out a roar and sprang at me.

The monster might have been big and ferocious, but I'm not a soft pink family from the suburbs. I'm used to defending myself. I know how to fight and I know how to kill. I've done it often enough. Sometimes in Afghanistan they were faceless enemies; sometimes they wore terrified expressions. Sometimes they pleaded with me in a language I did not understand; sometimes they spat their hatred at me in the same language. Even without understanding the exact words, you get a feel for what they meant. Regardless, all those enemies ended up dead in the end.

Just like the second werewolf did. Adrenaline, training, and instinct can work wonders.

I tossed his carcass next to his companion's then climbed through the gap in the side of the RV where the passenger door had been.

The vehicle's interior was a bloodbath, limbs strewn about like discarded chicken bones on all-you-can-eat wings night back at the mess hall. At a quick glance, I could see enough body parts to make up a little boy and a little girl, lying about like the pieces from a Mr. Potato Head. There was even a mass of bloody fur—yes, indeed, the family yap-yap dog. Do I know how to call it, or what?

I heard a loud crunch and saw the third werewolf bite down on the head of a woman—Mom, I supposed. He crushed the skull as if it were the shell of a hard-boiled egg, then slurped out the brains. I thought zombies were the ones with a fondness for brains, but judging from the bloody mess and the mangled corpses, werewolves were not picky eaters.

He looked up, startled to see me there, with blood and gray matter oozing from his fang-filled mouth. His black fur bristled, his hackles rose; he challenged me as if I might be competition, someone intent on stealing his fresh kill. But I wasn't interested in his meal, and I wasn't his competition in the natural order of things. I *was* a threat, nevertheless.

After all my time out here in the desert, I've come to think of this as my territory, and I don't like anyone intruding on my territory, whether it's unprepared families in large RVs or big hairy monsters.

I killed the third werewolf and was done with it.

I drank in the sudden blessed silence for a few seconds before tiny background noises intruded: blood and gore dripping from where it had spattered on the walls, the hum and low drone of voices and static from a poorly tuned radio station…then the whimpering groan of one of the victims, not quite dead. The father.

I saw that his forearm had been torn off, noticed a detached hand lying on the floor, still gripping a pistol. The weapon hadn't done him much good. Dear ol' Dad was twitching and mangled, half-dead from blood loss and fear.

On the radio, a reporter whose voice had an edge of urgency, spoke with breathy words beyond the usual gravitas of a "trusted news anchor." The reporter was Yuki Nitobe, the golden girl of Global Satellite News, and the reporter most directly connected with the story. Since the outbreak and the first V-War, she'd been all over the media. TV, newspapers, Internet and the radio. It was impossible not to know who she was. Her field reports had started off with a clear bias toward the anti-vampire stance taken by so many hardliners. More recently, though, she'd shifted in tone. She wasn't going rah-rah for the bloodsuckers, but her reports tended to include multiple points of view. A lot of what she talked about was the atrocities on both sides of this fight. From what she said, everyone seemed to be turning this thing into a no-rules gutter fight.

I frowned. Ever since I isolated myself in the desert, I haven't exactly kept up on current events. The world was a cesspool before I left, and it didn't sound as if it had gotten any better. Good riddance.

The dying father looked up at me, his mouth open and trailing blood. His eyes were glazed. As I leaned over him, he obviously didn't know where he was. His face buckled in terror, and he lifted his arm to fend me off—but he didn't have much of an arm left, and the stump wasn't much of a threat. He gurgled and coughed. Dying people aren't much for conversation.

The radio continued to talk about an invasion of vampires, werewolves, strange hybrids from dusty old folklore books, but it was all nonsense to me. I switched off the radio so the pure, beautiful desert silence could return. Why ruin it with talk radio?

The father died as I leaned over him, which was a relief for both of us. I didn't want the responsibility, and he didn't want the pain.

I climbed back out of the blood-soaked RV under the blue Utah sky. No wonder people came out here for vacation. I could just stare at the surrealistic landscape of red rocks for hours. Despite the similarities of rugged terrain, this did not look at all like Afghanistan, nor did it feel like that place.

Upon closer inspection, I saw that the RV did indeed have a broken axle as well as a flat tire. The driver must have been hauling ass, pursued by the hounds of Hell (which wasn't far from the truth, I guess). A driver has to exercise care and caution on rugged roads like this. I suppose they had learned their lesson.

Looking at what was left of the dead family, as well as the carcasses of the three werewolves, I pondered driving all the way to Mexican Hat to report what had happened. I didn't own a sat-phone or CB or any other way to make contact—on purpose. In the end, I decided it was none of my business.

I was pleased to discover that the RV had plenty of supplies: canned and dried food, containers of water, even toiletries. The suburban family had packed up and rushed out to the wilderness to get away from the horrors and complexities of the world. Right idea, lousy execution. Amateur survivalists!

163

But their RV wasn't going anywhere, and somebody may as well make use of their stuff. Why look a gift horse in the mouth? I loaded up my ATV with all their supplies, even unwrapped the dad's dead fingers from the handgun to add it to my own arsenal.

When I had secured the packages, I spun the ATV around and rolled off. I glanced over my shoulder at the wrecked RV, the mangled bodies strewn about. I considered giving them a decent burial or a funeral pyre, or…hell if I know. The Taliban liked to leave dead bodies around as a warning for others to see. Since this was far enough from my camp, I decided to let the desert take care of it. The circle of life and all that…

La, la, la.

Even the engine of the ATV grated on my nerves as I rolled off. This wasn't at all how I'd expected my day to go. It was going to be a long time before I could feel the silence settle inside me again.

– 2 –

On a clear, black night without a moon, the stars shine down like a billion bright eyes—and it's creepy to think about all those things watching you.

Heightened sensitivity, paranoia, PTSD—the military has developed plenty of handy labels, but not many cures. They like to package their cases up in neat categories and write prescriptions for the drug of the month, pat you on the back, assign you a counselor, and applaud themselves for the great job they did.

After Afghanistan, I found my own cure. Solitude works better than any number of pills, no matter what color they are. People, in fact, are the problem—with their noise, hatred, emotions, jealousies, ambitions, vendettas. For me, the best way to for a full body-and-mind cleanse was to turn my back on the world, let the VA seal my file, mark it "Case Closed," and worry about other things.

I know the feel of raw wounds, torn flesh. I've seen IEDs up-close and personal, watched a buddy get blown apart by a rocket-propelled grenade right when he was in the middle of telling a joke, and I never did figure out the punch line.

I even saw the flash of white teeth in a suicide-bomber's last ecstatic smile before he detonated his vest and headed off to his version of Heaven, some assembly required. And I remember those pearly whites flying at me like projectiles along with gobbets of flesh and blood. It wasn't bullets that injured me, but the sharp and jagged teeth of a terrorist.

But the Army decided the injuries still counted, so I earned my Purple Heart.

I didn't just get wounded in Afghanistan; I was *changed* there. That place, that war, changes everybody, one way or another. I don't think I'll ever get back to the way I was, but you gotta do what you gotta do.

I have my place out here in the desert, a shack made of corrugated metal reinforced with wooden walls, set into a natural alcove at the base of a canyon wall. My own private little lair. A long time ago, some uranium prospector or Navajo shepherd had abandoned it, and I fixed it up. I've got my sleeping bag, a cot frame, some clothes, plenty of supplies (thanks to the fortunate encounter with the RV today), a folding chair, and my fire pit. That's all I need.

And solitude.

The dark night smells clean, and the desert has few enough insects to make a bothersome noise. The burning mesquite logs send up tiny sparks like tracer fire, but that crackle is the right kind of sound, and it only adds to the silence. I can spend hours here alone, hands folded, thinking hard and *not* remembering.

After a while, you get attuned to the desert; you can sense things. I perked up, sniffed the air. I heard movement, something furtively pacing in the darkness beyond the ring of firelight. I heard the skitter of pebbles, claws moving on the ground, then a snuffle.

I levered myself out of the folding chair, which creaked. I stood, shoulders squared, hands loose, ready to flex. I inhaled deeply and let all of my senses broaden. I could sense beasts in the shadows out there, like Taliban. They were circling, probing, exploring…but this was *my* territory. They could sense that.

They probably knew what I had done to the three werewolves in the RV. They were assessing me, and I stood facing the darkness without a flicker of fear—not provoking them, but letting them know that it wasn't in their best interest to come closer. I put my hands on my hips, refusing to budge. I stood by my fire and saw muscular, bestial shadows moving out there. I waited, defiant.

Eventually, the beasts went away.

— 3 —

The dawn stillness in the desert is crisp, clear, and with a biting chill. It's like glass, so intense and transparent that it magnifies the surrounding world. And like glass, it can all too easily shatter.

I woke from a deep sleep that might have been classified as a coma. I had eaten well, rested well, and enjoyed the warmth of my sleeping bag and my extra blanket in my alcove. I boiled water for the morning coffee, rummaged in the supplies I had taken from the RV, and found packets of something called "cinnamon dolce latte mix"—what the hell was that? Amateur survivalists, indeed! It was sweet and not at all like anything I would have called "coffee," but I had learned how to adapt.

I moved about my camp, hoping for a quiet day. I thought I might explore the canyons before the day got too hot, or maybe I'd just stay here and watch the world, look at the red rocks, admire the endless kaleidoscope of sunlight and shadow on the formations. I didn't even need to move to get a good show.

Swallows were nesting high up on the slick rock cliff, and I could hear desert mice pattering around in the rock field. Most of all, the *stillness* had its healing effect on me, and I just drank it in. I was feeling calm and settled enough that I even endured a second packet of that powdered cinnamon dolce latte.

I saw the tiny human figure, a backpacker, making his way across the desert, stumbling through the bed of the wash and heading up into the deeper canyon, straight for my camp. He lurched along, clearly exhausted and in a hurry, but the enormous load on his back made him ungainly.

There used to be a certain camaraderie among hikers and backpackers. Out on the trail for long periods, you rarely saw anyone, but when you did cross paths with another hiker, you were expected to say a polite hello, share information about trail conditions, maybe exchange supplies if you needed anything. It was a brief and tolerable interaction.

This man, though, came directly to my camp. I could hear his breathing from a long distance away, hear the stutter-stumble of his footsteps. A shame. The day had started out so quiet, so pristine. This intrusion was as grating as a dentist's drill.

I waited for him, wary but resigned, not knowing what to expect but convinced that I didn't want his company…didn't want what he was selling. I was not interested in a "backcountry buddy."

As he came closer, I could see he was bearded, dust-streaked, gaunt, as if he'd been living on the run and in constant fear for a very long time. I'd seen that look on the faces of some comrades back in Afghanistan, especially the ones who had served three or four tours.

Some say that when you get that haunted, you'll never recover. I disagree. Solitude can even a person out. *Uninterrupted* solitude.

He was bedraggled, sweating, ready to drop as he staggered to my camp. "Thank God!" he said. "I saw your fire last night and I marked where you were, but…I don't travel at night. I found a safe spot, barricaded myself, and just hunkered down to wait. Did you hear the howling?"

I just looked at him, cold and silent, then finally answered, "I heard."

"As soon as the sun came up, and it was safe, I made a beeline here. I hoped you wouldn't leave your camp."

"This isn't just a camp, this is my home," I said. "I'm not going anywhere."

The backpacker looked around, studied my shack, my supplies, my chair. "So…you're safe here? It's secure? They leave you alone?"

"Nothing bothers me out here—until recently." I only have one chair and I sat in it. To make a point.

As if I'd invited him to join me, he unclipped the front straps, groaned, and swung around as he dropped the bulky frame off his shoulders. The backpacker didn't seem to understand subtleties.

"I see you had the same idea," he said. "It's sheer hell out there, and I decided the only way to survive that holocaust was to head out into the middle of nowhere. Be self-sufficient. It's monster against monster back in the real world, a menagerie of vampires—civilized ones and barbarian ones, all at each other's throats…and at *our* throats! We're just fodder to them—some of them at least." He shook his head and, seeing no other chair and receiving no invitation from me, he hunkered down on his pack. "It's all going to spin out of control. Cities are burning. Bombs are going off, and my scorecard isn't clear about who's throwing them. Can't trust anyone, can't trust anyone's word."

"I try to stay away from all that mess," I said.

"Me, too! Hole up out here in the deep desert, someplace where no one will find you, and let all those *things* sort it out back in the cities. Then we can come back when it's settled down."

"I'm not going back," I said. "I'm here for the peace and quiet."

He unzipped one of the front pouches of his pack, pulled out a sealed envelope of jerky. "I've got supplies. We can share. But it's not safe—some of those monsters have come out here, too. You and me, though…safety in numbers, right? The two of us could stick together, join forces. I'll watch your back, you watch mine."

I cut him off. "No thanks."

He looked crestfallen, then grew more desperate. "You're dead meat out here if they come. And I can make myself useful. Honest! Let's just try it for a week or so." He extended a grimy hand, pleading. "By the way, my name is—"

"I don't want to know your name. I don't want to know *you*. I don't want you here." I could feel my blood boiling, my hackles rising. I hate it when someone provokes me to anger. "You don't understand solitude," I said. The words sounded rough, like a growl.

The backpacker was slow to realize what was happening, and only in the last instant did he have fear in his eyes.

— 4 —

I dragged his body far from my camp. No need to have the smell of blood and death near where I live.

It took me half the morning to dig a grave deep enough in the rocky, sandy soil so that I wasn't worried about scavengers. I didn't mark the grave—what would be the point?

After all that, I was jittery and stressed. I had an edge to my mood. I don't like being disturbed; I don't like having my solitude shattered; I don't like all this nonsense. I went back to my camp, stretched out on my cot, closed my eyes, and just *breathed*, listening to the air, feeling the silence.

Far overhead I heard the roar of fighter jets, saw the vapor trails of dark aircraft racing across the sky…chasing after some other war. But it wasn't my war. I've already done that, and I left it behind.

I worked hard to calm myself, opening my hands, flexing fingers, making the claws retract. I felt as if I could just *wring* the silence out of the air, but it eluded me. No matter how long I stay here in the empty desert, it's hard to control the beast inside me, the one that's been there since Afghanistan.

At first I tried to crush it, kill it…but that wasn't going to happen. Now I revel in the wide open emptiness, the beautiful red rocks, the deep canyons with guillotine shadows, the painted terrain and the hardy plants and animals that know how to survive in a world that doesn't make it easy for them.

I like to let the beast out sometimes, but on my own terms, when I can be free to lope for miles, run across the desert and hunt whatever I like, stop and sleep in whatever lair I choose…

In the distance, even now during the daylight, I can hear a bestial howl, a call of some other monster. It sounds…lonely. I hope it doesn't track me down. Kindred beasts or not, I wish they'd just leave me alone.

"LET GOD SORT 'EM OUT" PT.1

Jonathan Maberry

– 1 –

Dover Air Force Base
Dover, Delaware
The Second V-War - Day 13

Their official designation was Vampire Counterinsurgency and Counterterrorism Field Team Victor-Eight.

Everyone called them V-8.

Their colleagues. The vampires. The press.

Themselves.

V-8.

Luther Swann had gone into the field with them sixteen times during the first V-War. Each time he'd seen shocking violence, casual indifference to suffering, incredible heroism, unexpected compassion, brutal callousness. And death.

Always death.

It seemed to cling to the team like an un-washable odor.

None of the original members of V-8 were still with the unit. Of the first line-up Swann had met, two were still alive, the rest were dead. One of the survivors was a paraplegic—the other was a double amputee. Of the fourteen replacement members during Swann's first run with them, only one remained:

Gunnery Sergeant Nestor Wilcox. United States Marine Corps.

Known as Big Dog.

That was his combat call-sign, and, Swann believed, the best possible definition of the man. A big dog. A junkyard dog.

Vicious, mean, unpredictable.

Heroic, reliable, a dependable leader.

All of those things and more.

Swann knew he feared the man. He was pretty sure he hated him.

But he was miles and miles away from understanding him.

These thoughts ran through his head while he waited for the V-8 team to arrive. The pre-dawn sky was dark red, as if the rising sun was poised to set the whole day ablaze.

Swann sat sideways on the front seat of a rental car, door open, his feet on the tarmac, big cup of Starbucks cradled between his palms. The engine was on and the radio was tuned to the national news.

None of it was good.

It was thirteen days since Hell Night. That was the name the press had given June 16. The day ninety-nine bombs had been detonated across the United States. The death toll soared to seven thousand two hundred and nine. Damage was estimated at fourteen billion.

The stock market dropped like a rock and if the president hadn't shut it down, it would have crashed. The Fed had only resumed trading two days ago with careful monitoring to make sure the flight-to-safety crowd didn't cause irreparable harm. Though everyone—even Swann, who was no economist—thought that the damage already done was beyond healing. Ninety-nine bombs on Hell Night had been enough to hammer cracks in the economy, the culture, maybe the American psyche.

Hell Night.

The Ninety-nine.

People used those terms. Like they used 9-11. You never had to ask what those numbers meant. You never had to ask, "Which towers?"

Hell Night.

The Ninety-nine.

Forever part of the shared American lexicon.

There had been no new attacks on families by the werewolf. Whoever or whatever he was. Or *she* was.

Over forty separate groups had stepped forward to take credit for the bombings. Most of them were the most radical—and, Swann thought, marginal—of the vampire groups. None of their claims were credible, as far as he was concerned. Even Jimmy Saint didn't seem to think the real bombers had come forth to put their trademark on it.

It was possible, of course, that the people responsible were already dead.

So many vampires were dead.

So many.

CNN was running a Death Toll clock. Aside from the thousands killed on Hell Night, the current tallies were staggering.

Deaths of vampires: Three thousand two hundred and six.

Deaths of humans (after Hell Night): Two thousand ninety-two. Of those, only one hundred and thirty-seven were military or police. The rest were civilian casualties caught in the crossfire between radical V-cells and SWAT, FBI Hostage-Rescue, ATF, NSA, National Guard, or Special Ops deployed on U.S. soil.

It was the biggest war-related death toll since Vietnam, far outpacing the Afghanistan and Iraq wars combined. Swann wondered if it would surpass the Civil War's total of two hundred and fourteen thousand.

He prayed not.

He feared so.

He waited for the bringers of death to arrive.

"MANIFEST DESTINY" PT.1

Weston Ochse

−1−

Bagram AFB, Afghanistan

Calder Lang was not a happy man. This was Maksimum Kriger's third back-to-back contract. Courtesy of NATO and their unwillingness to take down Vor Wakil themselves, Maksimum Kriger had been paid and was given a ridiculous deadline to not only remove the Haqqani terrorist leader from this existence, but also to destroy his organization's ability to project terror. Corporate intelligence said the stronghold probably held more then thirty Haqqani fighters. Calder knew that meant there was probably double that number, something which would be a real challenge for his burnt out team of ten men.

"You're scaring the men," Fell said.

Lang scoffed. "I doubt the men know how to be scared."

"No, but they're good at pretending for your sake. Seriously, do you know your fangs have descended?"

Lang felt them with his tongue and forced them to retract. The shit was really getting to him. He normally had a significant amount of control over his emotions and bodily functions. A retired Army Ranger Lieutenant Colonel, he'd had his share of stressful situations. These patriotic thrill kills shouldn't be getting to him.

Nevertheless, they were.

Lang forced his breathing to slow. After a moment he asked, "Has Leif checked the equipment?"

"You asked that twice already." Fell smiled, but it wasn't enough.

"Just fucking pretend I want to know a third time and answer the question." Lang regretted it the moment the words escaped, but there was no bringing them back.

Fell backed out of the seat and into the aisle. "Will do, boss," he said flatly. Fell was the only one of them with a tan—a result of a Mexican grandfather. He still had the blue eyes the rest of them shared, but had dark brown hair which was cut into a four-inch wide Mohawk.

Lang leaned back in the seat and closed his eyes. Maybe his wife was right. Maybe he was getting too old to play soldier. *The human mind can only take so much before it breaks*, she liked to say. *Please don't break on us.*

Somalia had been his first deployment. He'd done well until they'd put him in charge of the rescue mission for the Army helicopter pilots, Shugart and Gordon. He'd never been able to save them and even now, images of them being dragged naked through the streets haunted him. The popular war movie, *Black Hawk Down*, was a documentary to his failure. He'd spent the next fifteen years trying to make up for his absolute ineptitude. Each raid, each kill, each capture had put a layer between his heart and the hurt, but they also took him farther from whom he'd once been. No one would have believed he'd once wanted nothing more than to have peace in the world, live a simple life in Nemo, South Dakota, and make a home with his wife so that they could raise his son and two daughters together.

It was a dream. One that he'd almost managed had it not been for The Change.

They landed at Bagram Air Field an hour later. Since The Change all but a handful of soldiers had been pulled out of Afghanistan, so Maksimum Kriger had their own ground crew prepared to refuel their bird for the last leg of the deployment.

During such a significant cultural human event such as The Change, neither congress nor the president wanted American service members in far flung places. This they were able to agree on. Not only were they needed at home to help control the rioting, but with the addition of vampires in the ranks, the command structure was close to shattering. General May himself had put into motion the plan to form a special offensive vampire corps drawing from those men and women who changed. These he could control.

May had approached Lang to lead one of the teams, but Lang had already retired and was determined to carve out a life for his family. In fact, he'd also rebuffed North Sea oil billionaire Brandt Ostergard, who'd wanted him to lead his new enterprise Maksimum Kriger LLC. But Lang was done with fighting. He'd had enough.

Then Inger had contracted ovarian cancer. There were complications. Their bank accounts were sucked dry and because banks were reluctant to give vampires credit, Lang was forced to rethink his notion of living a life of peace.

Thankfully, Brandt's offer had still been on the table. Deploying with Maksimum Kriger—*the Maximum Warrior Program*—proved to be a godsend. That is until the idea of pay-per-view military ops became so popular that he found himself more on the road than at home. It was as if he'd never left the military, albeit this version had 360 degree Go-Cams and constant audio-visual feeds to Maksimum Kriger Network, providing a never-ending audio visual display of blood, gore, and the sort of mayhem that could only be created when Eleven Norse-blooded vampires went berserk through a well-defended terrorist position.

And the public couldn't get enough.

They were *Draugr*, or as one former sports broadcaster turned news announcer referred to them after Maksimum Kriger's first broadcast, *the insane Viking linebackers of the vampire kingdom.* This was because a *Draugr*'s bones were stronger and denser. Their hearts were not in their chests, but rather in their pelvis where they were protected by the hardened pelvic plates. They had extra bone plates in the chest and back to protect organs and their circulatory system had been rerouted to take advantage of this bone density. Because of this, it is almost impossible to kill a *Draugr* unless its head was removed.

The genesis of the berserker warrior in Norse mythology was believed to come from the *Draugr*. In those battles of the old times, a *Draugr* was like a tank, busting through the enemy and unable to die, chewing, clawing, stabbing, hacking, kicking, pummeling and pulping his adversaries. When the three extra adrenal glands began to pump, flooding the system with the adrenaline of four regular humans, the *Draugr* was incapable of inaction, its body forced to move in herking-jerking spurts across the battlefield and into the maw of war.

They filed out of the plane, with Lang bringing up the rear. Everyone wore sidearms, but were not yet wearing their battle kits. Not that they'd use their sidearms in battle. They were for everyone else. No sense getting all amped up just to take down someone stupid enough to fuck with the *Draugr* of Maksimum Kriger, but it did happen. Often enough for them to begin carrying sidearms. And in a place like Bagram, which had very quickly turned into an Afghan version of Tombstone or Dodge City in the 1800s, where gunslingers and the more war-minded congregated in order to ply their trades, it was absolutely necessary.

His men headed for the hanger Maksimum Kriger had rented. Like their Viking ancestors, they were an impressive bunch. All were above six feet tall. Several, like Ivar and Dagner, were almost Lang's size, rising six feet five inches. All except for Fell had blonde hair. Calder's hair was cut in a military buzz cut, but the rest of them wore their blonde hair long.

He kept his gaze straight ahead, but was well aware of the attention they received as other men stopped to stare. Some had seen them before and others hadn't. But one thing was for sure. Every damn one of them had heard of the *Draugrs* of Maksimum Kriger.

He was almost to the hanger when he caught a movement out of the corner of his eye. There, in the shadows of the hanger was a woman hunched over a man, feeding. She must have felt his gaze because she glanced up and snarled. Her pupils were gone, replaced by the whites and there were too many teeth in her mouth.

"Gunnar, to me," he called.

The men stopped and a young man who'd once been a lieutenant in the Minnesota National Guard ran back to him.

"Sir?"

Lang pointed. "Take care of that."

Gunnar turned to stare. When he saw his target, his mouth opened wide and an extra row of teeth descended from his upper jaw and grew from his lower. These weren't the flat molars of an herbivore, nor were they the incisors of a carnivore. These were razor-sharp and peaked like shark's teeth. His neck swelled as adrenaline surged through his body, bloating his vascular system until blood and fluids roared through his system.

The other vampire rose, one hand still holding her meat's collar. It had once been a man, his body armor useless against a creature intent on attacking the soft tissue of his neck. A contractor, wanna-be-badass, on the edge of the world in a Wild West air base who let himself be lured into the space between two buildings.

Lang could now see that the vampire wore the uniform of a mess hall server, which made her Filipina. She'd probably been beautiful and had lured the man between the buildings for the promise of sex. She didn't look like an *Aswang*, but she did look like a *Mandrugo*. Popular myth was that they had wings and could separate the upper half of their bodies from their lower. This was far from the truth but had come to be doctrine in Filipino culture. The truth was they had the ability to blend into whatever background they were near, much like a chameleon. The talons on their hands were sharp enough to rip through body armor, much less skin. They were ravenous and fed whenever they could. Unlike *Draugr* who were largely in control of their vampirism, *Mandrugos* had no power to stop themselves. They were also physically weak, which was why they had to lure their prey into situations where their talons or fangs could exact what they needed.

Two other *Draugr*, Colby and Dagner, ran up and joined them. When they saw the *Mandrugro*, they opened their mouths to begin their change.

Lang put his hands on their shoulders. "No, let Gunnar have this one."

Gunnar was the newest member of the team and had yet to get blooded. This was the perfect opportunity to let him feel his way through his new body. "Gunnar, now!"

Gunnar lowered both of his hands and extended his fingers. He leaned forward and began to run at the *Mandrugo*.

She picked up her meat and threw it at him, then backed into the shadows.

Gunnar batted the body aside with ease. It hit the metal side of the hangar and slid to the ground. Then he followed her into the shadows.

Whatever advantage she thought she had, a *Draugr* could see as good as any vampire in low light. Lang had no problem making her out from where he stood. The skin of her face and arms changed to match the rusted metal side of the building. Had she been naked it would have been much more difficult to see her.

Gunnar reached for her, but she clambered up his chest and over his head, swinging her body around, then latching her teeth into the back of his neck.

He tried to rip her free, but his increased neck size and the hulk of his shoulders wouldn't allow his arms to reach. He fell to a knee for a moment, then righted himself. He stood and slammed backwards into the hanger once, then twice.

She let go the second time and fell to the ground.

They'd dented the side of the hanger, making a body-shaped imprint five inches deep.

He wrapped one hand around her throat as she started to stand. He brought her to eye level and screamed into her face.

Lang shook his head. Gunnar was a noob, letting the adrenaline control him. The adrenaline was a tool to be used, not a drug to lose one's capacity for clear thinking.

She hissed in return and clawed the side of his face, ripping through the skin. Blood gushed.

Then Gunnar tore her apart, ripping her head from her body and wrenching her spine from her flesh. When he turned, blood and gore covered him like a giant Viking Carrie. He held her head in one hand and her spine in the other. The skin of her face changed from its chameleon colors to a sad, dead gray.

Fell appeared beside Lang, took one look and said, "Ooh, messy." Then he added, "Used to be when you deployed you could look forward to a little strange." Fell chuckled to himself and went inside.

Lang lingered a moment and stared at the shredded Filipina vampire. "Used to be bloodsucker was a metaphor, too. Now they're all over the damn place." Lang glanced at Colby and Dagner. "Get him cleaned up and calmed down." Then he followed Fell inside.

− 2 −

Black Hills, South Dakota

Laughing Horse's band had left Pactola Reservoir forty minutes ago and were nearing Nemo for the culmination of OPERATION RED CLOUD. Lakota from Pine Ridge had been dispatched into small bands, much like they'd been when the white men first came to take their land. Each had a target which would allow the people of the poorest and most neglected of America's reservations to shout the loudest to the world. Now more than ever was it important for people to stand up and notice, to stand up and realize that these changed beings, these vampires and changelings would most assuredly take their land, just as the people of the pre-change had once taken the land of the Lakota, the Iroquois, the Cherokee, and all the other peoples who'd lived on this land when Columbus made his terrible discovery.

Not just to take notice, but to take back. *Paha Sapa* belonged to the Lakota and they had the papers to prove it. That is until some smelly white man with bad teeth discovered gold and the sacred mountains were renamed the Black Hills, because of the darkness of the ponderosa pine.

Laughing Horse sat in the passenger seat of an 82-foot RV, while Dancing Dog drove. Seven of his men sat in the back, while another twenty followed in the reconditioned reservation school bus. They carried a mish-mash of weapons, as well as explosives. But their deadliest weapon was their conviction.

They passed through Paradise Valley, heading north on Nemo Road. Never a large town, even at the height of the gold rush, Nemo's population was only about five hundred. Of those five hundred, Laughing Horse only cared for five of them. And as he directed Dancing Dog to pull into a dirt road, they saw a mailbox with the name LANG stenciled on the side. This was the right place. This is where his band was going to make the world stand-up and take notice. This was his brainchild. This would be his calling card to the universe.

$$-\,3\,-$$

Bagram AFB, Afghanistan

"Lang, are you listening?" The Maksimum Kriger intelligence analyst stared bluntly at their Maximum Warrior team leader who appeared not to be listening at all to what he was saying. David Margules was tired of telling people things and them not listening. That was one reason he'd left the CIA. The other was because he couldn't stand working for the vampires in the head office. And now look at him. Here he was working for vampires again. His last girlfriend was right. He had an advanced case of *schadenfreude*. "I asked if you were listening."

"Hold the tone," Fell said, an edge to his voice.

David knew these men could break him in two, but he didn't care. He was hired for his brain and he was damned if he was going to let a pair of genetic mutations get in the way of his mental gymnastics.

"No, it's all right." Lang held up a hand. "You're right. I should have been paying attention. Please, proceed."

David gave Fell a heavy-lidded look, then turned back to the flat screen on the wall. "The compound lies in a mountain valley in the Chora Khwar. It's south of Torkham Gate and west of Peshewar, Pakistan. The area was cleared during the Afghan War, but when NATO and the US pulled out—"

Fell interrupted, "The Germans still hold Mez."

David let Captain Obvious have his moment and continued. "Despite the German's controlling Masr-e-Sharif, no other NATO forces, including the U.S. reside in Afghanistan. Nature abhors a vacuum and every right-wing Muslim nutjob swooped in to proclaim victory. As I was saying, this area had been cleared, but a Taliban commander, former Shadow Governor of Jalalabad, one Vol Wakil has created a compound from which he's sending out hunter-killer VBIED teams to eliminate NGOs. The latest attack occurred when a Fiat 500 was parked beside a tent housing the operations of *Doctors Without Borders*. It detonated killing seventeen people, including three American doctors, seven Australian nurses, and seven children."

Fell sat back and crossed his arms. "That's all very sad and I think Wakil and his crew should all be screwed into the assholes of camels, but why does NATO care? They're out of this."

David gravely hoped this tactical situation briefing wasn't going to become a lecture in the effects of targeted violence on socio-economic constructs. Even if he had the time, he wasn't sure if he could find words small enough for these hulking giants to understand. "Let's just say they are willing to pay to have Wakil removed and it gives us the opportunity to double dip by broadcasting it to all of your blood-thirsty fans."

"How many men does he have?" Lang asked.

"Forty. But they've also brought their families."

Fell turned to Lang. "What's our ROE?" he asked, meaning rules of engagement.

"We're indemnified for accidental and wrongful death, but it has to be within reason. Right now the *Draugr* of Maksimum Kriger are heroes. We go around killing women and children, we'll soon become the same bad examples of vampires people are seeing on the nightly news. We'd also probably be sued."

"So no collateral damage."

"Unless absolutely necessary."

They turned back to David.

"Weapons?" Fell asked.

The word sounded more like a grunt. With all of the words in the English language, why someone would settle for one word questions was beyond him. "Standard weapons inventory. They have everything from AK-47s to 1875 Enfields. Sources say they have several hundred pounds of military grade explosive and a ton of ammonium nitrate."

He went over the layout of the camp and showed where the commander resided, as well as the buildings suspected of housing the explosives.

Half an hour later and a dozen inane questions from the one with a verb for a name and he was gloriously done. They stood and left. Watching them, he couldn't help but wonder what it was like being on the front lines. He'd fought three wars from a desk in a SCIF, briefing commanders and shooters alike, and had always wanted to see what it was like on the other side. What it would be like to actually hold a weapon, stare through the sights at a bad guy and to really pull the trigger. He imagined it for a moment, then turned back to his computer. It was probably about the same as his HALO games, but probably a lot smellier.

Yeah. He was glad to be behind a desk. It was a much more tidy existence.

– 4 –

Nemo, South Dakota

Laughing Horse sat on a stool in the modern kitchen of the Lang Family. Inger Lang sat across from him. She'd been scared at first, especially when they'd rounded up her daughters, each of them now bound and gagged and dumped on the living room floor. But when he'd calmly explained to her that they weren't going to do anything, she'd calmed down. They still had to find her son. He had most of his men doing just that.

"Please call your husband."

"I still don't see what this has to do with us," she said.

White men called her type pretty. With mousy blonde hair and freckles across her face, she wouldn't make the covers of any magazine, but she had a way of moving her facial features that was intriguing. Laughing Horse had seen younger versions at UCLA and they always ended up with the school's superstars, leaving the raving beauties wondering why they'd been ignored.

"Really? Let's just say that you're in possession of stolen property and we're here to reclaim it."

"But we didn't do anything?"

"Yet you still live on stolen land."

"We didn't know." she tried a half-hearted imploring smile.

Laughing Horse returned it. "*Ignorantia legis neminem excusat!* Ignorance excuses no one. Now call your husband."

Her hands shook as she dialed her Facephone app. Times had surely changed. It wasn't but twenty years ago when soldiers would wait days if not weeks to hear from their loved ones. Now with the glories of wifi, they could not only have instantaneous connections, but also face-to-face communications.

The Facephone rang for a full minute before she turned it off. "He was scheduled for another operation. He might be—"

"Try again."

This time she connected.

"Inger, what's wrong?"

"Cal, there's a man who wants to speak with you." She handed the tablet to Laughing Horse.

Laughing Horse delighted in seeing the stony features of Calder Lang narrow, crumble, then resolve back into granite.

"Who are you and what are you doing in my home?"

"Greetings, Lieutenant Colonel Calder Lang. My name is Laughing Horse. I'm from Pine Ridge and am here to take what's mine."

"What do you mean what's yours?"

"Everything. I'm here to take everything. But first we need to cleanse the land. I think your son is around here somewhere. He's changed like you, isn't he? Like father like son."

"If you harm my family I will—"

"What? Jump up and down? Cry? Punch a baby? What? You're seven thousand miles away and there's nothing you can do to stop me."

Calder bit the inside of his lip, but other than that, it was the only indication he'd heard. Finally, "I'm sure we can talk about this."

"Like you talked to the men in the town in North Mali and gave them a chance to surrender? Oh, no. You didn't do that. It would have hurt your ratings. Or what about the cartel leader on the Baja Peninsula?

Did you and your Viking vampires talk to him before you ripped apart thirty-seven of his men, then him and his wife, all in IMAX 3D glory?"

Calder shook his head. "Wait. Is this political? Do you have a problem with Maksimum Kriger business model or do you want to reclaim your land? I'm not getting this."

"The confusion is all yours, Lieutenant Colonel Lang. But then I suppose it would be since you carry the responsibilities of so many injurious deeds."

"You're crazy. Listen, let my family go and I'll give you what you want."

"Good old Elisabeth Kubler-Ross. Now there was a genius. She was able to label the five stages of grief so perfectly. You're now on stage three. Having gone through denial and now anger, you've arrived at bargaining. So tell me, Lieutenant Colonel Lang, what is it you think I value?"

"You can have anything you want as long as you leave my family alone?"

"Including your life?"

"Absolutely."

Laughing Horse couldn't help himself. He laughed. The man's devotion was absolutely stunning if not remarkably predictable.

"What's so funny?" Lang said unable to keep the anger from his voice.

"That you think you're even able to bargain. To play poker, Lieutenant Colonel Calder, you need to have chips. And I have them all."

Lang whispered, "Seriously. Anything you want. Anything. Just let them go."

"Do you know what the next two stages are?"

Lang stared blankly from the screen.

"Depression and finally acceptance. Some people get to acceptance right away and for some it takes a lifetime. Good bye, Lieutenant Colonel Calder. I'll be contacting you shortly. And do your family a favor. Don't tell anyone about this conversation. We see anyone coming for us and we'll burn the bodies along with the house."

Laughing Horse snapped off the tablet and set it on the table.

"What is it you're going to do to us?"

"It's best to keep some surprises for later." Then he leaned over halving the distance between them. "But between you and me, it's going to be a stunner."

– 5 –
Bagram AFB, Afghanistan

"What are we going to do?" Fell asked, suddenly by his side.

Lang's head was reeling. How had this happened? His family was supposed to be safe. How had they even found them in such a back-water town?

Fell grabbed his shoulders. "Calder? What are we going to do?"

Lang shrugged free. "I need to call Ostergard and get on the first flight home."

"Seriously? Its twenty hours of air travel no matter how you meas-ure it unless you get a ride in an SR71." Fell paused for a moment as if he had an idea, but then he shook it away. "And what about the madman's directive not to tell anyone?"

Lang spun around and punched the air. He wanted to hurt some-thing, break something, rip it apart. He felt his lips receding as his fangs began to descend. He fought it hard. He needed to have his wits about him. He got himself under control. "Do we have anyone local we can call?"

"There's a crew of *Draugr* up at St. Olaf's which puts them eight hours by road. We could probably get them on a slick and have them there in three hours."

"Who are they? Are they experienced?"

"All I know is that I was asked to visit. They have a Mead Hall and wanted me to regale them in the behind the scenes. They're big fans."

Lang paced back and forth. "Can we get them there and near site but not have them attack? I'd like to have them on hand."

"Do you have a plan?"

"Not yet. But it's better to have them and not need them than to need them and not have them."

"For all we know it could be just this one madman."

Lang shook his head. "There's been trouble brewing since well before The Change. I think this is bigger."

"So you think he's organized?"

Calder nodded. "Definitely."

Canute came running. "They've moved up the timeline and contacted the subscribers. We leave in an hour."

Fell shot a look at Lang. "Who moved up the timeline?"

"The analyst. He has intel indicating that the Taliban are going to vacate tomorrow morning. We have to do this now."

"I don't like the idea of being rushed," Fell said. "Slow is smooth and smooth is fast. You start out fast and it all get's fucked up."

Three uniformed men approached. One wore German fatigues. The other wore U.S. combat multicams. All the uniforms were sterile, but it was clear that the German was in charge.

"You are from Maksimum Kriger." His English held a Bavarian accent as well as a little worry.

Lang nodded. "We are but we're leaving."

"You can't leave until you help us with a problem."

Fell raised his eyebrows as he mouthed the words *can't leave*.

Lang shook his head. "Negative. We have a mission in sixty mikes. Sorry."

The two Americans glanced at each other as the German forced a smile. "Sad to say, sir, that we're conducting runway maintenance. No planes in or out for the foreseeable future."

"You have got to be kidding me. You're strong-arming us?"

The German clasped his hands in front of him. "I'd prefer to say that if you can help us with our problem, we can most certainly help you with yours."

Lang only took a moment to answer. "Fine. Fell, get the men. And you," he jutted a finger at the German. "Show us your problem."

Fifteen minutes later they were standing in front of the mess hall. All the while, versions of his family were living and dying in rapid-fire clarity in the front cortex of his mind. Each time they rose from the dead and glared at him, hate-filled eyes condemning him. But as the full spread of the German's problem was relayed to him, he had to force thoughts of his family away to attend the situation at hand. After all, he had a second family, and the men of Maksimum Kriger deserved his complete attention.

Third country nationals had been abandoned after NATO and the U.S. pulled out of Afghanistan. Mostly from the Philippines, but also from Indonesia and Bangladesh, these persons had been contracted to clean, feed, and transport soldiers on a daily basis. When everyone pulled out, so did their contracting companies, along with their passports. They weren't allowed to leave the air force base because they had no identity papers. Many of these TCNs had been trapped in this twist of fate and the law for years. And then The Change had happened. What had been a population of unhappy workers passively complaining about their situation became an even more serious problem as many of them became vampires. That so many had become *mandrugo* spoke to an ethnic similarity which could have been the result of familial relationships, especially if a large portion of them came from the same community.

"We let them feed on themselves, I'm afraid." The German shrugged his shoulders. "There was nothing more we could do. We inherited the problem and just wanted it to go away."

One of the Americans jumped in. Crew cut and a deep tan, he looked to be about fifty and a hard-ass from way back. "We convinced them to take the old mess hall as their new digs. It was the best way to keep track of them. We had guards on the doors, but they were overwhelmed two weeks ago and no one is willing to pony up any more men."

"What was your plan?" Lang asked.

"We thought of using explosives, but we just couldn't bring ourselves to do it."

Lang didn't believe that for a moment. They didn't want to use any more of their materials in what was clearly a losing battle. "And you want me and my men to remove your problem."

The German at least had the good sense to smile apologetically. The two Americans, on the other hand, nodded happily.

"And when we do this, the runway will be fixed, right?"

They nodded again.

"How many are in there?" Lang pointed to the door.

"It started as 324 TCNs, but a lot of them were eaten."

"So you really have no idea how many there are."

"No. Like I said it—"

"Wasn't your problem. It's something you inherited. Got it." Lang turned to Fell. "Make sure we get this recorded. We can use it to get bonuses for the men. Have Maksimum Kriger set up some sort of limited time special subscription. Spin up the cams, test the compiler, and let me know when you are ready. I'm going to see if I can't get a layout of the interior."

"On it." Fell took off at a jog.

Lang couldn't remember the last time they'd fought a concerted battle against vampires. In fact, he believed that this might be the first time. This found opportunity might be the thing that let him stay home, especially if his agent could negotiate residuals for him. Sudden thoughts of home brought back an avalanche of worry. This Laughing Horse man was going to be a problem.

"LET GOD SORT 'EM OUT" PT. 2

Jonathan Maberry

– 2 –
Dover Air Force Base
Dover, Delaware
The Second V-War - Day 13

An engine roar split the darkness and Swann got out of the car and turned to see a strange machine descending through morning mist. It looked like some grotesque hybrid of airplane and helicopter. It had two huge props tilted upward to slow the vertical descent to the landing strip, and the rotor wash blasted the coffee cup from his hand and splashed his new blue jeans with house blend.

Swann cursed and slapped at the steaming stains on his trousers as he crouched backward against the car.

The machine touched down with surprising delicacy for so big a craft, and immediately the engine whine changed and a side door slid open. Two figures jumped down to the ground, spotted him, and began walking purposefully in his direction.

Even with combat helmets on, Swann recognized the figure on the right. He was five inches over six feet, with bullish shoulders packed with muscle, and a chest that seemed as big around and as solid as a bear.

Big Dog.

The other soldier was shorter—maybe five-nine—and female. Without a doubt, female. Long-limbed and athletic, she had the easy grace of one of an Olympic volleyball player. A rifle strap was slung slantwise across her chest, and as she approached, she pulled off her helmet, revealing a black woman with medium-brown skin, intense eyes, and a smile that was as warm as arctic ice.

Big Dog removed his helmet, too, and his big face was split into a wide grin of what appeared to be genuine pleasure. He thrust a hand toward Swann.

"Doc!" he roared and proceeded to remodel Swann's hand bones. "Good to see you. Happy to hear you volunteered to roll out with us. This one should be a nut-buster."

"I didn't exactly volunteer," said Swann, trying hard not to wince as he took the remains of his hand back. "This was General May's idea. I think he wanted me out of Washington."

"Be good for you. The real deal is what's happening in the field."

The "field" was America's cities and towns. The battlefield and the home front had become the same thing. That terrified Swann but seemed to pump the Big Dog up.

"Let me introduce you to my good right hand," said Big Dog. He clapped the woman on a shoulder and, Swann noted, she held her ground and didn't budge. Swann had received that same comradely swat on several occasions and had nearly fallen to his knees. He imagined it was like what being shot would feel like. "This is Staff Sergeant LaShonda Forbes. Don't let her movie star looks fool you. She's a ball-buster like no other."

Swann offered his hand and winced as she took it, but her shake was merely firm and dry. She gave his hand a single pump and let it go without further damage.

"Pleasure. Seen you on TV, Dr. Swann," she said. She had a Baltimore accent with a light brush coat of Deep South. That was a phenomenon Swann had noted with most military people. Somehow every soldier below the rank of lieutenant seemed to become a little mush-mouthed if they were in the military long enough.

He mumbled something to her and nodded to the craft they'd arrived on.

"What on earth is that?"

Big Dog looked at it as if surprised to see it sitting there. "That? That's our new ride. V-8's been upgraded. Special equipment, special treatment, special assignments."

"Special bullshit," said LaShonda.

"Yeah, yeah, yeah," agreed Big Dog. He jerked a thumb at the machine. "This little honey's an MV-22 Osprey. A multi-engine, dual-piloted, self-deployable, medium lift, vertical takeoff and landing tilt-rotor aircraft designed for combat, combat support, combat service support, and Special Operations missions worldwide."

Swann stared at him. "I have no idea what you just said."

Big Dog brayed like a happy mule.

"It's a tactical aircraft," said LaShonda. "The rotors tilt so it can take off and land like a helicopter, but then tilt down for long-range flight as an airplane. Allows us to go more places faster, and get in and out easier. And we can carry out a full team and all the gear we need."

"She's my interpreter," said Big Dog. "She speaks civilian."

"That'll be useful," said Swann.

Big Dog looked him up and down. "You got coffee on you."

"Before that thing came at me, it was in a nice paper cup."

"Ah, well, we got a coffeemaker on board."

"Really?"

"Fuck no. But we do have some gear for you. You can't go into battle dressed like a fucking stand-up comedian."

Swann wore a tweed jacket over a checked dress shirt and jeans. It was what he wore to teach classes at New York University. It's what he wore back when he was teaching at UCLA.

"Come on," said Big Dog. "We're burning daylight."

The sun had been up for less than a minute.

"MANIFEST DESTINY" PT. 2

Weston Ochse

– 6 –
Nemo, South Dakota

It never got boring seeing the look of abject fear on the faces of those who'd kept his people down. So many of them argued that it wasn't their fault, they weren't involved, they minded their own business. If it hadn't been for the advent of the Indian casino, the Lakota would still be the poorest nation. And to think they once brought down the pride of the American fighting machine only to have become the poster child for poverty, malnutrition, and the slovenly drunken Indians.

Laughing Horse's idea about his future changed when he'd first heard Sherman Alexie speak while attending UCLA. The Spokane-Coeur d'Alene Indian novelist and poet spoke about the five centuries of colonization and the new Native American identity. Laughing Horse had been fleeing his entire life from the poverty, alcoholism, and despair of Pine Ridge. And here in one of the shrines of his captors, a place where O.J Simpson, James Dean and Jim Morrison began their life journeys, it took a poet to point out to him that by running away from his obligations he condemned another generation. He realized that white America's idea of Manifest Destiny—that they had a spiritual and moral imperative to take all of America and remake it into some agrarian model white society—was an absolute insult to his people. That members of congress like South Dakota's own senators would promulgate the idea by denying the enforcement of previously-made and congressionally-ratified treaties was injurious.

Two days later he quit school and returned home.

Two months later came The Change.

At first, he despaired that this was yet another thing happening to them for which they had no control. But noticing the ever increasing rise of murders and disappearances as The Changed began to feed on each other, Laughing Horse saw opportunity and perhaps even providence. The Change was the White Buffalo his people had been waiting for five hundred years. Living forever in the shadow of the *Paha Sapa*, the Black Hills, he knew now was the chance to free them of the crippling grip of his captors.

And he would begin with The Changed.

War Eagle caught him deep in his thoughts. "Ground surveillance radar has detected movement northeast of here."

Laughing Horse looked up. "Is it the son?"

"We think so?"

"Is the trap ready?"

War Eagle nodded.

Laughing Horse stood and glanced at the three females tied to their chairs, wild, tear-streaked eyes shining above their mouth gags. All blonde, they had the strong Scandinavian features he'd seen on the popular girls at UCLA. Once upon a time he would have liked them. But he'd changed as much as the vampires had. Beautiful or no, he'd eventually have to kill them.

He and War Eagle moved onto the porch. The house was a large two-story cabin, built from hewn and polished timbers. A matching barn stood across a paved parking area. Everything was nestled in a small clearing with towering ponderosa pine all around. The ground was covered with Micah flecks and pine needles. The reflective rock sometimes caught in the light, making the ground wink, as if it was magic.

"We don't want to kill him, yet."

War Eagle spoke Lakota low into the communication set strapped to his body armor. Beneath the armor he wore a t-shirt and jeans. Military boots with Vibram soles covered his feet. He had a Bowie knife and Sig Sauer P226 pistol.

Two of Laughing Horse's men ran from the back of the house to the barn, posting themselves on each corner. They wore dark camouflage made to take advantage of the dark pines. Their hair hung long in battle braids. Silver reflective ballistic glasses covered their eyes. Each of them had personalized battle paint. They carried military model M4 rifles with folding stocks. Tactical comm wires ran from a receiver/transmitter module attached to the front of their black body armor.

"Movement within fifty meters," War Eagle said. "Do you want to call him now?"

"No, but make sure we get this videoed. It might be something we can use to our advantage." He glanced around trying to spot his men in the treeline. He was their philosophical and political leader, but War Eagle, true to his name, was the military tactician. He'd spent seven years in the Marines before coming back with a chest full of medals and PTSD. "And our men are ready?"

War Eagle smirked. "You'll have to trust me on this. All the men have been trained and know their mission."

All Laughing Horse could do was nod.

A few seconds later a young man stalked through the trees and into the clearing on the other side of the barn. He was well over six feet, was broad-shouldered, and had a shock of blonde hair. He was definitely his father's son. He carried a compound bow in one hand and a rasher of rabbits in the other. A quiver of arrows hung at his side. Three steps in and he saw Laughing Horse and War Eagle. He paused for a moment and glanced around. Seeing nothing, he continued. Concern on his face as he neared.

Laughing Horse stepped down from the porch and walked a few meters further. "Been waiting for you." The trick was to act as normal as possible.

"Who are you and what do you want?" He sped up his stride as he took in the weapons and body armor on War Eagle standing behind Laughing Horse. He passed by the corner of the barn and was so intent on the armed man on his family's porch, he missed the two Indians.

One fell in behind him. The one on the far corner, knelt slowly and aimed his rifle at the boy, balancing an elbow on a knee.

"You're Brand Lang, right?" Laughing Horse offered him a smile. "I was just speaking with your father about you."

Brand's eyes narrowed as he tried to parse the information.

"He told me not to kill you."

Brand's eyes went wide as his grip tightened on his bow. "What'd you tell him?"

"No promises."

Brand dropped the rabbits and moved to pull an arrow free from his quiver when the Indian behind him pushed the barrel of his M4 into the back of the boy's head. Brand stopped immediately.

Laughing Horse clapped his hands. "Such great irony. How is it that you have a bow and arrow and we have guns? A hundred years ago it would have been much different."

"A hundred years ago there weren't vampires." Brand's mouth pulled back as his gums began to recede.

"If you change I'll kill your sisters."

The battle for control raged over the boy's face. It was clear he didn't know what to do, that he'd wanted to succumb to the change. He squeezed his fists together so hard that the bow snapped in his hand. He let it fall to the ground, then fell onto his knees. His face returned to normal. His body began to shake uncontrollably.

"Why are you doing this?" he managed to say through the flood of adrenaline.

"What is it with this family? Everyone wants to know why? Why not be suitably fucking terrified and just do what I tell you to do?"

He turned and walked back to the house. As he passed War Eagle he said, "Get him tied up. It's almost time to call his father."

– 7 –
Bagram AFB, Afghanistan

It's been argued that real soldiers don't wear Go-Cams, but for the *Draugr* of Maksimum Kriger, the suite of Go-Cams each of them wore were essential for battle. In fact, without working Go-Cams inclusive of real-time syncing and satellite uplink, Maksimum Kriger wouldn't even consider fighting. After all, when they smeared the earth with blood, subscribers in over 134 countries paid ridiculously to be part of the action. Whether it was the standard 19.99 Euros per minute, or a complete battle package for 5,000 Euros, the unwashed masses of the unchanged, which comprised the great majority of the audience, desired nothing more than to feel like they've been changed, if only for a single moment.

This is what Maksimum Kriger brought to the world. Even when England and the U.S. tried to ban it, the governments couldn't deny the income-generation possibilities. So it was through a *gleefully-applied tax* that allowed the battle streams to flood American and British living rooms. Amazing how morals and ethics could be mollified by the promise of more free money. The intrigue of death, which had always been a fleeting possibility on the nightly news, or something one could find if they looked hard enough on the Internet, had been democratized allowing all races, ethnic groups, and religions the ability to relish how amazing blood and brains appeared when rendered with high definition cameras and in surround sound.

194

The standard *Draugr* Go-Cam set-up incorporated three cameras. The chest and back cams were identical, providing 170-degree views. The chest-cam view provided the extra ability to view the hands and arms, giving viewers a chance to pretend they are actually in the combat themselves. The back-cam allowed for extra dramatic tension as the viewers saw what was coming behind the *Draugr*, most of the time something which could possibly hurt them, or even kill them. These were connected with Kevlar webbing which allowed for not only a secure connection to the body, but also provided channels for the backup transmission cables, which were used when the wireless connection failed. The 360-degree fish-eye rested atop each of their helmets like a marble.

Fell, Brandt, Canute, Colby, Dagner, Fell, Gunnar, Ivar, Leif, Sten, and Tait stood in two lines before him. They wore black uniforms, wore black boots, and had Kevlar gloves covering their hands. The uniforms had Kevlar threads mixed in a 1:30 ration, making the cloth not necessarily bulletproof, but mostly fang proof. On their heads they wore Viking helmets which could have come straight out of the Middle Ages, had they not been created using composites and containing electronics. While each of them had different stylized horns—some curved, some straight, some twisted, some rotated down—each horn contained a video compiler and a transmitter which allowed the combined footage to be uploaded via SatCom. The helmets were strapped on to keep them from being ripped off. The only thing these Maximum Warriors didn't carry were weapons and that's because they were the weapons.

Canute and Ivar were already changing. They couldn't help themselves. The excitement of the upcoming battle was making them into *Draugr*. The others were under control, but not for long. Lang hurriedly briefed the plan and sent them into three teams.

Fell, Brandt, Canute, and Colby would breach the front entrance. Gunnar, Ivar, Leif and Sten would breach the rear door. Tait stood by with Lang to reinforce if it became necessary.

Lang directed them to their posts and pulled out a tablet on which he could see each man's three-way footage. To the uninitiated it was a confusing sight. But he'd been doing this long enough that he could parse the information as easily as normal sight.

Just as the men began to move, his phone buzzed in his pocket. He cursed. He'd left it on in the event the Indian would call. Checking the caller ID, it was confirmed. His wife's darling visage greeted him, but he knew that if he was to answer, it would be that Indian trying to manipulate him.

Fell paused and let the other three *Draugr* continue. "I wouldn't take it." His voice was already getting rough from his change. "Let's get through this. I have another option."

Lang wanted to know what this man was doing to his family, but he didn't have enough time. He stared at the phone for a moment, then reluctantly shut it off. Although he was desperate to know what was going on seven thousand miles back in America, he had a responsibility to his men in the here and now. They were about to combat a den of *mandrugo*, something which no one had ever done before.

"It better be good," Lang said. His voice was choked with worry.

"Oh, it is. Now let's kill us some vampires."

Lang swallowed and nodded. "Get in position."

"Wilco."

− 8 −

Nemo, South Dakota

Laughing Horse tried to call for the fifth time and was now furious at Lang's willful ignorance of his previous command. Did the man not believe they would do terrible things? Did he think he was playing? The Native Americans had been called savages not merely because of the way they lived. In fact, the word had become associated with the way someone or something was treated. Savage.

Laughing Horse was savage and he'd be damned if that Viking vampire wanted to see it then he'd have the opportunity.

He tried one more time to call but with the same response.

He found himself staring furiously at the girls of the Lang clan.

Savage.

Savage.

He'd fucking show Calder Lang what a savage really was.

"LET GOD SORT 'EM OUT" PT. 3

Jonathan Maberry

— 3 —
Dover Air Force Base
Dover, Delaware
The Second V-War - Day 13

The interior of the Osprey was more spacious than Swann was used to. His previous missions with V-8 were always aboard cramped Black Hawks. Apart from Big Dog and LaShonda there were twelve soldiers aboard, all of whom were strangers to Swann. Ten men, two women. Typical of the SpecOps shooters Swann had met, while on the job they called each other by combat call-signs instead of names. And nobody wore a nametag. He noticed that V-8 had a new unit patch with the words ELITE SPECIAL OPERATIONS running in a circle around a stylized V8. Black lettering on a blood red disk.

LaShonda—called Thriller by the team—and a gaunt white kid called Spooky, helped Swann get kitted out. His new gear included a bullet-proof vest, armored limb and shoulder pads, and a helmet with a visor. This last bit was very high-tech and once activated sent digital data to one of the lenses. The combined data-stream included laser-distancing, a combat mission clock, a data-stream for mission support, and facial recognition. As he turned his head to try it, the call-signs of each of the soldiers popped up. ZMan, Sweetheart, Thor, Porkchop, Groucho, Dingo, Genghis, Tiktok, Spooky, King Kong, Blackjack, Big Dog, and Lonely Boy.

Who comes up with this shit? Swann wondered.

"Only use call-signs from here on out," cautioned LaShonda.

"Okay."

"Which means," said Big Dog, "that you get one, too."

"Oh. Not sure I want to know what mine is." A whole bunch of nick-names ran through his head, including epithets hung on him during his last outings with Big Dog. Pussy, pain in the ass, dickhead, walking target, vampire bait. Like that.

"Van Helsing," said Big Dog.

The other soldiers yelled it out and applauded.

"Fuck yeah," roared ZMan and Porkchop. "Fucking Van Helsing the vampire hunter. Booyah!"

As nicknames went, thought Swann, it could have been worse.

Van Helsing.

He nodded, accepted fist bumps, forced a smile.

"Do I get a gun of some sort?" he asked.

"You any good with a gun?" said LaShonda.

"Not really."

"Ever fire one?"

"I had a BB rifle when I was a kid."

"Then...no."

"Oh."

Tiktok patted his arm. "We'd all take it as a favor if you wouldn't ever touch a gun. Like...ever."

"Got it."

"Seriously."

"Loud and clear."

She beamed at Swann.

He felt naked without a weapon. Not that he wanted to use one. Not that he really wanted to shoot anyone—human *or* vampire. But the ferocity of the werewolf attacks stayed with him. They haunted him.

He could not understand them.

Not at all.

The Osprey lifted off and leaned into the wind. Swann looked out the window to see the big rotors slide forward and lock into position for standard turboprop flight. The machine—now configured like an airplane—gained speed and altitude.

Once they were underway, Big Dog hunkered down in front of him and the rest of V-8 clustered around. There was the usual rough language and rougher humor that Swann had come to expect and, to a degree, understand. The jokes, the trash talk, it was all part of the process of helping otherwise ordinary human beings prepare for doing extraordinary things. Like killing. Like running headlong into fire-fights. Like being the life takers they bragged about being. It was a kind of armor, every bit as important and useful as their limb pads and ballistic helmets. It was part of the process of transforming from citizen to soldier.

Swann had no such armor. He couldn't do the trash talk. He didn't know or fully understand that language, and wasn't sure he wanted to. It was as important for him to remain a civilian as it was for them to become soldiers.

It's a mad, mad world, he thought. *And none of us are sane.*

"What's the op?" asked LaShonda.

"You'll like it," said Big Dog with a smile. "It's cowboys and Indians. We got hard intel on a V-Cell that's using an old farm near New Hope, Pennsylvania, about thirty miles north of Philly, right on the Delaware. Local law got word to the ATF, who sent a couple boys to take a quiet look. Pinged their nitrate sniffers something fierce, so we think they're making bombs."

"Mission objectives?" prompted LaShonda, and Swann realized that this was a rhythm with them. She threw out questions so that Big Dog could be the answer man. He assumed she already knew the answers. She and the big man seemed to be a team.

"We need to determine if they are making bombs. That's first. Then we need to collect samples to determine if the shit they're making has the same chemical signature as the Ninety-nine."

"Rules of engagement?" asked LaShonda.

Big Dog's smile turned into a grin. Very wolfish, not at all pleasant. "If they have fangs then they'd better be unarmed or they'd better be right with Jesus. We take zero shit."

The team laughed and traded punches and more of the he-man rough humor. Swann was already finding it tiresome, and more than a little frightening.

"But," added Big Dog, holding up a finger, "that doesn't mean this is the O.K. Corral. You pick your targets. I don't want to hear about civilian casualties. And I don't want a friendly bullet in my balls because you pack of Girl Scouts got the wedding night jitters."

They laughed. They nodded.

Swann wished he had an eject button that would dump them all out of the plane.

Tiktok nodded in his direction. "What happens to the professor here when we deploy? He staying here on the bird?"

"No," said Big Dog. "Van Helsing is with me. He'll be on the team channel, which means anyone who has a question about the fang gang asks him." He took a moment to let them react, and there were plenty of dubious expressions, so he jumped on that. "Before you ladies get your panties in a bunch, remember this—I've rolled out with him enough times to know that what he's got in his head kept me alive. First time I went up against a *craqueuhhe*...if the professor didn't warn me about how fucking fast they are, and how strong they are... shit, I'd have been dead and drained right there and then. Same for when I got into that nest of *nuentoters* up in Amish County. Shit. I was going to go hand-to-hand with those ugly sonsabitches, but the professor starts yelling at me about how their bodies are covered with pustules. Fuckers are a walking inventory of deadly pathogens. I fell back and dropped a frag on them and dove into a horse trough. So... yeah, if Van Helsing is riding with us then we got a damn good chance of staying ahead of these bloodsucking pricks."

"Oorah!" growled LaShonda, and the others chimed in.

Swann noted, with bizarre detachment, that one of the soldiers said "Hooah" instead, and one said, "Hooyah." He'd been around the military enough to recognize the variations from Marines to army to navy. Like most of the Special Ops teams working with the V-Division of Homeland, V-8 was a mixed bag of first-team shooters from all branches of the military.

LaShonda opened a laptop and called up a satellite image of their target. Swann was only vaguely familiar with Pine Deep. He knew that it was a small town whose economy was split between farming and craft businesses that drew shoppers in for Halloween and Christmas. The town had also had its share of troubles, including some violence caused by white supremacists. The news stories at the time all mentioned that Pennsylvania had the nation's largest population of Ku Klux Klan members, and it had for some years. Swann found that so strange, since Philadelphia, Bethlehem, Doylestown and Pittsburgh were such fiercely liberal towns. The farming communities were far more conflicted.

An ugly thought occurred to him.

"Um, Big Dog?" he began, feeling as awkward using the call-sign as he always did. "Is there any indication of a connection between the people at this farm and the werewolf murders?"

Big Dog glanced at him and Swann saw shutters drop behind the man's eyes. "First, professor, these are vampires—not *people*."

Swann clamped his mouth shut on the reply he wanted to give.

"Second, no. Those murders have nothing to do with this. They sent the Big Dog and his pack out to sniff up the pricks that bombed half the fucking country. Our brief does not include looking for whoever played slice and dice with a bunch of crossbreed families. Personally, I couldn't give a rat's hairy ass about those murders. And I suggest you don't let concerns about that cloud you for this operation. Are we clear there, Professor?"

Swann said nothing.

After a moment, Big Dog nodded as if he'd gotten the answer he wanted.

"Okay, everybody check your weapons and gear. We're on the ground in fifteen minutes."

The team moved off to get ready, which left Swann and Big Dog alone for a few minutes. The sergeant turned slowly to Swann and leaned toward him, dipping his own energy through the walls of Swann's personal space. It was a deliberately intrusive act.

"We're not going to have a problem, are we, Doc?"

It was not an invitation to a conversation, and it was very clear Big Dog did not require an answer. The smile on the soldier's face went exactly one millimeter deep.

However, the sergeant paused to make a final comment.

"Look, Doc…I've been following you in the press. I know that you've done everything you could to keep this war from happening. And, even though I don't agree with your politics, I admire that you stood up for what you believe. You built a case to show that the vampires weren't a unified enemy force, that maybe the war was a byproduct of a lot of misunderstandings, a lot of people's kneejerk reactions, a lot of fear. Maybe even a lot of people wondering if the whole universe is wired the way the Bible says it's supposed to be. You tried to calm it all down before everything went to shit. You took a stand even when everyone else was trying to shout you down. That was gutsy. That showed you got some balls on you. And I admire that you want to be fair to everyone on both sides. You're a peacemaker, not a soldier. It even made me take another look at the whole 'us versus them' thing, and maybe I can see some things the way you do. More than I did last time we rolled out together."

Swann was surprised and moved by these words. He said, "I—"

But the Big Dog cut him off. "That was before those evil mother-fuckers set off ninety-nine bombs. You gave them a chance, Doc, and they pissed all over you just like they pissed all over everyone who tried to make the peace work. This time there's no question about whether the Bloods are united. There's no question about whether they're an enemy force. There's no question about whether they *want* this war. This is Pearl Harbor, this is 9-11. They picked this fight. No, let me say it the right way. They *started* this war. Them. The Bloods. No fucking doubt about it. Ask anyone in America today. Ask Joe Public if there's any doubt left. What choice do we have but to respond with appropriate force? What choice do we have but to go at them with a will and heart, because if we don't they won't stop. They can't. What they did was so big that even if they wanted to, they could-n't step back from this. This is war, Doc. War. It really is *us* or *them*. It's up to each one of us to decide which side we're on."

Swann stood up slowly, and Big Dog rose with him. Swann was a tall man, but the Marine was taller, broader, more imposing in every way that mattered in that moment.

All Swann could do was to slowly and deliberately turn his back on the sergeant.

It felt like the defeat it was.

"MANIFEST DESTINY" PT. 3

Weston Ochse

— 9 —
Bagram AFB, Afghanistan

They breached both doors simultaneously, expecting to find the *mandrugo* ready and waiting for them. But they saw nothing. The place was empty.

"Fell, move into the room," Lang commanded.

Fell and his team did as they were told.

Lang observed from all the Go-Cam feeds. Tables, overturned chairs, walls, but no *mandrugo*. Had this been a ruse by the German to get them inside? Had there even been vampires in this place? He remembered the looks on the Americans' faces and couldn't believe the relief they'd shown could have been acting.

Still…

He ordered Gunnar's team to move forward as well and watched through their camera feeds. More of the same. Nothing.

What was going—

And then he saw it. It was miniscule, but he thought he saw part of a wall shift slightly. No more than a wobble, like a mirage might do in the desert at high noon. It was something he barely noticed, but it was enough. After all, walls don't wobble.

He spoke slow and calm. "Fell, Gunnar, be ready. They are all around you. They are blended into the background. Each team get back to back and prepare."

The men snapped into position, facing outwards.

The first attack didn't come from the walls, however. It came from above as a piece of ceiling fell on Ivar. The image reconciled into a *mandrugo* which was already clawing away the skin from the *Draugr*'s face. Lang's man screamed and that scream brought everything alive.

The walls moved and surged towards the *Draugr*. Not just part of the walls, but the entire walls, which had been constructed by fifty or sixty *mandrugo*, side-by-side and on top of each other. Chairs unfolded to become *mandrugo*. A table separated as five *mandrugo* became independent parts. What had once been a cohort of Filipina women desperate to make a living in a far-away land had now become vampire and something from which they would never return. And every last one of them was hungry.

"Stay in formation," Lang commanded, then he grabbed Tait and ran into the building.

Absolute pandemonium.

The shrieks of the *mandrugo* mated with the screams and roars of his men to create a vampyric cacophony of violence and battle lust. His men ripped and broke the smaller, weaker *mandrugo* whenever they could get one, but there were so many.

Sten was covered in five of them which had latched on like lamprey.

Colby was down and Brandt was on one knee.

Lang pointed and Tait dove into Fell's fray, ripping the *mandrugo* from where they covered Sten.

Lang surged towards Fell and pulled Brandt to his feet. Colby's eyes and throat had been ripped out. A *mandrugo* fed on his blood. Lang brought up a boot and crushed the creature's head, then left his foot there.

"Men of Maksimum Kriger," he screamed loud enough for everyone to hear, "Berserk!"

They shook and twitched and began to move in surges of energy. Slow then impossibly fast, then slow again. They seemed to transport themselves from violence to violence, as if they invented the idea of bodies being torn apart. *mandrugo* began to run from them as they realized the power and fury that was now before them.

Lang felt his own adrenal glands feeding him and he let himself become lost for a time as he surged across the floor, hands ripping and tearing, his mouth chewing, reveling in the sweet heat of *Mandrugo* blood. And for a time he forgot about his family and about the crazy Indian who held them. For a time his worry was gone, replaced by the need to kill, to feed, to protect his men.

Cornered and with nowhere to go, a clutch of *mandrugo* moved to him like rats and flowed across his body. He couldn't see or breathe. Their combined weight made him stagger. He flailed with his arms and tried to grab them but they moved too fast. He fought to stay on his feet. He knew that if he fell, he'd lose the last bit of advantage he had.

He panicked a moment, then knew what he needed to do and began to chew. Chew, swallow, chew, swallow. He began to eat the *mandrugo* covering his face. It shrieked and fell away.

For a brief second he gulped in air. He screamed, "To me!" then was covered once again.

But it only lasted a moment as his men roared and came from every direction to rip the *mandrugo* from his body. He grabbed two of them by their long hair and began to swing them. He brought them together hard enough that their heads exploded, showering everything with delightful gore.

His wounds began to heal even as he fought, making him stronger and stronger. Soon he was at full strength and began to laugh. His men began to laugh with him as they fought, killing the *mandrugo* and producing a product for which the world would pay a handsome sum.

Oh, but life was grand.

– 10 –
Bagram AFB, Afghanistan

Lang held out his hand. "Give me back my phone."

Fell shoved it in his pocket. "No way. Get in the vehicle and you can take it from there."

Although exhausted, rage was still alive in Lang's eyes. "I don't have time for this." He shook his outstretched hand again. "Especially coming from you."

"Yes, you do."

"I need—"

"First of all, you won't be able to use it where you're going. Second of all, it's going to do you no good to know what's going on there. Third, I need it to coordinate the St. Olaf *Draugr*."

Lang stared hard for a moment, but then realized he was displacing his anger. A Humvee pulled up. Their intelligence analyst sat in back.

Gunnar was behind the wheel.

"Now get in the vehicle. You'll be home in four hours."

"But that's impossible. Unless…"

"Ostergard has his own private SR-71. He thinks it's better than a Concord."

"Certainly faster," Margules interjected. "I don't mean to ruin this surprise party, but you know it only has room in the cockpit for two. A pilot and him." He pointed at Lang. "Like I've been trying to tell this galoot," now he pointed at the driver. "There isn't room for three of us in the cockpit."

Fell gave him a stern and steady gaze. "You're not riding in the cock-pit."

"Then where will I…" Margules gulped.

Lang climbed in the passenger seat. "Ostergard went for this?"

"Went for it? Hell, we're going to film it."

"This is my family we're talking about."

"After this, no one will ever think of messing with your family. Now get going." He held up the phone. "I'll see what I can do to stall that fanatic."

Lang got out of the Humvee and put a hand on Fell's shoulder. "You're a good man, Fell."

"I'm *your* man, Calder."

Both men stared at each other for a moment, then Lang let go and returned to the Humvee. Gunnar put it in gear and they were off, winding along the road that encircled the field and the 10,000 foot runway. Fourteen minutes later they pulled up to an SR-71 Blackbird. Officially retired from the U.S. defense inventory in 1998, there were still a few in service as part of special programs. Most were sent to the Boneyard in Arizona, but it seemed as if a few were sold to private investors. Lang should have known Brandt Ostergard would have one. Any man who owned his own submarine would own the fastest plane ever to carve the ionosphere.

The pilot helped him climb into an oxygen suit, while a technician assisted Margules to do the same. Capable of flying at 80,000 feet, they'd need the suits if they wanted to stay alive. His Go-Cams, armor, and weapons were placed in a bag. They were in the air within half an hour. Lang sat behind the pilot. Margules lay in a life support coffin in payload.

− 11 −
Bagram AFB, Afghanistan

Fell sat in the hanger with the rest of Maksimum Kriger, leaderless for a while until Lang could save his family. Until then, he was in charge. They'd lost two to the *mandrugo* and five more were wounded. The beasts had been like rats and were all over them. If it hadn't been for their altered forms, more than two of them would be dead. Still, it had been a joyous battle. They'd never fought other vampires, much less gotten footage of it. He'd already been in contact with the Ostergard Group and subscriptions were selling like crazy. This one might make it so they could all see their families. Not like they didn't enjoy the battles, because they couldn't survive without them. But there needed to be a balance to their lives. They needed time to heal, time to be with their families, time to refuel their need to fight.

He went to each of the men and spoke to them, checked on them, just as he knew Calder would have done if he had been there. Then he found a place at the back of the hanger and sat down. He drew his knees up and Face-dialed the Indian. It was picked up on the second ring.

A face appeared in livid purple.

"Where have you been? Where's Lang?"

"He was injured. He wanted me to call and ask that you hold off. Shouldn't be long. He's just—"

"You should have never turned off the phone! You should have kept the lines of communication clear."

A sense of worry began to fill Fell. He needed to manage this man's emotions, but he also needed to understand what was going on. "What did you do?"

"It's not what we did. It's what you caused us to do."

"We were in the middle of a battle. We couldn't answer even if we wanted to."

"Excuses!" Laughing Horse shouted. "That's what you decided. You made the choice." He turned and looked at something off screen, then back at the phone camera. "What happened is your fault."

"What have you done?"

"I'll send you the link. You can see for yourself."

Then he hung up.

Fell stared at the phone. Something terrible had happened back in Nemo, South Dakota while they'd been fighting the Mandrugo. He was almost too afraid to find out.

The phone made a sound and a message appeared on the screen with a web link. His finger hovered above it for a moment as he knew that he didn't want to see what he was about to see, but knew he had to. He pressed the link. The screen went black. Then it went to a video.

The first time he watched it, his jaw dropped.

The second time he watched it with tears in his eyes.

The third time he watched it, he knew that the man was going to die.

He called Laughing Horse again.

This time the man was calmer. His face had lost its purple hue. In fact, it was as if he'd never done thing inhumane things Fell had witnessed in the video.

"So you watched the video."

Fell had to lick his lips to get them working. "I did," he managed to say.

"You men of Maksimum Kriger charge for your videos. Mine are free."

"You never should have done this. You know you're going to die now."

Laughing Horse scoffed. "I know no such thing. What I do know is that this is no worse than what the white man did to my people. You might not remember Wounded Knee but we will never forget it."

"I'm sure it's part of your cultural memory, but it's not part of ours. Mainly because it had nothing to do with us. You're blaming an entire race of people on something a few did."

"If I could punish them, I would. Your kind is my proxy."

"I thought you were a thinking man. Did you not think that Calder might chase you down and do to you what you did to his family?"

"It's why I left one alive. If he wants her to live, then he must let me go."

Fell shook his head. The man had no idea what he'd just done, but for the sake of the girl, he had to make it look like there was hope. "You better keep her alive, though. She's your only bargaining point."

Laughing Horse nodded. "Still, if he had answered my calls, this never would have happened."

"Seriously. A man doesn't answer his phone so you punish him by doing what you did to his family?"

"That's putting it a little simply."

Fell was about to say something when the truth dawned on him. "You never had any plans to keep them alive, did you?"

"Someone had to be the first. We had to plant our flag on someone. With your association with the offensive subscription-based reality thrill kill show it seemed like the perfect merging of planning and opportunity."

Fell wished he was aboard the SR-71 now, too, so he could get his pound of flesh. But he kept his face clear. "Calder will be contacting you."

The man smiled. "I'm sure he will." Then he hung up.

"I just spoke to a dead man," Fell said aloud.

He closed his eyes and counted to a hundred. The he called the St. Olaf *Draugr*. They were already in place. He told them to hold and that in less than two hours Lang would be there. They sounded excited. They revered Lang like a hero. They were about to see first-hand just how bloody heroes got.

– 12 –
Black Hills, South Dakota

Lang's ears still hadn't popped by the time he and Margules climbed into the South Dakota National Guard AH-60 Black Hawk. The ground crew closed the door behind them and the pilot lifted off. They were soon racing north from the airfield just outside Rapid City to Nemo. The Black Hills were on their left and served as a dark Western Horizon. The sun was directly overhead giving them six good hours of daylight left. More than enough time.

They'd given him a headset and he keyed the mike. "Have you had any word from my people?"

"We're informed that communications gear will be awaiting you," the co-pilot said.

Lang turned to Margules. "I wasn't briefed on the mission. Why are you here exactly?"

Margules's eyes rolled and his face turned a deeper green as the Black Hawk turned sharply.

"You going to be sick?" Lang asked.

"Ulp. Hope not." He brought a hand to his mouth and managed to swallow down whatever it was that had tried to escape. "Mr. Ostergard wants UAV oversight. Wants to make sure—ulp—that we have good footage. I think I can also help by helping you prep the battlefield by establishing an operating picture."

Lang nodded as he took in the information. "Think it's going to be that difficult?"

"These are the same Indians that defeated Custer."

"But Laughing Horse is no Crazy Horse."

"He thinks he is. Oh—" Margules grabbed one of the sick bags and almost made it. He puked mostly on his hands and the floor of aircraft. The interior filled with the violent smell of bile.

"He better clean that up," the co-pilot said.

Lang looked out the window and dialed down his nerves as best he could. One thing he'd never considered was that his family would be at risk because of his occupation.

Flight time was short and they soon found themselves landing on the baseball field for Nemo High School. Ten *Draugr* awaited him, their shoulders and jaws and frontal ridges like a calling card to their *changed* forms. But where his men were in top physical condition, these were a study in fast-food eating and hard drinking. Too much time in the Mead Hall talking about being a Viking rather than being one. Several were easily over four hundred pounds with their weight disturbed along their equators. Still others had flab. One wore animal skins and a horned helmet like some Haggar the Horrible parody.

He exited the craft and let the kid clean up his own mess. A man in reasonably good shape, his hair painted purple and cut Mohawk style like Fell's, detached himself from the others and approached.

He was as tall as Fell, but not as tall as Lang. He put his right fist over his heart and said, "I am Joshua from St. Olafs. My men are at your service."

Lang put his fist over his heart as well. "Thanks. But do you have contact with my men? Any communications?"

Joshua pulled out a smart phone. "Fell sent a link for your review, but asked that you call first."

Lang took the phone. "See if you can get your men to unload. They're wearing Go-Cams and might need help putting them on."

Purple Mohawk's eyes widened. "We're going to be part of the show?"

Lang grumbled and turned away. He dialed his number, then thought better of it and moved to the bleachers. He was all alone as he clicked the link. While he waited for the video to spool up, he glanced at the field. He'd sat in these very bleachers once last year when his son played baseball. Brand had hit a homerun and a triple. The triple had been the most exciting. Lang had been in awe of his son's athleticism as he rounded the bases and slid into third before the ball arrived.

The video began to play. He rested his elbows on his knees and watched as Laughing Horse appeared on the screen.

"You decided this when you chose not to answer my phone call. You decided this when you chose to move into stolen property and live in our stolen home. You decided this when you felt that you could viciously attack others for profit and never considered that people might do the same thing to your family. Everything that is about to occur is your fault and you will forever live with the fact that you weren't there to stop it.

Laughing Horse shifted the view to where his wife was bent over the kitchen table. Her arms had been tied to the table legs on one end, while her ankles were tied to the table legs on the nearer end. She was naked and bruised as one of the Indians moved in and out of her, pounding his penis into her over and over.

Lang's heart lurched as the entirety of it hit him.

The camera angle changed as it moved to the side so he could see the action better, then to her front where he could witness the animal ecstasy on the face of the Indian as he fucked his wife from behind.

Laughing Horse provided a voice over. "This went on for several hours. We have all the footage but wanted to share this part with you." He reached down and grabbed a handful of her lank blonde hair and pulled her head up so Lang could see her face. It took a moment to realize that she was dead. "Alive or dead, this is what the soldiers did to my people. You all want to pretend it never happened. Convenient. Receipt of stolen property is a felony right?" The camera moved in close to her dead eyes as her face moved in motion from the way the Indian fucked her.

"Inger. Oh no, Inger." He said to himself. He rocked back and forth as he watched, transfixed.

Then the camera moved to the cutting board to where his oldest daughter was tied… where an Indian did the same to her as had been done to her mother, plunging in and out of her.

"Amelie. No!" This was beyond too much. Why hadn't the man waited? What had he done to his family? Lang saw it all but was having difficulty understanding.

The camera moved to his daughter's face to reveal her still alive and crying, agony and terror storms in her eyes.

"Don't kill her. Please, don't kill her," he said to the image.

"You used to like to take souvenirs to prove you'd killed my people. You'd scalp us. Much like we're going to do now."

Lang watched in utter horror as an Indian took a knife and began to saw at his daughter's face. Her screams and her cries of *Oh, Daddy* entered his soul like battle rockets and didn't subside until her scalp had been removed completely and shaken in front of the camera like a terrible trophy. Then, mercifully, she died, her last breath hitching, then exhaling, then no more.

The image shifted to Laughing Horse's face.

"But wait, there's more." The camera moved through his kitchen to his front door then outside. "You're going to love this one. It's something you brought over from England.

His son was in the middle of the driveway but in not in any position Lang had ever considered. He hung suspended, each of his limbs pulled tight by chains, the chains attached to the rear bumpers of four cars.

"Dismemberment is a grisly thing, don't you think? I daresay worse even than scalping."

His son was in full-on berserk mode pulling, thrashing, fighting against the restraint, but the chains were too well made.

Lang was squeezing the phone so tight he was afraid it might snap. Try as he might, he couldn't figure out a way let the grip go.

"Ever seen someone's head cut off? Not quickly, mind you, but slowly, inexpertly, like I'm about to do to your boy now."

Lang kept his jaw shut. He no longer pled to the image. This man had sealed his fate and with each word was dooming another generation. Lang's anger was balanced on the keen edge of reason and he held it there, even as Laughing Horse brought a wood saw and began to saw through his son's neck, even as his son's eyes went from berserker anger to fear, even as the head fell to the ground and Laughing Horse kicked it, and even as the cars revved their engines and pulled the body of his little boy apart…the boy who'd hit the triple last year during his senior year of high school.

"There's one more member of you family left," Laughing Horse said, positively glowing with his unbelievable accomplishment. "Sigrid will remain alive if you call me. But time is ticking, tick tock, tick tock, tick—"

Lang hung up the phone, then with a shaking hand punched in his number.

Fell answered right away. He was about to say something, then changed it. "You saw."

"I saw." Both words dropped with a metric ton of anguish.

"I told them to tell you to call me first. Only reason I sent the link was in case the comms—"

"Doesn't matter now."

"No, I suppose it doesn't." Fell paused a moment. "I'm so sorry, Calder."

Lang nodded. "Are the men okay?"

"We're fine. Don't worry about us. Take care of what you need to take care of and we'll be along as quickly as we can. Ostergard is moving us to your position."

"Has he seen the—"

"Yes, he has. Most of the planet has. He arranged for legal protection. We're officially assisting with local and state law enforcement in apprehending Laughing Dog and his men."

"I don't think they'll be apprehended."

"I didn't think so. Either way, it's a Dead or Alive mission."

"He wants me to call him."

"I'd pay him a visit instead. I wouldn't give him a chance to do something else."

Something Else. What else could Laughing Horse do? Lang had just asked himself a question for which he never wanted to learn the answer.

"I gotta go."

"Calder?"

"What?"

"Just that… hell… I'm just so damn sorry."

Lang hung up. He stood shakily and took a moment to find his balance. He glanced at the third base where he'd once seen his son

slide to fame. Then he walked over and handed over the phone to
Purple Mohawk and said, "Let's meet your men."

— 13 —
Nemo, South Dakota

Laughing Horse was feeling moderately depressed. After all that
hard work he wasn't getting any feedback from Calder Lang or anyone
for that matter. The website already had more than a million hits, but
what he needed was personal connectivity. He needed to see their
faces when they saw what he did. Of course he knew the world was
against them right now, but that had been the plan all along.

Shock them.

Get their attention.

Then explain the situation.

He was sure that given the time he'd be able to bring them around
with logic and reason, explain how he was merely doing what the
American government had already deemed as lawful by their willful
ignorance of their own treaties and agreements and allowing others to
steal over and over and over. They'd established the precedence at
Wounded Knee. The world would soon be on his side. After all, they
hated America, and once her great secret was exposed, it would give
them the poisoned bait they needed to cripple the superpower.

He knew he came across as an insane sadist killer, but they'd
forget about that. They'd forget the terrible deeds, even with the
video on the site, they'd forget. It's human nature to do so. It's human
nature to forgive. The people of the world had done it before and
they'd do it again.

Just look at Russell Means. He'd been a prominent leader of the
American Indian Movement, masterminding takeovers of Mount Rush-
more, the Bureau of Indian Affairs office in Washington D.C., as well
as participating in the takeover of Wounded Knee, resulting in the
deaths of several white federal officers. He should have been hated,
but instead became a famous Hollywood figure staring in movies such
as *Last of the Mohicans*, *Natural Born Killers* and *Thomas and The
Magic Railroad*.

Laughing Horse began to feel better. He strode through the house.
The wife was still tied to the table. The daughter was tied to the
butcher block. The pieces of the son were stacked on the right side of

the porch, already drawing flies. The other daughter had been tied to a chair and been forced to watch and listen to her family. She'd survive this event, probably, but she'd never be the same again. Now she was held by one of his men. They'd pulled the RV into the drive and she was inside awaiting the negotiations.

Speaking of the negotiations, where was Lieutenant Colonel Lang? Last he'd heard he was with the doctors. He held up his phone and checked the power and reception bars. He thought about calling, but he didn't want to put himself in a position of less power.

Machine gun fire made him look up.

He called for War Eagle but got no response.

Another round of machine gun fire, but this time from the other direction. Were they under attack?

He spun towards the sound and called again. Still no answer. He ran to the edge of the barn and peered around it.

Suddenly gunfire was all around. All of his men were firing. He heard screams. Then he saw movement. An impossibly fat vampire was running down the hill towards him.

He took a step back in shock and fear, but stopped when the vampire fell, tumbling the rest of the way into a heap at the base of the hill. The vampire worked its way to its feet and wobbled. Fat as it might be, it was undeniably a *Draugr*. It wore a Go-Cam rig. Its two-horned helmet had broken, one horn hanging by wires. The vampire turned to assess and saw him right away. It began to run. Its lips were already pulled back and teeth had descended. Fat or no fat, this thing wanted to kill him.

Laughing Horse turned and ran for the house. "War Eagle. Where are you?"

He burst through the front door and ran into the kitchen. He reached for a knife on the counter and spun towards the doorway. He glanced at the knife, then the bodies, and decided it wasn't enough. He ran into the living room and up the stairs. He tripped up the last few stairs, almost falling on the knife. But he righted himself and ran to the front of the house. He found the son's room and went to the window.

The fat *Draugr* stood in the middle of the driveway looking around. Then he spied movement in the RV and ran towards it. He slammed into the side of the vehicle hard enough to shake it on its wheels. The *Draugr* backed away and ran at it again. This time he got it on two wheels, but it fell, rocking violently back and forth. But the *Draugr* wouldn't be stopped. It ran at it over and over until it had it back on two wheels, and this time it kept the vehicle from coming back, tipping it over the rest of the way. As the RV crashed to the ground the front windshield shattered. The *Draugr* took immediate advantage and began to claw its massive rotund body inside.

Things were not going as planned.

Where'd this attack come from? Maksimum Kriger was on the other side of the world. Were there more groups? What the—

A man on the hillside drew his attention. To the right and left of him *Draugr* engaged his men in close combat. His Sioux warriors were possibly the best hand-to-hand knife fighters on the planet. But they were human and couldn't match the speed, strength or stamina of a vampire. One of his men shot a *Draugr* six times in the chest, but it seemed to do no damage. But all this was secondary to the vision of the man on the hillside who seemed to be staring straight at him.

Calder Lang.

How?

The *Draugr* leader strode down the hillside and into his driveway like the King of the Universe. He kept striding towards the house, never once breaking eye contact with Laughing Horse. When the peak of the roof broke their gaze, Laughing Horse found himself hyperventilating as fear took him. He heard Lang step onto the porch, then he roared.

He'd seen his son.

The roar continued until the *Draugr* was out of breath then repeated itself.

Everyone, even the warriors on the hill paused for a moment to witness the anger and anguish that echoed through *Paha Sapa*.

Then Lang went inside and the roaring grew louder.

He'd seen his wife.

His daughter.

The sound of breaking.

The sound of crying.

Then the sound of rage as he thundered up the stairs like a hate train.

Laughing Horse found himself standing in the middle of the son's room, a knife in his hand, which was trembling so much he couldn't hold it straight.

Lang fumed in the doorway. His forehead ridge was more pronounced. Two inch-long fangs descended from a lipless mouth curled into a corpse smile. The eyes were enraged slits and emanated raw power. But even with all of this, Laughing Horse was drawn to the lens on the Go-Cam on the *Draugr*'s chest.

"I don't think you understand," he said.

He meant to say more, but Lang was on him. Breaking his hand, then crushing his fingers in a bestial grip. Then Lang did it to his other hand. Someone was screaming and it took Laughing Horse a moment to realize it was himself. Then Lang broke his forearm and twisted, removing the entire lower half of the arm. He ripped the skin and meat away from the bone with his teeth, swallowing, and some of the gore fell from his chin, sliding across the lens of the Go-Cam and turning the world a blood red for the subscriberverse.

Lang held Laughing Horse's ulna in his hand like a knife and began to jab the broken end repeatedly into the indian's stomach. Five. Ten. Fifteen times.

A miniature helicopter appeared at the window, a small camera it's only payload.

Lang shot his face into Laughing Horse's stomach and began to eat. The sensation of being consumed unleashed something inside Laughing Horse that made him begin to shriek. He wanted to explain. He wanted to show the world what he really meant. He wanted to provide them a rational reason supported by international law why the *Paha Sapa* should be returned to the American Indian, but he couldn't because there'd be nothing left of him because the best of him was ending up as fuel for a fanatical Viking vampire who wanted revenge for...

...killing

...raping

...dismembering

...his family.

Laughing Horse left his body and watched like the world watched the *Draugr* savaging him. What he hadn't seen was what was happening to the rest of him. For as the *Draugr*'s face was buried in his stomach, his hands had broken both of his legs, shattered his spine in three places and ripped free his lower jaw.

If only he'd had the time to explain.

— 14 —
Nemo, South Dakota

Lang's rage was vast and contained a universe of need.

He ran after an Indian who was hell bent on escaping. But nothing escaped Calder Lang. Nothing could escape a *Draugr* when it wanted something. He was unstoppable and carried the DNA of the greatest marauders to ever live. They were Vikings. They lived in history as a people who came and took other people's things, relatives, and land, and made it their own. They'd been takers, men in longboats landing on peaceful sands, returning with what they could rape from the land and people. The very idea that a lunatic wouldn't realize this was incredible. Manifest Destiny and the idea one could own the land was not in his DNA. These were other people's constructs and not those of a Viking.

Lang ran through the forest in full berserk mode. His thoughts were his own, but were so far disconnected from his muscles as to belong to someone else's. He caught up to one of the fleeing Indians and pulled him down by his war braid. Once down, he fell upon the screaming fool, ripping out his jugular with one hand while his other broke the spine.

He twisted the head from the torso and brought the base of it to his mouth. He sucked bone marrow, spinal fluid, blood and brains, chewing, eating, fueling, berserking.

His eyes were caught by movement as he saw another dashing through the trees. He chased this one down using the head of the other as a weapon, swinging it and launching it through the air. He fed again, chewing on the jugular he held in his gore-dipped hands like it was a root. He tied the two war braids together and took with him his battle-made bolo and brought down the next two.

He had fuel for a thousand days. His son had been killed in the name of some false idea. His family had been shattered because of the need to right old wrongs. If they believed in retribution, then he was there to explain it to them—explain to them how he would right a new wrong, how he would chase them down, all of them, every last Sioux Indian, every reservation, every person who pretended to be an Indian, even children playing silly games, until the planet was free of their kind, until the universe had forgotten them, until he'd forgotten they'd ever come to his home and soiled his life.

That was his Manifest Destiny.

That was his God-given DNA-provided right.

To take everything.

And it was all on Go-Cam.

Somewhere he knew Brandt Ostergard was laughing.

Somewhere he knew people were entertained by his folly.

But he didn't care. The footage would serve as his warning to the world, as his business card to those who would do his kind harm, and as a foreshadowing of those he was going to kill.

He swung a pair of bolos made from the heads of his enemy and everything ran before him. The universe stepped aside while his anger fed, and the people of this great wide earth applauded.

"LET GOD SORT 'EM OUT" PT. 4

Jonathan Maberry

Pine Deep, Pennsylvania
The Second V-War - Day 13
— 4 —

Luther Swann could feel his heart beating with such force that it felt like he was being punched repeatedly in the chest. Sweat poured down his body, soaking him. He could smell his own fear in the acrid sweat-stink that rose from his armpits.

V-8 was poised to hit the farmhouse. They all wore black BDUs, with helmet-cams and full assault gear. They were split into two teams of six soldiers and one team leader. Each team had five soldiers with Heckler & Koch MP-5s, one man with a handheld breeching tool, and a point-man with a Glock .40 and a ballistic shield. LaShonda anchored B-team at the front door, a Remington 870 pump held ready. Big Dog had the same gun and was ready with the A-team out back. Swann was behind him, crouched and quivering, unarmed and feeling stupid and vulnerable.

Big Dog spoke a single word into the mike.

"Now!"

The riflemen smashed out the door-glass and Big Dog flung a flash-bang into the living room. It flashed and banged with all the roar of a sudden close-range crack of thunder.

Big Dog signaled to King Kong to breech the door. The soldier swung the heavy ram with practiced ease and the door burst inward in a shower of splinters. Then A-team was rushing inside, guns up and out, yelling at whoever might be in there, ordering them to disarm and drop.

It all went to hell.

The vampires were waiting for them.

Twenty of them. Men and women. Most of them wearing body armor. All of them carrying weapons except for a towering giant of a man with a face like a jackal and a mouthful of shark teeth. It was a vampire species Swann had never seen before. He bellowed out a warning as the giant rushed at King Kong, tore the breeching tool from the man's hands, and swung it at him with shocking speed and power. King Kong tried to duck, tried to ride the blow.

It hit him full on the side of the head.

The impact was shockingly loud, dreadfully wet. King Kong's ballistic helmet flew to pieces. As did his head. Blood shot upward driven by hydrostatic pressure. The geyser splashed the kitchen ceiling. King Kong was falling, collapsing, dropping into an artless heap inside of a microsecond.

That's when everybody started shooting.

Big Dog wheeled around, raised his shotgun and fired at the giant. The first round took him in the stomach, but the body armor and the monster's sheer mass sloughed it off. The thing swung the breeching tool at the team leader, who dropped flat and avoided the blow by inches. He rolled onto his side, jammed the barrel of the Remington pump at the giant's ankle and fired.

The blast tore the ankle and foot to rags.

The giant screamed and canted sideways, still trying to smash Big Dog with the tool. Big Dog twisted out of the way and fired again, this time upward, between the giant's legs, catching him in the crotch at point blank. He jacked another round and shot the monster in the face.

The giant flopped backward, dead. Ruined. Utterly destroyed.

Swann ducked down behind the kitchen counter, arms wrapped over his head as several vampires began firing from behind an overturned dining room table. The rattle of automatic gunfire filled the air.

The soldiers found whatever cover they could—the stove, the refrigerator—and returned fire. Bullets chewed at the furniture and appliances, chipping pieces away, filling the air with flying splinters. Swann was afraid to look…and afraid not to.

He saw a vampire take two rounds to the face and pitch backward, the back of his head blown off. Another of them stood up to hurl a grenade and as he raised it, Tiktok shot him in the chest. The vampire's body armor stopped the bullets, the impact knocked him back and the grenade went flying into the dining room.

The vampires tried to scramble out of the way, but the bullets and their own barricade trapped them in the moment.

The grenade exploded.

Everything inside the blast radius was torn to red pieces.

But there were more of them. They boiled out through the cellar doorway, firing, firing.

Sweetheart, one of the female soldiers, was closest to the cellar and she went down under a pile of them. Lonely Boy rushed to her side, firing at the pale killers. But then he went down, too. Blood sprayed the walls, shooting up between thrashing arms and legs.

Genghis and ZMan rose up and hosed the vampires, emptying full magazines into them, and then dropped down to reload as Thor and Dingo stood up to take their place.

There were more vampires than soldiers. Many more. But the vampires were not soldiers. The training, the teamwork, the high-tech weapons—all of that mattered.

The vampires began to fall.

Suddenly one of them—a young woman in a house dress and sweater—came rushing through the crowd toward Groucho. She had no visible fangs and she carried no weapon.

Groucho hesitated for a moment—just for a moment—his doubt and compassion making him uncertain. The woman smacked his rifle barrel aside and threw herself at him, grabbed him, and buried her teeth into his throat. Even without fangs the bite was devastating. Blood splashed her face as she bore Groucho to the floor.

Big Dog kicked at her but couldn't dislodge her. He jammed the shotgun against her temple and fired. Her face disintegrated into pulp, but even as she fell sideways her teeth remained locked on Groucho's windpipe. He twitched and gurgled and drowned in his own blood, locked in an embrace with his killer in a parody of intimacy.

Swann saw all of this.

He saw the vampires rally.

He saw Blackjack go down with a knife socketed in the hollow of his throat.

He saw Lonely Boy fall with a small black dot over his eye and the back of his head blown out.

He saw Thor get hit with a sweep of bullets that blew his thighs apart.

He saw people die.

He saw vampires die.

He saw so much death.

And all the time, he hid in the corner behind the kitchen counter, unable to contribute, unable to help, able only to scream. And because that was all he could do, he kept doing it.

"FORCE MULTIPLIER"

Larry Correia

−1−

There were four guards manning the Russian security checkpoint. Two were inside the guard shack, huddled next to an electric space heater. The other two were outside, next to the DhSK heavy machine gun mounted on a tripod.

He clicked his radio. "Execute," Kovac ordered.

The snipers fired simultaneously. The wet impact of the bullets was far louder than the suppressed rifles. The soldiers next to the machine gun emplacement collapsed, leaving behind a fine red mist floating in front of the spotlight. Clean shots.

A split second later a shadow moved inside the guard shack and was immediately followed by a large quantity of blood splattering against the interior of the window. Basco's genetic heritage was Indonesian, and his mutation made it so that he could move like a fucking magic ninja.

There was no alarm. Quick and quiet, just like they'd practiced.

The smell of torn open bodies and fresh blood wafted over. It made him hungry. Kovac keyed his radio again. "Checkpoint is clear. Bring up the trucks." He lifted himself out of the snow bank he'd been lying in for hours. Cold didn't bother him anymore, and his body seemed immune to frostbite or hypothermia, that was one welcome change among many.

Kovac used hand signals to order his squad to move out. Ten figures rose from the snow. Their snipers would remain on the mountainside and cover their approach. Everyone knew their individual assignments, and responded quickly. A few of them were so fast that they seemed to simply vanish, while others were slower, but nearly invisible in the dark.

There was only one road in. The terrain here was unforgiving, consisting of iced-over rock, steep angles, and deadly cliffs. It was an excellent location for a secret research facility. Assaulting this place would have been suicide for humans.

In typical old Soviet military architectural style, the facility was a concrete cube. The main doors were designed to stop a tank. Breaching those would take too long, and the Russians would call for reinforcements. Instead his squad moved down the mountain, toward the side that the Russians considered impossible to climb. The snow here was a thick, clinging slush, but most of the squad had no problem moving across it at an incredible rate of speed.

Their intel said the Russians ran constant patrols through this area, normally consisting of two men and a dog. Kovac sensed the approaching patrol before the guard dog smelled them. He flashed a signal at Meeker, who gave him a nod, then disappeared into the trees. Thirty seconds later, there was some commotion as the possessed German Shepherd latched onto its surprised handler's throat. There was a thud as Meeker eliminated the other guard, and then a yelp as he dispatched the confused animal.

Meeker reappeared, covered in steaming blood, carrying an AK-74 in each hand, and wearing a new fur hat he'd taken as a trophy. He grinned, revealing a mouth filled with hundreds of needle shaped teeth.

Gregor was the fastest, so he took point. Kovac ran after him, down a narrow rock shelf. The closer they got to the facility's wall, the more treacherous the footing became. One slip would mean a three hundred foot drop, but he wasn't worried. It was hard to imagine that he used to have to concern himself with things like balance. The mutations took on various forms, so he'd given out assignments to the team based on their different abilities. The slowest would bring up the rear and would need help scaling the wall, while the quick ones eliminated the opposition and secured their entrance.

Kovac was running out of mountain. He studied the rapidly approaching edge of the cliff. There was a twenty-foot leap to the icy wall on the other side. Gregor's ancestors were from Ghana, where their legends told of vampires living in trees. He had already jumped across and was climbing so quickly and effortlessly that that bit of folklore seemed very plausible.

Kovac didn't hesitate. Hurling his body across the gap felt as natural as breathing. He hit the smooth concrete on the far side and began to slide, but he latched on and clung there like a spider. Wind and weather had created handholds that he never would have found when he'd been human.

He waited a moment to make sure his impact hadn't made too much noise. There was a flashlight moving high above, but the patrol wasn't lingering. There was no adrenalin in the guard's scent. They were unaware, dull from the aching cold. Kovac began climbing upwards. His bare skin stuck to the wall, and it burned each time he had to peel his hand away. It took him nearly twenty seconds to scurry up the side. The others, who were physically capable, had jumped across and were following him. They'd throw down ropes for those who were not so athletically gifted, but even the least of his men were more than human.

Kovac reached the top and hesitated, listening, smelling, and feeling. He could sense that the humans had their backs turned. He'd developed an instinct that told him where human eyes were lingering, and how to put himself in the places where people weren't looking. There were several soldiers up here. His senses were so sharp he could smell the grease on the bolt carriers of their AK-74s and what brand of cheap cigarettes they were smoking. The squeak of boots against the metal catwalk told him their position, their stance, even their weight.

Gregor was already over the railing and moving down the catwalk, stalking a guard. Kovac picked another guard and went in the other direction. This soldier smelled old. His sweat had vodka in it. In the old days he'd have used a knife for this kind of business, but he didn't need to do that anymore. Instead he simply reached out, took hold of the back of the guard's neck, and dug his fingers in until he had a handful of spinal column and twisted. Lowering the body to the catwalk, Kovac noted that Gregor was feeding on his victim and Bennett had secured the climbing rope for the others. Silent as a ghost, Kovac had snapped two more necks before the next member of his squad arrived.

It took him a moment to find Lila, and that was only because of the leathery rustle of wings. He couldn't actually see her. In fact, when she was in her hunting form she was nothing but a dark blur, until you caught her out of the corner of the eye. He turned his head until she appeared in his peripheral vision. She was crouched, naked, on top of a railing, her bare feet curled around the pipe like a raptor's claws. Security cameras didn't have peripheral vision. He'd tested her, and knew that her presence would be confusing every camera within a hundred yards. It was nothing too overt, more like a simple blur. The guards watching the monitors would probably think that snow had gathered on the lenses, nothing more.

Kovac wiped his bloody hand on his pants and unslung his AKS-74U. Stomach rumbling, he stepped over the last dead man, confident he'd feed later, preferably on someone that didn't taste like bad cabbage. Gregor finished and tossed the partially drained human over the side. The soldier was too weak to scream on the way down. Gregor went to the door, tilted his head to the side and listened. "There is no one on the other side," Gregor said as he tested the door. Of course it was locked.

The roof door was reinforced steel, but he'd brought flexo linear-shaped charges in case they needed to breach, though he was hoping to be deep inside the facility before they went loud. As soon as Doroshanko came floating over the edge, Kovac signaled for him to move up. They kept him masked and hooded, because otherwise the weird pale glow his skin gave off would give them away. Though not worth a damn in combat, it turned out Moldavian DNA possessed some handy traits. Their vampires could go anywhere they felt like. Doroshanko took his glove off, revealing oddly translucent flesh that gave off a glow like a lava lamp, and placed his hand on the door handle. The handle began to vibrate, and that spread out through the whole door. He moved out of the way. "It is unlocked. There will be no alarm."

They stacked up, ready to enter. Some would fight with firearms, others with their natural gifts. Most of them would stick together, but a few were better suited ranging around on their own as solo killers.

Kovac keyed his radio. "Strike team is in position."

"Extraction team is in position."

"Over watch is ready."

Those were the responses he'd been expecting. There was a heat in his chest, and this wasn't like the rush he'd used to feel before an op. This was different. This was better. He'd found them, brought them together, given them a mission and a purpose. Kovac had taken several individual apex predators and molded them into a lethal pack. Now they were going to fulfill their destiny.

"Execute."

— 2 —

Every country reacted differently to the I1V1 virus. When it was revealed that latent vampire DNA was activating among a small percentage of the population and causing strange predatory mutations, some governments saw this evolutionary offshoot as a threat and immediately cracked down. Others were more lenient, and tried to reconcile with their new vampire citizens.

Neither response would work.

The outcome had been inevitable from the minute Patient Zero was made known to the world.

There were two things he had studied exhaustively during his mortal life: war and history. The topics were hopelessly intertwined and rather complex. History was clear about what happened whenever a superior group clashed with an inferior one—the inferior society was always eventually conquered, absorbed, subjugated, or eliminated.

The real question was, which species was the inferior?

Evolution had made the vampire physically and mentally superior. Humans were their food. On the other hand, humanity had vastly greater numbers, established command and control, and infrastructure. It was now believed that vampires had existed before, hence the various cultural myths about them, as the folklore about their various subtypes was turning out to be far too accurate otherwise. If that was the case, despite the vampire's evident superiority, humans had wiped them out once before. He knew that many of his fellow vampires— those with enough sense to actually think about the future at least— assumed that it would happen again. It was just a matter of time.

Kovac had pondered on the implications of this prior loss. It suggested that humanity was better suited to win their competition and vampires would eventually be hunted to extinction once again. Of course vampires had lost last time. Individuals, no matter their skill, would eventually be destroyed by the side with superior numbers and logistics. Direct action between the two would always end the same way.

History demonstrated that there was only one way for a smaller force to defeat a much larger one.

The last twenty-five years of his mortal life had been spent learning the ins and outs of asymmetrical warfare. He'd spent a decade fighting an army made up of illiterate Third World goat rapists. His side had been armed with drones, satellites, and cruise missiles, while the other side had been armed with the technological equivalent of a Radio Shack and whatever the Iranians could smuggle in, and they'd managed to remain a pain in the world's collective ass the whole time. Approximately twenty thousand jackoffs in a country the size of Texas had held out against the most advanced military coalition ever assembled. They were motivated. They had direction. They could disappear among the locals. And most importantly, their opponent's political leadership did not have the stomach to go far enough to exterminate them because of collateral damage.

Vampires were spread across the world. Most of them could blend in, and in fact, millions of them were living and feeding off of the humans around them now with no one being the wiser. On their own, they were nothing. Vampires were pests, vermin, just murderers and cannibals with super powers. They were lone wolves that would be hunted down and eliminated, just like last time.

But if all vampires had direction, motivation, and coordination, the only way man could stop them was if they had to guts to kill everyone they suspected might be a threat. The minute mankind faltered and lost their nerve, when they lacked the balls to get the job done, then the competition would be decided.

To fight this war, he would need an army.

It was a good thing the Russians had already done so much recruiting for him.

— 3 —

"Status?" Kovac asked as he walked into the secret prison's command center. Bodies were strewn everywhere. Very few of them were in one piece. Shell casings rolled underfoot. His own AK was still smoking from the heat. He'd just shot a lot of people. Basco and

Gregor, who'd both had extensive military experience during their mortal lives, were waiting for him.

"We're secure," Basco reported. "Most of the humans are dead."

"Prisoners?"

"Ours or theirs?" Gregor shrugged. "We beat the shit out of the surviving humans and crammed them all in a few cells. We're freeing the vampire prisoners and loading them in the trucks now. Some of them are pretty fucked in the head. I'm talking psycho crazy, Boss, like they've gone feral."

His best intel had estimated that there were a hundred vampire prisoners being experimented on here. It turned out there was nearly twice that. They didn't have enough room on the trucks to get all of them out. "Anyone who doesn't cooperate, leave them. We don't have time to fuck around with drama queens..." Kovac checked his watch. Seven minutes had passed since the first shots had been fired at the checkpoint, and two minutes since the alarm had been sounded. They'd have a good head start. This place was so isolated that it would take time for reinforcements to arrive by helicopter, but if there were a bunch of savage vampires running loose in the facility, it would take time for the Russians to get the place secured enough to realize it had actually been a prison break. "Last thing we do before we leave is unlock all the cells. They're on their own."

"We should kill the rest of the humans," Gregor spat. "I cleared the medical wing. They were dissecting us. The vampires in there were still alive, but they were being peeled like fruit."

Basco nodded. "The cells aren't much better. They were penned in their own filth. It looks like most of them were being fed pig blood through hoses."

"On second thought, toss the surviving humans in with the vampires we leave behind. Maybe a good meal will cheer them up. Good work, men." They'd only taken one casualty, with Clark getting his brains blown out by an alert guard, and Meeker was missing, but it could be assumed that psychopath was off somewhere playing with his food. They'd killed at least a hundred Russian soldiers and an unknown number of support staff. He noticed that there was a human lying under a desk. He couldn't see her, but he knew she was trying to control her breathing so as to not make much noise. He could even smell that there were salty tears streaming down her cheeks. "Who is that?"

"One of their doctors, I believe," Basco answered.

She certainly didn't smell like cabbage. "Leave her to me."

There was a muffled squeak from beneath the desk.

"Tell Lily to take off. We need the cameras to work. Take video of the worst-looking captives, those shitty cells, and that medical wing. We'll stick it on the Internet. That's propaganda gold. Get moving. We're out of here in five."

"Do you still want to leave your message, Boss?" Gregor asked as he removed a small video recorder from a pouch on his vest.

"Of course. The more scared they are, the harder they push, the better we recruit." Kovac went to the desk, grabbed the doctor by the hair, and pulled the now screaming woman from her hiding place. "That's half the fun."

— 4 —

Langley, Virginia

The man in charge of America's vampire response shook hands with a CIA operative whose job didn't officially exist.

"Thank you for coming on such short notice, General."

"You know my time is valuable, so this had better be good." General May glanced around the situation room. Considering the level of spooky mischief that was decided in this place, it was remarkably humble. It looked like a conference room you'd find in any corporate office building. There were three CIA men shifting nervously in their seats, clutching folders sealed with literal red tape. He only knew one of them by name and the others hadn't made an effort to introduce themselves. "I've got a global crisis to avert, so let's make this quick."

"I'm really sorry." The CIA pukes seemed more squirrelly than usual, and that was saying something. "How is the containment going?"

"Get to the point, Stuart. V-8 is on an op right now. A couple vamps kidnapped a school bus and took a bunch of kids hostage. Nasty business. We're going in soon, so I'd much rather be watching that live than listening to your bullshit."

That just made Stuart's minions even more jittery, but they didn't realize that Director Stuart and the General went way back. He had been at Special Operations Command before his current posting at Red Storm, so he'd been giving Stuart—head of the National Clandestine Services branch of the CIA—grief for years.

"I'm afraid we've got a complicated situation on our hands."

Terrorists, vampires…for General May, it didn't really matter who the bad guy was. Men like Stuart would feed him the intel, men above them both would give the order, and then it was his job to figure out how to get his boys in place to pull the trigger.

"The situation is only as complicated as you make it out to be, which knowing you fuckers are involved, means it's probably bad," the General snapped. Director Stuart had always reminded him of Mr. Rogers. He even wore a sweater at work. How the hell could a self-respecting spymaster wear a fuzzy sweater? But General May knew that looks could be deceiving, and Stuart was a fellow merciless badass who knew how to get the job done. "So what's the deal?"

It was one of the unnamed minions who asked him the question. "Are you familiar with a Lieutenant Colonel Marko Kovac, US Army Special Forces?"

"Yeah, from Seventh Group. We first met at SOCSouth in Panama, only it was Captain Kovac back then, but I'm sure you already knew that."

"What do you know about his record?" asked the other.

This was a rather suspicious line of questioning. "Enlisted man, 82nd if I remember right. Then Rangers. Went OCS, made it through Selection, got his long tab. Went to the War College. In between that he volunteered for every deployment in every war we've had since Panama." The General pointed at the man's folder. "I've got a feeling that's all in there. Somalia, both Iraq wars, a couple trips through scenic Afghanistan, and every other shitty FID mission the Army could find, and that's just the official part…and I know that you know about Libya when he wasn't supposed to be there, and you probably know of some deployments that I'm not even cleared for. When he died in that helicopter crash it was a sad day for the Army."

"How would you assess Kovac's leadership capabilities?"

"Superb."

"And his loyalty?" added the other.

That hung in the air like a poisonous cloud.

He slammed his hand on the table. "Loyalty? Are you fucking kidding me?" General May had a terrible poker face, and the minions unconsciously pulled back from the table as a result of his angry glare. "I'd say that he was one of the best soldiers I've ever had the privilege of knowing. Who is talking shit? Is that what the CIA brought me in here for? Somebody is accusing Marko Kovac of selling state secrets or something? Bullshit. There's no way."

"And you're certain of that?" Stuart asked.

"Let me put it this way—if he was still alive when all of this I1V1 vampire virus crisis started, Kovac would have been the very first man that I requested for Operation Red Storm. The man was a tactical genius. He was like a Green Beret poster child. You can always tell the real quality of an officer by his men's loyalty, and anyone who served under Kovac in combat would gladly follow him into hell. Whatever turncoat son of a bitch you rolled up selling classified intel is trying to cover his ass by implicating a dead officer who isn't around to defend his name. We've seen it before."

"You have no idea how much I wish that was all this was about…" Stuart took a deep breath and held it for a moment. He exhaled, then shoved one of the folders across the table toward May. "Okay. Here's the deal. Lieutenant Colonel Kovac wasn't killed in a helicopter crash three years ago. That cover story came out of my office. He was MIA on an op in Syria."

"I didn't know we'd lost anyone in that aborted clusterfuck of a mission." That was terrible news, but not unheard of in his old line of work.

"We had Kovac checking out possible allies, but some of the rebels turned on us."

"There was a meeting with the rebel leaders, but it was a trap. It turned into a firefight," said one of the minions. He was younger than the other two, and he was in extremely good shape, which suggested he was a field agent rather than an analyst. "I had to pull us out."

"We don't leave men behind."

The man looked him square in the eye. "We were outnumbered a hundred to one and hanging in the wind with no backup, deniable and expendable. I saw Marko get shot. I had six other guys who were still alive and half of them were injured. I made the call and we ran…I did what I had to do…I thought he was dead."

General May stared back at him. He sensed no lies, distortion, or bullshit. It was the simple truth, one warrior to another. The General nodded. Explanation accepted.

"Turns out I was wrong," the field agent muttered.

"Play it." Stuart gestured at the other minion, who promptly began pushing buttons on a remote control. A giant TV on the far wall came on. "This video was made a little while after the Syria incident, but only recently discovered."

When the CIA was that fuzzy on dates, it meant that they had something to hide, but General May held his tongue and watched.

The picture was a close-up of a man with his face wrapped in cloth, concealing all of his features, except for a fanatic's eyes. He was speaking in Arabic. The camera pulled back, revealing that two more masked thugs, and a third man down on his knees between them, shirtless, filthy with dried blood and scabs, wrists zip tied together. They jerked his head back, and through the swelling, bruises, and lacerations of repeated beatings, General May could barely recognize the face of Marko Kovac. He struggled, but one of the rebels slugged him in the mouth.

The original speaker held up a rusty old butcher knife for the camera.

The office minion began to translate. "He will demonstrate to the Great Satan what happens when we meddle in their affairs—"

Stuart shushed him. They had all seen this sort of thing before.

The thugs shoved Kovac face down on the floor. They'd laid down a tarp. He struggled. Kovac was an excellent fighter and extremely fit for his age, but he was severely injured, his hands were tied, and he was being held down by two giant slabs of meat. There wasn't much he could do. One of them pulled back on his jaw, exposing his neck, while the other knelt on his back. The speaker went to them, placed the edge of the knife against the side of Kovac's neck and began to saw.

"Jesus…" General May had to look away. This was a friend.

"You're going to want to keep watching," Stuart suggested.

There was blood all over the tarp. The knife was dull. Kovac was thrashing. The speaker was still shouting propaganda as he worked. There was blood up to his elbows.

It was hard to tell what happened next. Kovac's hands had gotten free somehow. He placed them on the tarp and lifted himself off the floor. The speaker stepped back, confused. The two thugs tried to push him back down. One started kicking him, putting the boot to Kovac's ribs. Blood was still pumping from his neck as he struggled upward. Kovac stood. One hand flashed out, hitting a terrorist so hard that the thug flew off the screen in a blur. More blood splattered the tarp, the walls, even the ceiling.

"What the hell…"

The camera jerked wildly as the cameraman stumbled backwards, revealing that they were in the living room of an apartment, with average furniture and decorations on the wall, then back to Kovac and the terrorists. The other big man had wrapped Kovac up and was lifting him off the floor while the speaker slammed the knife into his chest. Kovac moved and it was almost too fast for the camera to track. He broke free of the thug and sent the speaker crashing away. Kovac grabbed the thug by the arm and…ripped it off.

He'd just pulled it right off the man's body. "Holy shit."

The cameraman must have been too startled to run, as his friend thrashed and screamed, blood spraying out of his torso, because he kept it focused on the action as Kovac walked toward the speaker and clubbed him with the severed arm. Kovac reached down, hoisted the speaker into the air, and dragged the screaming man next to his body. For the briefest instant, the camera picked up a flash of long white teeth, and then Kovac was biting down on the speaker's neck.

But he didn't just bite that son of a bitch—he shook him like a terrier with a rat. The speaker screamed and screamed as Kovac ripped him from side to side, flinging him about with impossible strength. Kovac drove one of his hands through the terrorist's flesh and into his guts. The cameraman came to his senses, dropped the camera, and probably ran for his life. They could hear him crying for help. The camera landed on the ground, but they could still see Kovac's legs, planted solid, and the lower half of the speaker's body thrashing about. Droplets of blood splattered against the lens as Kovac tore him apart.

There was one last, wet gurgle, and the speaker's mangled corpse was tossed aside to crash against the wall. Kovac's bloody, bare feet came toward the camera. He got down on his hands and knees. The hilt of the butcher knife was still sticking out of his chest. Kovac's blood-soaked face filled the screen. The laceration in the side of his neck was still drizzling. His eyes had turned solid red, like the orbs had filled with blood. His canines were far too long. When he spoke, his voice was far too deep.

"You wanted to send a message to the Great Satan? Well…I'm listening."

Kovac looked up and let out an animal growl. There was a noise off screen. It was the clack of a Kalashnikov's safety. He launched himself upward and was gone. There was gunfire. Then crashing and a sound like the ripping of wet cloth, more gun shots, and so much screaming.

The minion hit stop. "The sounds go on like that for a long time."

General May put his hands on the table. They were shaking.

Marko Kovac was a vampire.

Stuart was studying him. "We tracked this video back to a village outside of Damascus. Thirty seven men, women, and children were killed there in one night. The rebels blamed the regime and the regime blamed the rebels. Now we know what really happened. Lieutenant Colonel Kovac had been infected with the I1V1 virus, and was one of the unlucky ones. He underwent a mutation while being held prisoner by the rebels and we just saw the results."

"Please tell me they found Kovac's body in that village."

"No."

It had been too much to hope that the terrorists would actually do them a favor for once. The General leaned back in his chair and rubbed his face in his hands. It was all a genetic crap shoot who ended up getting their junk DNA activated by I1V1. Talk about shitty luck. If Kovac was still out there… "Gentlemen, this is bad."

"We were hoping you could help us assess the situation. You're the expert on vampires."

"No, Stuart. There's no such thing as an expert with these things. It's all too new. We've documented almost a hundred types of vampire now, and they're all over the board, abilities and psychology. Some go bug nuts murder crazy. Others hide it. Some are supposedly playing nice and trying to be good, not that I buy that for a second, but they can at least be semi-rational. Some vampires have wild personality changes. Who knows? I'll need a copy of this for my tech guys. They at least might be able to guess what genetic type he is. Damn it all to hell, I can't think of a worse person to end up infected."

"Lieutenant Colonel Kovac was cleared on many of our top secret operations," the analyst minion said.

The General snorted. "Cleared? That's nothing. I don't think you realize the magnitude of the situation. The US Army has spent the better part of the last thirty years teaching that man how to overthrow countries and wage guerilla wars. He knows all our dirty tricks and came up with a bunch of new ones. He knows our responses, our defenses, our plans, and how we think, because he is us. At this point I'm just hoping that Kovac does fall into the bat-shit crazy blood-lust category, because I can deal with that. That's just another animal looking for its next meal. But if he retains all his knowledge and reason? Holy shit. There are smart vamps out there forming terror cells, but I can deal with amateurs. The last thing we want is somebody like Kovac on the other side capable of plotting and molding those cells into a real fighting force. That would be a nightmare."

The CIA men shared frightened glances.

He felt a sinking feeling deep in the pit of his stomach. "Oh no…"

"We got this video a few hours ago from our liaison at the FSB. There was an attack on a facility the Russians were using to hold vampires."

The Russians were far more direct in their vampire response than this administration had allowed Red Storm to be. "Facility, as in one of their secret prisons they're using to experiment on vampires…come on, I'm not stupid. All professional courtesy to my Russian colleagues, those boys don't fuck around. When a Russian grows fangs and starts eating people, they don't stop to open dialogs about civil liberties."

"This recording is from a few days ago," said the minion with the TV remote.

"That's remarkably forthcoming by Ivan's standards."

"The FSB really thought we should see this," Stuart said.

The camera had been set on a desk or something of equivalent height. It showed a room filled with computers and monitors. There was blood spatter and bullet holes on the walls. The angle wasn't quite right to see for sure, but there were hints of bodies—a bit of red-stained clothing peeking around the back of a swivel chair, a shape in the corner that might be an outstretched hand, and peeking into the edge of the picture was a mass of blonde hair without any clue what it was attached to.

Blood began to pool under the hair.

There was movement in front of the camera, and a torso appeared, wearing Russian body armor and covered in mag pouches. The man pulled up a chair and sat directly in front of the camera. His face was momentarily covered, and the General realized that was because he was wiping blood from his mouth with a rag…no…a lab coat. Face cleaned, he tossed the lab coat aside.

"I am Marko Kovac. This is my declaration of war."

He appeared entirely human, though he looked much younger and stronger than the last time they'd met in person. Marko was in his fifties, but what was age to a vampire? They still weren't sure about that. But his eyes…they were different. They were frighteningly vacant of anything approaching humanity.

"This message is for the leaders of the efforts against vampires, and especially for my old friend, General May, of America's Operation Red Storm. I can't say that I was surprised to hear that you got the job. I have just finished liberating a vampire prison in Siberia. I'm sure most of you know of the place, even if you won't ever admit it. By the time you watch this I'll be long gone, but don't worry. I took a few souvenirs. All those millions of vampires that are still sitting on the fence, thinking they can sneak by, or live in peace with you? Once they see that humans consider us nothing more than lab rats, they'll join the cause."

"The videos are already all over the Internet," Stuart supplied. "NSA is trying to track the origins."

But that wasn't the part that had concerned the General.

When Kovac smiled he didn't even have fangs. "You heard me correctly. Millions. Not thousands…millions. I've seen your estimates. You have no idea how wrong you are. Most of us are hiding in plain sight. There are more of us every day. The virus has swept the planet, but the awakening isn't instantaneous. For some it is faster than others. So far, you've only seen the tip of the iceberg. The newly awakened have an advantage over the first of us…they know how the humans around them will react. So they'll continue playing at their mortal lives, pretending to be like you. They'll live with you by day and hunt you by night. The more they kill, the more you fear them, the more desperately you search. You've got no choice. The vampires among you have access to your food, your infrastructure, your money, even your secrets, so you can't afford not to eradicate us. So you have to push, and that means you'll make us push back. There are suckers on both sides who think we can work this out, but that's wishful thinking. You know it, and I know it, but the rest of the world hasn't caught on yet. I will convince the undecided."

General May knew exactly where this was going, and he didn't like it.

"One of the first things you taught me, General, was that if you're going to fight a war, you fight to win. Anything other than a total commitment gets your men killed. Your governments are weak. They want peace. They don't realize they should want survival. Your hands are tied. Mine won't be. Vampires are coming for you. I will train them. I will arm them. I will forge them into the scythe that will harvest you like wheat. There won't be any frontal assaults in this war. This is a war of attrition and time is on my side. This is a war of shadows and that is where we live. Every time a dam breaks or plane crashes, when vampires bomb your cities or poison your water, you'll wonder if that was me. Only you'll never know the answer for sure."

His voice had gotten deeper and deeper as he spoke. There was no trace of the good man General May had known before. Kovac got out of the chair and picked up the video camera. The view temporarily shifted to show that the hair belonged to a young woman missing half her neck, then it was back on Kovac's face

"From this point on my existence is like a black hole. You will only know I am real by the absence of light."

The picture went black.

<h2 style="text-align:center">– 5 –</h2>

Fort Bragg, North Carolina

General May studied the latest reports. Killings were happening all over the country, and they were occurring at a steadily increasing pace, and beneath those average murders, he looked for a pattern. His search was interrupted by a knock on the frame of his open office door. It was one of his V-8 strike team leaders. "You wanted to see me, General?"

He returned the salute. "Yes, I did. Close the door and take a seat, Captain."

He was a handsome young man, and all indications were that he was one hell of a soldier. His strike team loved him. It was saying something when a twenty-six-year old, newly promoted Captain could command that much respect from a group made up of hardened combat vets. The Captain waited, probably suspecting that he'd done something wrong, because why else would the General in charge of Red Storm call him in for anything other than an ass-chewing.

"I read your report on Peoria. Moving that soon after hitting the ground was a gutsy call."

The Captain tried to think of a good response that might lessen the expected ass-chewing. "I assessed the situation. The lead vampire seemed erratic. I recognized what type he was, and how he was behaving made me think the hostages were in imminent danger, so I made the call."

"You smoked four vampires, rescued twenty school kids, and your men didn't get so much as a scratch on them. Excellent work."

"I have an excellent team, sir. They train hard."

"Take the compliment, Captain. I don't give them very often."

That put him slightly more at ease. He even smiled a bit. "Thank you, sir."

This was more difficult that he'd expected it to be, but he had to plow forward. "I'm putting together a team for a special assignment. I'm thinking you might be an asset for it, but first I need to ask you a few difficult questions. I want your no bullshit response. This isn't a Power Point to make the General happy. No political correctness. I need to know the God's honest truth of how you see some things, Captain."

It was obvious he hadn't expected General May to call him in to discuss philosophy. "Yes, sir."

"I think you know vampires better than anyone. You've worked with Luther Swann several times now and I know you've read all his stuff. He thinks we can coexist with vampires. Do you?"

"That's a tough one, sir. Personally, I like Dr. Swann. I think he's a smart guy and he means well. The President says that we can and we should try to—"

"This is off the record. Don't blow smoke up my ass. Can humans and vampires coexist peacefully?"

"Some of the types? Maybe. There are a few mutations where they can survive without feeding off of humans. Them, you can treat it like a genetic disorder."

"And for the rest."

"Most of them..." The Captain paused, probably deciding how bad he wanted to sabotage his career. "No. Not only no, but hell no. I'm sorry, sir, and I know we answer to a civilian authority, so I will follow my orders, but I don't think they realize what we're up against out there. The people talking about coexisting are living in ivory towers. This is an academic thought-exercise for them. They've not crawled down in the corpse piles like I have, or looked some ghoul in the face while it's eating a baby it just sucked out of pregnant woman."

"So you think that our direction is incorrect?"

The Captain swallowed hard. He was treading on dangerous ground and he knew it. "We're their food, sir. Sure we can coexist, just like we do with cows."

"And what about their civil liberties?"

"I'm a very big fan of the Constitution, General, and I took a solemn oath to defend it. I had to think long and hard about that when I accepted this assignment. All the guys on the strike teams have to. These aren't foreign soldiers. They're not even terrorists. A little while ago they were regular folks who got a disease. I believe all men are created equal and should enjoy equal protection under the law, but these…things, the feeders, and the ghouls, and the suckers, and freaks, the heart stealers, and the spear tongues, they are not men anymore. If somebody gets infected, turns, and they never harm a fly, I've got no problem with them, but the others? Give me a clean shot and I will put them in the ground."

The Captain was a tough one, but considering some of the weird, violent shit he'd seen over the last year, it wasn't a surprise. "And what about the regular folks that turn? They were good people before. Hypothetically speaking, do you think they're actually still the same person they were before? Do you think they've just been overpowered by the disease?"

"No, General, they aren't the same person they were before. The way I see it, once they've crossed that line, there's no coming back. They have to be destroyed. By their fruits, ye shall know them."

"Are you a religious man, Captain?"

"Does it matter?"

"For this assignment, yes."

He nodded. "I wasn't before I had this job, but when you've seen what I've seen, there comes a point when blaming a virus doesn't cut it. This may sound crazy, General, and I don't know what else to call it, but I believe in the soul…I know that in some of these vampires at least, when they turn, that human soul is gone. It's extinguished. Replaced. By what, I can't tell you, but it is evil. Pure, absolute, literal evil."

"That'll do…" General May picked up a folder which had been sealed in red tape. He handed it across the desk. "We need to talk about what really happened to your father. I'm afraid I've got some bad news for you, Captain Kovac."

"LET GOD SORT 'EM OUT" PT. 5

Jonathan Maberry

— 5 —

Pine Deep, Pennsylvania
The Second V-War - Day 13

Swann could actually see the moment when the battle turned. It started with a vampire rushing through the smoke toward Big Dog, who had knelt to reload his shotgun. The vampire came too fast for the soldier to avoid. A hand flashed out and the shotgun went spinning away. The vampire's second blow caught the sergeant across the face. The blow actually lifted the Big Dog's whole body into the air and sent him crashing into the dining room table barricade.

With incredible, blinding speed, the vampire leapt after the sergeant and pounced on him.

Other vampires rushed the remaining V-8 soldiers and in an instant the battle changed from a gunfight to the most brutal hand-to-hand combat Swann had ever seen. Everyone was kicking, striking, clawing, gouging, biting. Everyone.

LaShonda was locked together with a wiry Asian vampire. Both had knives. Both were bleeding. The vampire kept lunging with powerful thrusts, but LaShonda moved like a dancer, twisting aside each time and slashing with small, short cuts to her attacker's arms and chest. The vampire was much faster and stronger, but it was clear LaShonda was the more dangerous knife fighter.

In the entrance to the dining room, however, Big Dog was not faring as well. The vampire he fought was one of the most terrifying and powerful European vampires—a *nelapsi* from the Czech Republic. Swann had written extensively about this kind of monster. It was driven by an insatiable bloodlust, a true appetite for destruction. There were folkloric accounts and legends of *nelapsi* destroying entire villages, killing every human and every animal, leaving nothing behind but blood-soaked ground and wreckage. The *nelapsi* delighted in tearing their victims apart or crushing them in a bone-snapping embrace.

Big Dog was fighting back with every ounce of his own prodigious strength and all of his deadly combat skills. He drove a knee into the vampire's groin, smashed him across the face with two lightning-fast elbow smashes, tore out a fistful of hair, and chopped it across the throat. The blows rocked the vampire, but none of them seemed able to stop it. Swann racked his brain for the secrets of what made this vampire vulnerable. Every vampire was in some way, even the most feared—the dreaded *Draugr* and the ferocious *Alp.*

Heart, he thought. And then he shouted it into the team radio. "Big Dog! Go for the heart! It's the only way!"

The *nelapsi* raked the sergeant with his claws, ripping the whole front of the Kevlar vest to ribbons. Big Dog responded by head-butting him with the rim of his helmet. The *nelapsi's* nose exploded into red, but it only laughed, energized by its own pain and blood. Big Dog tore his knife from its sheath and thrust it just as the vampire darted forward and sunk its teeth into the Big Dog's shoulder. The sergeant screamed in pain. The vampire merely grunted as the blade stabbed into his heart.

Into his heart.

Heart.

"Jesus Christ," yelled Swann. "No!"

The *nelapsi*, unique among all vampires, did not have a single heart. It had a second one, and only by destroying them both could the monster be killed.

The creature worried at Big Dog's shoulder, tearing and slashing, spraying the floor with blood.

"Two hearts!" shrieked Swann. "*It has two hearts!*"

Swann did not remember getting up. He did not remember even thinking about it. He was up. Moving. Running through the smoke. Running past figures locked in bloody battles. Running.

Running.

He reached the shattered table. Without breaking stride he kicked at one of the legs. It cracked. He kicked it again and again until the oak splintered and the leg fell to the floor. Swann stooped, snatched it up, reversed it in his hands, raised it, and with a savage cry of mingled horror, terror and rage, drove the jagged point of the broken end down into the back of the *nelapsi*.

In the movies staking a vampire always looks easy. As if there's no toughness of skin, or density of muscle. As if there's no bone.

The spike went in only two inches and stuck fast.

The *nelapsi* screamed, though. It reared back from Big Dog, twisting around, lashing out. Swann felt himself falling. He had no memory of the blow that struck him. None.

His left eye seemed to go black. His left side felt empty. Gone.

He looked up with one eye at the monster as it rose above him, a knife buried in its chest and the table leg in its back. He reached around to claw at the spike. Blood dribbled from its chin, blood ran down its body, but it was still alive.

Still alive.

It was going to kill him.

Then it was going to help the other vampires kill the rest of V-8.

The rest of the humans.

It was going to kill *us*.

They're going to kill us all.

That was how Swann's brain framed the thought. They. Us.

Down deep in his soul the civilized man he was screamed at the wrongness of everything that was happening around him.

Then a shape rose up between him and the vampire. Huge. Bloody. A creature of rage that bellowed like a monster. Like a bear.

Like a big dog.

The sergeant threw himself at the vampire and knocked it backward against the wall. The impact was so loud and wet. The *nelapsi* froze, his eyes going wide with shock.

Big Dog cocked his fist and punched him in the chest, right in the center, right over the sternum.

Again.

And again.

And with each blow the vampire fell closer and closer to the wall.

On the fourth punch, the front of the vampire's chest tore apart and the jagged point of the table leg burst through.

That fast the vampire was gone. The light went out of its eyes, the power fled from its limbs.

The knife and the spike.

The creature died.

Big Dog spun around. His face was bloody but he was grinning with the madness of battle.

Dear God, thought Swann. *He's enjoying this.*

Big Dog stooped and picked up a Sig Sauer automatic that had fallen from some dead hand. He aimed and fired, aimed and fired, aimed and fired.

LaShonda pushed away the corpse that a moment ago had been trying to tear out her throat. She rolled to her knees, drew her sidearm, aimed and fired.

And that was how it ended.

The surviving members of V-8 hunted the last of the vampires down and killed them all.

There was no attempt to take prisoners.

That moment had passed.

The slaughter was complete.

The battle was…

Swann could not bear to use the word "won."

Nor could he say that it was over.

Darkness wanted to take him. It clawed at him.

And he let it take him down.

"THE HIPPO" PT. 1

Scott Sigler

— 1 —
Cry and Cry Again

The little girl cried.

She cried loud. She cried non-stop. The sound of it echoed through the night, bounced off the walls of abandoned buildings, burnt-out cars, reached up to the star-blocking clouds.

Harry sat very still. He watched—from a distance, of course. He couldn't make his move too quickly just because that girl made enough noise to wake the dead. Bloods were fast. Bloods were strong. And, lately, the bloods were *organized*.

Those cries would draw them in, Harry knew, and if he and Rebecca didn't mind their Ps and Qs, the monsters might catch him off-guard.

The girl was still alive, obviously. Too stupid to stay quiet, too weak to know her mewling put her at risk. She probably always got a trophy in kids' soccer even though she didn't do shit to help the team win, and hell, these days it didn't matter if the team won at all. Coddled parents didn't even bother to keep score for their second-generation coddled children. Fucking kids these days…no grit in them at all.

Harry wished he could find the child psychologists responsible for that horseshit and kick them dead square in the nuts, and/or vajay-jay—Harry wasn't sexist, mind you. Why would he do that? Because coddled kids weren't *tough*; they didn't know what it meant to get the shit knocked out of them, didn't know what it meant to *lose*. Losing teaches awareness. In a game of soccer, awareness matters a lot. In life—especially in Oakland—awareness keeps you alive.

Out there, the little girl was crying her damn fool head off instead of staying quiet and finding a good place to hide. She wanted someone to come and get her instead of realizing she was on her own.

"We're all on our own, sweetie," Harry whispered. "Ain't that right, Rebecca?"

Rebecca didn't answer. She rarely did.

The crying girl didn't understand what she was really doing: she wasn't calling for help—she was calling for her own death.

Harry would save the girl if he could. She'd been going on like that for maybe ten minutes, long enough for him to know that if there were any Bloods in the area they were already on the way.

So, he and Rebecca would wait. And while waiting, why not have a bit of a snack?

Harry rolled a little to his right side so he could reach inside his long coat. Slowly, silently, he pulled out a small, square Tupperware container. The container wasn't that deep, just large enough for four mini-cupcakes pressed in so tight they were almost square instead of round.

Red velvet. Cream-cheese frosting. Harry made them himself, using his father's recipe. A wonderful way to pass the time between outings.

Slowly, silently, he took one out, set it on the ground in front of him. Slowly, silently, he sealed the container and slid it back inside the inner coat pocket.

Slowly, silently, he peeled the paper from the cupcake.

– 2 –
Cry and Cry Again, Part II

Tavena couldn't see the girl, but she heard her. Tavena could almost taste those cries.

Cries of fear…cries of *pain*.

"Gotta be wounded," Peter said. "Easy pickings."

His words sounded wet. Was he drooling? Tavena would have yelled at him, but she was damn near drooling herself. A wounded little girl? Didn't get any better than that.

Peter reached inside his dark-blue denim coat and drew his sidearm. He flipped off the safety. Two weeks ago, Tavena would have called that a *gun*, or maybe a *piece*, back when she still called magazines *clips*.

But now she knew better.

She looked at his weapon. "You think the person making that noise is going to hurt us? You scared, Pete? Hell, maybe you should be—she sounds at least seven."

Peter started to shake his head in annoyance, then stopped. His eyes squinted shut. He pinched the bridge of his nose with his free hand.

"Pete, you all right?"

He nodded lightly. "Yeah, headache is still a bitch."

"You want a Tylenol?"

"Does Tylenol even work on us anymore?"

Tavena shrugged. "I don't know. I haven't had a headache since I changed. And when I said *you want a Tylenol*, I meant *stop being a fucking pussy already*."

Peter opened his eyes, blinked rapidly. "Oh, sorry, I didn't understand you at first. I only speak *bossy-ass bitch* as a second language. I'm rusty."

Tavena sighed. She didn't like Peter. No one did, really. No one except Charlemagne, apparently. And if Charlie liked him, did the opinion of anyone else really matter?

Nope, not one bit.

Peter fucked up left and right, yet he got private meetings with Charlie. Hell, he'd been in her truck for two hours before this very mission. Maybe Charlie saw something in Peter that no one else did. Maybe they were screwing each other silly—Tavena didn't know.

Whatever their relationship, Charlie had finally sent Peter out on this mission, making him do some actual work for a change. Unfortunately, she'd assigned him to Tavena.

Peter stopped blinking, made an obvious effort to control his pain.

"I'm fine," he said. "I'm okay."

"Didn't ask if you were."

"Thanks for caring."

"You and Charlie do tequila shots in her truck or something? Maybe you're hung over."

"No shots," he said. He thought for a second, then shrugged. "Maybe hung over, though, or something like that."

"Which happens without booze, how?"

"Gas," Peter said. "She had this doc there, asked me to be a guinea pig, see if gas would work on us."

Well, at least they weren't screwing. Not unless Charlie liked her men unconscious.

"What kind of gas?"

He shrugged. "How would I know? The kind that works on us, that's what kind. I was out the whole time."

Well, that was just great. Tavena wasn't just saddled with the group fuck-up, she was saddled with a *stoned* version of the group fuck-up.

"You sure you're good for this, Pete? Oakland is no place to screw around, and there's a psycho killer somewhere out here, in case you forgot."

"I haven't forgotten *anything*," he snapped. "I'm just hungry is all. I know how dangerous it is out here, I got shot just last week. Twice. Doesn't feel that good, you know?"

Tavena did know. Ten days ago, she'd taken a round in the leg. She got the guy who pulled the trigger, of course. She'd taken her time with him. He'd been a big one, maybe six-three and at least two-thirty. Before her change, a guy like that would have fucked her up, then probably gone ahead and actually fucked her. That's what big guys did to women. But *after* the change? He'd begged her to stop.

Paybacks are a bitch.

"I'm hungry," Pete said.

"So I've heard."

"Let's get the girl."

And there it was, one of the many reasons no one liked Pete.

"We're supposed to be looking for a killer," Tavena said. "It's not snack-time."

"Napoleon said an army marches on its stomach."

Fucker was always quoting shit. He thought it made him smart. Well, he *was* smart, for sure, smarter than she was and she knew it, but Peter was also a coward. Even with the strength and speed that came with his change, he was always so cautious, so careful. Every time the guns came out, he angled to be the last one into the fight, if not just stay behind altogether and "protect the rear," as he liked to call it.

That was why Charlie had put Tavena in charge. Peter hated both a) blacks, and b) women, which made serving under Tavena a real pain in his lily-white ass.

Still, the boy had a way with words. He could almost always talk people into getting what he wanted.

"Come on, Tavena," he said, his voice smooth and sweet. "We'll just take a look. We're still following orders…were *supposed* to look around, right? We'll just *look* where that girl happens to be."

Tavena's stomach rumbled. She wondered if he heard it. The smile on his face told her that he had.

"You know what, Peter?"

"What?"

"One of these times, that clever-ass mouth of yours is gonna get you into trouble."

His smile faded. "Is this one of those times?"

Tavena unslung her shotgun. Her eyesight had improved with the change, but hadn't helped the fact that she still couldn't shoot for shit. With the Remington 870, however, she didn't have to hit something dead on—just aim in the general direction and let the spray do the rest.

"Nope," she said. "This isn't one of those times. I'm hungry, too. You go first."

Peter looked at her weapon, a thoughtful frown on his face. "You know, with that shotgun and your foot speed, maybe it makes more—"

She lowered the barrel until it pointed at the man; he stopped talking.

"Keep trying to put thoughts in my head, Pete, and *one of those times* is gonna come a whole lot faster than you'd like."

He glanced down at the black shotgun's barrel—which was aimed right at his nuts—then back to Tavena.

He smiled. "How about I go first?"

"Good idea," Tavena said. "You're always so full of good ideas."

– 3 –
Cry and Cry Again, Part III

Harry ate a second cupcake. Delicious. The frosting was what set off a proper red velvet, and his frosting was the bomb.

He put the wrapper in an outside pocket, where it joined the first. You couldn't leave anything behind, not even a scrap of paper from a delicious mini-cupcake. Back in his cop days, scouring the scene around a murder always meant looking for not only shell casings and footprints, but also food wrappers and even crumbs—any detritus that could tell you *this is where the perp was*. So, no paper left behind. And no crumbs, either, but that wasn't a problem because

Harry made some *seriously* fucking moist cupcakes. Crumbs were the mark of either an amateur, or one of those vegan motherfuckers and their gluten-free bullshit sawdust recipes. Seriously, if you want to live like a herd animal, then stop cooking and just go eat some grass.

Movement.

It was dark, but Harry's eyes were well adjusted to what little light there was. The man was fifty meters out, sidearm in his right hand. Thick coat, black, or maybe dark blue. Harry watched him cut across the lawn of a small ranch house, move onto the sidewalk outside the next house in line, then hunker down by the back bumper of a Toyota with no tires.

The guy didn't look like much. A twitchy type. Seemed to be moving cautiously, though, and that was…

Other movement. Smaller person—a woman, probably—carrying a shotgun. Harry couldn't make out the model. She passed wide of the Toyota, kept going, then came to a stop fifteen meters further down the street, fifteen meters closer to the crying girl. The woman raised the shotgun to her shoulder and swept the area in front of her. After about ten seconds, the man stood and advanced past her.

Motherfucker—they were leapfrogging.

Someone was training them. Not a good sign.

Harry licked his fingers. He wiped them dry against his coat, and then settled down to wait.

— 4 —
Kids These Days

Tavena slid to a stop by a burned-out Ford F150. Recently burned, judging by the greasy, melted-plastic smell oozing out of the charred interior. A block ahead, the girl was just sitting there, her butt on the pavement, back leaned against the front right wheel of a boxy, graffiti-covered truck. The truck's sides had panels halfway up, the kind that were hinged at the top. How ideal: the girl was resting against a food truck.

She was still crying, the face-wrinkling kind of cry that shut her eyes tight, left her mouth open. A string of dangling drool caught light from the streetlamp above.

The girl was directly under that streetlamp…the only light still working on the street, the only illumination at all, really, as the people left in Oakland knew well enough to shut their run-down houses up tight and keep everything dark. House lights at night were the equivalent of neon signs saying, "*Come kill us!*"

Just the one light…and the girl right under it.

And then, Tavena smelled blood.

The girl was *wounded*.

Tavena's hunger spiraled up, almost made her leave her position and just rush forward, but she stayed put. Charlie had taught her better. Discipline. Charlie said self-control turned brawlers into soldiers and soldiers into armies. Charlie said it took an army to win a war.

Think, Tavena, think…ignore the hunger and the smells and the sounds…something isn't right.

A gleam of metal, on the ground by the girl's butt. A weapon? No, not a weapon…the girl's hands were behind her back, the gleam was—

Peter shot by, all speed and intensity. He wasn't moving to the next logical leapfrog position, he was moving as fast as he could, going straight for the girl.

The coward attacking the weak, attacking the girl who was *chained* to the truck.

Tavena started to shout out a warning, but stopped: if there were Beats around she couldn't reveal her position, but she had to warn Peter, order him back. Indecision froze her for a few seconds, which was all the time Peter needed to close in.

The girl saw Peter coming—her screams rose higher and louder and faster.

The sound of snapping metal rang through the night; Peter's feet stopped cold while momentum threw his body down in a violent arc that slammed his face against the pavement. Something on Peter's feet, glinting under the streetlamp.

A *trap*? Someone used a little girl as *bait*?

No…not *someone*…

Tavena had to let Charlie know, but she had to help Peter, couldn't leave one of her own behind.

She sprinted around the F150, her beyond-powerful legs closing the distance to Peter in seconds.

The girl, still screaming, still *bleeding*, her face a wet, red mask of terror hiding behind a sheet of thin, blonde hair.

Peter, his left leg pinned between two half-circles of blackened metal. Triangular trap-teeth buried in blood-soaked denim, Peter's leg flopping sickly below the half circles. He screamed, too, a whiney bellow that would have sounded more at home coming from the little girl's throat.

Tavena stopped, her hands flexing on the shotgun. The smell of the girl's blood had short-circuited her brain…she was in the open, under a streetlight, lit up like a solo dancer at center stage.

Lit up like a *target*.

In that moment, Tavena knew she had blown it, knew that Charlie would be so disappointed, then a *crack* echoed off the mostly abandoned houses as something slammed into her left hip. Heightened senses let her hear the bone cracking, *splintering*, let her feel shrapnel-shards of the same exploding and driving through flesh from the inside out, let her sense the bullet tumbling, gouging its way through muscle and vein until it exploded from her inner left thigh in a meat-pie spray.

The streetlamp spun above her; Tavena found herself on the ground.

You've been shot…put pressure on it…

She was changed, she could heal so fast. Could she die? Stupid question—of course she could die. Plenty of her kind had fallen to the San Francisco mercs—and to the psycho.

The pain pummeled her all at once, a steamroller of agony that squashed the air from her lungs.

Tavena rolled to her back. Her right leg worked, so did her arms, but the left leg just *screamed* and held her in place like an anchor wedged deep in ocean-floor rock.

"Tavena! Get up, you dumb bitch!"

Peter, shouting at her.

"You stupid whore, get *up*! Help me…I've almost got it, just get up and help *get this fucking thing off of me!*"

She lifted her head, looked down the length of her body. Peter had jammed his fingers between the trap's triangular teeth. He was pulling them apart, slowly, arms trembling with the effort. An impossible task for a normal man, and just the tiniest bit beyond his enhanced strength. If she could move to him, help him, the ruined leg would slide free.

The goddamn girl kept screaming.

Why did she have to smell *so good*?

Boot heels on the pavement. Coming quickly, but not running. Tavena turned to her right, to the source of the sound.

A fat man—beyond fat, *obese*, but moving with purpose—stepped into the streetlamp's outermost illumination. Black trench coat hanging heavy, flat-black material making him more a blob of shadow than a man. He carried a rifle, also black, like an M-16 but stretched out with an oversized mag and some kind of rectangular thing on the end of the barrel. Black boots, black pants, black skin, not a shiny spot on him save for two eyes set deep back below fat black cheeks and heavy eyebrows.

Tavena blinked, tried to process what was happening, but could only think one clear thought—that fat man was *handsome*.

"*Tavena*, help me! Goddammit, get the fuck *up*!"

Peter, pulling hard against the trap's jagged-toothed half-circles, his arms trembling, needing just a little more space to free his ruined leg, but that was silly because he wouldn't be able to run and where would he go and it was really kind of too bad that he couldn't actually turn into a bat and fly away like the old legends said.

The fat man stopped five feet from Peter.

"Oh, don't get up on my account," the fat man said, then put the rifle stock to his shoulder, aimed, and fired.

Peter's left hand *popped* in a cloud of blood and bone that caught the streetlamp's gleam, a red and white firework mist that sparkled in the air before drifting away. The trap snapped back together again, triangular teeth punching in even farther than before. Tavena wondered if Peter's soaked jeans were the only thing that kept his shin and foot from falling free.

At least Peter stopped screaming. That was *something*, wasn't it?

Peter lifted what was left of his hand, held it in front of his shocked face. A ground-up mess of red. Raw hamburger on a stick. The pinkie was still there, and most of the thumb, but the rest of his fingers were nowhere to be seen. He could heal, yeah, but not *regenerate*—Peter was fucked.

So was Tavena. She knew it. Her body started to shiver. So cold all of the sudden, as if the temperature had just plummeted fifty degrees.

The man took another step toward Peter. The little girl screamed even louder.

Peter looked up at the shambling mound of black-clad black man.

"I'll kill you," Peter said, trying to sound fierce but not getting anywhere near it.

The man let out a lip-flapping huff of air, like he was casually impersonating a horse.

"Probably not," he said. He raised the long rifle and fired again. Peter's upper body spun away and down. He lay on his side, much of his right shoulder just *gone*, blood pouring from the wound to slicken the shreds of his blue coat.

The fat man turned to the little girl.

"You should shut up now," he said. "Unless, of course, you want to do this again tomorrow night?"

The crying instantly ceased. The girl's lips quivered and her whole body trembled, as if the cries inside of her were fighting hard to swell her up and rip out. She was more afraid of the fat man than anything else in the world.

The fat man turned to Tavena, swinging the strange weapon as he did until she was looking straight down the wide barrel.

"Evening," he said. "Believe it or not, you can heal from that wound. If you be good and stay still, you get to live. At least a little while longer, anyway, and can any of us really ask for more?"

Tavena stared at him. So cold. Pain crashed through her, consumed her.

"I asked you a question," the man said. "Will you be good?"

Something inside of her wanted to say, *Yes, Daddy, I'll be good*, something bottled up from way back when, something that she'd thought had evaporated forever after her change, but it was still in there, just waiting for this monster to chip it out of her soul.

She nodded.

"Good," the fat man said. He slung the rifle. He reached into his long, flat-black coat and pulled out a keychain. He knelt next to the girl, his wide body blocking any view of her. A rattle, then the man stood, folded a pair of handcuffs and made them vanish inside his coat.

The little blond girl stared up at him. Tavena had killed a dozen men, a half-dozen women, even two children. All of them had looked at her with utter terror in their last moments, but all of those expressions combined couldn't match the girl's horrified stare.

The man jerked a thumb at the spray-painted truck. "If I was you, I'd get into the back and come with me. First-aid kit is in there and your cut isn't that bad. I'll call Academi and tell them to come get you. Maybe they'll take you in as a refugee. You're young enough, they might not have the heart to leave you on this side of the bridge. If you don't want to come with me, I doubt you'll make it through the night."

Tavena couldn't keep her head up. She let it slowly fall back to the pavement, then heard the pitter-patter of little feet sprinting away. The fat man was right: the girl wouldn't make it. The smell of her blood would bring out the loners and the strays. By sunrise, she'd be dead—if she was lucky, and didn't wind up with the kind that liked to keep prey alive as long as possible so the meat stayed fresh.

The little footsteps faded away.

"Kids," the man said. "Amirite?"

Tavena didn't answer him.

Peter moaned softly. "Help...me..."

The fat man laughed. "Ain't that a hoot? I bet you've heard people say that a bunch, and you know who helped them? No one. Your time's up, asshole."

Tavena lifted her head again, saw the man reach into his coat and wondered just how many pockets were inside of it, a coat so big it could be a tent. The fat man pulled out something short and stubby, something that fit perfectly in his large fist. The streetlamp's light glinted off something circular attached to the end of it.

The man pressed a button; the circle spun with a soft whirring noise. A saw. A *bone* saw.

The fat man put his knee against Peter's neck, leaned all his weight against it, pinning Peter's head to the pavement. The saw descended, brought forth a new kind of high-pitched scream.

Peter's good leg kicked, but not for long.

– 5 –
Harry Comes Home

Dawn broke as Harry closed in on home. The single garage slot was just wider than the truck, not quite two inches to spare on either side, less than an inch clearance from the roof.

Once inside, Harry stopped the truck. He cracked the window and listened—nothing.

He rolled down the window all the way.

"Dad? I'm home."

His father was much further inside the high school and couldn't hear him, but that wasn't the point. The salutation served another purpose: letting any trespassers at the abandoned McClymonds High know that someone had already squatted here. Buildings like this drew thugs, bums, wandering homeless that didn't speak English, and—of course—the occasional Blood scouting for a place to hide from the local vamp-hunting militia. Calling out the phrase "I'm home" let anyone present know the school only *looked* abandoned. Most of the time that was enough to make people—the smart ones, anyway— find a quiet way out. Sometimes they announced their presence to Harry, saying they were leaving and that they didn't want any trouble. Harry usually let those people go.

Some people didn't leave, or actually *wanted* trouble. Those people left, eventually—or at least their corpses did.

And, sometimes, the visitors ran into Dad. When that happened, the problem kind of took care of itself.

With his right hand, Harry reached inside his long coat and drew Big Baby. He slid the driver's door open, eased off the seat to the internal step and then down to the dirty concrete floor.

He moved to the truck's rear, pulled the chain that lowered the roll-down garage door. He pulled it slowly, making as little noise as possible. When it shut, he finally allowed himself to relax a little. He wasn't safe by any means, there could still be trespassers in the halls and rooms, but at least he wouldn't have to fight his way out of the loading dock.

– 6 –

Tavena's Tour

Tavena knew she didn't have long to live. No one could hurt this much and survive, not even one of the Changed.

She lay on her back, strapped down tight to a dolly. Her right shoulder was wedged against what she thought was a stainless steel sink, her left shoulder not quite touching what she knew was an oven. She'd recognized those things when that monster of a man put her in here.

He'd also set something on her chest. Some kind of plastic container. Tupperware, maybe? Tavena couldn't really see her chest because the asshole had put a metal mask over her mouth, which blocked the view even when she could muster enough energy to open her eyes.

Just above her head, the food truck's rear doors swung open. A fat hand reached in, lifted the Tupperware container from her chest and set it aside. She was pulled back, heard the grind of poorly-oiled wheels on the truck's stainless steel floor, then she was out and upright.

She was in a small, industrial garage of some kind. No light, but she didn't really need light to see anymore.

The man tugged at the straps around her chest and arms, around her stomach, her thighs and her shins, straps that held her tight to the dolly. She'd tried to break free during the drive here, but she felt so weak from the wound. That, and the straps were made out of something far stronger than canvas. Had she been at her full strength, she wasn't sure if she could have broken free. The efficiency of the restraints made one thing horrifyingly clear—the fat man had done this before.

She realized he was only using one hand to test the straps. The other hand held a giant-sized revolver. It was so big it looked almost comical. Focusing on it was better than focusing on the endless pain.

"What the hell is that thing?"

The metal mask made her voice sound tinny. He walked in front of her, looked at her. And there was something else to focus on, another mental life preserver to keep her afloat in a sea of agony—this morbidly obese black man had *blue* eyes.

The man lifted the handgun, which seemed just as overweight as he was. The barrel alone had to be almost two feet long. She'd held a Magnum revolver once, and the fat man's weapon was much bigger than that.

"Oh, this?" He held it closer to her face, barrel pointed away so she could see it in profile. "This is just Big Baby. Say, *hello*, Big Baby"

The man then talked out of the corner of his mouth in a high-pitch voice, an amateur's impression of a ventriloquist.

"Hello, you nasty piece of shit. I hope you die."

The fat man clucked his tongue in disappointment.

"Oh, come on now, Big Baby," he said. "This woman is a guest in our home. If she behaves, we'll let her go."

"That's a fucking mistake, Harry."

Tavena stared at him. She didn't know what to think. Was he fucking with her?

"A mistake, I tell ya. Have me give this cunt a six-hundred caliber money-shot right now and be done with it."

The fat man laughed, shook his head. "Oh, I'm sorry about him—Big Baby has a bit of an attitude problem."

How much more fucked-up could this get? She'd seen a girl chained to a truck as bait, had her hip destroyed by some kind of super-sized sniper rifle, been strapped to a dolly and set in the back of a food truck, and now the psycho who had done all of it was having an insane conversation with the biggest handgun she'd ever seen.

The man slid the weapon inside his coat, came out with both hands held up, fingers wiggling.

"See? No worries."

"What are you going to—"

The words froze in her mouth as a new wave of pain rattled her like a loose window in a windstorm. Without the gun to focus on, the agony came back as inexorably as a rising tide.

"Do with you?" the man said. "I'm just going to ask you some questions. I usually don't do that, but the way you and that twitchy friend of yours were acting makes me wonder."

"I won't…won't talk."

The man smiled. "If you say so, shorty." He reached back into the food truck and pulled out the Tupperware container. Clear plastic with a blue top, filled with water and also something that took up most of the available space. He held it in front of her face.

Inside it, a brain.

Peter's brain.

The man tilted the container slightly. Peter's brain pressed against the side, round ridges suddenly flatter.

"If you don't talk, I have a container that matches this one," the man said. "Target had a sale on a four-piece set. I expected more, and paid less."

He stepped up into the food truck. Tavena saw the whole truck drop down slightly on its suspension. The man fumbled about for a bit, then came out once again, this time with that long rifle slung across his back. He'd left the Tupperware container somewhere inside.

He walked behind her, then tilted the dolly back—Tavena stared up at the ceiling, wondering when it would all end.

"Sorry, honey," he said. "I had to put the leftovers in the fridge. Come on, pumpkin', it's time to meet Dad."

He rolled her forward.

− 7 −

The Reporter's Inside Info

Karin squatted by the body. Yep, definitely the work of the Hippo. That made this a win for everyone. The reporter wanted special info and access, and she was willing to pay for it. Pay *well*.

The reporter was about to get what she wanted, so the reporter won.

Karin liked money, so she won, too.

And since Karin worked for Academi, and since Academi was a for-profit company complete with a PR department, a hard-hitting reporter being escorted around by a friendly-if-capitalistic Academi lieutenant meant the reporter got a positive, behind-the-scenes look at Academi's equipment, personnel and competence. And that meant Academi also won.

A win-win-*win*, so to speak.

Karin cupped her hands to her mouth. She had to shout to be heard over the roar from the Apache hovering overhead.

"Yuki, come on out! The area is secure!"

Karin couldn't blame the woman for wanting to stay in the armored vehicle. The black Conquest Knight XV looked like the love child of a limo and an Abrams tank. It was safe in there…mostly. The Bloods could strike anytime, anywhere, but they didn't have a lot of heavy weapons at their disposal. The Bloods that had survived this long weren't stupid. With an Apache hovering overhead, another on-station not too far away, two Grizzly armored personnel carriers—one fifty meters in front of the Knight, one fifty meters behind, with five well-armed troops deployed from each—the vamps weren't coming anywhere near Yuki Nitobe.

Unlike San Francisco, no one in the East Bay could afford Academi's services. That meant the Bloods ran wild, opposed only by a decimated police force and bands of loosely organized militia. Humans were in control, but according to Academi's intel people, not by much. That made this hostile territory as far as Karin was concerned, and she didn't want to be here any longer than she had to be. Academi's "Deceased in Service" bonus was a windfall for grieving families, but Karin wanted to pay for her niece's college the old-fashioned way, not with a DiS.

Yuki peeked her head out of the Knight's armored door. That long brown hair, soft and gleaming in the sun like it belonged in a shampoo commercial's slow-motion toss. Those dark eyes. The red-lipstick lips that always seemed right on the edge of a blow-me-a-kiss pucker. The reporter wore a flak jacket. Made her look even cuter than she normally was, which was already damn cute.

Such a beauty. And smart, too. With book deals, her freelance on-location reports in demand by every network in the world, Yuki was a journalistic rock star. She even *smelled* good. Too bad she was so high-class—a woman like that would never be interested in Karin.

Yuki stepped onto the running board then down to the street. She adjusted her shoulder bag, clutching it so tightly it seemed like more of a life preserver than the oversized purse it was.

Karin waved her over. "This is what you wanted to see."

Yuki hated being here, that much was obvious. She did much better in San Francisco proper, where the Fairmont Hotel staff treated her like a VIP, where the city's elite wanted to be seen at her side. Yuki never looked afraid in San Francisco, but that made sense—with a private army patrolling the streets and rooftops, it was one of the safest places on the West Coast. Easy to be brave with a thousand highly trained spec-ops soldiers backing up the SFPD, and an Army division stretched from SFO to Pacifica, effectively cutting off the peninsula from unwanted incursions.

Yuki joined Karin at the corpse.

"Oh, my," Yuki said. She pointed down. "Is that a goddamn bear trap?"

Karin nodded. She didn't know anything about hunting, but it looked like the bear traps she'd seen in movies.

"You wanted to experience the Hippo's work first-hand," Karin said. "This is it."

Yuki knelt next to the ravaged corpse. The dead man lay on his right side, face down. Mangled left hand, shattered right foreleg, nothing left of his shoulder except for a few shards of bone…the vamp had suffered mightily, even before the killer had applied the gruesome finishing touch.

"So, it's true," Yuki said. "This psycho takes their brains? That's messed up."

If Yuki was horrified by the jagged, irregular cut that marked where the top of the vamp's head had once been, she didn't show it. In fact, she sounded downright excited.

Yuki removed a small HD camera from her bag. So small, in fact, that after she took establishing shots of the body and close-ups of the face, she slid the camera all the way inside the skull and turned it around slowly.

She finished with a shot of the severed skull top—a blood-smeared, shallow white bowl—then stood and put the camera away.

"What the hell did all that damage to his shoulder? A grenade or something?"

"A sniper rifle shooting a fifty-caliber bullet," Karin said. "We've never recovered a shell casing, though. He cleans up after himself, even digs the rounds out of the bodies." Karin reached into her pocket, pulled out a .50-caliber cartridge. "Something like this, we think."

Yuki's eyes went wide. Her delicate fingers took the round like it was some kind of holy relic. She rested the bottom of the cartridge on the heel of her palm: the round's point reached almost to the tip of her middle finger.

"My God. It looks like a little artillery shell."

Karin laughed. "You could call it that, ma'am."

"Karin, do I look like a *ma'am* to you? Call me *Yuki*."

Something fluttered inside Karin's chest.

"Okay, Yuki."

The reporter again looked at the round in her hand, then the dead vamp's shoulder.

"This bastard must have come in fast to not see a bear trap," she said. "He must have wanted something. Any idea what was used for bait?"

Karin pointed to the right. "There's blood over there, only a few hours old. Probably human."

Yuki's eyes widened even further. She smelled a story, a big one— Karin couldn't decide if she was impressed with Yuki's excitement, or disgusted by it.

The reporter pocketed the shell. "You said the killer did something to their faces, too?"

Karin hooked her boot heel on the vamp's hip and pulled, flipping the corpse onto its back.

"Oh," Yuki said. "Oh my."

She again pulled out the camera and went to work.

Whatever device the killer had used to cut off the top of the skull had also been used to saw a chunk out of the vamp's face. The lips had been cut away and tossed aside; flat lumps that looked like tomatoes deflated from rot. The killer had cut upward from where the corners of those lips would have been, then horizontally below the nose.

"He took the teeth," Yuki said. "He took the vampire's *teeth*."

"Uh-huh," Karin said.

"As a trophy, you think?"

Karin shrugged. "I couldn't say, ma'am. Sorry, I mean *Yuki*. But if you've got the footage you want, we should be on our way."

Yuki looked around quickly, suddenly remembering where she was.

"Yeah, sure," she said. "I'd better get back and file this story."

Karin signaled for her teams to mount up, then walked Yuki back to the Knight VX's luxurious interior. In minutes, the three-vehicle detachment—escorted by the low-flying Apache—was headed back to the I-80 Bridge and the safety of San Francisco.

Or, as Karin and her Academi co-workers called it, "Fortress SF."

San Francisco had had plenty of money even before things went to shit. When things started to get really bad, the bright boys and girls in Silicon Valley realized how spread out that area was, how hard it was to protect. One couldn't turn a profit if one's talent kept turning up dead. So the tech community pulled up all roots and moved north, knowing that a peninsula offered a better chance to completely control a large area.

In a world struggling with global recession, if not an outright depression, property values in the City by the Bay had actually gone *up*.

A peninsula, sure, but still a large area—properly protecting it required an army. Several Fortune 500 companies quietly pooled their resources into a new firm, the Gateway Collective, which promptly acquired Academi—the all-services-available outfit once known as Xe, and before that, as Blackwater.

The motorcade rolled along I-80 until it reached the fortified wall that blocked off access to the bridge. A few months back, the government had accepted Academi's proposal for bridge security, further cementing the company's hold on the city of San Francisco.

A flak-jacketed, fatigue-wearing young man leaned into the Knight VX and politely checked the IDs of both Yuki and Karin. He checked Karin's first, handing it back with a sharp little salute. He then checked Yuki's, smiling wide when he handed it back to her.

"Thank you, ma'am," the man said. "We're glad you're back safe."

He leaned back out of the car and shut the door, leaving Karin and Yuki alone once again. Karin noticed that Yuki hadn't asked the young man to call her anything *but* ma'am. Did it mean something that she'd given Karin different rules?

The motorcade rolled onto the bridge. With the checkpoint stopping all vehicles, there was little traffic ahead other than a black Abrams tank rolling the opposite way.

"I admit, I'm pretty impressed," Yuki said. "I didn't expect Academi to be so...*polished*. Your budget must be huge."

"I bet you say that to all the girls."

Yuki laughed and blushed. "Funny. But seriously, this limo-tank? All the hardware your team brought? I just saw a *tank* roll past and couldn't miss the Academi logo on the side, and above us, a damn *Apache*? I knew private armies had money, but if this is what you roll out for a reporter looking into a story, I can only imagine what you have set aside for actual combat. Come on, Karin—what's Academi's hardware budget?"

The reporter flashed the smile that was as big a part of her stardom as her writing skill and story-getting tenacity.

Karin shrugged. "I couldn't say how much. The Gateway Collective co-founding companies included Google, Cisco, HP...and another company rumored to have a little bit of money in the bank, something called *Apple*. Maybe you've heard of it?"

Yuki laughed again. Karin liked that laugh, and started to wonder if, just maybe, she had a shot with the rock star reporter. One could never account for taste, as Karin's mother had often said—maybe the hot-like-fire Yuki was into the soldier thing, and butch lieutenants in particular.

"I wasn't aware Apple was in on it," Yuki said. "But that makes sense considering that ten billion dollar headquarters they're building downtown. Can I quote you that Apple is part of Gateway?"

Karin raised her hands in a defensive posture. "That was off the record, ma'am, per our agreement."

Yuki affected a pout. Damn if it didn't make her look even sexier.

"All right," Yuki said. "A deal is a deal."

Karin nodded, knowing full well Yuki would run with that information as part of the Hippo story, or as a follow-up. And that was fine,
because everything Karin had said *off the record* had been previously approved by her superiors. Academi *wanted* everyone to know about their bottomless resources—the more money people thought the company had, the less likely the Bloods would organize raids on San Francisco proper. The job was keeping the city safe by any means necessary—no one cared if that came by brute force, or by controlling the media.

Karin had been tasked with spoon-feeding Yuki exactly the information Academi wanted Yuki to have. When Yuki had been just another reporter, Karin hadn't had a problem with that. Now that she'd spent some time with her, though, it didn't feel right. Manipulation was just another form of lying. But, that was Karin's mission, and she'd carry it out. She hadn't climbed to lieutenant on dumb luck—she got the job done, whatever that job might be.

The convoy drifted right onto the Fremont Street exit.

"So, Karin, you haven't told me the most basic part of all of this—why do you call him *the Hippo?*"

And there it was, the moment Karin had been told to wait for.

"One of our drones got footage of the guy," she said. "He's a big fella."

In that moment, Karin wondered if the beautiful and classy Yuki Nitobe might crap all over herself.

"You have *footage* of this guy?"

Karin nodded.

"Why the fuck didn't you tell me?"

Karin shrugged. The real answer was, *because it's supposed to be your idea.*

Academi wanted to find out who the Hippo was. And also, hopefully, find a way to contact him. Eventually, the US Government would organize a total clear out of Oakland, return the area to the full rule of law and wipe out the pockets of Bloods holed up all over the city. To do that the Army needed intel, intel that Academi could potentially provide for the right price. The Hippo left a trail of bodies all over the East Bay, which meant he knew the area, possibly even something about Blood numbers and locations. Sure, he was a .50-cal-toting, dead-shot, skull-saw-wielding psychopath that collected teeth as trophies, but he was the best boots on the ground available without sending additional personnel into an area overrun with the Blood species known as *Kallikantzaros*.

Little was known about that strain. They were created by the Ice Virus just like the rest of them—or "reborn," or whatever the scientists called it—yet they seemed to be a particularly nasty bit of business. The Greek legends didn't do them justice. Fast and strong, they healed faster than anyone thought possible. Unlike many Blood strains, the *Kallikantzaros* lived up to the legends in one disturbing way: they really did eat human flesh, and they really did drink human blood.

Academi had sent two field operatives out looking for the Hippo: DiS bonuses had been paid to the families of both. No one knew if they'd died at the hands of the Hippo, or run into a cell of *Kallikantzaros*. Judging by the state of their remains—gnawed-on bones, mostly—odds were on the latter.

After that, Academi had tried hiring local PIs. One was still missing, the other had turned up sans throat.

Four people sent to find out about the Hippo, and all four were dead.

So, the brass switched tactics: why pay for PIs or risk writing DiS checks when reporters didn't cost anything at all? An anonymous email to Yuki that Academi was tracking some kind of serial vamp-killer had her calling the main office just minutes later.

Yuki held up her hands in exasperation. "Well? You have footage of the guy, but you don't know who it is? From what you said, it sounds like he's ex-military—didn't you run the footage through facial recognition databases?"

"The squints did that," Karin said. "They came up blank. It wasn't a great shot of him, but they said it should have been enough to ID him if he served in the military or any metro police department. Which means they think maybe he was Special Forces, black ops kind of shit. Or maybe CIA wet squad, FBI undercover, any number of areas where the people in charge went out of their way to make sure there was no facial recognition pattern on file. These days, bad guys can run a face-scan just as easily as the good guys."

Yuki looked forward, seemed to think on that for a moment.

"The footage, she said. "Can you get me that footage? I'll pay."

Karin smiled. Not only were reporters free, they actually *gave* you money to do the job you were supposed to do anyway.

"I'll see if I can get my hands on it," Karin said.

"LE BELLE DAME SANS MERCI" PT. 1

Jonathan Maberry

– 1 –

Doylestown Hospital
Doylestown, Pennsylvania
The Second V-War - Day 14

When Luther Swann opened his eyes the first thing he saw was Special Agent in Charge Jimmy Saint. He was seated comfortably in a guest chair reading the *New York Times*. Swann could see the headline.

U.S. FORCES ELIMINATE V-CELL
HELL NIGHT ORGANIZER KILLED

The picture was of the farmhouse in Pine Deep. Beside the picture was a photo of the *nelapsi*.

That brought all of the images back in a sickening rush. Swann raised a weak hand and touched his head. It was wrapped in gauze. Both eyes weren't bandaged, however, and seemed to be working normally.

Saint noticed that Swann was awake and folded the paper and gave him a warm smile.

"Hey, Luther, welcome back to the land of the living. How do you feel?"

"Wh-what day is it? Where am I?"

Saint told him and added, "You took a hell of a knock. Minor concussion. Nearly cracked your skull. Probably feels worse than it is, though."

Swann said, "Ugh."

"The doctors here want you to rest. But…they say that you'll be fine."

Swann said nothing. He doubted he would ever be fine again.

"You're quite the hero," said Saint.

"Hero?"

"Your actions during the raid saved the life of Gunnery Sergeant Wilcox, and that turned the tide of the battle. The Big Dog is now your number one fan. I think he wants to adopt you."

"Shit."

Saint grinned. "The good guys won," he said and tapped the newspaper. "Says so right here."

"Don't believe everything you read in the papers."

"I work for the government. Of *course* I don't believe everything I read." Saint shrugged. "Even so, there's no doubt that you guys did take down a nest of bad guys."

"Yeah. I guess."

He looked around the room. There were at least a dozen bouquets of flowers, two fruit baskets, cards taped to the walls, and an open box of chocolates. Saint followed his gaze. He pointed to the biggest floral display.

"From the president," he said as he plucked the card from among the brightly colored flowers. He read: "With the thanks of a grateful nation."

"Jesus Christ."

Saint took a chocolate out of the box. "Help yourself," said Swann dryly.

The agent chewed the chocolate and washed it down with some of the water placed bedside for Swann.

"Listen, Luther," he said, leaning his forearms on his thighs, "they're running with this. They're making you out to be a hero. They're going to continue doing that."

"Why?"

"Why do you think? You were the voice shouting loudest against open war. Now you actually *killed* a vampire during a battle with a terrorist cell."

"I didn't kill that vampire."

"The official story says you did, and every man and woman on V-8 will swear to it. I think they even believe it. Like it or not, you're now the face of *our* side of the fight. You're not in the middle anymore."

"That's bullshit. I'll go right to the press."

Saint's face lost all trace of humor and he leaned a little closer, spoke a little more quietly. "Luther...this is me talking here as your friend. Don't fight this. We're at war now. And this war isn't going away. Everyone in the country—hell, everyone in the *world*—is terrified by what's happening. They need a voice of reason, of balance. They need to know how to make the right choice."

"All out war is hardly the right choice, Jimmy. And I *don't* support that. I never have and I sure as shit never will. You know where I stand on this—I don't think that the V-cells represent the majority of the vampire population. Even with the Ninety-nine, I think we're seeing a small percentage. Well-organized and clearly well-funded, but small. Most of the vampires are as uninvolved in this war as most ordinary human citizens are. They don't want this fight."

"The fight is here, Luther. They don't have a choice."

"And...what? We demonize all of them because of a radical minority? Correct me if I'm wrong but hasn't that mentality been our problem for a long time now? When has it *ever* turned out to be the sanest, most intelligent or most *honorable* course of action? When has it ever been justified?"

Saint shook his head slowly but said nothing.

"I won't advocate ethnic genocide, Jimmy," Swann continued. "I was against it from the start and nothing that's happened has changed that. Nothing."

Saint sighed and stood. "Okay, Luther. That's your call."

"Yes, it is. And what's more, Jimmy, if we keep going the way we're going, I think we're going to make this a worse problem than it already is."

Saint's brow furrowed. "How the hell could it get worse?"

"Because right now, as I keep saying, this is a small group. If we start killing everyone who's become infected, if we kill the innocent—and you *know* that will happen—then we'll be creating martyrs. The radicals could use that to build a real majority within the vampire community. And it could get even worse than that."

Saint winced. "I know I don't want to hear this, but tell me anyway."

"Right now there's no leader, no face of the vampire movement," Swann explained. "If we force them to really organize into an army then, believe me, they *will* find that leader. All great armies have had them. They'll find someone with the right charisma, the right energy, the right words. Maybe even a true believer who has a dream and the skills to organize and plan. Is that what you want? If that what we want to see? The rise of a charismatic leader? Do we want them to find their Genghis Khan? Their Hitler? Or maybe their Moses to lead them out of bondage?"

Saint walked slowly to the door, opened it, then paused.

"You have friends out there, Luther. You do. But you also have enemies. I honestly couldn't say who's who, and I doubt you can, either. *I'm* your friend, though, so please listen to me when I tell you that you have to be very careful. There are powerful people who want this war. Very powerful people. Doing the 'right thing' is noble, but it could get you hurt."

"I don't care about that."

"You should. No man's an island, Luther. You're a family man. You have kids. You've seen what the people who want this war are willing to do to make sure we keep fighting. What do you think they'd be willing to do to you if they thought you were in their way?"

Swann felt as if the room was tilting downward. He gripped the sheets with both fists.

"Word to the wise, Luther." Saint gave him a last small, sad smile and went out.

"THE HIPPO" PT. 2

Scott Sigler

— 8 —
Tavena Meets Dad

Tavena had hated high school. How shitty was it that she would die in one?

The fat man rolled her down the hallway, one hand on the dolly, the other on a powerful flashlight. When she could open her eyes—the searing volcano in her hip forced them shut most of the time—she saw that school janitors served more of a role than she'd ever guessed: the place was trashed.

"Where are you taking me?"

"The gym," he said. "To meet Dad, like I told you."

Everything slurred to darkness. A sound brought her back to reality, a sound she remembered from her days in school—that signature *chunk-click* of a heavy gym door opening.

When reality returned, the fat man was rolling her onto a small basketball court. The room caught every sound and kept it alive in a fading echo. Skylights let in some of the morning sun, but much of the gym remained shrouded in deep shadow. On the floor, she saw the usual markings—the painted key, the three-point line, the baseline—but also a long curve done in scratched duct-tape. Bits of black outlined the gray tape, as if the strips had been there for a while.

He stopped her five feet shy of the strange, curving line, then set her upright.

The gym felt still. Unnaturally so.

"What's with the tape?"

"I call it the line of death," the fat man said.

The stillness broke as something moved, moved *fast*, coming out of the shadows and at them: a black man, naked and snarling. The man crossed the floor running on all fours, growling like a wolf, coming *so fast* that Tavena wanted to run but she couldn't move.

The man leapt, fingers extended, teeth barred—

—his head snapped back; his feet continued the original path. The man fell on his back, thumping against the hardwood floor.

"Hi, Dad," the fat man said. "How was your day?"

The pain faded a bit as Tavena watched the naked man scramble to his feet. She saw he was wearing a collar—thick and made of steel—that connected to a metal cable running up to the ceiling. She looked skyward: the cable ran to a spool set up in the gym rafters.

The man—an old man, in his sixties Tavena could now see—leaned against the cable, trying to reach her. Drool spilled from his lower lip. Tavena had no doubt that if the man could get free, he would tear her to pieces and start eating her.

"That's my dad," the fat man said. "He's not feeling all that great lately." He pointed up to the spool of cable. "That keeps him in place, but gives him some range of motion. He's got to be able to move a little until he gets better. He's restrained, sure, but he's not an animal."

That's exactly what he is, Tavena thought. Whatever strain this man was, it wasn't *her* strain. She'd seen people like him before, though, and she'd killed them. Charlemagne even organized hunts, because creatures like the psycho's dad killed Blood just as often as they killed Beats.

"He's not going to get better," Tavena said. "He's already gone."

"Oh, *pshaw*," the fat man said. "Dad's going to be fine. Just have to make sure he gets enough to eat."

Tavena heard a rustling, then the man reached around in front of her, showed her a small remote control. It looked like a car alarm remote, the kind that would hang on a keychain. Someone had scraped off the labels and written in new ones with a silver pen: *Loosen* instead of *Lock*; *Retract* instead of *Unlock*; *Buzz* where the *Trunk Open* would be, and above the red panic button, the word *Release*.

"That collar Dad wears gives him a little jolt if he tries to get out any of the main doors," he said. "Usually he's chained up, though. I can give him a little zapparoonie with this if I have to. It's really only safe to move him if he has a full belly. Dementia, you know. It's hard on a family."

Dementia. The old man was a walking killer, the kind that would slaughter anything he came across—human, werewolf, vamp, probably even his own son if he got the chance. And the fat man called it *dementia*? Someone was crazy, all right, and it wasn't the drooling old man.

"Dad earns his keep," the fat man said. "Sometimes he helps get rid of trespassers." He turned to face his father. "Dad, I'm taking her back to the truck and putting in a batch, okay? I'll bring you some cupcakes when they're done."

The old man just growled.

"You too, Dad," the fat man said.

Then, Tavena was tilted backward and was rolling again.

– 9 –
Yuki Cracks the Case

Karin wanted to take Yuki into the Academi HQ, show the place off a little, but the reporter had yet to leave the Knight XV.

"It's more comfortable in the building," Karin said. "You don't have to sit in the parking lot, you know."

"Shhh," Yuki said. She had a tablet computer in her lap, was focused on a video.

Karin sighed and watched Yuki watch the video.

As far as Karin knew, Yuki hadn't dated any famous men. The rock star reporter would be great paparazzi fodder for actors, athletes, businessmen and such, and yet, nothing. So, maybe, just *maybe*, Yuki wasn't interested in guys at all.

A girl could always hope.

The video wasn't great quality. Shot at night, from a drone, it showed a shambling mound of a man handling a dead body. The whole clip was only about fifteen seconds long, from the time the man came into view until he stood and aimed a Barrett sniper rifle at the drone taking the video. Then a flash of light, then static.

Yuki played it again.

The big man in the video carried the four-foot-long M82A2 like it was nothing more than a common carbine. The .50-caliber weapon fired the same massive 12.7x99mm rounds as a Browning machine gun. In the right hands, it could kill from a distance of over 2,000 meters: the Hippo could probably take you out from over a mile away.

No matter how many times Karin saw it, the end of the video still blew her mind; the man shoulder-fired the Barrett and took out a drone that wasn't more than a few feet across, a drone that was probably 200 feet above him.

Yeah. The Hippo knew what he was doing.

Yuki finished watching the video for the fifth time.

"All of the…well, *decapitations* isn't the right word," she said.

"How about *cleavings*?" Karin offered.

Yuki's nose wrinkled up. "Not quite right, but it'll work until I can riff on it. All the cleavings were in Oakland?"

Karin nodded. "Or close to it. We've found six so far."

"You've *found* six. So it's probably more?"

"Probably a lot more," Karin said. "Those are just the ones we've come across during various recon missions. It's not like we're trying to stop this guy, if you know what I mean."

Yuki's fingers drummed against the tablet's glass. "I would guess he's got ties to the area. Otherwise, why Oakland?"

"That's what we figured, too," Karin said. "But like I told you, facial recognition came up with nothing. We have a list of people who lived in the area and might have had experience with the Barrett or access to one when the first V-war got bad. Special Forces training, SWAT, arms dealers, even competitive target shooters. My guys say from the way the corpses were shot and the way the man handled the Barrett, he's not someone who just picked up a fifty-cal rifle for the first time. We've cleared a bunch, but fifty-two people on that list are missing. You know how it is these days—with all the violence, there's no way of knowing who's dead and who just decided to drop off the grid."

Yuki nodded. "Ain't that the truth?" She pulled absently at her lower lip. A trace of lipstick smeared onto her forefinger and thumb. "You said fifty-two?"

Karin felt her heart sink a little. She'd been giving Yuki nothing but good news until now. Even with help, a reporter trying to track down fifty-two missing people in an area overrun with Bloods, it was—

"That's *great*," Yuki said.

"It is?"

"My God, Karin, only fifty-two names? You've handed me this amazing story, *and* done most the legwork? I could kiss you."

"Please do." The words were out of Karin's mouth before she thought to check them.

"Huh?" Yuki blinked. "Oh, right!"

Her little hands reached out to Karen's face, and Karen's chest thrummed with surprise. Yuki cupped her cheeks, pulled her in…

…and planted a single, firm smooch on Karen's forehead.

"Karin, you're the *best*."

"Thanks," Karin said. "I try, I try."

A kiss on the forehead? What was that? Did that mean something? Or was Yuki just caught up in the moment? But those lips, so soft, so warm, she—

"We have to find the connection to the Oakland area," Yuki said.

Karin nodded. "Sure, but I told you, Yuki, we checked all the available records."

"Right idea, wrong kind of records. This level of violence isn't survival—it's *personal*. Let me cross-reference your list of names against news stories. If I'm lucky, whatever happened to your *Hippo* happened early on before news crews stopped going to Oakland."

– 10 –
Batch It Up!

Tavena watched the psycho slide three cupcake trays of red velvet batter into the food truck's oven. It wasn't like she could do anything else. Still tied to the dolly, she was just inside the closed rear doors: her entire field of view was this obese asshole playing Home Ec.

The truck/kitchen would have been cramped for a normal-sized person. She wasn't sure how the fat man got around so well. Everything was so compact: the oven, the fridge, metal cabinets, the sink set in the stainless steel counter, some kind of ammo-making rig bolted onto that counter. The same efficiency he used for cooking applied to that rig: neatly-stacked Tupperware containers held what she assumed were shell casings, bullets and other things.

The round that had destroyed her hip? He'd probably made that with his own hands.

The killer slid into the oven two metal pans with what looked like meatloaf, and a glass casserole dish with what looked like eggs and broccoli.

"I like to batch things up," he said. "If the oven's already hot, why not conserve energy, amirite?"

Tavena didn't answer.

"And that phrase, *batch it up*," the fat man said. "If I ever get a cooking show, I think that could be my signature, like *Bam!* Or *Yum-O!* Know what I mean?"

"Just kill me," Tavena said. "I hurt…so bad. Just get it over with."

"You kids these days," the psycho said, "always in a hurry." He shut the oven door. "While that's cooking, I'll do the icing. That's what I wanted you to see, really. The trick is in the preparation. For this batch, I'll use your buddy. If you don't start talking, the next batch will be you."

Batch could be *her*? What the hell was this lunatic talking about? The pain made it hard to track, hard to think.

"He wasn't my buddy," Tavena said. "We were just…assigned together."

The fat man smiled. "Assigned? Someone put you two together? Someone *in charge*?"

Dammit—she'd said something without meaning to. She had to stay sharp, not give up anything on Charlie. Charlie had a vision, a destiny that went beyond the life of one soldier.

"Who's in charge, girlie? Tell me and I'll make the pain go away."

Tavena found the strength to shake her head.

The big man opened a small fridge, pulled out the Tupperware container.

Inside that container: Peter's brain, bobbing about in pinkish water.

The fat man turned to the truck's small sink. He turned the faucet on halfway, let the water run. He opened a cabinet and pulled out a metal colander, his movements definitive and precise—this mobile kitchen was tiny, but it was *his*, and he knew it well. He set the colander next to the Tupperware container.

"You don't have to die, you know," he said. "I mean, if I was going to kill you, would I have let you use Dad's mask and dolly?"

"You…you put your father in this rig?"

The fat man nodded. "Sure, how else am I going to get him around? We have another place we stay in sometimes, just to make sure we're not too predictable."

He removed the Tupperware lid and gently lifted out Peter's brain. Water ran down the folds and dripped first into the Tupperware, then into the colander as the man set the brain inside. Tavena saw that bloody water drain through in rivulets, run down the counter to flow into the sink, kept away from the floor by the counter's raised edge.

"You have to soak it for about an hour," the man said. "Helps get the blood out of there. Nobody likes blood, really, nobody except for you animals."

278

He gave the colander a quick, firm shake to knock off excess water, then held it in front of Tavena's masked face.

She stared at it, couldn't even close her eyes to block out the sight. Peter's brain, all that he had ever been, now nothing more than a grayish pink mass of folds in that all-too-familiar shape. Chunks of bone dotted the surface, as did more than a few strands of blond hair.

"Take a good look," the man said. "This is how you end up if you don't tell me what's going on."

Tavena's last bit of resilience faded away, perhaps bludgeoned by the sight in front of her, perhaps finally lassoed and dragged away by the soul-piercing fire in her hip. She had gone through the change, she had become a taker of life and an eater of flesh.

Tavena was supposed to *be* the nightmare, not be *in* one.

The brain…all those folds…where was the part that made up Peter's annoying personality…which part held his selfishness and laziness … where were the parts on *her* brain that made her who she was…

"Okay," she said. "I'll talk."

The blue-eyed fat man nodded. "Mmm-hmm. I know."

He turned back to the sink. He set the colander under the gently running water, then started picking bone bits off the brain.

"You gotta rinse it," the fat man said. "Bone dust, mostly, but sometimes the saw kicks off little splinters. Those are *not* fun to bite into when you're trying to enjoy a cupcake. And I'm sure you've eaten food with a hair in it—that's just gross."

She stared at his broad back. She could see the big lump under his arm, where the handle of that obscene handgun distended his black jacket. She wished she could break free, sink her fingers into his fat neck and tear it to pieces, but she had nothing left with which to fight. She…

Wait a minute…just wait a goddamn minute…

"You said the hair…are you going to *cook* Peter's brain?"

"Mmm-hmmm," the fat man said. "Going to boil it. It keeps its shape, mostly, but when it's cooked it's all creamy. Some butter, some cream cheese, some sugar, then *batch it up* and you've got frosting."

The tentacles of pain squeezed her, caressed her, slid all around her in a constant embrace. *Frosting.* The cupcakes the giant freak had just put in the oven. He was going to make fucking *brain frosting* to put on cupcakes.

" I'll talk," she said. "Told you that, I'll talk. What do you want to know, just ask me. I can't take this anymore, I can't—"

He turned sharply, all the humor gone from his eyes.

"I'm cooking right now," he said. "Show some respect."

"You're fucking *insane!*"

"*I'm* insane? You don't see me eating people, do you?"

"You put goddamn brains *in cupcakes,* you psycho piece of shit!"

Suddenly, his hand was on her throat, so strong, so *crushing,* squeezing hard enough to make her forget about her hip if only for a moment.

"*You monsters eat BABIES! You have to be PUNISHED! All I'm doing is making some motherfucking CUPCAKES!*"

He squeezed harder. Tavena didn't even close her eyes, just prayed *please, God, please*…prayed to die *but please don't let him use my brains as icing*—

The fat man let go. He turned back to the sink.

"Batch it up," he said calmly.

She drew in a desperate breath.

He continued, voice as deep and smooth as it had been before he grabbed her throat.

"Batch it up, amirite? So, with the brain cleaned, we boil it for twelve to fifteen minutes."

He put the brains in a pot, filled the pot with water, then put the pot on the tiny stove. The *whuff* of lighting gas, then the hissing of the same.

"Twelve to fifteen minutes," he said. "That's all the time you have to answer my questions, and answer them *correctly,* or today I'm making a double batch."

− 11 −
Secret Recipe

It was old hat to Harry. Keep the perps talking, make them repeat things, see if the story stayed the same in the retelling. Mess up particular details and see if they are corrected.

"So this Charlemagne, guy—he's organizing a Blood army?"

"She," the girl said. "It's…Charlie is a woman."

Harry had to listen carefully to make out her words. The monster was almost gone, all used up. Strength, speed, quickness, aggression, all good for keeping a body alive, but without blood? In the end, even a vamp can bleed out.

He'd been killing the monsters for months now, more months than he could remember. A year? Two? He wasn't sure. Only in the past few weeks, though, had he seen the monsters behave like trained soldiers: moving in pairs, sometimes in groups of four or five, leapfrogging, using a lot of cover—and *always* armed. That made things harder.

At first, killing them had been easy. Overconfidence breeds stupidity, and these things were so high on their strength and speed that they didn't think anything could hurt them.

They were wrong.

Blow off a bastard's head, doesn't matter what that bastard is made of, that bastard dies.

Rebecca did the dirty work. She killed just fine up close or from a distance. Harry hadn't had a chance to use Big Baby just yet—something Big Baby complained about non-stop. Harry was saving Big Baby for an encounter of the up-close and personal kind.

Yeah, it had been easy at first, but the stupid Bloods had died off early, and after the first war ended only the smart ones were still alive. Harry'd had to start luring them in, finding people who could be used as an attractant, so to speak. Bait usually worked. Sometimes those people lived, sometimes they didn't.

The wounded woman started to shiver. Shock was setting in; she wouldn't be of use that much longer.

"Charlemagne trains you by Colby Park, right?"

Her head hung low, chin to chest, as if the metal mask weighed a million pounds.

"Greg Brown Park," she said. "Other places. Moves it around a lot."

That bit of information was also consistent; Harry knew Tavena was telling the truth. She was clearly just a foot soldier in this young army—or maybe *militia* was a better term—and she didn't know much. Charlemagne's real name? Tavena had no idea. Troop strength? She'd seen no more than ten Bloods gathered in one place at one time, and usually different faces. That meant there could be twenty of them, or a hundred, or a thousand. No way to know for sure.

The oven timer dinged.

"Ah," Harry said. "Now we're ready to *get in the mix!*"

He turned off the burner and moved the pot to the counter, then stared at the girl. She didn't look up. Dammit. He'd thought maybe *get in the mix* was better than *batch it up*, but she hadn't even noticed.

Kids these days.

"I have some bad news for you, Tavena," he said. He used wooden spoons to carefully lift the brain from the boiling water and place it into a mixing bowl. He tipped the bowl over the sink, draining the water from the folds. The knurled tissue steamed slightly and gleamed a little from the truck's overhead lights.

She lifted her head with great effort. He could see some of her mouth through the mask's opening, could see lips curled back to show her constant level of pain. Her eyes looked hollow and sunken, as if she was already dead but they hadn't *quite* got the message.

"Lemme…guess," she said. "You're going to…kill me anyway…right?"

"Bingo! It's not personal, it's just that you're a baby-killing fuck-stain of a monster and your kind has to *go*. But! Before you die, I'm going to show you my mixing technique." He set one spoon down. He held the bowl in one arm, turned and held it right in front of her hanging head. If she was dying right this minute, the last thing she'd see would be what he would do to her after she shuffled off to Buffalo.

"Boiled brains have a creamy consistency," Harry said. He pressed the wooden spoon into the mass. It squished down, then through, almost like it wasn't a brain at all but a mass of soft dough shaped like a brain.

The restrained, masked, wounded vamp let out a soft moan.

"It's soft because brain tissue doesn't have any sinew or fiber," Harry said. He kept lifting the spoon, then slowly mashing it down again. Each time it made a squelching sound. When he brought the spoon up, clumps of brain stuck to it. "When I add the melted butter, oh, man, it blends *so nice*. And then the cream cheese is the best—"

The wooden spoon *crunched* into something.

"Crap," he said. "Must have missed a bit of bone. Sometimes the splinters drive *way* into the brain."

He set the spoon on the counter, then reached into the bowl. The brain tissue squished around his fingers.

"Still warm," he said.

The monster moaned again.

Harry's fingertips searched for, then felt, the mystery bit of hardness...that didn't feel like bone.

He pinched his finger and thumb on it, then lifted, shook his hand to drop most of the grayish clumps back into the bowl, and looked at what he held.

A tiny piece of green plastic, no bigger than a grain of rice.

Some kind of transmitter.

"Uh-oh," Harry said.

The monster started to laugh, a pain-wracked sound that didn't fully hide her tone of contempt.

"Peter's...headaches," she said. "Charlie...she must have put that in him. She...she knows about you, you *sick fuck*. And that means she's coming for you."

Harry's balls seemed to shrivel up, tried to crawl into his stomach.

RFID, maybe? He'd put the brain in water back when he'd collected it, but if the transmitter was supposed to work while inside that dead dude's head, it could obviously function in a liquid environment. Maybe the boiling had destroyed its ability to send or receive, but if so it didn't matter—it had been here, at the high school, *before* boiling, so whoever put this in that vamp's head might have gotten a signal.

"This is bad," Harry said. "Real bad. I'm going to go check on Dad. You wait here for me, okay?"

Tavena didn't respond.

Harry lifted her head. All life had left her eyes. She was gone.

"Crap," he said.

He grabbed a towel and wiped the brains off his hands. He turned the oven off, but left the oven door shut—maybe he'd get lucky and get the cupcakes out before they were ruined.

"Big Baby?"

"*Yeah, Harry?*"

"I hope you're ready to play."

"*I've been waiting, motherfucker! Cock the hammer, bitch, COCK IT!*"

Harry drew the Pfeifer Zeliska. Thirteen pounds of bad-assery firing a .600-caliber Nitro Express round that could blow a head-sized hole in a cinderblock wall. Arguably the biggest handgun in the world, and Harry was just the big sonofabitch to put it in play. If the Bloods were coming to his home—his *home*, for fuck's sake—Big Baby would be there to welcome them.

"*Let's do some damage,*" Big Baby said. "*Let's whip that ass.*"

Harry nodded. "Okay. First, let's go get Dad."

— 12 —
Other People's Money

Yuki offered Karin the tablet.

"There's your guy," she said.

Karin felt her nose wrinkle in disbelief. "You're shitting, me, Yuki."

"I shit you not."

"We've tried for weeks to find out who this guy was. We have a whole department doing it. You've been working on it for a couple of hours, and in the back of a vehicle. You found out who he was from a crappy video and using nothing but a tablet?"

Yuki nodded. "If I ran a city and wanted it protected, I'd call you. You wanted someone to do some basic reporting, so you called me."

The words took Karin aback. "We didn't call you, you said you wanted—"

"Give it a rest," Yuki said. "Don't play a player, Karin. Or if you do, next time, try not to be so obvious about it."

Karin's face grew hot. She'd thought she'd been spoon-feeding Yuki the information, but the reporter had known exactly what was happening the whole time.

Yuki smiled. "Don't worry, I'm not going to write an article on how Academi tried to manipulate me. I won't get you in trouble with your bosses."

Karin felt some of her anxiety slide away. Some, but not all.

"Why would you do that?"

"Because I still have a great story," Yuki said. "*Two* stories, actually—the fact that there is a serial killer called *The Hippo*, and also that man's identity and tragic back-story."

Karin reached for the offered tablet; Yuki pulled it away at the last second, just out of reach.

"Not so fast," she said, and smiled. "You think this kind of information is *free*?"

More of that strange anxiety again.

"I don't understand," Karin said. "You, uh, want me to give back the money you gave me?"

Yuki rolled her eyes. "Oh, Karin, I hope you're really good at you Academi job, because you aren't exactly the most perceptive girl I've ever met. And besides, that was the network's money, not mine. The Hippo's identity will cost you *two* things. First, I need another heavily-armed escort into Oakland—for me and a cameraman—so we can do a remote at the Hippo's house."

Karin instinctively started searching for words to make it sound like that was a huge favor to ask, and that she'd have to burn personal capital to get her superiors to play along, but one look at Yuki's bemused smile made Karin give it up—Academi would love the PR, and the reporter knew that.

"Fine," Karin said. "I don't think that will be a problem."

"Awesome," Yuki said.

"And the other thing?"

Yuki handed over the tablet. "Take some of that money that isn't *my* money, and take a girl out to dinner. I've been in San Francisco for a week now, and haven't had a single date."

Karin felt her face flush red again. "I'd like that," she said.

She couldn't look at Yuki's smile anymore, so she took the tablet and read.

– 13 –
High School Blues

They moved so quietly.

If Harry hadn't found the transmitter, he wouldn't have known those sounds—nothing more than a bird on the roof, a mouse on the floor—were Bloods who had come to kill him. But he had found it, and he did know.

Harry stood just inside the chemistry lab, his back against the wall, the open doorframe to his left. The metal door hinged inward ninety degrees on the other side; the handle pressed against a rubber doorstop sticking out of the brick wall. A photocopied flier about a basketball game still clung to the door, just below a thin window made of wire-lined glass.

The gym wasn't far away. If they found Dad, they would kill him, too, and Harry couldn't let that happen.

He couldn't lose his father…family was everything.

Two mice, coming down the hallway to his left. So quiet, *so quiet*. Then, to his right, closer to the gym, he heard the skitter of a small piece of glass kicked across the hard floor. He listened carefully, decided there were two Bloods in that direction as well.

Which meant Harry was up against four of them.

Four against one: impossible odds.

Another noise echoed through the hall, a noise the vamps couldn't muffle because door latches worked the way door latches worked: *chunk-click.*

Dad. They were going into the gym.

Harry heard the two vamps to the left coming closer, so close they couldn't hide booted feet stepping on dirt- and rubble-strewn school floors.

Maybe just ten feet away…

These were Charlemagne's people, which meant they were trained, which meant they were likely approaching with weapons up and at the ready. Did they have shotguns like Tavena? Shotguns that would tear into Harry's big belly, splatter his innards against the wall …

Closer still…five feet from the door, maybe less.

Hitting a vamp from sixty meters with a Barrett was one thing; tackling *two* of them at close range was another. That was where Big Baby came in handy: if Harry hit a vamp with Nitro Express round, that vamp would go down and *stay* down. He'd seen the Bloods shrug off normal rounds like they were no more than a bee sting.

But even if he took out the first Blood, that left him face-to-face with the second, an untouched monster only a few feet away…

Harry needed an advantage.

Four against one? Four against *two* was much better.

Three feet, at most…

Slowly and silently, Harry pulled the remote control from an inner pocket: he pressed the button labeled *Release.*

Sounds rushed through the hallway from far down on the right: a deep growl, then a scream of surprise, then a shotgun's roar.

The two Bloods near the door suddenly rushed forward to help their comrades, their silence forgotten. As they moved past, Harry raised Big Baby in both hands and leaned out the door behind them.

The barrel's tip was only a foot from the back of the first vamp's head when Harry pulled the trigger.

A deafening roar: the thirteen-pound gun jumped in his hands as a skull exploded, a burst water-balloon spraying wetness in every direction. Harry saw a detached lower jaw skid across the filthy floor in one direction, a spinning shotgun in the other.

The second vamp spun fast, *so fast*. He had a shotgun, too: he brought it up and aimed just as Harry dipped back into the Chem Lab. The shotgun's deafening sound dominated the hallway air; a burning sting in Harry's cheek, part of the door frame denting in a spray of lead and paint.

"*Kill that motherfucker!*" Big Baby screamed.

Harry cocked the revolver's hammer as he pressed his back flat against the open door. He heard the *chack-chock* of the vamp putting another round in the shotgun's chamber.

Harry dropped, ass cheeks on his heels.

The shotgun barrel peeked around the door and fired right above his head—had he been standing, the blast would have taken his face clean off.

Chack-chock.

The vamp had pumped another round, but it was too late for him— Harry held Big Baby in his left hand, reached across his chest to the right, angled the barrel out the door and pulled the trigger.

The massive recoil was too much for one hand: Big Baby spun away to clatter on the hallway floor.

Harry had a split-second to realize that if he'd missed, he was dead, then he heard the thump of a body and a choked moan of surprise and fear.

His ears rang from the combined assault of the shotgun and Big Baby's .600-caliber detonation.

Harry stood, peeked around the door. The vamp lay on the floor, blood-smeared hands clutching desperately at his crotch.

"*Pick me up, goddamit!*"

Big Baby. Harry grabbed the vamp's shotgun, then found his revolver and picked it up.

"*You dropped me when you fired—that's a real rookie move, Harry, a real bitch move,*"

"My bad," Harry said.

He aimed the Big Baby at the wounded vamp.

"*I'll be damned,*" Big Baby said. "*Harry, I blew his nards off!*"

Harry slung the vamp's shotgun. "Vampires have nards?"

"Well, not this one, not anymore. Lemme finish him! Please?"

There was an instant of understanding where Harry looked at the moaning vamp, a burst-moment where he realized that not only was he talking to his handgun, but his handgun was *talking back* and had used a line from an old movie that Harry had seen as a kid, a movie a handgun couldn't have seen because *handguns did not watch movies*, which meant Harry was bug-nuts crazy, and then that instant vanished as fast as it had arrived, leaving no trace of its existence.

"Okay," Harry said. "Go ahead and finish him."

He cocked the hammer back again, then let Big Baby do his thing.

"LA BELLE DAME SANS MERCI" PT. 2

Jonathan Maberry

— 2 —

Doylestown Hospital
Doylestown, Pennsylvania
The Second V-War - Day 16

When Luther Swann was released from the hospital, a car came to pick him up. It was a standard government Crown Victoria. The driver was a tall, poker-faced man in a black suit with a wire behind his ear. He flashed an NSA badge and helped Swann into the backseat, closed the door, and drove away.

Five blocks from the hospital the car pulled into a parking lot of a Starbucks.

"Why are we stopping here?" Swann asked.

The driver got out and walked away.

A moment later the door opened and a woman climbed into the back seat. She was Asian, pretty, and she did not speak once.

"What's going on?" demanded Swann, fear hammering in his chest.

She held up a finger to her lips for silence, then opened a laptop and punched a button. The screen resolved immediately into a live video stream of a woman seated on an ornate hand-carved throne. The woman wore a mask of ivory and only her dark eyes were visible.

"Professor Swann," she said. "I am glad to see that you are well."

"Who the hell are you and what the hell is going on?"

"For reasons I'm sure you'll appreciate I won't give you my real name. Here in the Court I'm called the Crimson Queen. A theatrical name, I grant you, but useful."

"The 'Court'? What—?"

"My Court. I speak to you now as the voice of the united vampire peoples. We are becoming a global nation, Professor Swann. We are few now, but every day our nation grows. Soon we will be many."

She spoke in a soft and lilting southern accent. Her phrasing was formal and Swann guessed that it was ritualistic. That this was something she had said many times in exactly this way. A litany.

"Are you responsible for the bombings?" he asked.

The Crimson Queen shook her head. "No, we are not."

"Who is?"

"We don't know."

"But they're vampires. That much is clear."

"Is it?"

"Of course. Who else?"

"That, Professor Swann, is the question I hoped you would ask yourself. It is, without doubt, the most important question anyone alive today could ask."

"I don't understand…"

"Yes," she said, "I believe that you do."

Swann said nothing, his mind racing.

"We are not your enemies," said the Crimson Queen. "But we are not your friends. We are a new race. Or, perhaps, we are an old race alive again. Take your pick. Either way, we are not governed by the laws and rules of human society. You understand this, I believe. You are the only voice of reason on your side. Or, at least, the only one being heard."

"I wouldn't put too much on how much they're listening to me right now."

"Then make them listen," she said. "It's not too grandiose a statement to make that the future of our world stands on a knife edge. Right now the vampire nation, the Court of the Crimson Queen, is not a party to this war. We are doing what we can to pull our side back from the brink. We don't want this war. We never did. But listen to me, Professor Swann, if things continue the way they are going, the humans take away our ability to choose a better path. You know this, don't you?"

"Yes," he said weakly.

"If you force us to fight, we *will* fight." She took a slow breath. "*All* of us will fight. And, Professor Swann…there are many more of us than you think. Many more."

The screen went dark.

Without a word, the Asian woman folded the laptop, gave him a small and very toothsome smile, and got out. She walked away. A few minutes later the driver returned, got in, and in total silence drove Luther Swann all the way to Washington, D.C.

"THE HIPPO" PT. 3

Scott Sigler

– 14 –
Harry Interrupts Dinner

Harry ran down the hall toward the gym. He didn't hear any struggle, didn't hear any gunfire. Was Dad okay? Had those two fuckers killed him?

Harry kicked at the gym door's handle and knocked it open—*chunk-click-BAM*—then rushed in, hollering, hoping to startle the vamps enough to get one of Big Baby's last two shots off before they could react.

But, no one was standing.

There, in a spreading blood-pool at center court, his naked father perched over two dead bodies. Dad had torn the arm off of one, held it in both hands like it was an oversized chicken wing. He bit down on the bicep, ripped free a chunk that was both bloody shirtsleeve and ragged muscle.

Dad chewed, smiling.

"Mehhhh," he said, then pulled the severed arm close to his chest as if Harry might try to take it from him.

Harry nodded, slowly stepped back a few steps.

"Sorry, Dad," Harry said softly. "Just finish eating. It's okay, Dad… it's okay."

Harry kept up the calming tone until his butt hit the gym door's handle—*chunk-click*—then he backed out and let the door swing shut. Before it fully closed, he heard a growl and a squelch as his father tore off another big bite.

Harry tried to control his breathing. He listened, but didn't hear anything other than the sound of his father chewing.

Charlemagne had sent four vamps to take him out, and he'd survived. Those four would be expected to report back soon, which meant Harry had to get the hell out of there.

He reached into his coat of many pockets and pulled out his cell phone. He set the timer for five minutes—it was all he could spare. Yes, he had to get out of there, but things would be so much easier if he just let his father eat for a few minutes.

Five minutes, then they'd head to the backup place.

−15 −
The Report

"This is Yuki Nitobe, reporting live from Oakland, California. I am standing in front of the former house of Harold Chamberlain, one of the change's early victims. What happened here was an unbelievable nightmare involving the death of a six-year-old girl and the destruction of an American family, but that tragic story pales in comparison to what came next, and to the shocking revelation of what Chamberlain is now doing to Oakland's vampires. The whole story at eight, right here, on Global Satellite News. "

Yuki lowered the microphone. "How'd that look, Cory?"

Cory lowered his shoulder-held camera. "Tip-top, Yuki. And you look hot as hell."

Karin fought the urge to slap the man in the back of the head. She had to admit, though, that Cory was right—Yuki had opened her blouse another button, made her eye makeup darker, and put on a shade of purplish-red lipstick that Karin couldn't stop staring at.

Yuki waved Karin over.

"Karin, how do my eyes look? This is a somber report, too much shadow?"

Yuki batted those eyes, and Karin's insides melted.

"Um…they look great."

Yuki tipped her head toward the house. "And from where Cory is standing, you can't see any of your people, right?"

Karin smiled a little. It was quite an image Yuki wanted to present: the brave reporter, standing alone on the dangerous streets of Oakland, in front of a half-burnt-out ranch house. Nothing behind her but peeling white paint, broken glass, charred wood, and two equally ruined homes on either side.

Off to the left—out of the camera's view, of course—two squads of Academi heavies. Off to the right, two more squads. A Grizzly blocked either end of the street, and another—along with a fifth and sixth squad—was on the street behind the house to make sure no unexpected guests came through the back yard.

Mid-afternoon, plenty of sun by which to see any threats, and enough firepower to kill anything short of a platoon's worth of organized vamps. That made this street about the safest spot east of the Bay Bridge. With those assets off-camera, however, the public would see exactly what Yuki wanted them to see, or, rather, exactly what she *didn't* want them to see.

Yuki was a master of casual manipulation, both visual and verbal, and Karin was already halfway to smitten. Dating Yuki, she knew, would not end well.

But it could be a whole lot of fun in the mean time, and you never know what her heart might find...

"Thirty seconds," Cory called out.

"Got it," Yuki said to him. Then, to Karin: "You're sure I look good for this?"

"Not good," Karin said. "You look...just *amazing*."

Yuki smiled. "Awww, you're sweet." She reached up and cupped Karin's cheek—the skin felt cool from the afternoon air, yet electrifying at the same time—then gave that same cheek a light pat.

"Off with you now," Yuki said. "It's show time."

– 16 –
Harry Comes Home, Part II

Harry made sure the remote control was firmly in his hand before he cracked open the food truck's back door. If the old man needed a shock from that collar, that's just the way things were.

"Dad?"

No answer.

Harry opened the door a little more, held it at arms length, the remote in his other hand and held near his hip.

"Pops, you okay?"

"Mehhh," the old man said.

Harry opened the doors the rest of the way. Dad was, of course, strapped to the dolly, the brass mask that had recently covered

Tavena's face now where it actually belonged. Dad's eyes were half-lidded. He looked like he needed a nap. His burgeoning belly jutted forth from between the tight straps just above and below it.

"Dad, you shouldn't have ate so much."

"Mehhh."

The old guy was so cute when he was sleepy.

"Come on, Pops," Harry said as he pulled the dolly from between the stove and the sink. "Let's get you settled into your new home."

The old building had once been a warehouse, then a transmission shop, then something to do with motorcycles, Harry wasn't sure. Whoever had owned it wasn't around anymore, obviously, nor were the people who had stored their vehicles here. All victims of the first round of violence, probably.

There were several non-running trucks inside, along with a couple of boats covered by tight, dusty tarps. The food truck fit nicely between some rich dude's Chris Craft and a rust-eaten delivery truck with a faded Frito-Lay logo on the side.

The building was cold and drafty. Not as nice as the school. But it was safe, probably, and that was enough.

Harry rolled the dolly through an open, heavy fire door. Maybe this room had once been used for painting cars; now it was Dad's room. Harry set the dolly upright.

Up above, attached to a ceiling girder, was a winch spooled with steel cable. Harry pulled a second remote from a coat pocket and pressed a button: the winch hummed to life, lowered the cable down like an industrial spider just starting a web. He clipped the cable to his father's shock collar.

"This is your new place, Dad."

"Mehhh," Dad said.

"I hear ya," Harry said. "Hard day. Same-old, same-old, amirite?"

He loosened the dolly's straps. His father managed two steps before sagging down to the concrete floor and immediately falling into a snore-punctuated doze.

Harry removed the mask.

"Sleep well, Dad. I love you."

Harry rolled the dolly out of the room and shut the heavy door behind him.

Dad was a kook. No doubt about that. But he was family, and family was all that mattered.

Harry walked to one of the abandoned vehicles, an old RV. It wasn't a bad setup, really: a bed, a little couch that was almost comfortable, a tiny sink, a small flat-panel TV, and—of course—a working stove and oven. There was also a stall that doubled as both shower and toilet. Getting his bulk into that narrow space was quite a challenge, he already knew.

He opened the RV door. The smell of baking cupcakes welcomed him like an old friend. He'd put in a batch as soon as he'd arrived. The RV was old and smelled a little funky—the odor of good cooking would drive out that funk, make the small space downright homey.

The RV's oven was smaller than the food truck's, but big enough for one batch. Just twelve cupcakes, enough to last tonight and tomorrow.

Harry slid off his coat. Thing had to weigh a hundred pounds, at least, what with all the bells and whistles in there. He set the coat over the back of the driver's seat, then drew Big Baby from the custom shoulder holster.

Finally, Harry sat his fat ass down on the couch, Big Baby on the cushion next to him.

"*Helluva day at sea, eh, Harry?*"

"Been trying to tell you," Harry said. "Oakland's a dangerous place."

"*You did good, kemosabe. Dad's alive. I'm alive. You took one lousy pellet to the cheek, other than that, you're fine. Four of those fuck-nuggets are dead.*"

Harry nodded, then realized he'd left the batch of cream cheese frosting in the food truck. Ah, screw it—he would get it later. He just needed to rest his bones for a few minutes.

He picked up the remote and turned on the TV. The very first image he saw was a KRON: SPECIAL REPORT logo across the bottom, above it, a ridiculously attractive Asian woman standing in front of…

…in front of Harry's old house.

"It was here, just over a year ago, that the Change destroyed a family," the woman said. "One of many families, to be sure, but this story is still affecting the Bay Area. Here in the East Bay, in Oakland, a serial killer is on the loose. When the nation, and indeed the world, is deluged daily with images of death, why is yet another serial killer significant? Because this one isn't a Blood, this one *hunts* Bloods, exterminates them as if they were vermin and not people. I warn you, the following images may be too disturbing to see, even for those of your numbed by the nightly parade of death and destruction."

The image on the screen changed to the vampire Harry had put down just last night.

"*Serial killer? What's that crazy bitch talking about?*"

"Shut up, Big Baby."

The camera showed the open skull, then moved inside the skull. A circle of light played off the already-drying red smears inside.

"Thus far, seven victims have been found," the reporter said. "All with the tops of their heads cut off, all with their brains removed. And, all appear to have gone through significant physical trauma before death. In short, they were captured, tortured, killed, and then their bodies were mutilated."

Harry listened to her, watched her, but only partially. He couldn't stop looking *past* her, to the half-burned house. That bird-feeder in the front yard...Harry had put that in himself.

"While authorities could find nothing about this killer, I, Yuki Nitobe, was able to discover his identity. Serial killer or self-appointed vigilante? We still don't know. What we do know, now, is his name— Harold Chamberlain."

The image changed to a picture of a smiling, handsome black man with blue eyes, wearing a police uniform. It took Harry a split-second to recognize the man.

"*Sweet Jesus,*" Big Baby said. "*Look how skinny you used to be, you big fat fuck. It barely even looks like you.*"

"Shut up, Big Baby."

Yuki again. "This man was a gun collector and member of the Oakland Police Department's SWAT team, highly decorated for his service to the public. What is he now? Perhaps you can decide for yourself—just look at what Harold Chamberlain does to his victims."

The image changed to another vampire Harry had put down, a white woman he'd taken out a week ago. A ragged line of bone bordered the negative space that had once been her upper jaw. The top of her head, missing. Dried blood flaking off her skin. One eye gone, the other staring out.

"*I remember that one,*" Big Baby said. "*She screamed a lot.*"

"She did," Harry said.

He wondered if all of his work looked that sloppy.

"Chamberlain was a Marine for eight years," Yuki said. "In the Marines, he was a sniper. After he got out, he became a police officer in Oakland, eventually joining the SWAT unit, where he served for another three years until the change. SWAT stands for *Special Weapons and Tactics*. Already armed with lethal skills, Chamberlain received further training as part of the SWAT unit."

"You were a Marine? No shit?"

Harry stared at the screen. His thoughts felt out of focus, kind of fuzzy, like he couldn't lock them down, like trying to read a piece of paper someone was waving in front of your face.

"I wasn't," he said. "I don't think I was…"

Yuki turned and walked toward the house, moving slightly sideways so that she could continue to look at the following camera.

"Chamberlain was a family man," she said.

The image on the screen flashed up a picture of a woman. Hispanic, dark complexion, brown eyes, a roundish face etched with laugh lines.

"Chamberlain married Doris Meraz seven years ago, and four years ago, they had a daughter, Rebecca."

The image changed again. This time, a little girl, her skin a perfect milk chocolate, but the eyes, the *eyes*, they blazed blue, the color of a clear sky an hour before the sun sets.

"Jesus H. Christ," Big Baby said. *"You had a daughter? Man, you never tell me anything."*

"Shut up, Big Baby."

Yuki stood at the charred front door.

"It was in this house that Chamberlain lived with his wife, his daughter, and his father, Allan Chamberlain, locally known as the owner of Bup's Cups, an Oakland pastry shop. A year ago, police were called to this house because Harold Chamberlain had allegedly murdered his wife and daughter. It was assumed he changed, and as a result, killed those closest to him. Before he could be brought to trial, a wave of violence submerged Oakland in riots and overwhelmed the city government. In this chaos, Harold Chamberlain escaped and has never been heard from again. As for the death of his wife and daughter, I was able to find some pictures of the crime scene on the Internet. Again, the images you are about to see are disturbing in the extreme. If you don't want to see such horrors, please, turn away."

"Oh, she's good," Big Baby said. *"Milking the drama like that. She's—"*

Harry picked up Big Baby and cocked the hammer in one smooth motion. He pointed the barrel at the TV—using both hands, this time—and fired. The gun leapt. A fist-sized black spot appeared in the screen, haloed by spiderweb cracks, but the slightly darker picture kept playing.

"These are the images of murder," Yuki said. "These show—"

Harry cocked and fired again.

The screen went black.

He cocked and fired again.

And again.

And again.

He cocked the hammer and pulled the trigger: the hammer clicked on empty.

"Jesus," Big Baby said. *"Overreact much?"*

Harry tossed the gun forward. It hit the dashboard and fell somewhere in front of the passenger seat.

"Asshole," Big Baby said, but the revolver's voice sounded far away.

Memories rose up in Harry's thoughts, glowing tendrils of recollection, flash bulbs of bits of images he couldn't remember, that he had pushed away, pushed *down.*

His daughter…screaming…the taste of blood…a vampire did it, not *him,* he'd served his country and then his community, he'd protected people against those monsters…it was the vampires, the *Changed,* one of *them* killed his daughter, one of *them* killed his wife—not his father, his father could never have done that, *never.* The monsters had done it, it was the monsters that had to be punished, it was the monsters, the monsters, they had to be *punished—*

The oven timer beeped.

Harry opened his eyes. The cupcakes were done. That was the problem, that was why he felt so fuzzy, because he hadn't eaten in a long time. He'd feel better after he ate a cupcake or two. Or three.

He stood and removed them from the oven, set them on the counter to cool.

No, not the cupcakes themselves…he felt fuzzy unless he had that frosting, that special frosting…the food truck, there was a batch of it in the food truck. He only felt right after the frosting.

Harry shuffled to the RV's door and stepped out onto the dirty concrete. It wasn't him, it was *them*, the monsters, he was one of the good guys.

He killed monsters.

He *punished* monsters.

And now those same monsters, those baby-killers, they were organizing, becoming even more dangerous.

No, one monster in particular was organizing them—Charlemagne.

Harry walked through the dark space toward the food truck. He would have a little snack, a little frosting, get some sleep, and then he'd start planning the next mission.

Charlemagne had to be punished.

"MONSTERS IN THE DARK"

Jonathan Maberry

The Mine
Department of Defense Advanced Bioweapons Research Facility
Six Hundred Feet below Willis Mountain
Buckingham County, Virginia

Dr. Andrew Chu stood well behind the soldiers. They had the guns and the flamethrowers. He had a clipboard. There were eighteen soldiers in the lab. Not official soldiers, though each of them had gone to war under some or other flag. Most were American, Chu thought. One of them at least was Australian and another was French. Each was a brute. Hard-faced men with heavy arms and dead eyes. Their team leader, a bruiser named Derek Tatum, was a barrel-chested bear with a shaved head and an iron gray goatee. He was shorter than everyone in his team, but there was deep cunning and a total lack of mercy in his eyes.

Even so, even with all that, Chu could feel the fear in the room. It was like an odor, a miasma. It filled every corner of the lab.

Deep fear.

Dread.

Each of the men stood with their rifles slung—but fingers lay ready along the curves of trigger guards. They were hyper alert to the point of stress.

Chu couldn't blame them. If he hadn't gone to the bathroom ten minutes ago he'd have probably peed his pants by now.

They all stood in a loose half-circle around a big gray box. The box stood on the steel arms of a forklift. Six bands of quarter-inch steel cable bound the box shut. Each band was sealed by a huge lock of case-hardened steel.

"Waiting on you, Doc," said Tatum.

Chu licked his lips. "O-okay," he said, tripping over the word. "Let's…um…do this."

It was the best he could do. He would have liked to say something profound or even witty, but all he could manage was a nervous stutter.

Still, none of the hard men called him on it. They were all sweating. They were all that scared.

"Ready on the line," said Tatum as he approached the box. He reluctantly let his rifle hang from its strap as he unclipped a ring of keys. He selected one, fit it into the top lock, but paused and turned to his men. "Hear me and hear me good. As of right now we are at alpha-one alert. We need to get the sample in this case into the development tank and we need to get it right the first time. We lose control of this situation and we're all fucked. Do you read me?"

"Sir!" shouted the men.

"But we don't take chances. If something goes wrong, you put this fucking thing down like a dog, do you read that?"

"Sir!"

"Even if I'm in the way. This thing cannot be allowed to escape."

The men said nothing. They knew. They understood.

Tatum turned to Chu. "Ain't that right, Doc? You tell them."

Chu sputtered for a moment, but he managed to get it out. "This specimen is unique. It's the result of months of research and forty million dollars in developmental capital. This is the weapon that will win us the war against the vampire insurgents."

Their eyes flicked from the case to him and then back again.

"We can't lose this specimen. It would set our weapons program back a year at least. China and North Korea are breathing down our necks on this."

No one spoke.

"So…we have to keep it safe."

"Right," snapped Tatum, "safety first. Got it. But the bottom line is that we don't take stupid risks. We manage the situation exactly as drilled. Follow the protocols, remember your training and this is over in two minutes. Fuck up, forget what you know, and you will get every man in the room killed. And you'll probably get half of North-fucking-America killed. If this gets out and if the Bloods get hold of this—and I'm not even talking about the Koreans and the Chinese—then we are all well and truly fucked. *Do you understand?*"

"Sir!" they growled.

Tatum studied them. Taking his time to look each man in the eye. Then he nodded to Chu.

"Okay, Doc, let's do this and fuck us if we're stupid."

Chu nodded. He took a tranquilizer dart gun from a table and hastily fitted the high-pressure air hose to it. But his hands were shaking so badly that the barrel wobbled dangerously in Tatum's direction. One of the soldiers stepped forward and took it from him.

"I got it, sir," he said. The soldier set his feet and raised the dart gun in a two-handed grip.

Tatum licked his lips and turned the key. The first steel band fell away. He unlocked the second, the third.

One by one the heavy steel cables slithered down the sides of case and coiled around it like dead snakes. The soldiers raised their weapons. Trigger fingers twitched. No one dared blink.

Tatum tossed the keys aside and raised his own weapon, holding the automatic rifle in one hand as he reached for the doorknob with the other. He turned it slowly and the room was so silent they could all hear the metallic click. The door immediately began swinging outward, and Tatum jumped backward, taking his rifle in two hands.

However, the door swung open slowly. Without force. Without haste.

It opened halfway and then swung the rest of the way open on its own. Light from the overhead floods filled the case and melted the interior shadows away.

A figure stood there.

A man.

But, Chu knew, that was a lie.

It had been a man.

Long ago.

Before the Ice Virus.

Before the firing of the V-gene.

Before transformation and manifestation and metamorphosis.

Now it was something else.

Tall. Powerfully built. Naked, except for a pair of dark blue shorts. Skin as pale as milk. Eyes as red as blood.

A smiling mouth.

"Hello, Doctor Chu," said the thing in the box. He took a step forward and watched as the soldiers all retreated with identical nervous jerks. The thing laughed. Its voice was deep, deformed by an unnatural timbre. It sounded like distant thunder. It looked, as Tatum had looked, from one man to another. Each of them. All of them. He laughed at the sight of all those big men and all of their guns.

Chu shifted around and moved over to a tall glass cylinder. He tapped a button on a computer pedestal and the glass tube rose into the air on hydraulics that squealed like a pig.

The thing cocked an eyebrow. "Really?" he drawled, amused. "In there?"

"If you p-please," stuttered Chu.

"And if I don't please?"

Tatum raised his rifle and braced the stock against his shoulder. "Then we find another volunteer."

The thing smiled as if that was a very funny joke. And he winked at Tatum as if they shared the secret of its punch line. Chu saw Tatum's eyes tighten and his knuckles go white with tension.

"'Volunteer'," said the thing. "Such an interesting word. Don't you think, Dr. Chu?"

Chu found that he was unable to reply.

The thing nodded as if an answer had been given. He stepped down from the case and walked past the line of soldiers. If he cared about the row of gun barrels that tracked him, it did not show. He stopped only briefly when he reached the outer edge of the platform that had been enclosed by the cylinder. There he turned and looked at Chu. They stood less than ten feet apart.

So close.

So close.

The smile momentarily faded from the thing's face as he met the doctor's eyes. "Do you know why I volunteered for this, doctor?"

Chu could only shake his head.

"Because I love my country," said the thing. "That's why I joined the navy. That's why I volunteered for the SEALs. That's why I reenlisted when this war started."

Chu said nothing. No one did. The thing looked around at the other men.

"You people probably think that when we change, vampires stop being soldiers, stop being citizens, stop being Americans. We don't. Not those of us who can think. Not those of us who are masters of what we are. And there are a lot of Bloods like me." He paused and briefly looked down at his massive arms, at the thick black claws that sprouted from his fingertips. "Well, not *exactly* like me. But you get the point."

He paused and took a half step toward Chu, who was so frightened that he was unable to retreat. Tatum edged forward and shifted around so the vampire was aware of him.

The thing ignored the soldier. He ignored all the soldiers.

"It's important that you understand that. You waste too much of your time on contempt for all vampires. That's stupid. It's ignorant. And it makes you blind to the most powerful allies you have in this war."

He turned and stepped into the center of the platform.

"Until now," he said. He smiled once more. "*That's* why I volunteered, Dr. Chu."

Chu's mouth was as dry as paste. He pressed the button and the glass cylinder began to slide downward. The walls of the cylinder were ten inches thick and tempered to a hardness greater than steel.

In the last second before the cylinder banged down into place, Chu heard the vampire's last words.

"God bless America."

Then the seals locked into place. Chu could see the monster's face, see the smiling mouth, but he could imagine what the sound of its laughter must be like.

Hell itself must sound like that.

V-WARS CORRESPONDANTS

KEVIN J. ANDERSON has published 125 books, more than fifty of which have been national or international bestsellers. He has written numerous novels in the *Star Wars*, *X-Files*, and *Dune* universes, as well as a unique steampunk fantasy novel, *Clockwork Angels*, based on the concept album by legendary rock group Rush. His original works include the *Saga of Seven Suns series*, the *Terra Incognita* fantasy trilogy, the *Saga of Shadows* trilogy, and his humorous horror series featuring Dan Shamble, Zombie PI. He has edited numerous anthologies, including the *Five by Five* and *Blood Lite* series. Anderson and his wife Rebecca Moesta are the publishers of WordFire Press. Wordfirepress.com.

JAMES A. MOORE is an award-winning author of over thirty novels, including the critically acclaimed *Serenity Falls* trilogy and the *Seven Forges* fantasy series. His recurring anti-hero, Jonathan Crowley, has appeared in half a dozen novels with more to come. You can find him at http://jamesamoorebooks.com/ and he's normally lurking around Facebook and Twitter when he should be writing.

JOE McKINNEY has been a patrol officer for the San Antonio Police Department, a homicide detective, a disaster mitigation specialist, a patrol commander, and a successful novelist. His books include the four-part *Dead World* series, *Quarantined*, *Inheritance*, *Lost Girl of the Lake*, *The Savage Dead*, *St. Rage*, *Crooked House* and *Dodging Bullets*. His short fiction has been collected in *The Red Empire and Other Stories*, *Speculations*, and *Dead World Resurrection: The Complete Zombie Short Stories of Joe McKinney*. His latest works include the werewolf thriller, *Dog Days*, set in the summer of 1983 in the little Texas town of Clear Lake, where the author grew up, and *Plague of the Undead*, Book One in the *Deadlands Saga*. McKinney is a two-time recipient of the Bram Stoker Award®. For more information go to http://joemckinney.wordpress.com.

JONATHAN MABERRY is a *New York Times* bestselling author, multiple Bram Stoker Award winner, and freelancer for Marvel

Comics. His novels include *Code Zero, Rot & Ruin, Ghost Road Blues, Patient Zero, The Wolfman*, and many others. Nonfiction books include *Ultimate Jujutsu, The Cryptopedia, Zombie CSU*, and others. Several of Jonathan's novels are in development for movies or TV including *V-Wars, Extinction Machine, Rot & Ruin* and *Dead of Night*. He's the editor/co-author of *V-Wars*, a vampire-themed anthology; and was a featured expert on The History Channel special *Zombies: A Living History*. Since 1978 he's sold more than 1200 magazine feature articles, 3000 columns, two plays, greeting cards, song lyrics, and poetry. His comics include *Captain America: Hail Hydra, Bad Blood, Marvel Zombies Return* and *Marvel Universe vs the Avengers*. He lives in Del Mar, California wih his wife, Sara Jo and their dog, Rosie. www.jonathanmaberry.com

LARRY CORREIA's *Monster Hunter International*, despite being self-published, reached the *Entertainment Weekly* bestseller list in April 2008, after which he received a publishing contract with Baen Books. *Monster Hunter International* was re-released in 2009 and was on the *Locus* bestseller list in November 2009. The sequel, *Monster Hunter Vendetta*, was a New York Times bestseller. The third book in the series, *Monster Hunter Alpha*, was released in July 2011 and was also a *New York Times* bestseller. Correia was a finalist for the John W. Campbell award for best new science fiction/fantasy writer of 2011. *Warbound*, the third book in Correia's *The Grimnoir Chronicles* series, received a nomination for the Hugo Award for Best Novel in 2014. *The Dead Six* series started as an online action fiction collaboration with Mike Kupari (Nightcrawler) at the online gun forum "The High Road" as the "Welcome Back Mr Nightcrawler" series of posts. These works predated the publishing of *Monster Hunter*.

SCOTT SIGLER is the *New York Times* best-selling author of fifteen novels, six novellas and dozens of short stories. His hardcover horror-thrillers are available from Crown Publishing and Del Rey. He also co-founded Empty Set Entertainment, which publishes his YA *Galactic Football League* series.

WESTON OCHSE is the author of twenty books, most recently *SEAL Team 666* and *Age of Blood*, which the *New York Post* called "required reading" and *USA Today* placed on their "New and Notable Lists." His military science fiction novel profiling PTSD called *Grunt Life* is an instant classic. Weston is a military veteran with 30 years of military service. He moonlights as a Superhero for Rent, Literary Stuntman, and Yakuza of the written word. You can find him in the *Yellow Pages* under Badass.

YVONNE NAVARRO is the author of twenty-two novels, including the *Dark Redemption* series and the apocalyptic vampire novel, *AfterAge*. She's also had well more than a hundred short stories published, plus two editions of a writer's reference book, *The First Name Reverse Dictionary*. She is wife to author Weston Ochse, and mommy to a people-friendly parakeet named BirdZilla and four rescued Great Danes: Goblin, Ghost, Ghoulie and Grendel. She lives in southeastern Arizona, and you can find her most easily on Facebook.